D0185867

Nelson Richard DeMille was born in New York City on August 23, 1943 to Huron and Antonia (Panzera) DeMille, then moved with his parents to Long Island. He graduated from Elmont Memorial High School, where he played football and ran track.

DeMille spent three years at Hofstra University, then joined the Army where he attended Officer Candidate School and was commissioned a Lieutenant in the United States Army (1966–69). He saw action in Vietnam as an infantry platoon leader with the First Cavalry Division and was decorated with the Air Medal, Bronze Star, and the Vietnamese Cross of Gallantry.

After his discharge, DeMille returned to Hofstra University where he received his bachelor's degree in Political Science and History. He has three children, Lauren, Alexander, and James, and he and his wife reside on Long Island.

DeMille's first major novel was *By the Rivers of Babylon*, published in 1978, and is still in print as are all his succeeding novels. He is a member of American Mensa, The Authors Guild, and is past president of the Mystery Writers of America. He is also a member of International Thriller Writers and was chosen as ThrillerMaster of the Year 2015. He holds three honorary doctorates: Doctor of Humane Letters from Hofstra University, Doctor of Literature from Long Island University, and Doctor of Humane Letters from Dowling College.

For more information on Nelson DeMille, go to:
www.nelsondemille.net
Facebook: NelsonDeMilleAuthor
Twitter: @NelsonDeMille
Instagram: @NelsonDeMilleAuthor

NOVELS BY NELSON DeMILLE

NELSON DEMILLE

THE CUBAN AFFAIR

sphere

SPHERE

First published in the United States in 2017 by Simon and Schuster
First published in Great Britain in 2017 by Sphere

1 3 5 7 9 10 8 6 4 2

Copyright © 2017 by Nelson DeMille

The moral right of the author has been asserted.

*All characters and events in this publication, other than those
clearly in the public domain, are fictitious and any resemblance
to real persons, living or dead, is purely coincidental.*

All rights reserved.
No part of this publication may be reproduced, stored in a
retrieval system, or transmitted, in any form or by any means, without
the prior permission in writing of the publisher, nor be otherwise circulated
in any form of binding or cover other than that in which it is published
and without a similar condition including this condition being
imposed on the subsequent purchaser.

A CIP catalogue record for this book
is available from the British Library.

Hardback ISBN 978-0-7515-6588-1
Trade Paperback ISBN 978-0-7515-6587-4

Printed and bound in Great Britain by
Clays Ltd, St Ives plc

Papers used by Sphere are from well-managed forests
and other responsible sources.

MIX
Paper from
responsible sources
FSC   FSC® C104740
www.fsc.org

LONDON BOROUGH OF WANDSWORTH	
9030 00005 6932 3	
Askews & Holts	21-Sep-2017
AF THR	£19.99
	WW17010251

To the memory of Bob Dillingham—

My bighearted father-in-law.

And to the memory of Pat Dillingham—

My free-spirited sister-in-law.

PART 1

PART I

CHAPTER 1

I was standing at the bar in the Green Parrot, waiting for a guy named Carlos from Miami who'd called my cell a few days ago and said he might have a job for me.

Carlos did not give me his last name, but he had ID'd himself as a Cuban American. I don't know why I needed to know that, but I told him I was Scots-Irish-English American, in case he was wondering.

My name is Daniel Graham MacCormick—Mac for short— age thirty-five, and I've been described as tall, tan, and ruggedly handsome. This comes from the gay clientele in the Parrot, but I'll take it. I live here on the island of Key West, and I am the owner and skipper of a 42-foot deep-sea fishing charter boat called *The Maine*, named for my home state—not for the American battleship that blew up in Havana Harbor, though some people think that.

I usually book my charters by phone, and most of my customers are repeats or referrals, or they checked out my website. The party just shows up fifteen minutes before sailing, and off we go for marlin, sailfish, tuna, sharks, or whatever. Or maybe the customer wants a sightseeing cruise. Now and then I get a fishing tournament or a romantic sunset cruise. Whatever the customer wants. As long as it's legal.

But this guy, Carlos, wanted to meet first, coming all the way down from Miami, and he sounded a bit cryptic, making me think we weren't talking about fishing.

The barmaid, Amber, inquired, "Ready for another?"

"Hold the lime."

Amber popped another Corona and stuck a lime wedge in the neck. "Lime's on me."

Amber is pretty but getting a little hard behind the bar. Like nearly everyone here in what we call the Conch Republic, she's from someplace else, and she has a story.

I, too, am from someplace else—Maine, as I said, specifically Portland, which is directly connected to Key West by U.S. Highway One, or by a cruise up the coast, but Portland is as far from here as Pluto is from the sun. FYI, I spent five years in the U.S. Army as an infantry officer and got blown up in Afghanistan. That's the short story of how I wound up here. The long story is a long story, and no one in Key West wants to hear long stories.

It was about 5 P.M., give or take an hour. The citizens of the Conch Republic are not into clocks, which is why they're here. We're on sun time. Also, we have officially seceded from the United States, so we are all expats. I actually have a rainbow-hued Conch Republic passport, issued by the self-appointed Secretary General of the Republic, a guy named Larry who has a small office over on Angela Street. The passport was a gag gift from my first mate, Jack Colby, who like me is an Army vet. Jack got screwed up in 'Nam, and he's still screwed up but in an old-guy sort of way, so my customers think he's just grumpy, not crazy. His favorite T-shirt says: "Guns Don't Kill People. I Kill People." Maybe he is crazy.

I wasn't sure of the time, but I was sure of the month—October. End of hurricane season, so business was picking up.

Amber, who was wearing a tank top, was sipping a black coffee, surveying the crowd. The Green Parrot's regular clientele are eclectic and eccentric and mostly barefoot. The owner, Pat, is a bit crazy himself, and he tells the tourists that the parachute hanging on the ceiling is weighed down with termite turds.

Amber asked, "How's business?"

"Summer was okay. September sucked. Picking up."

"You were going to take me for a sail in September."

"I did a lot of maintenance on the boat."

"I thought you were going to sail to Maine."

"I thought so, too."

"If you ever go, let me know."

"You'll need a sweater."

A customer called for another and Amber moved off.

I've never actually slept with Amber, but we did go skinny-dipping once off Fort Zachary Taylor. She has a butterfly tattoo on her butt.

The place was starting to fill up and I exchanged greetings with a few people. Freaks, geeks, loveable weirdos, and a few Hemingway look-alikes. He used to live here, and you can see his house for ten bucks. You can see mine for free. Bring a six-pack. Anyway, Key West's official motto is "One Human Family." Well, they haven't met my family. And they haven't been to Afghanistan to see the rest of the human family. Or, like Jack, to Vietnam. Or if they have, they're here, like me and Jack, to float in a sea of alcohol-induced amnesia. I've been here four years. Five is enough to forget why you came here. After that, you're not going home.

But, hey, it could be worse. This is paradise. Better than two tours in Allfuckedupistan. Better than freezing my ass off in Maine. And definitely better than 23 Wall Street, where I worked for a year after graduating from Bowdoin College. If I'd stayed with Hamlin Equities I'd now be dead from boredom.

Instead, I was captain of *The Maine*, and a former captain of infantry with a fifty percent combat disability and a quarter-million-dollar bank loan on my boat. The fifty percent disability is for pay purposes and I have no physical limitations except for housecleaning. The bank loan is a hundred percent pain in the ass.

But when I'm out there on the sea, especially at night, I am free. I am captain of my own fate.

Which was why I agreed to meet Carlos the Cuban, who was not interested in fishing. That much I understood from our short phone conversation. And I wouldn't be the first sea captain who got involved with these people.

Well, I'd listen and see if I could make an intelligent decision—like I did when I left Wall Street and joined the Army for adventure. How'd that work out, Mac?

Being captain of your own fate doesn't mean you always make good decisions.

CHAPTER 2

A well-dressed man came through the open double doors and I knew it was Carlos. He was good-looking, maybe late thirties, with a full head of well-styled brown hair and pale skin. He wore neatly pressed beige linen slacks, Gucci loafers, and an expensive-looking Polo shirt the color of my lime wedge. I had the impression of a man who had stood in his air-conditioned walk-in closet this morning trying to figure out what to wear to Key West to blend in. Unfortunately he failed. But no one here is judgmental, and in fact some of the gay clientele seemed intrigued.

I'd chosen to dress up a bit for the meeting and I wore clean jeans, boat shoes instead of flip flops, and a designer T-shirt that said: "Designer T-Shirt."

I knew Carlos hadn't picked me out of the Yellow Pages, so he knew something about me and he'd determined that Daniel Graham MacCormick might want to work for him. Well, maybe I did, but I damn sure wasn't going to make a midnight run to Cuba.

Carlos spotted me at the bar and walked toward me. He put out his hand. "Carlos."

"Mac." We shook.

"Thank you for meeting me."

When someone thanks me for meeting him, he has something to sell me. Or Carlos was just a polite gentleman. He was probably third generation and he had no Cuban accent, but you can tell that these people are bilingual by their well-modulated English and their slightly skewed syntax. Also, a lot of them used their Spanish first names, so he wasn't Carl. I asked, "What are you drinking?"

He looked at my Corona. "The same."

I caught Amber's attention and ordered two Coronas.

Amber checked out Carlos, liking what she saw, but Carlos didn't notice because he was checking out the Green Parrot, not sure of what he was seeing. I could have met Carlos on the boat, but something told me that I should meet him in a public place, and he had no objection to that, which was good for starters. Plus, he could pick up my bar tab.

Amber gave Carlos his Corona with a lime and a smile, and slid mine across the bar.

Carlos and I clinked and he said, "Cheers."

I noticed he was wearing a Rolex. I asked him, "You been to Key West?"

"No."

"How'd you come?"

"I drove."

It's about a four-hour drive from Miami, down U.S. One, known here as the Overseas Highway, which connects the hundred-mile-long archipelago of islands, bridge by bridge, until it reaches Key West, the last island, ninety miles from Cuba. Some people say it's the most scenic drive in America; others find it a little nerve-wracking and take a boat or plane the next time. Or never come back. Which is fine with some of the full-time residents of independent means. I, however, depend on mainland customers. Like Carlos. Who drove four hours to see me. "So what can I do for you?"

"I'm interested in chartering your boat for a cruise to Cuba."

I didn't respond.

"There is a fishing tournament, sailing from here to Havana in a few weeks."

"Does the Cuban Navy know about this?"

He smiled. "This is an authorized event, of course—the Pescando Por la Paz." He reminded me, "We are normalizing relations. The Cuban Thaw."

"Right." I'd heard about the new fishing tournament with the double-entendre name—Pescando Por la Paz, Fishing for Peace—but I wasn't involved in it. Back in the Nineties, before my time, there used to be regular fishing tournaments and sailing regattas between the U.S. and Cuba, including the seventy-year-old Hemingway Tournament, but George II put a stop to all that. Now it was opening up again. The Cuban Thaw. The Key West Chamber of Commerce even had a new slogan: "Two Nations, One Vacation." Catchy. But not happening yet.

Carlos asked, "So, are you interested?"

I drank some beer. Well, maybe this was all legit, and Carlos didn't want me to sail into Havana Harbor and blow up *The Maine*, or rescue some dissidents or something.

I had some questions for Carlos—like who was he—but questions mean you're interested. And that means the price is open to negotiation. "I get twelve hundred for an eight-hour day. Tournament rates depend on variables."

Carlos nodded. "This is a ten-day event, beginning on Saturday the twenty-fourth, and returning on Monday, November second—the Day of the Dead."

"The . . . ?"

"What we call All Souls' Day in the U.S."

"Right. Sounds better." A fishing tournament is usually four to six days, but Carlos explained, "The tournament fleet first makes an overnight goodwill stop in Havana, then the fleet sails to the tournament in Cayo Guillermo, a day's cruise east of Havana. Do you know this place?"

"No."

"It was the favorite deep-sea fishing place of Ernesto." He smiled. "Hemingway, not Guevara."

That must be an old Cuban joke.

He continued, "It was the setting for his famous book, *Islands in the Stream*. Have you read it?"

"I have."

"So you know the place already. Some of the best pelagic fishing in the world."

I was impressed that he knew what "pelagic" meant. The price just went up.

"The tournament is for bill fish—sailfish, swordfish, and marlin. Are you available?"

"Maybe. That's a lot of diesel. Let's say three thousand a day."

He seemed to be doing the math, and if he was good at it, that came to thirty thousand. Which I could use. I don't usually do a pitch, but I told him, "The Maine sleeps four comfortably, or five close friends. My first mate and I give up our berths. Price includes fishing gear, fuel, bait, and whatever. I assume this is catch and release, because I can't keep big fish on ice. You supply the food and drink, and I need to see your license and permits for Cuba." I reminded him, "Florida does not impose a sales tax on charter fishing, so thirty thousand is the total with no extra charges except a tip for the first mate at let's say ten percent. I don't take tips." I also told him, "I'd have to cancel some previous bookings."

"Your website shows only one booking in that time period."

"Really? I need to update that. So, that's the price."

"You drive a hard bargain, Mr. MacCormick."

"Captain."

"Captain." He glanced around. "Let's get a table."

"Why?"

"There are some other details you need to know."

Well, I was afraid of that. "Look . . . Carlos, I do charter cruises. Fishing, sightseeing, sometimes a party cruise. I guess I can do a tournament—even to Cuba—but I don't do other things. Understand?"

Carlos didn't reply and his silence said it all.

"But thanks for thinking of me." I asked Amber to give the bar tab to Carlos and I wished him a safe trip back to Miami.

He replied, "Two million."

"Excuse me?"

"You heard me."

I said to Amber, "Hold that tab." I said to Carlos, "Let's get a table, amigo."

CHAPTER 3

We took our beers to a back table and sat.

I can't imagine how many shady deals have gone down in this place over the last hundred and twenty-five years, but if the Green Parrot could talk, it would say, "Show me the money."

"Two million," I said.

"Correct."

"For a fishing tournament."

"No. That's thirty thousand. Certified check up front. The two million is cash, payable on completion of a job in Cuba."

"Sounds like a tough job." I asked, "With whom would I be doing business?"

Carlos took a business card out of his pocket and slid it across the table.

I looked at it. *Carlos Macia, Attorney*. He had a good South Beach address, but there was no name of a law firm.

He said, "I'm well-known in Miami."

"For what?"

"For being heavily involved with anti-Castro groups."

I left the card on the table and looked at Carlos Macia. Odd as it sounds, I was happy to be dealing with a lawyer. Some of these anti-Castro guys were cowboys, sometimes hare-brained, and often dangerous to themselves and others. I looked at him. "Who recommended me?"

"Amigos."

"Explain what you need, Counselor."

He looked around the crowded room. "The walls have ears."

"Actually, they have termites. And no one here cares what we're talking about. Look, Mr. Macia, you have offered me two million dollars and it will not surprise you that I could use the money, but—"

"You can pay off your bank loan on The Maine."

"But I will not do anything illegal for the money."

"I would not ask you to. I am an attorney."

"And your amigos? Are they attorneys?"

"No. But I can assure you, the only laws you'll be breaking are Cuban laws. Does that bother you?"

"Only if I get caught."

"And that's the point. If you don't get caught you are two million dollars richer, and you have broken no American laws." He smiled. "Unless you don't pay your income tax on the money."

On the subject of death, taxes, and getting caught, I asked Carlos, "How dangerous?"

"That's for you to determine when you hear about the job."

"How dangerous, Carlos?"

"Cuba is dangerous."

"You expect me to risk my life for a measly two million taxable dollars?"

He looked at my bare arms. The shrapnel and burn scars didn't tan well. "You risked your life for far less in Afghanistan."

"It was a government job. Free medical."

"You were awarded the Silver Star and two Purple Hearts. So you're no stranger to danger."

I didn't reply.

"This is why we thought of you."

Again, I didn't reply.

"And you have a good boat." He smiled. "And I like the name. The Maine. Very symbolic. Part of our shared history."

"I named it after my home state. Not the battleship."

"Yes, you're from Portland. And you have no family responsibilities here, and no one to answer to except yourself. Also, we know that as a former Army officer you are a man we can trust."

"Sometimes I drink too much."

"As long as you don't talk too much. Also, you have no ties to the anti-Castro groups, and I assume you have no positive feelings toward the Communist regime. Correct?"

"Between you and me, Carlos, I don't give a damn one way or the other."

"So you say. But if I had to bet money—and I do—I'd say you'd like to see those Communist bastards gone." He smiled again. "You could run charters to Havana."

"I can do that when relations improve."

"Don't hold your breath. Meanwhile, I have two million dollars on the table."

I looked at the table. There was nothing there except his card and an ashtray. You can still smoke in this joint. I said, "The thirty thousand for the tournament sounds good."

"Captain, I don't really care about the tournament. That's just the cover, as you know. In fact, you will not be sailing to Cuba on The Maine. Your first mate, Jack Colby, will. We will supply another crew member along with three avid fishermen. You will be flying to Havana on an authorized charter with one of my clients, and at some point after your job is done you will meet up with your boat and sail it out of Cuba."

"With what onboard?"

He leaned toward me. "About sixty million dollars of American currency. Two of which are yours to keep."

"Five."

Carlos looked at me. "You'll have to negotiate that with my clients."

"Okay. And how's my first mate compensated?"

"That's up to you." He informed me, "Mister Colby does not need to risk his life, and therefore does not need to know many of the details."

"Who else is risking their lives?"

"A few others."

"You?"

"No. I am persona non grata in Cuba."

"Right." Well, I'd promised myself in the hospital that I'd be more careful in the future. But . . .

Carlos glanced at his Rolex. "I think I've given you enough information for you to decide if you'd like to hear more from my clients, who are available now."

I thought about that. The mission briefing. I'd volunteered for dangerous missions because it was for my country. This was for money. A lot of it. And maybe it wasn't as dangerous as Carlos thought. For Carlos, a Miami lawyer, driving back to Miami after dark was dangerous. But for me, the danger bar was so high that even now, four years after Afghanistan, I felt there wasn't much I couldn't handle. But maybe that's how I wound up in the hospital.

Carlos said, "My client, who will fly with you to Havana, can speak to you tonight. She will be very honest with you."

She?

"Also, to be honest, we are interviewing others for this job."

"Take the lowest bidder." I stood. "And please take care of the bill."

Carlos stood. "I can have my two clients at your boat in fifteen minutes. You should hear what they have to say."

"I've heard enough."

He looked very disappointed. "All right. I'll let my clients know. Or . . . I have an idea. You can let them know yourself. Can we charter your boat for a sunset cruise tonight? What do you charge for that?"

Carlos was slick. Or thought he was. I should have said, "Adios," but I said, "Make me an offer."

"Two thousand."

"How many people?"

"Three, including me."

"Meet me at my boat in half an hour. What do you drink?"

"Cuba Libre." He smiled.

"See you later. Give the barmaid a good tip."

I walked through the noisy barroom, waved to Amber, and

went out to Whitehead. Close by was the Zero Mile Marker for U.S. Highway One, the literal end of the road that started in Maine. I've had a lot of profound thoughts about that, usually fueled by a few beers. And I just had another thought: A journey of a hundred miles to Havana begins with a single misstep.

CHAPTER 4

Key West is only about a mile wide and four miles long, so walking or biking is a healthy way to get around, especially if drinking is in your plans. I'd walked to the Green Parrot from my rented bungalow on Pine Street, so I began walking to the marina. There was a nice breeze blowing through the palms, and it was a clear day, so it should be a two-thousand-dollar sunset.

I texted Jack, who was supposed to be getting the boat cleaned up in case the Cuban guy had wanted to see it: Got 3 customers for sundowners. Cuba Libres, ASAP.

Well, if nothing else, I made two thousand bucks tonight. What would I do with a couple million anyway?

I turned onto Duval, Key West's main street, which is a mile of bars, drag shows, T-shirt shops, boutique hotels, and a street scene that makes Mardi Gras look tame. I especially enjoy Fantasy Fest on Duval in the week leading up to Halloween, when lots of ladies wear nothing but body paint—which I'd miss this year if I was in Cuba.

I got a text back from Jack, who has a flip phone and just learned how to text on it: This the Cuban guy you met at Parrot?

I replied, Yes. And stop asking the captain questions.

I wanted to get to my boat before my customers, so I flagged a cab to take me to Charter Boat Row.

Key West has about twenty-five thousand people, excluding tourists, but it feels like a smaller town and the full-time residents tend to know each other, and I knew the cabbie, Dave Katz, who used to drive a taxi in New York. He asked, "You sailing tonight?"

"Sunset cruise."

"Good. How's business?"

"Picking up."

"I hope." He said, "When they open Cuba, we're all screwed."

"Why's that?"

"Tourists are gonna fly to Havana. Cruise ships won't even stop here any more."

I reminded him, "Two nations, one vacation."

"Bullshit. We're screwed."

I also reminded Dave, "They don't have Fantasy Fest in Havana."

Dave laughed, then said, "In five years, Havana will look like it did before Castro. Sex shows, gambling, teenage prostitutes, cheap rum and cigars. How we gonna compete with that?"

"I don't know, Dave. Haven't thought about it."

"You should. The Cubans know how to make money. Look at Miami. They own the place. Soon as the Commies are gone, Havana will be like Miami. But with gambling. And cheaper. We're screwed."

Fortunately it was a short ride to Charter Boat Row, and I gave Dave a twenty and some advice. "Buy a fifty-six Buick and move to Havana."

"Not funny, Mac. You'll see. People'll be fishing out of Havana for half what you charge. You'll be cutting bait, working for the Cubans."

I might already be working for the Cubans. "Adios, amigo."

"Screw that."

The sign outside the marina said: HISTORIC CHARTER BOAT ROW. EXPERIENCED CAPTAINS. That's me.

I walked along the finger dock and a few captains and crew, experienced and otherwise, called out greetings while knocking down the suds, so they weren't sailing tonight. But business should pick up. It always does. And I had a bank payment due on *The Maine*. And an engine overhaul bill. Maybe I'd be happier cutting bait in Havana. Or maybe it was time to go home.

I had intended to sail *The Maine* to Portland in September to explore that possibility, but I didn't. So now I was thinking about calling my father to talk about that. But like most down Easters, my father was a man of few words. If I'd gotten killed overseas and he had to put my obit in the *Portland Press Herald* at twenty dollars a word he'd be Yankee frugal and Maine taciturn and just say: <u>Daniel MacCormick died.</u> If it had to be a six-word minimum he'd show his practical side and add:<u> Car for sale.</u>

Well, maybe I'm being hard on the old man. He was proud of me when I joined the Army, and before my second deployment to Afghanistan he advised, "Come back." Well, I did, and he seemed pleased about that, but a bit concerned about my physical injuries, though not so much about post-traumatic stress, which he doesn't believe in. He liked to say he came back from Vietnam the same as when he left, which, according to my mother, is unfortunately true.

Regarding war, the MacCormicks have fought for their country since they arrived in the New World in the early 1700s, killing Indians, Frenchmen, Brits, Confederates, Germans, Japanese, and assorted Commies without regard to race, religion, or ethnic background. My older brother Web fought in the second Iraq war, so we also have dead Arabs on the family hit list, and I knocked off a few Afghanis to ensure true diversity. But if you met my family or knew my ancestors, I'm sure you'd think they were all fine, peaceful people. And we are. But we've always done our duty to God and country, which sometimes means somebody has to die.

After I killed my first Taliban, the men in my company gave me a T-shirt that said: "The Road To Paradise Begins With Me." Jack loved that shirt so I gave it to him. He has an interesting collection.

My father, Webster senior, is a weekend sailor and a weekday certified financial planner, very risk averse with his clients' money and tight as a crab's ass with his own. I'd love to sail home with a few million in the bank and flip the old man half a million to invest for me. My mother, June, a Bedell, is a third-grade teacher at a private elementary school, though she doesn't particularly like children, including maybe her own. Most of the MacCormicks and Bedells are college grads and according to my father the youngsters have all been educated beyond their intelligence. He may be right.

Like a lot of New Englanders, my family's politics are a mixture of progressive and conservative. We believe in taking care of the less fortunate, but we don't want that to cost us money. As for me, I am apolitical, and as for Yankee frugality, I missed that class. If I had, for instance, two million dollars I'd buy drinks for the house at the Green Parrot and take Amber on a long cruise. My financial advisor is Jack Colby, who likes to say, "I spent most of my money on booze and broads and I wasted the rest of it."

Well, I guess it goes without saying that Portland and Key West, though connected by the same ocean and the same road, are different places. And it also goes without saying that unlike my father, I am not the same man I was when I left home. But we are all One Human Family, fishing for peace. Meanwhile, I'd listen to what Carlos and his clients had to say about fishing for money. Costs nothing to listen. Better yet, I was getting paid for it.

CHAPTER 5

I came to the end of the dock where *The Maine* was tied. The bank and I own a beautiful 42-foot Wesmac Sport Fisherman, built in 2001 by Farrin's Boatshop in Walpole, Maine. The original owner had custom outfitted the boat with a tuna tower, a hydraulic bandit reel, two fighting chairs, and other expensive boy toys. *The Maine* is powered by a Cat 800-horsepower diesel, and even with the tuna tower and other commercial extras she cruises at about twenty-five knots, which gets her out to the usual fishing spots quickly.

If Cuba was in her future and mine, she could make Havana in under five hours, burning thirty gallons of diesel an hour, which was about a quarter of her six-hundred-gallon fuel capacity. She'd burn about three hundred gallons getting to Cayo Guillermo, then an unknown amount of fuel for the six-day tournament, so she'd have to take on fuel before heading back to Key West. But to keep her light and fast, only enough fuel to get us home. And how much does sixty million dollars weigh?

But why was I doing that math? Well, because I was thinking that you shouldn't turn down two million dollars before you've heard the deal.

I jumped aboard and saw that Jack wasn't back yet with the rum and Coke.

I went below to the galley and got myself a bottled water from the fridge. The galley and cabin seemed shipshape and I used the head, which looked like it could pass an inspection from the Cuban lady. Jack is, if nothing else, neat and clean, a holdover from his Army days.

The Maine has a wide beam—16 feet—so there's room below

for two decent-sized staterooms that sleep four, as I told Carlos, though a ten-day sail with provisions onboard could be a bit tight. And where was I going to stow sixty million dollars? I guess that depended on the denomination of the bills and how much room they took up. I'm sure we'd figure it out. Or, better yet, I'd just tell Carlos, "You need a bigger boat. Find someone else."

I went into the cabin and checked out the electronics, which had all been updated about a year ago at great expense. To stay competitive in this game you needed the best and the latest in chart plotters, radios, radar, sounder boxes, and all that. Plus I had a flat-screen TV in the cabin, a DVD player, stereo, and four new speakers. I don't even have that stuff in my crappy house.

I bought this boat—formerly named the *Idyll Hour*—from a rich guy from Long Island named Ragnar Knutsen, who had discovered that a pleasure boat was not always a pleasure. He'd sailed to Key West with his buddies for a fishing trip four years ago, then put a FOR SALE sign on his boat at Schooner Wharf. Someone at the Parrot knew I was looking and told me to check it out. I did, and made a deal with Ragnar for three hundred thousand, though the boat, new, had cost him about twice that—which should have been my first clue that I was buying a bottomless money pit. But I already knew that from growing up in Maine.

I also knew, as did Ragnar Knutsen, that the two happiest days of a man's life are the day he buys a boat and the day he sells it. Ragnar, though, hid his happiness and told me he was practically giving me the *Idyll Hour* in thanks for my service to the country.

My father, of course, thought I was making a bad investment, a bad career choice, and an immature decision. I knew he was right, so I went ahead with the deal.

The bank liked the deal more than my father did, and for fifty thousand down—my Army separation pay and savings—I was able to sign a quarter-million-dollar note, and rechristen the boat as *The Maine*. With luck, I could get two-fifty for it, pay off the loan, and get a job back on Wall Street. Or I could go home and live on my disability pay. Or, holy shit, learn the financial planning business. Or, better yet, go back to school for a graduate degree in something. Never too old to waste time in school. I went to Bowdoin, as I said, the oldest college in Maine and one of the oldest in the country. When I was there, it was ranked the fourth best liberal arts college in the nation, but more importantly the second best drinking college. We got beat by Dartmouth, though I don't know why. I did my part.

Anyway, grad school was also an option, and the Army—as a way of saying sorry about that Taliban RPG that almost blew your balls off—would pick up some of the tab.

Or . . . I could listen to what Carlos and his amigos had to say. As I used to say to my men, you gotta die someplace. And Cuba was as good a place to die as Afghanistan. And maybe that was better than wasting away here in Margaritaville, or on Wall Street, or in Portland. Lots of options. None of them good. Except maybe the Cuba option. Maybe this was my lucky day. Maybe not.

CHAPTER 6

Jack wheeled a cart alongside *The Maine* and called out to me, "Are those Beaners onboard yet?"

Well, if they were, they'd take offense and leave. Jack Colby does not embrace political correctness, cultural diversity, gender equality, or whatever is in fashion at the moment. He's okay, though, with Key West's gay and transgender population. "Everybody's gotta get laid," he believes.

Jack and I unloaded the cart, and I saw he'd scored two bottles of contraband Cuban rum—a liter of Ron Caney and a liter of Ron Santiago. He'd also bought Coca-Cola, limes, a bag of ice, and God-awful snacks. *The Maine* is not a party boat, per se, but I've had some interesting charters over the years, including a few drunken orgies. The captain and mate can't drink, of course, but we *can* get laid at anchor. This job does have its moments.

We stowed everything below and Jack went topside, sat in the fighting chair, and lit a cigarette. He asked, "Who are these people?"

I opened a can of Coke and sat in the opposite chair. "The guy I met in the Parrot is a Miami lawyer named Carlos. There are two other people. One is a woman."

"Why did this guy want to meet you at the Parrot just to talk about a sunset cruise?"

"He wanted to see the famous Green Parrot."

"Yeah?" Jack took a drag on his cigarette. After three years of working for me, he knows he asks more questions than I care to answer, but before the Cubans arrived I'd tell him about the fishing tournament. And the other job.

Jack Colby was about seventy, tall, lanky, and in pretty good shape. His thinning brown hair was long and swept back, he had a perpetual three-day stubble, and his skin looked like it had been left in the toaster oven too long. Jack always wore jeans and sneakers, never shorts or flip flops, and today he'd chosen his favorite "I Kill People" T-shirt.

I suggested, "The Maine T-shirt I gave you would be good tonight."

"Yes, sir."

He doesn't mean "yes," and he doesn't mean "sir." He means "Fuck you." Sometimes he calls me "Captain," and I never know if he's using my former Army rank or my present title as a licensed sea captain. In either case he means "Asshole."

Jack had been an enlisted man in the Army, and no matter how short a time you served, the military pecking order stays with you all your life, and as Jack would sometimes remind me, "You are an officer and a gentleman by an act of Congress, but an asshole by choice."

The military also discourages fraternization between officers and enlisted men, and that, too, stays with you, but Jack and I share the unbreakable bond of combat—same mud, same blood—and though we rarely socialize, we're friends.

Jack asked, "How much did you clip them for?"

"Two thousand."

"Good score."

"I'll split it with you."

"Thanks. I hope this Cuban broad is a looker."

"She's a Cuban American lady. And what do you care? You're so fucking old, the only thing you can get hard is your arteries."

Jack laughed. "Yeah? And I think you spent too much time in the foxhole with your gay soldiers."

I think we've been together too long, and I notice that when I'm around Jack, I use the F-word more than I usually do, and I mimic his wiseass attitude. I hope he's not rubbing off on me. I've got enough problems.

When Jack Colby first came aboard *The Maine* looking for a job, wearing a T-shirt that said: "Wounded Combat Vet—Some Reassembly Required," he said he'd heard I was ex-Army, and in lieu of a résumé he showed me his DD-214—his Army discharge paper—which he kept neat and safe in a plastic case, as it was an important document, loaded with military acronyms that defined his service. Box 13a told me that he'd been honorably discharged in 1969, and another box showed me he'd served a year overseas. Among his decorations, medals, and commendations was the Vietnam Service Medal, the Combat Infantry Badge, the Bronze Star, and a Purple Heart. I recalled that his home of record was Paterson, New Jersey, and that his last duty station had been Fort Benning, Georgia. Jack's service number had an RA prefix, indicating Regular Army, meaning he'd volunteered for a three-year stint. His MOS—Military Occupation Skill—was 11-B, meaning infantry, and his Related Civilian Occupation said, "None." Same as mine. He'd attained the rank of Private First Class, which is not much rank after three years and a tour in Vietnam, and I deduced that he'd either been busted or he had a problem with authority. Probably both. But he had received the Bronze Star for valor and a Purple Heart, so I hired him.

I imagine that Carlos knew that Jack was ex-military when he was searching for idiots to go to Cuba, and I also wondered if Jack would be up for a late-in-life adventure. Carlos said that Jack's life would not be in danger, which was true regarding the fishing tournament, but not true regarding sailing out of Cuba with sixty million bucks onboard if Cuban gunboats were on our ass. If we made it that far.

Well, we'd see what Carlos and his clients had to say. If nothing else, I had lots of experience calculating the odds of survival, and as we used to say, any odds better than 50/50 were too good to be true. And the biggest clue about how dangerous this was, was the money. They weren't offering me two million dollars to walk into the Bank of Cuba with a withdrawal slip for sixty million.

"What's on your mind, Captain?"

"Just thinking about the Cuban Thaw."

"They're all fucking Commies." He quoted from one of his T-shirts: "Kill A Commie For Christ."

"You been to Cuba?"

"Hell, no. Place sucks."

"Could be interesting."

"Yeah. Like 'Nam was interesting." He remembered something and said, "Hey, I saw a great T-shirt on Duval." He smiled. "'Guantánamo—Come For The Sun, Stay For The Waterboarding.'" He laughed.

Jack's life was becoming more and more informed by T-shirts. I guess if you don't own a car, you can't collect bumper stickers. But Jack might be onto something: The Book of Life was a collection of T-shirt jokes.

I didn't know much about Jack's life after he'd left the Army and before he showed up on my boat, but he told me he'd stayed in Columbus, Georgia, after his medical discharge because of some local girl whose husband had been killed in Vietnam. He wound up marrying her, and I assume the marriage ended, because he was here alone, though he never mentioned a divorce. Maybe she'd died.

As for my own love life, I was once engaged to a woman— Maggie Flemming—from Portland whom I'd reconnected with on one of my Army leaves. We sort of grew up together and my mother approved of the lady's family, which was more important than approving of the lady.

Long story short, my two overseas deployments and my stateside duty stations kept Maggie and me apart, and then my hospital stays and rehab put a further strain on the relationship. Also my head was in a bad place, and when you're screwed up, you screw up, and that's what I did, and I took off for Key West, where nobody notices. My mother was disappointed about the broken engagement, but my father didn't comment. As for Key West, they both thought I'd be back soon.

As for Portland, it's a nice town of about sixty-five thousand people, historic, quaint, and recently trendy and touristy, with lots of new upscale bars and restaurants. In some ways it reminds me of Key West, mostly because it's a seaport, though nobody swims nude in Portland, especially in the winter. The family house, a big old Victorian, is haunted, though not by ghosts, but by memories. Portland, though, was a good place to grow up and it's a good place to grow old. It's the years in between that are a challenge to some people.

But maybe if I scored big on this deal, I'd give it another try. Maggie was married, and my parents were still crazy, and my brother had moved to Boston, but I could see myself in one of the old sea captain's mansions, staring out to sea . . . I actually missed the winter storms.

I finished my Coke, stood, and looked down the long dock, but I didn't see my customers. It was possible they'd had a conversation and decided that Captain MacCormick wasn't their man. Which would be a relief. Or maybe a disappointment, especially if no one else came along with a two-million-dollar offer this week.

Jack asked, "Where are these Beaners?"

"Jack, for the record, I think Mexicans are Beaners."

"All these fucking people are like, mañana, mañana."

"No one around here is good with time, either, including you, gringo."

He laughed.

Jack's world view and prejudices are a generational thing, I think, and he reminds me in some ways of my father, who grew up in what amounts to another country. Jack Colby and Webster MacCormick are unknowable to me because their screwed-up heads were screwed up in a screwed-up war that was different from my screwed-up war. Also, I had the impression from both of them that they'd like to go back to that other country. My generation, on the other hand, has no nostalgia for the past, which was screwed up when we arrived. In any case, as my father once said to me in a rare philosophical moment, "Memories about the past are always about the present."

As for the future, that wasn't looking so good, either. But it might look better with a few million in the bank.

I spotted my customers at the end of the long dock. Carlos, an older guy, and a young woman. "Our party is here."

Jack swiveled his chair around. "Hey! She's a looker."

"Look at *me*—and listen."

He turned his attention to me. "What's up?"

"Carlos, the lawyer, has offered me thirty Gs to charter The Maine for the Pescando Por la Paz."

"Yeah? So we're going to Cuba?"

"I haven't accepted the job."

"Why not?"

"I wanted to speak to you first."

"Yeah? Well, I accept."

"You will be skippering The Maine."

"Me?"

"Right. You sail to Havana for a goodwill stop, then a place called Cayo Guillermo for the tournament, then home. Three fishermen onboard, and—"

"These three?"

"No. Just shut up and listen. They'll supply you with a mate. It's a ten-day cruise. I'll give you half."

"Yeah? I'll take it. But how come you're not going?"

"I fly to Havana. Then meet you, probably in Cayo Guillermo."

"Why?"

"Because I have a job to do in Cuba."

"What job?"

"You don't want to know. But we sail back to Key West together."

Jack stared at me. "Are you outta your fucking mind?"

I didn't reply, though I knew the answer.

Jack stood and got in my face. "Listen, sonny, your luck ran out when you got blown up. You got no luck in the bank. If you get involved with these crazy fucking anti-Castro—"

"That's *my* decision, Jack. All you have to do is join a fishing tournament."

"Yeah? And if the shit hits the fan, I'll be trying to outrun Cuban gunboats with a bunch of wetbacks onboard."

"We're not smuggling people out of Cuba."

"Then what are you doing in Cuba while I'm fishing?"

"I don't know yet."

He put his hand on my shoulder and gave me some fatherly advice. "If you say yes to this, I'll rip off your head and shit down your neck."

"I want to hear what they have to say."

"No you don't. And I'm not going."

"Okay . . . but there's a lot of money involved. More than thirty thousand."

"Yeah? You need money? Sink this fucking boat and collect the insurance."

"I missed an insurance payment."

"Then rob a bank. It's safer. And they don't torture you here if they catch you."

Carlos and the other two approached. The lady was wearing white jeans and a blue Polo shirt, and had long dark hair topped with a baseball cap. She looked about my age, mid-thirties, and she had a nice stride.

"Mac? You listening to me?"

"Yeah . . . look, Jack, they're offering me . . . us . . . two million."

"Two . . . *what*?"

"I said I'd listen and make a decision."

"Yeah? And if you listen and turn it down, then you know too much and you could wind up—" He made a cutting motion across his throat. "Comprende?"

"Your share is half a million."

Jack was uncharacteristically quiet, then said, "Make sure you listen good. 'Cause I don't want to hear anything."

"And they don't want you to hear anything."

Our charter guests arrived and Carlos said, "Beautiful boat."

Jack and I simultaneously reached out to help the attractive young lady aboard. She had nice hands. I pictured us together in Havana.

CHAPTER 7

Carlos introduced his clients, Eduardo and Sara—no last names—and we shook hands all around.

Eduardo was a distinguished-looking gentleman, older and taller than Jack, and with better posture. He was dressed in black slacks, sandals, and a white guayabera shirt. A gold cross hung on a chain around his neck. Eduardo had a heavy accent and I could easily guess at his personal history: He and his family were rich in Cuba, they escaped the godless Communists with just the guayaberas on their backs, and Eduardo was still pissed off.

Sara, like Carlos, had no accent and she seemed a bit reserved and not overly smiley, but her eyes sparkled.

We made small talk for a few minutes and I thought that Carlos was trying to determine if Sara or I seemed interested in a trip to Havana together. Also, my customers were checking out Jack's T-shirt, maybe wondering if he was crazy.

Carlos said, "Looks like it'll be a good sunset."

Time, tide, and sunset wait for no man, so I told Jack, "Cast off," and I went into the cabin and started the engine.

Carlos and Eduardo made themselves comfortable in the fighting chairs and Sara sat on the upholstered bench in the stern, looking at me in the cabin.

Jack yelled, "Clear!" and I eased the throttle forward. Within ten minutes we were out of the marina, heading west toward the Marquesas Keys.

The smell of the sea always brings back memories of Maine, of summer in the family sailboat and lobster bakes on the beach at sunset. Good memories.

I ran it up to twenty knots and took a southwesterly heading. The sea was calm, the wind was from the south at about five knots, and the sun was about 20 degrees above the horizon, so we'd have time to anchor, make drinks, and salute the dying sun.

Jack came into the cabin, sat in the left-hand seat, and lit a cigarette. "Want one?"

"No."

"They're gluten-free."

"Go set up the drinks."

"Who are these people?"

"I told you."

"Who's the broad?"

"The lady may be flying with me to Havana."

"Just fuck her here."

"Jack—"

"If you go to Havana, you don't want a pair of tits watching your back."

"All I'm doing tonight is listening."

"Who's the old guy?"

"Your guess is as good as mine."

"And make sure you understand how, where, and when the two million is going to be paid. For that kind of money, they'd rather kill you than pay you."

"I'd rather kill *you* than give you half a million."

He laughed, then said seriously, "If you decide to say no to this, I'm okay with that. And if you say yes, then I'm with you because I trust your judgement."

"My judgement sucks, Jack. That's why I hired you. But trust my instincts."

We made eye contact and Jack nodded.

I said, "Go change your shirt. That's an order."

Jack went below.

I cut back on the throttle and stared out at the horizon. Jack Colby and I don't agree on much, but we agree that after surviving frontline combat duty we were both on borrowed time. My former fiancée, Maggie, told me that God had another plan for me. I hope so. The last one didn't work out so well. But to be fair to God, the combat thing was my plan. Man plans, God laughs.

I idled the engine and checked the depth finder. Lots of shoals out here and I didn't want to drift onto them. I toggled the windlass switch to lower the anchor, then cut the engine.

I came out of the cabin and saw that Jack was wearing a *The Maine* T-shirt, and he'd set up a folding table with the bags of snacks, rum, Coke, ice, and five plastic tumblers with lime wedges.

Carlos did the honors, choosing the Ron Santiago, and made Cuba Libres for everyone. The alcohol rule for the crew is twelve hours between bottle and throttle, but Jack says you're just not supposed to drink within twelve feet of the helm. I say never refuse a drink when you need one.

Eduardo proposed a toast. "To a free Cuba. Salud!"

We clinked and drank.

Carlos commented on the Cuban rum and said, "Those Communist bastards nationalized the Bacardi factory, stole it from the family, but it's still good rum."

In my infrequent dealings with Cuban Americans, I've learned that "Communist bastards" is one word. Well, I guess if the Conch Republic ever nationalized my boat, I'd be pissed, too. But I was still surprised at the depth and duration of the hate.

I glanced at Sara, who was looking out at the setting sun. She hadn't said much, though Carlos said she'd be honest with me about the dangers of this trip to Cuba. But maybe she was thinking that I wasn't the guy she wanted to trust with her life. I had the same thought about her.

Jack, picking up on the theme of Communist bastards, told our customers, "I killed a lotta Commie bastards in 'Nam."

Eduardo smiled and drank to Jack.

Carlos, warming to the subject, asked, "Did you know that Cuban Communists participated in the torture of American prisoners of war in the Hanoi Hilton?"

Jack replied, "I heard about that."

Carlos continued, "What most people don't know is that about twenty American POWs were taken to Havana's Villa Marista prison and subjected to brutal interrogation experiments, including mind-altering drugs and extreme psychological torture. They all died in Cuba, but they are listed as missing in action in Vietnam."

Jack said, "Commie bastards."

Carlos was obviously psyching up the troops to hate the inhuman enemy. But when you do that, you also run the risk of frightening the troops. Havana wasn't looking so good to me.

Sunset cruises are supposed to be two or three couples getting romantic, and I had great mood music, like Bobby Darin singing "Beyond the Sea," or if my customers are younger I put on one of my Adele CDs or Beyoncé. But this group wanted to hear "Onward Christian Soldiers."

To change the subject I asked my customers, "Do you know about the green flash?"

They didn't, so I explained, "When the sun dips below the horizon, there is sometimes a flash of green light. Some people see it, some don't. But if you see it, it means you'll have good luck."

Carlos, being a lawyer, said, "People will lie."

"If you lie," I told him, "bad luck will come to you."

Carlos had no comment, but Sara said, "I've heard it told differently. If you're already blessed and chosen, then you'll see the green flash. Those who are not favored will not see it."

I said, "I've heard that, too. But I assume all my paying customers are blessed."

She smiled.

Eduardo produced five Cohibas and said, "Made in Cuba by slaves, but still hand-rolled in the traditional way." He passed them around and Sara also took one.

Jack had a Zippo lighter and lit everyone up. He showed his Viet-era Zippo to his fellow septuagenarian, and Eduardo read the engraving: "'Yea, though I walk through the valley of the shadow of death, I fear no evil, for I am the meanest motherfucker in the valley.'"

Jack and Eduardo got a laugh out of that.

Well, Jack had a new friend. The cultural divide narrows when you hit seventy.

We smoked our contraband cigars and drank our contraband rum. I got my binoculars out of the cabin and scanned the horizon. To the south I saw what appeared to be a Coast Guard cutter. Also, I'd seen at least two Coast Guard helicopters overhead.

The Straits of Florida between the Keys and Cuba are well-patrolled waters. The Coast Guard and the Drug Enforcement Agency are on constant alert for drug smugglers, human smugglers, and desperate refugees from Cuba trying to make the short but dangerous sail to freedom.

If you live in the Keys, you know that thousands of Cubans set out each year in homemade boats and unseaworthy rafts—the balseros, they were called. The rafters. They prayed for calm seas, favorable winds, and no sharks, and put themselves into the hands of God.

Of the thousands who attempted the crossing each year, I don't know how many made it, how many drowned, or what happened to those who were caught by Cuban patrol boats—but I did know that under the current refugee policy, if the U.S. Coast Guard picked them up at sea they were considered "Wet Foot," and returned to Cuba. But if they made it to land in the U.S. they were "Dry Foot," and allowed to stay. Which seemed to me to be a cruel and arbitrary process, an affirmation that life is randomly unfair.

I and most of my fellow charter boat fishermen agreed that if we ever picked up a balsero at sea, we'd take them ashore.

I passed the binoculars to Sara, and she, Carlos, and Eduardo scanned the horizon to the south, consciously or unconsciously looking for their countrymen.

Carlos said, "The sea is calm, the winds are from the south, and there will be a moon tonight."

Everyone understood that this was a night for the rafters.

Carlos freshened everyone's drinks and asked me some questions about *The Maine*. He then mentioned the Pescando Por la Paz and said to me and Jack, "I hope you'll consider that."

I didn't reply, but Jack said, "I hear I'm skippering The Maine."

"Yes, if Captain MacCormick agrees."

I said, "We can talk about that later."

Carlos asked us, "Do you have passports?"

Jack replied, "Yeah. Issued by the Conch Republic." He laughed.

Carlos didn't get the joke, but said, "You can both get an expedited passport in Miami. I can help with that."

I actually had a real passport, and I'd made Jack get one in case a customer wanted to sail to a Caribbean island. I said, "We're good."

The sun was red now, dropping into the sea, and we all looked out at the sparkling horizon. I can't believe I get paid for this.

On that subject, Carlos said, "If I see the green flash, I'll pay double. If I don't, this trip is free." He looked at me.

This was a sucker's bet, but really a test. Did I trust Carlos? No. Was I a gambler? Yes. Did Carlos want to screw me, or did he want to incentivize me with a two-thousand-dollar tip? One way to find out. "You're on."

Everyone was quiet now, staring at the red ball as it sunk below the horizon. A fiery light hung for a moment above the darkening sea, then disappeared, and the day slipped into night. I did not see the green flash.

Carlos, however, said, "Yes, I saw it. So I am blessed. Or will have good luck."

Jack said, "Lucky you just lost four thousand bucks."

"And worth it."

I was sure it wasn't his money he was gambling with. Or his life.

Eduardo admitted he didn't see the green flash, but Sara said, "I think I saw something." She looked at me. "And you?"

"I would like to see the green flash of four thousand dollars."

Everyone laughed. Even Carlos, who fished an envelope out of his pocket and handed it to me. "Here's two. Two later."

"Two is enough."

Carlos made another round of drinks—straight rum this

time—and we all sat, except for Jack, who went below and put on one of his Sinatra CDs. Frank sang, "When I was seventeen, it was a very good year . . ."

Carlos and Eduardo had returned to the fighting chairs and I found myself next to Sara on the upholstered bench.

The boat rocked in the gentle swells and the breeze died down. The lights of a few other boats were visible out on the dark water, and if you looked almost due south, you could imagine the lights of Havana, less than fifty miles away.

In fact, Carlos pointed his cigar and said, "That is hell over there. Here, it is heaven. But someday, in my lifetime, Cuba will be free."

We all drank to that, and Eduardo said, "And that bastard, F.C., who has created hell on earth, will burn in God's hell with his father, the devil."

F.C. is what the Cuban Americans call Fidel Castro, though I don't know why. Anyway, Eduardo's damnation sounded very solemn in his Cuban accent.

I think I understood where Carlos and Eduardo were coming from, but Sara was a cipher. She still seemed a bit reserved, but she liked a good cigar, drank straight rum, and wore a baseball cap. She'd also slipped off her loafers and was barefoot. Jack says that women who go barefoot are hot. Sounded plausible.

Jack came up from below into the cabin to turn on the running lights and check the radar to make sure a cargo ship wasn't bearing down on us.

We sat silently with our own thoughts, smoking and drinking, listening to Sinatra, and enjoying the majesty of the sea and sky. Life is good.

Until Carlos said to me, "I think there's some fishing business for you to discuss with Sara and Eduardo. I'll go below and watch TV. Jack can join me or stay in the cabin." He looked at me. "Captain?"

I nodded.

Carlos went into the cabin for a word with Jack, then disappeared below, leaving me with his clients.

Sara said to me, "I think you're the man we're looking for."

I didn't reply.

"We can't evaluate you any further. But you can evaluate us, and see if you're interested in working with us." She asked, "Do you want to hear more?"

I looked at Eduardo, whose face seemed expressionless in the darkness. He drew on his cigar and stared out to sea.

I turned my attention back to Sara. "I told Carlos I wasn't interested."

"But you *are* interested. Or we wouldn't be here."

Well, the moment for an important decision had arrived, as it had so many times in Kandahar Province. I stared at the red glow of my cigar, then looked at Eduardo, then Sara. "Okay."

CHAPTER 8

Sinatra was singing, "I did it my way," and a bright moon began to rise in the east, casting a river of light on the dark water.

Sara looked at me and we made eye contact. She said, "You probably want to know who we are before you hear what we have to say."

She had a soft voice, but it commanded attention. "That's a good start."

"I'm Sara Ortega and this is Eduardo Valazquez, though you should not repeat our names to anyone."

"I ask the same of you."

She nodded and continued, "I'm American born, an architect by trade, living and working in Miami. You can visit my website."

"Married?"

She glanced at me. "No."

It was Eduardo's turn and he said, "I, too, live in Miami and my life's work is the destruction of the Communist regime in my homeland."

"Website?"

"No."

Well, there were thousands of Cubans in South Florida and elsewhere in America who belonged to any one of several dozen anti-Castro groups. It was like a small industry in Miami, but getting smaller as the younger generation of Cuban Americans lost interest in the crusade. The third generation had no memory of old Cuba and no personal experience with the Communist regime to fully understand the hatred that their parents and grandparents clung to. Also, the CIA was not funding these groups like they used to, so maybe this was why Eduardo and his amigos needed sixty million dollars.

Sara said, "In my private life, I'm a supporter of Eduardo and his friends, but in my public life, I've shown no interest in exile affairs."

"So you won't be arrested as soon as you step off the plane in Havana?"

"Hopefully not." She added, "There are many like me who keep a low profile so that we can travel to Cuba."

"Have you been?"

"Once. Last year." She asked, "And you?"

"I haven't had the pleasure."

"I hope I have the pleasure of showing you around Havana."

Normally, I'd say, "Me too." But I didn't.

She also let me know, "I speak perfect Cuban Spanish and when I wear clothes bought in Cuba I can pass for a native."

I wasn't so sure about that.

She asked, "Do you speak any Spanish?"

"Corona."

"Well, that's not important."

What *was* important was that this sounded like we were going on a secret assignment together, and this was the mission briefing. I said, "I think we're getting ahead of ourselves."

"Well, then, catch up to me. I'm in Havana. Are you?"

That was a bit sassy. "Let's go back to Miami. Who else knows about this?"

Eduardo replied, "A few of our friends, but each person knows only what he needs to know. And only a few people know your name."

"Hopefully the Cuban secret police are not among those people."

He replied, "I would be lying to you if I said there was no possibility of a security leak. But our experience in the past has been very good, and our friends in American intelligence assure us that no secret police from Cuba have infiltrated our group. As for

Cuban American informants in our midst, we have always identified these traitors, and they are no longer with us."

I didn't ask for a clarification of "no longer with us." I did ask,
however, "How about all these thousands of new refugees escaping from Cuba?"

"We have little to do with them. We help them, especially if
there are family connections, but we can't trust them all so we remain separate from them." He added, "For the most part they hate
the regime as we do, but for different reasons. My goal is to return
to a free Cuba. Their goal is to get out of Cuba. To get a job in
America." He editorialized, "Unfortunately, these people have not
done an honest day's work in their lives."

"They will when Starbucks gets to Cuba."

Eduardo ignored that and informed me, "Everyone in Cuba
works for the government, and everyone makes the same money—
twenty dollars a month. Slave wages. There is no incentive. That is
Communism."

Actually, I've had a few months where a twenty-dollar profit
would look good. That's Capitalism.

Eduardo continued, "The people are hungry. There is malnutrition."

"Sorry to hear that. But to return to the topic of security and
this . . . mission being compromised—"

"You think like a military man," Eduardo said. "That's good."

"Right. So—"

"There is always a chance that we will be betrayed. I will not lie
to you. We have lost people in Cuba."

I had a flashback to the battalion ops bunker where some colo-
nel was saying, "I won't lie to you, Mac. This is going to be tough."

I looked at the cabin and saw that Jack was still there, having a
smoke. I could see the flickering light of the TV coming from the
stateroom below. Maybe Carlos was watching reruns of "I Love
Lucy."

This might be a good time to announce that the sunset cruise
was over.

Sara said, "I'd understand if you didn't want to go to Havana with me. There's an element of danger, and maybe the money isn't enough of an incentive. But for me, it's personal, so I'm going."

"How is sixty million dollars personal?"

"The money will be returned to those it belongs to—including my family. And some of it will go to our cause. And, of course, you will be paid." She added, "Carlos says you want five million. Will you take three?"

"Let's talk about the element of danger."

"We'll come to that. But first, now that you know who we are, we'd like you to know how we became who we are." She nodded to Eduardo.

Well, as I said, I could almost guess Eduardo's history, but I know that the Cuban exiles like to tell their story, and he began, "My father, Enrique, was a landowner in Cuba. Mostly sugar plantations and sugar mills. When Castro took power, my father and my older brother, also Enrique, were arrested, held in prison, starved, then shot by firing squad. Their last words, according to witnesses, were 'Viva Cuba.'"

Eduardo paused, then continued, "The Communist bastards would sometimes drug those who were to be executed so they had no last words. Or they would starve them, or even bleed them. They wanted no martyrs, no defiant words at the execution wall."

"Sorry to hear that."

"But there's more. My mother and I were forced out of our home into communal barracks, and sent to work in the fields we once owned. My sister, who was ten years of age, became ill and was taken from us and never seen again. My mother died of overwork— or maybe a broken heart. With my family all gone . . . there was no reason to stay, so I escaped and made my way to a coastal village, where I and a few others stole a small sailboat. But there was no wind and we were six days at sea. An American Coast Guard cutter saw us and brought us aboard, as they did in those days before the rules changed, and they took us to the Coast Guard station in Key West." He paused, then said, "I will be forever grateful."

And forever pissed off. And who could blame him? I didn't grow up in South Florida, but I've been here long enough to hear similar horror stories from people of Eduardo's age. Like Holocaust survivors, they're not forgetting, and there's no reason they should. But it's a heavy thing to live with. I didn't know what to say, except, "I'm sorry for your loss."

"I believe that God saved me so I could bring justice to all who have suffered at the hands of these godless monsters."

I really didn't want to engage in this conversation, but I asked Eduardo, "If you and your friends ever overthrew the regime, would you take revenge? Like shoot Communists?"

"Every one of them."

Sara interjected, "All we want is justice. The return of our property, and the right to return to Cuba. We seek the establishment of human rights, and the freedoms we have here."

That should be easy after Eduardo shoots all the Commies.

Eduardo said, "Sara has designed a beautiful monument to be built in Havana, dedicated to all the martyrs who have been murdered by the regime."

I'm never sure what to say when I'm in the presence of anyone who's committed to a cause. My mother says I'm self-absorbed. She's probably right. But I had to say something appropriate to what I'd just heard, so I said, "I hope you get to build that."

Sara finished her rum, then said to me, "As for my family, my grandfather was a bank president, working for an American bank in Havana. I can't tell you his name or the name of the bank and you'll understand why."

Eduardo's cigar had gone out and Sara relit it with her own. There was some obvious affection between them. She continued, "My grandfather often said that most people in Cuba were in denial about Castro's forces, which were growing stronger in the Sierra Maestra mountains. And the Batista government and the newspapers mocked the revolutionaries, and my grandfather said there was a false sense of security in Havana."

Substitute Kabul for Havana and I've been there.

"But my grandfather was a smart man and he could tell that the days of the Batista government were numbered even before Castro's forces moved out of the mountains toward Havana."

All this talk about Castro, Batista, and 1959 made me think about The Godfather Part II, which I'd just seen again on TV a few weeks ago at 2 A.M. I remembered that Michael Corleone had come to the same conclusion as Sara's grandfather: Batista was finished.

Sara continued, "My grandfather gathered all the American and Canadian dollars in his bank, and also jewelry and gold coins kept in the safe deposit boxes. He also asked his customers to transfer their other assets to his bank so he could have it all flown to his bank's headquarters in America. Everything was packaged individually with the names of the depositors on the packages, and receipts were issued by my grandfather." She looked at me. "This money never got out of Cuba."

"And here we are."

She nodded. "There were also land deeds and other monetary instruments in these packages, as well as about sixty million dollars in currency, which was a lot of money in 1958."

"It's actually a lot of money now."

"Yes, but then it was worth almost a billion dollars in today's money." As the granddaughter of a banker, she reminded me, "There is over half a century of lost interest on that money."

"That's what happens to money when you hide it under the mattress."

"It's actually hidden in a cave."

"I'm not sure I want to know that."

"There are over twenty thousand caves in Cuba. Cuba is riddled with caves."

"And I assume you know the one where your grandfather deposited his clients' assets."

She nodded.

"How do you know that no one's made a withdrawal?"

Eduardo replied, "The cave was sealed by Sara's grandfather. It is still sealed."

I didn't ask him how he knew the cave was still sealed, but he must know or we wouldn't be talking about going to Cuba. I was starting to see a picture of me with a pick ax.

Sara poured herself a Coke and continued, "On New Year's Day 1959, Castro's forces entered Havana and Batista fled the country. My grandfather wasn't immediately arrested because he worked for the American bank, and Castro was telling the world that his revolution was not Communist. Which, of course, was bullshit."

The obscenity coming from Sara's nice lips caught me by surprise and I smiled, but she wasn't smiling, so I nodded.

"My grandfather was questioned by the revolutionary police about the bank's assets, and he said that his wealthy depositors had sent their money out of the country months before because they were frightened about the revolution. He actually kept a second set of books to show to the police. In fact, a few wealthy Cubans had gotten their money out, but most delayed too long in getting themselves out."

Eduardo interjected, "The collapse of the Batista government was very sudden. Havana celebrated New Year's Eve as Castro's forces began marching on the city and Batista's soldiers began to flee. The upper classes, government officials, and senior military who couldn't escape were arrested. We know that some of these people were bank depositors who may have revealed under torture what they knew about Sara's grandfather hiding his bank's assets."

It wasn't looking good for Sara's grandfather, but she had a happy ending. "My grandfather, with the help of his bank in America, was able to board one of the last commercial flights out of Havana. He arrived in Miami with nothing, except my grandmother and their three sons, one of whom was to become my father."

"Your grandparents were lucky."

"Yes, and my grandfather continued his career in Miami. He called it a temporary corporate transfer. He died in Miami ten

years ago. My grandmother is still alive, as are my parents, waiting to return to their home in Havana." She added, "We'll see this
house when we go there."

Or send me a picture.

She continued, "Before the revolutionaries closed the American bank, my grandfather was able to wire transfer all the records
of these assets to the bank headquarters in America. The families
who escaped to America were located and given receipts—or
still had their original receipts. Those who remained in Cuba
and who survived may also have their original receipts. In any
case, there's a record of everything in the American bank headquarters, and the money will be returned to its rightful owners
or heirs."

Minus some expenses, like my fee. "Okay, so the paperwork's in
order, and all you need now is the money."

"It's waiting for us." She looked at me. "My grandfather was a
very brave man. He risked his life to protect his clients' property
and his bank's property from falling into the hands of the Communists. So you can see why this is personal for me. I want to finish
my grandfather's work."

I nodded. If I was my father, which I'm not, I'd ask Sara how
these wealthy Cubans got their money. Batista's government, as I
understood it, was an extension of the American Mafia. Gambling,
drugs, prostitution, and pornography. Also the factory owners and
the landowners like Eduardo's father were often not enlightened
employers, which was why so many of them were arrested after the
revolution. I also wondered if the American Mafia used Grandpa's
bank and had some money in that cave. Behind every great fortune
is a crime, but probably some of this money was earned honestly.
And all of it had been kept out of Castro's hands. I don't make
moral judgements—well, I do, but in this case, I'd withhold judgement. At least until I decided if I wanted to take a three-million-
dollar cut of the cash.

Sara asked, "What are you thinking?"

"I'm thinking, why now? Why not leave the money where it

is until relations improve? The bank and the depositors should be able to make a legal claim on the money. That's my advice. No charge."

Sara replied, "The problem is actually the improved relations. From what we are told, the contemplated treaty between the U.S. and Cuba will address the question of compensation for American assets that were seized when Castro took over. These are now worth billions. But in exchange, the regime insists that the U.S. legitimize their appropriation of all private property and money that was seized from Cuban citizens. So for the Americans, they'll have a legal means to recover what they lost. For the Cubans who lost everything, there will be nothing."

Well, I thought, someone has to get screwed. That's the art of the deal.

Sara continued, "It could happen that this American bank, when dealing with these issues of compensation, may inadvertently reveal to the Cuban government that their former depositors in Havana—Cuban and American—have receipted assets still in Cuba. We've discussed this and spoken to lawyers, and we feel we need to move on this and recover the money before it becomes an issue in the negotiations."

I guess I could see that happening. No one knew what lay ahead as the two governments began talking after a half century of silence. I was sure that it would take another half century to unravel the questions of who owned what, who was going to get compensated, and who was going to get screwed. If it was my money—and three million of it might be—I'd go get it now.

Eduardo added, "With improved relations comes tourism. Already thousands of Canadians, Europeans, and others who have no travel restrictions to Cuba are exploring the country. Hiking and camping are becoming popular. And when tens of thousands of Americans start to arrive . . . well, one of them may accidentally discover the hidden entrance to this cave."

That should pay for their trip. And I guess that could happen, even with twenty thousand caves. I asked, "Did anyone ever try to recover this money before now?"

Eduardo replied, "No one but Sara knows the location of this cave."

I looked at her and she said, "I will explain later."

"Okay . . . but do you have anyone in Cuba who can help you when you get there?"

"We do."

I wasn't sure if "we" meant me, but Sara said, "Let's move on."

That seemed to be a signal for Eduardo to stand and say, "I will leave you to discuss your trip to Havana."

Eduardo seemed to assume I was going, and I assumed he wasn't—he didn't want to wind up against that wall. Actually, neither did I.

He snagged the unopened bottle of Ron Caney and went below where Carlos was still watching TV.

I glanced into the cabin and saw Jack in the captain's seat, reading a magazine and eating from a bag of snacks. Hopefully he was watching the radar. For sure he was wondering if he'd be a half million dollars richer in a few weeks, or dead.

I looked at Sara, who was looking at me. Pretty woman. And smart. And brave. That was my evaluation.

"You look pensive, Mac. Can I call you Mac?"

"Of course."

"I know this is a lot to take in, and a lot to consider."

"Right."

"When you and I finish here, you'll be able to make an informed decision."

"Or justify a stupid one."

She smiled, stood, and poured us both some Coke. "Rum?"

"No, thanks, I'm driving."

She handed me my glass and touched hers to mine. "Thank you for listening."

"It's your boat tonight."

She sat in Eduardo's vacated fighting chair and swiveled it toward me, took a drag on her cigar, and tossed it overboard. She crossed her legs and said, "We will now go to Havana. Or do you want to go home?"

I wanted another drink, but I said, "I'm still listening. But I reserve the right to stop you at any time."

"Fair enough."

Jimmy Buffett was singing, "Wasted away again in Margaritaville." Which might not be my worst option.

CHAPTER 9

Sara stared out to sea, toward Cuba, then turned to me and began, "I went to Cuba last year at this time when we first heard talk of normalizing relations. As you know, the State Department doesn't allow American citizens to travel to Cuba for tourism. But they do issue licenses for group travel for cultural, educational, or artistic purposes, and that's how I went to Cuba."

I knew a few people who'd gone to Cuba with authorized travel groups, and even a few who'd circumvented the travel ban by going to Cuba via Canada, Mexico, or another country. Most Americans went to Cuba out of curiosity, or to have something to talk about at cocktail parties as they passed around Cuban cigars. Or, like the present mayor of New York City, who went to Havana on his honeymoon, some Americans wanted to experience the romance of socialism. And some Americans, I'm sure, went for clandestine purposes, and if you followed the news you'd know that some of those people were now in Cuban jails—and a few were never heard from again, as Eduardo admitted.

Sara continued, "I went with a Yale educational group." She added, modestly, "I graduated from the Yale School of Architecture. We were in Cuba for twelve days and we saw a lot of beautiful old colonial architecture, much of it collapsing, unfortunately, and a lot of ugly Soviet architecture, also collapsing, fortunately."

"Did you see your grandparents' house?"

"Yes, a beautiful mansion in the Old Town. It's now a squalid tenement filled with families. I also saw the bank that my grandfather managed. It's now a government office where people come to sign for their libretas—their monthly food ration booklets." She added, "It's sad ... actually, it made me angry."

I nodded. Revolutions usually replace one group of incompetent autocratic assholes with another, and the real losers are everyone else.

Sara said, "If you go to Cuba with me, we'll be going with a Yale educational group."

"I went to Bowdoin."

"I'm sorry to hear that."

She had a sense of humor. That's good. She'll need it.

She assured me, "Anyone can join the group if there's room."

I assumed I was already booked.

She continued, "These authorized tours are very tightly run, and you need to account for all your time. There are few opportunities to separate from the group, and the Cuban tour guide may be reporting to the police. Breakfast, lunch, and most dinners are with the group, and you spend most of your day on a tour bus with the group and the Cuban guide, and there are lectures most evenings before dinner given by the two Yale faculty group leaders or by a local Cuban university instructor."

"What time is cocktails?"

"Generally speaking, you're free to explore Havana after dinner, but during the day it's more difficult to separate from the group, though there are opportunities. If, for instance, you're sick—and many people develop gastrointestinal problems—you can stay in your room, or pretend to be in your room, and no one checks on you."

"As long as they hear the toilet flushing."

"Please be serious."

"Sorry. Look, I get this. Let's move on to where the rubber meets the road. What happens in Havana? Do we meet someone?"

"Yes, maybe the person I met last time. Or maybe someone else."

"And they take us to the cave?"

"No. Our contact in Havana will assist us in getting out of the city, to the province where the cave is located. We will be met there by someone who will give us shelter, and give us a vehicle to transport the money from the cave to Cayo Guillermo."

That sounded like two too many people in Cuba who knew about this.

She saw my brow darkening and said, "These contacts don't know about the cave or the money." She assured me, "These are trustworthy people. This part will go well."

"And how about the next part?"

"Getting from the cave to Cayo Guillermo with the money is the most difficult ... dangerous part of the plan." She let me know, "We need to be resourceful and smart."

Actually, we needed to be Superman and Superwoman. But for three million dollars, I could be resourceful and smart. I asked her, "How about getting the money aboard *The Maine*?"

"There are several possibilities. We'll know before we get to Cayo Guillermo."

Transferring the money to *The Maine* sounded like the weak link in an already weak chain of events. But this wasn't my problem if I wasn't going. And as of now, I wasn't. But to do due diligence, I asked her, "And you know the exact location of the cave?"

"I'm the only one who does." She explained, "My grandfather gave a map to my father, with detailed instructions for locating the cave. My father gave it to me."

"Okay." That was more than my father ever gave me. I asked, "Why you?"

"My father was the favorite of my grandfather, and I was the favorite of both of them."

"I see." Using that method of inheritance, I'd never see a dime.

She added, "I'm the best suited to do this."

"I'm sure you are." Anyway, I tried to imagine a fifty-five-year-old treasure map with detailed instructions on finding a cave somewhere in a province. Well, half my time in Kandahar Province was spent looking for bad guys in caves. Everyone wanted to find Osama bin Laden. But we kept coming up empty. Turns out the asshole was in Pakistan. I could have the same experience in Cuba with the money. Wouldn't *that* be ironic? "Okay, so you have the treasure map. And if you're stopped at customs or stopped by the police on the street—"

"I've copied the map, and altered it. And I've hidden the map in plain sight by labeling it, 'A great hike through the Camagüey Mountains.'" She added, "And it's all in English now."

Clever lady. "I hope nothing was lost in the translation."

"That's for me to worry about." She again assured me, "This part will go well." She further assured me, "My grandfather will be with me."

I thought he was dead. "Okay, I'm good with caves. And land navigation. And hiking." And guys trying to kill me while I'm doing all that.

"I assumed you were. So is that a yes?"

"That's a theoretical, conditional maybe." I asked her, "What happens when we leave the tour group and the Cuban tour guide notifies the police?"

"That doesn't matter. When we're gone, we're gone, and we're not going back to Havana. We're going to the cave, then to your boat in Cayo Guillermo. Then to Key West, with sixty million dollars onboard."

"The devil is in the details."

"It always is."

I took a last drag on my cigar and dropped it over the side, then looked out toward Havana. Close, and yes, cigars. As for escaping from the Yalies, that would be much easier than escaping from the police and the military when we were reported missing. Also, there was the problem of how to get sixty million dollars—and maybe gold and jewels, which are heavier than paper—to Cayo Guillermo, then onboard *The Maine*. But these were the devilish details that we'd figure out or find out in Cuba. The Army likes to have detailed plans for everything, but everyone knows that even the best battle plans fall apart as soon as the first shot is fired. Then it's improvisation, instinct, and initiative that save the day. A little luck helps, too.

Sara continued, "There's a Yale educational group going to Cuba on October twenty-second. I'm signed up for it. So are you. I assume your passport is in order, but you haven't completed your paperwork for your visa."

"Did I put down a deposit?"

"You did. With a money order. You'll need to pay the balance."

"The word 'presumptuous' comes to mind."

"Let's call it optimism."

"And if I say no?"

"Then I go without you."

"How would you get the money out of the country without my boat?"

"There are other ways, as I discovered when I was in Cuba."

"Then you don't need me."

"Not good ways, as I also discovered. The Pescando Por la Paz is the best way." She explained, "It's perfect cover, and if we can get the money onboard The Maine . . . let's say hidden in boxes of provisions, then we don't have to resort to other methods that could be dangerous."

This whole idea was dangerous, but I didn't mention it.

She continued, "Also, sailing back to Key West with the tournament fleet won't present any problems regarding the Coast Guard or customs."

Right. We wouldn't want to get that far and have our sixty million confiscated at the dock. This was sounding easier every minute—or so she thought. The irony was that Sara *was* being honest with me, but not with herself.

She continued her pitch. "Yale groups go to Cuba two or three times a year. And there are other educational groups I can join. But this group tour, coming at the time of the fishing tournament, is a happy coincidence . . . a gift from God." She added, "You—and your boat—are the last piece in this plan."

Well, that sounded like pressure. This was a persuasive lady. I'd buy a boat from her and consider it a gift from God. But I wasn't sure I'd risk my life for her, or for the money. Also, there was another piece of the plan she hadn't addressed, and I asked, "If I said yes, how would you and I travel?"

"An authorized charter flight from Miami to José Martí Airport in Havana with the Yale group and other travel groups onboard."

She added, "The Yale group is booked at a good foreign-owned hotel in Havana."

That wasn't actually the question I was asking. "Are we traveling . . . as friends?"

She seemed almost embarrassed, then recovered and said, "We won't even know each other until we meet on the tour." She added to be clear, "Separate rooms."

Well, if I said yes, at least I couldn't be accused of thinking with my dick.

I waited for her to dangle the possibility of something more that might clinch the deal, but she said, "I have a boyfriend."

"Me too. This is Key West."

She smiled. "I've heard otherwise."

They really did their homework.

She continued, "As for the Pescando Por la Paz, Carlos has entered another ship in the tournament to hold a place. He can substitute The Maine for that ship."

That answered the question of why I never heard I was in the tournament. I was feeling like a rock star with a conniving manager who was booking me on a tour that I didn't know about—and didn't want to go on.

Sara also informed me, "Friends of Carlos chartered your boat in August."

I thought back to August and remembered two Cuban American couples on a fishing trip.

"They said you were a good captain."

"They're right."

"They also said you have guns onboard."

In fact, I have a 9mm Glock, and Jack has a .38 Smith & Wesson revolver that we can use if we're taking a shark onboard. Also onboard was a Browning 12-gauge shotgun for bird and skeet shooting, and an AR-15 semi-automatic rifle for protection. There are a lot of drug smugglers in the Straits and you don't want to run into them, but if you do, you need to be prepared. Bottom line, my arsenal is for sport, business, and protection against bad guys, which I guess could include Cuban gunboats.

Sara said, "Carlos says your guns can legally stay onboard in Havana and Cayo Guillermo if Mr. Colby declares them and doesn't bring them ashore. That is maritime law."

"Okay."

"But someone may have to bring a pistol ashore."

"Not happening."

"We can discuss that later."

"What else do I need to know that will get me arrested in Cuba?"

"Only what I've just told you." She admitted, "I have no specific details of anything else. This is compartmentalized information, doled out as we need to know it—in case we're questioned by the police in Cuba. You understand?"

I nodded, wondering what Sara did for a living when she wasn't designing monuments. I mean, you don't usually hear "compartmentalized information" from architects or many other people. Maybe she read spy novels. I asked, "How do you know our Havana contact is not being watched by the police?"

"In a police state, the people learn how to identify the secret police and how to lose them." She reminded me, "I had no problem meeting my contact last year."

Sara, having survived one trip into the heart of darkness, was a bit cocky. I've been there myself. And I have the wounds to prove it.

She also let me know, "There's a possibility that when we get to Havana, we won't be able to meet our contact. Or if we do, he or she will advise us, or get word to us, that it's too dangerous to continue, and the mission will be aborted. If that's the case, you'll be paid fifty thousand dollars for your time and trouble."

"Do I have to look at architecture for the rest of the tour?"

"You'll find all the cultural aspects of the trip interesting." She also told me, "If the mission is on, but you change your mind in Havana—"

"That will not happen."

"I didn't think so."

"Okay, if we're in Havana without a mission, will you go drinking and dancing with me?"

"It would be my pleasure." She made a show of looking at her watch. "We're going back to Miami tonight."

"Why don't you stay in Key West?"

"People are waiting for us in Miami."

"Okay." I stood.

She also stood. "I'd like your answer now."

"You'll have it before we dock. I have to speak to Jack."

"All he needs to know is what he needs to know."

"Carlos made that clear." I asked, "Will I be seeing Eduardo again?"

"Why do you ask?"

"I enjoy his company."

She stayed silent, then said, "He's an avid fisherman."

"He should fish in safe waters."

She nodded. "We'll see."

I called out to Jack, "We're heading back!" I said to Sara, "If you think of anything else I need to know, tell me before we dock."

"There is nothing else, except . . ."

"Yes?"

"I like your designer T-shirt." She smiled and tapped my chest. The hook was in.

She also said, "I feel confident that I can put my life in your hands. You survived two combat tours and you can survive Cuba."

"Well . . . it's not the same. I commanded a hundred well-trained men in Afghanistan, armed to the teeth, and each man was watching the other guy's back. In Cuba, it would be only me and you."

"But you have balls."

That sort of took me by surprise.

"And I have brains. And experience." She smiled again. "Team-work makes the dream work."

"Sounds like a T-shirt."

"Do you have confidence in me?"

"You seem to have confidence in yourself."

"What more do you want?"

Well, I'd like to get laid, but I'd settle for three million instead.

"Don't talk yourself out of this, Mac. There's a saying—'I'd rather regret the things I did than the things I didn't do.'"

"I actually regret both."

"We need you. This is also about justice. And about striking a blow against an inhuman system."

"I'll keep that in mind." I gave her my standard spiel. "Make yourself comfortable below, or stay on deck, but don't fall overboard. The Straits are an all-you-can-eat salad bar for sharks. We'll be back to port within an hour."

"Good cruise."

"I'm glad you enjoyed it."

As I moved toward the cabin I could hear the electric windlass raising the anchor. Jack started the engine. "How'd it go?"

"Okay."

"Are we going to be rich?"

"Not from fishing."

"Are you at least going to get laid?"

"It didn't come up."

He moved out of the captain's chair, but I said to him, "You take the helm."

"Why?"

"You need the practice."

Jack lit a cigarette and pushed forward on the throttle. "Trust your instincts, Mac."

"My instincts tell me you don't know what you're doing in that chair."

"For half a million, I can learn fast."

"I need your decision before we dock."

"What do I need to know before I make a decision?"

"Nothing you don't already know."

"Okay. I'll think about it." He reminded me, "We're on borrowed time anyway."

Indeed we are. And there was a payment due.

CHAPTER 10

We got underway, and Jack glanced at the GPS. "Is this the way to Key West?"

"Close enough."

Jack wasn't rated or licensed to captain a 42-foot motor vessel, but he's a natural sailor, with a gut instinct for the sea and the weather and a good feel for the helm. He's also a great fisherman. It's the ship's electronics that remain a mystery to him.

I asked, "You think you can handle the Pescando Por la Paz?"

"No problem."

Hopefully the mate that Carlos was going to provide knew how to navigate. I wouldn't want to get to Cayo Guillermo with sixty million dollars and discover that *The Maine* had run aground in Havana Harbor.

Well, that might be the least of my worries.

Jack opened the last bag of Doritos. "Want one? Gluten-free."

"You enjoy them."

Jack asked, "Do you know how they begin a fishing tournament in Cuba?"

"No. How?"

"On your Marx, get set—go!" He laughed. "Get it? *Marx*."

"Pay attention to the depth finder."

I could hear the SatTV in the cabin below. My satellite antenna sometimes works out here, and my customers seemed to have picked up a comedy show with lots of canned laughs that drowned out their conversation. Also, they were speaking Spanish, so I couldn't eavesdrop if I wanted to, but they were practicing good tradecraft by blasting the TV.

It occurred to me that I wasn't getting the whole truth from Carlos, Eduardo, or Sara. On the one hand, their story about the hidden money seemed believable and consistent with what happened in Cuba at that time. But on the other hand, it seemed like a story that was too well told. But maybe that was my natural skepticism getting in the way of a good opportunity to retire.

I wasn't trying to talk myself out of this, but when someone offers you three million dollars, you need to wonder if, (A) you'll ever see the money, and (B) if the job isn't more dangerous than it already sounds. I'm okay with dangerous, but when it crosses the line to suicidal I have to reboot.

Jack asked, "What are you thinking about?"

"I'm trying to figure out how I can screw you out of your thousand bucks."

"Yeah? Let me help you. Whoever turned down the other two thousand bucks should go back and ask for it. And the guy who didn't turn it down gets the two thousand in the envelope, so somebody owes me half of four thousand."

"Where did you learn your math?"

"On the streets of Paterson. Envelope, please."

I pulled the envelope out of my pocket and gave it to him.

He advised me, "Never turn down money—unless there are strings attached."

"There are always strings attached." I changed the subject and asked him, "How much ammo do we have onboard?"

He glanced at me, then replied, "Not much. Maybe half a box of nine-millimeter—"

"Take some of your ill-gained two thousand and buy at least four hundred rounds for the AR-15, a hundred for the pistols, and a few boxes of deer slugs for the shotgun."

Jack stared out the windshield, then said, "Combat pay in 'Nam was fifty-five dollars a month. Do you believe I risked my life for less than two bucks a day?"

"That wasn't why you were risking your life."

"Right. But even for half a million . . ."

"You need to think about this, Jack. I'm in, but if you're not, I need to know."

"*You* should think about it. All I'll be doing is fishing. Unless that broad told you something else."

"Only what you already know. You're driving the getaway boat. I—and Sara—are robbing the bank."

"What bank?"

I didn't reply.

He asked, "Are we being chased during the getaway?"

"I hope not."

"But if we are—?"

"That's where you earn your half million."

He nodded, then asked, "Do you take your two million out of the heist?"

"It's three now."

"Yeah? I guess it got more dangerous."

"Tell you what—if we get shot at, your combat pay is another half million. If you're in."

He thought about that, then smiled. "Okay . . . but if you don't make it to the boat, then I just sail home after the tournament and I sell your boat and keep the money."

Daniel MacCormick died. Boat for sale.

"Deal?"

I looked at him. "Deal."

We shook.

The moonlit water was calm, the winds had picked up from the south, and *The Maine* was clipping along at twenty-five knots. I could see the lights of Key West on the horizon.

Jack lit a cigarette and said, "I remember the Cuban Revolution."

"The one in 1898?"

"The one in the 1950s, wise guy. It was big news at the time."

"Not for me, old man. I wasn't born."

"I was a kid. But I remember it on TV." He seemed lost in thought, then said, "I can remember the priests in my church, St. Joe's, talking about churches in Cuba being closed down by the Communists, and priests being arrested. My Catholic school teacher said Castro was the anti-Christ." He laughed. "Scared the shit out of me."

I imagine that Catholicism and Communism didn't mix well in 1950s America. And Jack was having a flashback to those days of fading American innocence, which I found interesting.

He took another drag on his cigarette. "To make money, I sold the Catholic newspaper, The Tablet, on the sidewalk in front of the church after every Mass. Ten cents. The Tablet had all kinds of stories about people escaping from Cuba, and people getting executed. St. Joe's was raising money for the refugees, and I remember when the first Cuban family moved in down the street . . . They spoke pretty good English, and this guy, Sebastian, would talk to the neighbors about everything he lost in Cuba, a factory and some other shit, and the wife—can't remember her name—would cry a lot. The kids were young. Three of them. They were okay, but they always talked about the big house they had in Cuba. And servants. So I guess they all felt like they got fucked." He smiled. "Hey, I was *born* fucked in New Jersey."

There were two kinds of history: the kind you read about, and the kind you lived through—or were actually part of. For Jack, the Cuban Revolution was a childhood memory. For Sara, it was family history, and part of who she was. For Eduardo, it was a boyhood trauma and an obsession. And for me, it was irrelevant. Until today.

Jack asked me, "You trust these people?"

"My instincts say they're honorable people."

"That doesn't answer the question."

"They need us."

"Up until we're on this boat with the money you stole."

"We'll be armed. And they're probably thinking the same about us."

"Right. There's no honor among thieves."

"We're not thieves. We're repatriating money that rich Cubans stole from poor Cubans so it can be returned to the rich Cubans who stole it."

Jack smiled, then asked me, "You thinking with your dick?"

"Not this time."

"Okay." He asked, "How much money are you stealing?"

"You don't need to know. Also, it goes without saying that you will not breathe a word of this to anyone."

"Loose lips sink ships."

"You and I will write letters that names names and I'll leave the letters with my attorney in sealed envelopes, to be opened in the event of our deaths or disappearance."

Jack had no reply.

"And I will let our new amigos know that these letters exist."

Jack nodded.

Sara came up from below and stood with us in the cabin. She said to Jack, "I hope the tournament sounds interesting to you."

"Yeah, and the sail home could be more interesting." He asked, "Want a Dorito?"

"Thank you." She took one and looked at the electronic displays on the console. "Can you pull up Havana and Cayo Guillermo on the GPS?"

I got on Google Earth, typed in "Havana," and the screen switched to a satellite view of the city. Sara said, "If Christopher Columbus had Google Earth he would have realized he hadn't found India." She laughed for the first time. Nice laugh.

Sara pointed to a spot on the coast of the Straits of Florida, about four or five miles west of Havana Harbor. "This is the Hemingway Marina, where most of the tournaments used to dock. But to maximize the publicity for this new tournament, and to get good photo ops, the Pescando Por la Paz will sail directly into Havana Harbor." She pointed to the big harbor, and continued, "Here is the Sierra Maestra Cruise Terminal, just restored to the way it looked a hundred years ago."

I zoomed in on the structure, which appeared to be a long covered pier jutting into the harbor, attached to a large terminal building on the shore.

Sara said, "This restoration was done in anticipation of American cruise ships making Havana a port of call."

Maybe Dave Katz was right. The cruise ships would bypass Key West and I'd lose some of that business. Time to retire with three million dollars.

Sara continued, "The terminal building, as you can see, faces out onto a square—the beautiful old Plaza de San Francisco de Asís." She looked at Jack. "So when you get off this boat and step out of the terminal, you'll be right in the heart of the historic Old Town."

Jack stared at the screen, but said nothing.

Sara continued her sales pitch. "There might be a band waiting if it's been approved, and maybe a small crowd, maybe TV cameras and some reporters from Cuban TV and newspapers. Possibly also some Cuban government officials and some people from the American Embassy." She assured Jack, however, "You don't need to give an interview or pose for pictures if you don't want to."

Again, Jack said nothing. But if he agreed to an interview and photos, I'd strongly advise him not to wear his "Kill A Commie For Christ" T-shirt.

Sara said, "We don't know how much publicity the Cuban government wants for this occasion." She explained, "They're ambivalent. They realize that events are moving faster than they'd like, and they find themselves standing in the way of history."

Interesting.

Sara said to Jack, "There are lots of good bars, restaurants, and nightclubs in the Old Town."

I thought Jack was going to turn the boat around and head to Havana.

To put the rosy picture in better focus, I asked, "Do the crews and fishermen go through immigration and customs?"

"I guess they do. But as invited guests, I'm sure there won't be any problems. Why do you ask?"

Well, because you said that someone might need to bring a gun ashore. "Just asking."

I glanced at Jack, who seemed to be thinking about all this. He'd already signed on for the well-paying job, so Sara's soft sell was unnecessary. But it was good that she painted a nice word picture for him of his brass band arrival in Havana Harbor. If she could tell him where to get laid, that would clinch it.

Sara said to Jack, "I hope I gave you a good sense of what to expect in Havana."

Jack nodded.

Right. But not a good sense of what to expect in Cayo Guillermo.

I pulled back on the Google image to show both Havana and Cayo Guillermo, about two hundred and fifty miles east of Havana. Theoretically, it should be an easy sail along the coast.

Jack stared at the Google image and nodded to himself.

Sara said to me, "If Jack has the helm, let's have a drink."

I thought she was going to go below, but she walked out to the stern, and I followed.

She poured two rums and gave one to me.

Still standing, she said, "Eduardo is impressed with you and Jack, and he has no problem with three million." She asked, "Are you with us?"

"I am."

"Good. And is Jack with us?"

"He is."

She touched her glass to mine. "God will also be with us."

"Then what could possibly go wrong?"

We drank to that.

She said to me, "Carlos needs to meet with you, to give you the details of your educational trip to Havana, and there are papers for you to sign for your visa and a few other logistical things to discuss." She asked, "Can you meet him in his office tomorrow?"

"Sure."

"He'll let you know the time."

"I'll let him know the time."

She glanced at me. "Okay . . . and Carlos will come back to Key

West in a few days—at your convenience—to speak to you and Jack about the tournament. And to get a copy of Jack's passport and some information on The Maine. He'll have the permit for the tournament and a check to charter your boat." She smiled. "Secret missions begin with boring details."

"It's good when they end that way, too."

She looked at me. "This will go well."

That's probably what they said about the Bay of Pigs Invasion. Not to mention the CIA's hundreds of attempts to kill Castro. And let's not forget the Cuban Missile Crisis, the Mariel Boatlift, and the trade embargo.

As Jack might say, the U.S. and Cuba have been fucking each other so long that they both must be getting something out of it.

But we were now on the verge of a new era—the Cuban Thaw. But before that happened I had a chance to do what so many other Americans, including the Mafia and the CIA, had done before me—try to fuck Cuba. I probably had as much chance of doing that as I had of fucking Sara Ortega.

"Why are you smiling?"

"It must be the rum."

"Then have another. I like your smile."

"You too."

We had another, and she said, "Our next drink will be in Havana."

And maybe our last.

PART II

CHAPTER 11

It was about 8 P.M., and I was sitting at the bar in Pepe's, a Mexican chain restaurant located in Concourse E of Miami International Airport, drinking a Corona and looking through my Yale travel packet. Probably I should have read this stuff a few weeks ago when Carlos gave it to me in his toney South Beach office, but I kept thinking that this Cuba trip wasn't going to happen. Well, it was happening. Tomorrow morning. So, as the Yale Travel Tips suggested, I was staying at the airport hotel, located in the concourse about thirty feet from where I was now having a few beers. The Yale group would assemble in the hotel lobby at zero-dark-thirty—5:30 A.M. to be exact.

Jack had driven me to the airport earlier via the Overseas Highway in my Ford Econoline van, which is not my first choice of a midlife-crisis vehicle, but it's what you need if you own a charter fishing boat. In a few weeks I'll be trading in the van for a Porsche 911.

Anyway, I had used the drive time to rebrief Jack about his part in the Cuban caper, and I reminded him to pick up the extra ammo before he sailed.

I'd also reminded Jack not to top off in Cayo Guillermo because we'd want *The Maine* as light as possible if we needed speed when leaving—though stealth is what we wanted. Earlier in the week I'd given Jack a refresher course on the ship's electronics, so hopefully he could find Havana before he wound up in Puerto Rico. In fact, though, if he just followed the other boats in the tournament fleet he should have no problems.

Jack, while not overly enthused about his Cuban adventure,

looked forward to his half-million-dollar cut—though he was conflicted about getting shot at to earn his other half million in combat
pay. I promised him, "They don't have to hit you. I'll pay you even
if they miss."

Jack suggested I go fuck myself, then asked me how we were
going to get the loot aboard *The Maine*, and I told him, "I haven't
been briefed yet."

"When you find out, let me know."

"Someone will let you know—when you need to know."

"And what if I don't like the plan?"

"Whatever the plan is, Jack, I'm sure you won't like it."

"This is where I could get killed."

"Or get rich."

"Or neither. 'Cause I don't think you're gonna make it to the
boat with the loot."

"Problem solved."

I ordered another beer from the barmaid, Tina, and returned
to my thoughts. Before you go on any mission, you need to understand what you know, identify what you don't know, and try to
guess what could go wrong. And finally, getting there is only half
the fun; you need a clear path home.

So, to replay the last few weeks, after I met Carlos in Miami,
he'd come back to Key West, as promised, and Jack and I met him
aboard *The Maine*. Carlos had brought with him the paperwork
and permit for *The Maine* to sail to Cuba with the tournament, and
also brought with him *The Maine's* new first mate, a young Cuban
American named Felipe who seemed competent, and who also
seemed to know that this wasn't about fishing for peace. I didn't
know what they were paying Felipe, but I hope it included combat
pay.

Felipe and Jack had hit it off—as long as Felipe understood that
Jack was the captain—and they arranged to take *The Maine* out for
a practice run. Felipe had promised me he was familiar with the
boat's electronics.

I'd asked Carlos about the three fishermen who were ostensibly

chartering my boat, and he assured me they were actual sports fishermen who knew a rod from a reel so they wouldn't arouse suspicion. Also, these three men, whom Carlos identified only as "three
amigos," had made arrangements to fly out of Cuba on the last day
of the tournament with a destination of Mexico City. The three
fishermen were going to stay at a local hotel in Cayo Guillermo,
so if *The Maine* was sneaking out at night before the tournament
ended, the fishermen would not be onboard to complicate things
if we got into a shoot-out. So there would be only Felipe onboard
for me and Jack to deal with if this was a double-cross. And of
course, Sara would be aboard.

I had also asked Carlos if Eduardo had any intention of being
onboard *The Maine* and Carlos said no, because Eduardo was
persona non grata in Cuba and would be arrested if he stepped
ashore—or if Cuban authorities came onboard and checked his
ID. So despite my thought that Eduardo wanted to join us, it
seemed that he would not see Cuba on this trip—and probably
not in his lifetime.

I had also told Carlos about the letters to be opened in the event
of my or Jack's unexplained death or disappearance, and Carlos responded, "I would expect you to do that. But you can trust us."

As for timing, the Pescando Por la Paz fleet of ten boats was
scheduled to leave Key West on Saturday the twenty-fourth, two
days after my and Sara's Thursday flight to Havana with the Yale
group. The tournament crews and fishermen would spend Saturday night in Havana for their goodwill visit, but Carlos was em-
phatic that neither Sara nor I would meet up with anyone from
The Maine. Jack, however, wanted to buy me a drink in Havana, so
we made a date to rendezvous at the famous Hotel Nacional bar.
Carlos doesn't give the orders.

Carlos had also brought with him an article from the *Miami Herald* about the Pescando Por la Paz, and I'd seen similar articles in the
Key West Citizen. The Cuban Thaw had been big news recently, and
though most editorials and articles had been favorable, the hard-
core Cuban exile community remained adamantly opposed to

Washington's softening of American policy that had been in effect for over half a century. Basically, people like Carlos, Eduardo, and their amigos wanted F.C. and his brother Raúl gone—preferably dead—before any normalization took place. I myself had no strong opinion on that, as I told Carlos in the Green Parrot.

Also, I'd done due diligence and checked out Carlos' website and Googled him, and he was legit in the context of who he said he was—a rock star lawyer for the anti-Castro groups in Miami, and he was not shy about it online.

I'd also checked out Sara Ortega's professional website. She worked for a small boutique architectural firm and she had talent. Maybe, after I was rich, I'd hire her to build me a house somewhere. Her Facebook page didn't show much, not even a mention of her boyfriend, and there wasn't much about her on Google.

As for Eduardo Valazquez, he didn't exist on the Internet, but that wasn't unusual for a man of his age and occupation. He had, however, been mentioned in a few newspaper articles about the Cuban exile community—if this was the same Eduardo Valazquez—and I could see why he was not welcome in Castro's Cuba.

Bottom line about Internet sleuthing is that it's good as far as it goes, but you needed to take most of it with a grain of salt, and you needed some context to interpret what you read. In any case, my due diligence, for what it was worth, hadn't spotted any red flags, and here I was in Pepe's.

As for research and Intel about the People's Republic of Cuba, as I said, I'd convinced myself that this trip wasn't going to happen, so I didn't do much of what the Army called "Country Orientation." How much do you need to know about a place that sucks? More to the point, Carlos had given me a very good briefing, and he'd also assured me that Sara Ortega would be my main source of in-country information, and that aside from the Yale info packet and a Cuba travel guide there wasn't much I needed to read. Carlos also pointed out that I wasn't hired for my knowledge of Cuba; I was hired for my knowledge of survival in a hostile environment, i.e., Sara Ortega had the brains, Daniel MacCormick had the balls. Should work.

I'd also asked Carlos about the plan to get me, Sara, and the money aboard *The Maine* in Cayo Guillermo, and he assured me, "We will have the plan in place before you get to Cayo."

"And how will I—or Sara—know what the plan is?"

"We will get word to you—and Sara."

I didn't bother to ask him how he'd do that, or when, and we both knew that if the Cuban police were hooking up electrodes to my testicles, it was best if I didn't have this information.

Carlos also informed me, "We want no connection between you and The Maine, so I have the paperwork with me to buy your boat."

"How much?"

"I have a certified check for the exact amount of your bank loan, payable to your bank."

Well, now that I could dump this albatross, I wasn't sure I wanted to part with her, but Carlos assured me, "There is a buy-back clause in the contract, and when you return from Cuba, you can buy your boat back for the same price."

"Less if it has bullet holes in it."

He ignored that and said, "The chances of the Cuban authorities somehow connecting Daniel MacCormick the tourist and Daniel MacCormick the owner of The Maine are very slim, but if they do, it might arouse suspicion."

"I got that."

He then presented me with a sales contract, some registration paperwork, and the check payable to my bank and drawn on the Sunset Corporation, whatever that was.

"And to be extra cautious," said Carlos, "I've renamed the boat in the tournament paperwork."

"It's your boat."

"And I will have the new name painted on the boat." He smiled. "The Maine is now Fishy Business."

"I like it." But it would always be *The Maine* to me. And if I did buy it back, I'd have *The Maine* repainted on it, in gold, and sail it to Portland.

So I signed the paperwork and sold *The Maine* to the Sunset Corporation. In my next life, I want to be a Cuban American lawyer in Miami with an attaché case full of tricks.

And finally, Carlos had not forgotten the charter fee, and he gave me a certified check for thirty thousand dollars, which I split with Jack. Carlos also gave me a Cuba travel guide as a parting gift.

I congratulated Carlos on his new boat, and his last words to me and Jack before he and Felipe left Key West were, "Vayan con Dios."

And Jack's last words after he dropped me off at the airport were, "See you in Havana."

And mine to him were, "Don't wreck Carlos' boat." I also told him to use some of his money to buy four appropriately sized bulletproof vests.

———

I was working on my third beer and second bowl of nachos, half watching the Mets vs. Cubs playoff game on the TV above the bar while I flipped through my Yale travel packet. I glanced at a sheet of paper titled: *Thirty Frequently Asked Questions,* and read Number One: *Everyone says it is illegal to travel to Cuba. Is this trip legal?*

Yes was the expected answer. If it was *No,* there couldn't be twenty-nine more questions. But for me and Sara Ortega only part of it was legal.

I read on: *This program differs from more traditional trips in that every hour must be accounted for.* Even the time you spend trying to seduce one of the ladies in your travel group. Well, no, it didn't say that. But maybe it was implied.

I finished my beer and had a nacho. There were about thirty people in our group according to the roster in my travel packet, and I was happy to discover that I didn't know any of them. Except, of course, Sara Ortega of Miami, who was actually sitting at a table about twenty feet from me with two ladies who looked very serious and studious, and dressed to repel a second glance.

Sara, however, was wearing a pale blue sleeveless dress that barely covered her knees and loafers that she'd slipped off under the table.

I hadn't seen or heard from her since our sunset cruise, and as per her script we didn't know each other. But we'd made eye contact when she'd walked into Pepe's cantina, and I thought I saw a fleeting smile on her lips. Maybe a wink. I assumed she was also staying in the airport hotel, though apparently not with her boyfriend.

It appeared that there were other people from the Yale group in the restaurant who were staying at the airport hotel, and a few of them seemed to know one another, though a few had just walked up to a table and asked people if they were on the Yale Cuba trip, as Sara did before she joined the two ladies. Yalies, like vampires, can recognize one another in the dark. Similarly, Bowdoin alums can recognize one another in a bar—they're the ones passed out on the floor.

Anyway, I took my eyes off Sara, who was not looking my way, and went back to the travel packet. I read: *Each day has been structured to provide meaningful interactions with Cuban people.*

Which reminded me of one of Jack's informative T-shirts: "Join The Army, See The World, Meet New People And Kill Them."

I read on: *Please note that the Yale Alumni Association intends to fully comply with all the requirements of the general license. Travelers must participate in all group activities. Each individual is required to keep a copy of their Final Program, which could be requested by the Office of Foreign Assets Control at any point in the next five years.*

I didn't know this federal agency, but this sounded serious. I don't keep any paperwork more than five minutes if I can avoid it, but maybe I should have this Final Program with me if I wound up in a Cuban jail and someone from the newly opened American Embassy was allowed to visit me in my cell. "Do you have your Yale Final Program, Mr. MacCormick?"

"No, sir. I lost it when I was being chased by the police."

"Well, then, I can't help you. You're screwed."

Tina, without asking, took my empty and put a cold one on the bar. "Private joke?"

"Just thinking about my vacation."

"Where you traveling to?"

"Cuba."

"Why do you want to go to Cuba?"

"North Korea was sold out."

"Really?"

She was about ten years older than me, not bad-looking, and I thought if I flirted with her, Sara would notice, get jealous, and come join me. But that's the kind of silly thinking you get with a beer buzz.

"You staying here?" Tina nodded toward the hotel lobby.

"I am."

We made eye contact and she asked, "How're the rooms?"

Well, I can describe my airport hotel room, or show it to you if you haven't already seen a few. "I've slept in worse."

She smiled. "Me too." She added, "Beer's on me."

A waiter had drink orders for her and she moved down the bar.

Well, sleeping with the barmaid might not be a good way to begin this trip—or begin my romancing of Sara Ortega. It occurred to me that Sara, who lived in Miami, didn't need to stay at the airport hotel, so she was here to make sure I was here. But she wasn't here to have a drink with me. Maybe later.

Jack says women are like buses; there'll be another one along in ten minutes. But this one, Sara Ortega, was impressive. Like the Army women I once dated, Sara was ready to put her life on the line for something she believed in. And she'd somehow talked me into putting myself in harm's way again. The money was an inducement, of course, but aside from that I didn't want her going to Cuba alone or with someone less competent, and she trusted me to take care of business. *Balls*, she said.

Men are egotistical idiots, prone to female flattery, but we all know that. And even if Sara and I didn't hook up in Cuba, we'd always have memories of Havana. Unless we got killed.

I went back to the *Thirty FAQs*. Number Four informed me that I'd present one half of my visa card on arrival in Cuba, and it was *Essential* that I not lose the second half or I'd have trouble getting out of the country.

Well, if things went right, I wouldn't need the second half; and if things went wrong, the second half wouldn't get me out of Cuba.

I'm not a big fan of group tours—I did two group tours in Afghanistan. But I agreed it was good cover for this trip—until the time that Sara and I disappeared from the group. Then the alarms would go off. But if the Cuban police had any romance in their soul, they'd just think that hot Sara Ortega and horny Daniel MacCormick had slipped away to be alone together. And, as per Carlos, that would be our cover story if we were stopped by the police in the countryside. And the police might buy it—I mean, even if they're Commies, they're Latinos, right? But if we had sixty million dollars with us we'd have some additional explaining to do. That's where a gun would come in handy.

I looked again at the travel packet and read that it was illegal to use American dollars in Cuba, and therefore our group would go to a Havana bank to convert our dollars into something called CUCs—Cuban Convertible Currency, for use by foreigners.

Carlos had told me to bring at least three thousand American dollars, two of which I'd gotten from him to settle our bet. Never turn down money—even after you've turned it down.

Also regarding currency regulations, Americans in Cuba were not allowed to use the Cuban peso for any transactions, and Americans could not buy pesos at a Cuban bank. Unfortunately, said Carlos, our Cuban contacts wanted to be paid in pesos, because they weren't allowed to have or spend American dollars or CUCs. Therefore Sara would be carrying three hundred thousand Cuban pesos—worth about twelve thousand dollars—hidden on her person to be given to our Cuban contacts for risking arrest and imprisonment. That didn't sound like a lot of money, but it was about fifty years' salary in Cuba. I should have held out for five million. Dollars, not pesos.

I returned to my FAQ sheet and read that Wi-Fi was almost nonexistent in Cuba, and my cell phone would probably not have service. Carlos had mentioned this and pointed out the obvious, which was that communication between Sara and me would be difficult. It could also be a problem if, for instance, we tried to make an emergency cell phone call to the American Embassy. But as we learned in the Army, you go into battle with the equipment you have, not the equipment you want.

Sara and I could, of course, carry SATphones, but according to Carlos, that was a *very* big red flag for the Cuban authorities, and if you got stopped, you might as well be carrying a CIA ID card.

I took a long drink of beer and felt the alcohol seep into my brain, which sometimes makes me more honest with myself. Somewhere in the back of my mind I knew that this Cuban caper had less to do with money than it had to do with Mac's need for action and adventure, which had to do with my low tolerance for 9-to-5 work. That's why I quit Wall Street and how I wound up in combat for crap pay. And also why I wound up in a small boat on a big ocean—though the sea adventure never really got the adrenaline going the way combat did. Also, to be honest, I may be having daddy issues. But that analysis was for another time.

In any case, I now had a single elegant solution to my money problems *and* my midlife boredom problems. *Cuba.* And if I listened to Sara—and Carlos and Eduardo—I was also doing a noble thing, striking a blow against a repressive regime and righting an old wrong. But most of all, I knew, I was doing something for me. And Jack. And by extension, for all of us whose lives had been twisted by war.

On that subject, I admitted that like most veterans I was a better person for having served. My discharge papers, like Jack's, said *Honorable*, which was true. What was not true, however, was that my Military Occupation Skill—infantry commander—had no related civilian skill. Turns out it does.

I looked over at Sara's table. She was gone.

I asked Tina for another beer, but she gave me a note written on a paper napkin. It said: *Get some sleep. Tomorrow is a long day.* Signed: *S.*

Or, as I used to say to my men on the eve of a dangerous operation, "Tomorrow is going to be the longest or the shortest day of your life. It's up to you." And, of course, it was up to the enemy, and the gods of war, and fate.

CHAPTER 12

To get us into the spirit of adventure travel, the off-brand charter airline was flying an old MD-80 that had seen better days.

Sara was sitting about ten rows ahead of me in the window seat next to an older guy who appeared to be asleep, or maybe he'd died of fright during takeoff.

I was on the aisle, and the middle-aged guy next to me—who said he was with a people-to-people group called Friendly Planet— was staring out the window as I read about Cayo Guillermo in the travel guide that Carlos had given me. Cayo Guillermo, aside from being a fisherman's paradise, was also one of Cuba's seven certified entry ports, meaning customs, immigration, and security, includ- ing, I was sure, naval patrol boats.

I put down the book, yawned, and looked around. The Yale group of about thirty people were scattered throughout the cabin, which was full, and I could only imagine who these other people were, what groups they were with, or why they were going to Cuba.

The Yale group had assembled in the hotel lobby at 5:30 A.M., as per instructions, and we had been greeted by our group leaders, a young man named Tad and a young woman named Alison, both of whom were Yale faculty, but neither of whom inspired confi- dence in their organizational ability. Tad was maybe thirty, but he looked younger, a result no doubt of a cloistered life in academia. Tad needed three years in the Army. Alison was not bad-looking, though she seemed a bit severe, maybe even tight-assed. If I were alone on this trip, she would be my challenge. Anyway, Tad and Al- ison, according to the itinerary, would be giving lectures on Cuban culture, time and place TBA, which I think means To Be Avoided.

Sara had kept her distance from me during the group assembly, which was fine with me at 5:30 A.M. She was wearing black slacks, sandals, and a snug green Polo shirt. I wondered where she was hiding the three hundred thousand Cuban pesos.

My travel attire, like that of most of the men in the group, was casual—khakis, Polo shirt, and walking shoes. Also regarding attire, Carlos had said that Sara and I needed to look like hikers when we escaped to the countryside, so we had backpacks instead of carry-on luggage, and we'd leave our suitcases behind when we slipped out of our hotel in Havana, never to return.

After our group assembly and roll call we'd all gone to another concourse for what seemed like endless paperwork, passport and visa checks, and general bureaucratic bullshit. Finally, after we'd paid a twenty-five-dollar Cuban Departure Tax, we'd gotten our boarding passes for Wing-and-a-Prayer Charter Airlines, or whatever they were called.

It was during this drawn-out process that I checked out my fellow travelers. Most of the group were couples, and most of them were middle-aged, and many of them seemed like they were having second thoughts about their Cuban adventure. Me too. I also noticed seven or eight singles, including Sara and me, and a few older ladies of the type you always see traveling with groups, sometimes to exotic places where medical care is iffy. I give them credit, but I wouldn't give them my amoxicillin.

More importantly, I didn't see anyone in our group whom I'd consider suspicious—except Sara and me. Also, interestingly, Sara Ortega was the only person on the Yale roster with a Spanish surname. I hoped they didn't single her out when we landed in Havana.

Also on the roster was a name I recognized—Richard Neville, a bestselling author. I'd read one or two of his novels, which weren't too bad. I recalled his photograph on the book jacket and I spotted him standing away—or aloof—from the group. With him was a woman, Cindy Neville, according to the roster. She was young enough to be his daughter, but there was no physical resemblance, so she must be his wife. Cindy was a looker, and I wondered what she saw in him. Probably the bulge in his pants—the wallet, not the crotch.

Also on the roster was a man named Barry Nalebuff, a Yale professor who, with Tad and Alison, would be giving lectures, TBA.

Anyway, after the third or fourth head count and some confusing instructions from Tad and Alison, we had time for a quick cup of coffee and what might be my last buttered bagel on earth. Then to the gate.

Now, forty minutes out of Miami, we were already beginning our descent into Havana—or hell, according to Eduardo and Carlos. I could imagine what this flight was like in the 1950s; high rollers, movie stars, mobsters, and thrill-seekers from New York and Miami, flying on luxurious airliners to sinful Havana—casinos, prostitutes, sex shows, pornography, and drugs, all of which were in short supply in 1950s America. Old Havana must have been a deliciously decadent town, and it was no wonder that the corrupt Batista government fell like a rotten mango. I recalled that Sara's grandfather had gotten out on one of the last commercial flights from Havana to Miami. Now his granddaughter was back, and I hoped she shared his luck in getting out.

The Communists, like the radical Islamists I fought, are not fun-loving people, and when they take over, they become the fun police. I once told a captured Taliban fighter, through a translator, "Life is short, sonny. Get laid, have a few laughs and cocktails, and dance a little," but he had his own agenda.

The guy sitting next to me got tired of the view and said, "It's about time we normalized relations."

"Right."

"And end the trade embargo."

"Good idea."

"Our government has been lying to us."

"Now you tell me."

"Seriously, the Cuban people are like us. They want peace. And better relations."

Actually, they wanted to escape to Miami, but I said, "That's good."

"I think we're going to be pleasantly surprised."

I heard a chime and said, "The captain just turned on the no talking sign."

My companion turned back to the window, and I took the opportunity to fill out my customs declaration form. Was I carrying any firearms with me? I wish. Did I have any alcohol with me? Just what's left in my brain.

The form also asked if I was carrying Cuban pesos, and if so, how much. My answer was *No*, though I wasn't sure what Sara would decide to do. Honesty is the best policy, unless you could lie and get away with it.

I also had an immigration form to fill out. Was this my first time in Cuba? *Yes*. And last. Where was I staying in Cuba? *The Parque Central Hotel in Havana*. Should I mention the cave? No. As for my departure info, I wrote my return flight number and departure date—though I reserve the right to escape earlier by boat, under fire. I signed the form.

I looked up and saw Sara coming toward me. She didn't make eye contact as she headed for the lavatories in the rear. On her way back, however, she brushed her hand on my shoulder. I was getting into this secret relationship. It was exciting.

As we descended, I could see Havana in the distance, a city of over two million people, built around a large harbor that gave access to the Straits of Florida and the world beyond—if you could get there.

We made our final approach into José Martí International Airport, and I saw a few passenger terminals next to mostly empty parking lots. I noticed that one end of the airport was military, and the Cuban Air Force seemed to consist of five vintage Soviet MiG fighters, a few Russian-made helicopters, and an antique American DC-3 with a red star painted on its tail. Hopefully the MiGs and choppers were grounded for parts and repairs and I wouldn't see them overhead when I sailed out of Cuba.

I'd read in my guide book that José Martí Airport had been bombed by Cuban exile pilots in 1961, in preparation for the CIA-backed Bay of Pigs Invasion. The attack bombers were American-made, apparently provided by the CIA. I could see why the Castro regime might have some unresolved anger issues. Anyway, the airport looked okay now, but I was sure the memory lingered on.

The MD-80 touched down and I was in Cuba, a long ninety miles from the Green Parrot.

CHAPTER 13

We deplaned and walked in single file across the sweltering tarmac, under a blazing sun and the gaze of security police who carried Russian AK-47s. The last time I saw one of those, it was firing at me.

We filed into Terminal Two, a dark, unwelcoming structure, built, according to my travel guide, during the days of the Cuban-Soviet alliance, specifically to accommodate—or segregate—Americans arriving on charter flights. I looked for a sign saying <u>WELCOME AMERICANS!</u> but it must have been in the shop for repairs. Also, the air-conditioning was not working or nonexistent, but there were floor fans.

Tad was holding up a Yale sign and the group congregated around him. I also saw raised signs for cultural institutions and art museums, and signs for other college alum groups. Apparently Cuba was the hot new destination.

Tad was urging the Yale group to get closer, and I thought he was going to lead us in "The Whiffenpoof Song," but he shouted, "Please stay together!" Sara wound up next to me, and she looked a bit tense, which was understandable, so to buck her up I said, "Hi. I'm Dan MacCormick. What's your name?"

She gave me a quick glance. "Sara."

"First time here?"

"No."

"Do you know where I can buy cigars?"

"In a cigar store."

"Right. Are you traveling alone?"

She didn't reply but I saw a smile flicker across her lips, and I gave her a reassuring pat on her arm.

Alison had found a uniformed official who directed the Yale group to an immigration officer sitting in a booth behind a tall counter.

We formed a queue and Sara was several people ahead of me. She looked totally composed now, but somewhere on her body or in her luggage were three hundred thousand Cuban pesos that would need some explaining if she was searched. Also, she had a hand-drawn hiking map that might arouse suspicion if a sharp security officer asked to see the Yale itinerary.

The immigration officer motioned for the first person on line—who happened to be one of Sara's Mexican restaurant companions—to step forward into the booth.

The robotic officer took her immigration form, then matched her face to her passport and her name to a list that he had on a clipboard. He asked her a few questions that I couldn't hear, then asked her to step back, remove her glasses, and look at the camera mounted over the counter. I really didn't want my picture taken but I didn't think this was optional.

The immigration officer stamped the lady's visa, kept one half, then stamped her passport. He pressed a buzzer and motioned for her to go through a door and exit the left side of the booth. I wondered if we'd ever see her again.

The officer motioned for the next Americana, Alison, to step forward, and the process was repeated.

The line moved slowly, and at one point a couple approached the booth together and the immigration officer had a little shit fit and yelled out, "Uno! Uno!" like he didn't get the memo about the Cuban Thaw.

It was Sara's turn and she walked into the booth like she owned it.

The immigration officer took special note of Señorita Ortega, and I could see that they weren't getting along. She stepped back to have her picture taken, then collected her visa and passport and disappeared through the door.

The guy picked up a phone and spoke to someone, then motioned for the next person in line. I hoped he was calling about getting more ink for his stamp, and not about Sara Ortega.

After about fifteen minutes, it was my turn, and I walked into the booth.

The immigration officer stared at me with his dead eyes. I gave him my passport, my immigration form, and my visa tarjeta del turista.

He looked at my passport photo and flipped through the pages, discovering that I hadn't been out of the U.S. since I'd sailed *The Maine* to the Cayman Islands two years ago.

He asked in a heavy accent, "You travel with someone?"

"No." But I'm trying to screw that lady who pissed you off.

I was ready for my close-up, but he kept staring at my passport, and I wondered if I'd given him my Conch Republic passport by mistake.

Finally he said, "Step back, look to camera. No smile."

I stepped back, frowned, and had my picture taken for the secret police. The guy stamped my passport and visa, kept his half, and pushed the buzzer to unlock the door, which probably led to a hole in the floor.

I exited into the customs area where dogs were sniffing people and luggage, and I passed through a scanner as my backpack was X-rayed. The customs guy opened my backpack and examined my binoculars, which I thought would come in handy on our way to the cave and to Cayo Guillermo. He also found my Swiss Army knife and waved it at me. "Why you have?"

"To open my beer. Cerveza."

"No legal. Tax. Ten dollar."

I think he meant a fine, which was actually a shakedown, but I gave him a ten and he gave me my knife and said, "Okay. Go."

The bandito just made half a month's pay, but I was happy to see that official corruption existed in the People's Republic. It could come in handy.

I proceeded to baggage claim, which was a long counter piled haphazardly with luggage. I looked for Sara but didn't see her. I did, however, see Alison, who was directing everyone who'd gotten through customs to an exit.

I found my suitcase and wheeled it toward a customs agent who was collecting the declaration forms. Some people ahead of me had chalk marks on their bags, and they were directed to a counter where agents were searching the marked luggage. Another opportunity to levy a tax. Or be taken away to be searched. I was worried about Sara. I would have asked Alison if she'd seen her, but I wasn't supposed to know Sara Ortega.

My suitcase wasn't marked, and I gave the customs agent my Nothing to Declare form and headed out the door into the bright sunshine. There was a line of coach buses parked outside, each one with a sign, and I headed toward the Yale bus. Tad was standing near the bus, checking names off his list while a Cuban porter was loading bags into the luggage compartment.

I said to Tad, "MacCormick."

He found my name and checked me off. "You can give this gentleman your bag and hop aboard."

I turned his roster toward me and saw that most names had been checked off, but not Sara Ortega. I left my suitcase on the curb and headed back to the terminal. An armed guard at the door made it clear that I wasn't allowed to reenter the terminal, so I stood there, peering inside.

I had my cell phone, but it showed no service, and even if it did I didn't have Sara's number. We were supposed to exchange phone numbers sometime after we landed, on the off chance we had service in Havana.

A few people whom I recognized from our group came out of the terminal, but not Sara.

Just as I was thinking of reporting Sara's disappearance to clueless Tad, out came Alison and Sara, wheeling their suitcases and chatting away. Sara gave me a quick nod and Alison, who recognized me from the group, said, "We're all here. You can board the bus."

Sara hung back as Alison hurried to the bus.

Though I didn't know Sara Ortega, I offered to carry her back-pack as any single gentleman would do for a pretty lady who had caught his eye. She accepted my offer, and as we walked toward the bus, I asked, "What happened?"

"I was escorted into a back room and had my luggage searched. Got patted down and answered some questions."

"Do you think it was random?"

"Nothing here is random. Here, it's profiling. And paranoia. They have a problem with Cuban American tourists."

"Okay . . . the money? The map?"

"You should never try to hide anything. The map is stuck in my guide book and they barely noticed it. The pesos are in my back-pack, mixed with American dollars, which is what I did last time I was here. The customs agent asked why I was bringing pesos into the country."

I was sure she had a good answer, or she wouldn't be walking with me.

"I reminded him it was not illegal for me to possess pesos, it was only illegal for me to spend them, and I pointed out that I had declared the pesos. I showed him my receipt for the pesos that I'd bought from a Canadian bank and told him that I was giving the money to various Cuban charities—which is actually done by American aid groups and it's legal."

"Apparently he believed your b.s."

"He believed he'd made a good score." She explained, "Cuban customs is a gold mine for the customs officials. If they bust you, the government becomes their partner. If you pay them a fine, they pocket it."

"I got clipped for ten bucks."

"You got off easy. Cost me two hundred."

"We're in the wrong business." Señorita Ortega was a cool cus-tomer. I said, "It looked like you got off to a bad start with the pass-port."

"He was being obnoxious, asking why the Americana was com-ing back to Cuba for a second time, and how could I afford to stay at the Parque Central. He practically suggested I was a prostitute, and I said I was going to report him."

"I think he reported you to customs."

"Probably." She added, "I hate them."

"Right." It's usually *my* mouth that gets me in trouble. Now I had another mouth to worry about.

Tad and Alison looked impatient as we approached, and Sara took her backpack and moved ahead of me. Tad checked her off, the porter loaded her bag, and she boarded the bus.

Tad must have thought I was going to grab his roster again, so he held it to his chest.

I hopped on the big bus, whose air-conditioned interior was as cold as a well-digger's ass in Maine.

The bus had about fifty seats, so I was able to find two empty seats together and I sat next to my backpack. Sara was behind me, sitting with one of the older ladies.

Tad and Alison boarded, greeted everyone, and Alison said, "Well, that wasn't too bad." She introduced our bus driver, José, and led us in greeting him. "Buenos días, José!"

Group travel requires a certain level of voluntary infantile behavior. I had a flashback to my yellow school bus.

José pulled away and we were off to Havana, which my guide book said was twenty kilometers from the airport, giving Tad and Alison time to fill us in on the day's agenda. Our Cuban guide would join us at the welcome dinner at our hotel and answer any questions we might have about Cuba. Question number one: How do we get to Paris from here?

The bus was comfortable, made in China, and fit for Americans, though the lavatory was temporarily out of order and would probably stay that way until a plumber arrived from Shanghai.

This was Tad and Alison's second trip to Cuba, they told us, though not together. I hoped they'd hook up and made themselves scarce.

I tuned them out and looked out the window. The area around the airport was rundown—moldering stucco buildings with tin roofs—but the flowering vegetation was lush and tropical, hiding most of the squalor. The bus swerved a few times to avoid donkey carts, and the Yalies shot pictures out the window.

So here we were in hell. There's a TV series that documents the story of ordinary people who agree to smuggle drugs into or out of some shithole country. They get busted, of course, and I used to laugh at the stupidity of these amateur drug smugglers who risked ten or twenty years in a hellhole third-world prison for a few bucks. What were they thinking? I would never do anything like that.

CHAPTER 14

There was almost no morning traffic on the airport road and no sign of commercial activity—no shops, no gas stations, and no McDonald's. The only thing for sale was The Revolution, advertised on billboards, most of which showed the familiar Christ-like image of the departed Ernesto "Che" Guevara, and what appeared to be his quoted words praising LA REVOLUCIÓN. The only graffiti I saw was on the wall of a collapsed building—CUBA SÍ—YANQUIS NO.

If the martyred Che was the face of the revolution, Fidel was the man behind the curtain. My Yale info packet said that Fidel Castro had modestly avoided encouraging a cult of personality around him, so we'd see no images of F.C. or his brother Raúl, no statues, and no postcards or souvenirs showing F.C.'s or R.C.'s faces. I think the regime is missing an opportunity to make a few bucks on Castro Brothers T-shirts.

We reached the outskirts of Havana in about thirty minutes.

First impressions color future perceptions, and my first impression of Cuba was of decay. The buildings in Havana, like the ones along the airport road, were mostly in bad repair—except the buildings that were beyond repair. The good news was that the streets were litter-free, maybe because no one had anything to throw away.

There weren't many private cars on the streets, and the ones I saw were predominantly Soviet-era clunkers belching exhaust smoke, but I spotted my first vintage American automobile, a canary yellow Chevy convertible, maybe a '56 or '57. The Yalies took pictures from the bus.

There seemed to be a lot of people hanging around not doing much, including work crews, apparently on break from their twenty-dollar-a-month jobs. No one was in rags, I noticed, but a lot of the women wore the same dark Lycra pants and tank tops. If there was malnutrition in Cuba, as Eduardo said, it wasn't apparent in Havana, where many of the ladies seemed well-fed. The men, however, were leaner, and they dressed mostly in dark pants, sandals, and T-shirts, most of which sported American logos. I didn't see any children, but they were probably in school—or not yet born, since Cuba had one of the lowest birth rates in the Western Hemisphere, which is never a good sign of a country's future.

The bus continued, and Alison announced that we'd make our scheduled stop at the Plaza de la Revolución, which we did, and we all got off the air-conditioned bus into the sweltering October heat of Havana.

The plaza was huge, and Tad told us that a million people— ten percent of Cuba's population—had come here in 1998 to hear John Paul II say Mass. That's a lot of bread and wine for the Pope to hand out, and a lot of Porta-Juans. More importantly, for an officially atheist country, that was a lot of people showing up to hear the word of God.

The plaza was surrounded by mostly ugly buildings, one of which had on its façade a colossal metallic outline of a bearded and bereted Che Guevara, with the words HASTA LA VICTORIA SIEMPRE, which I thought might be Che's last words to his wife, Vickie, but which Tad said meant "Always toward victory." I needed to bone up on my Spanish. Corona, por favor.

Anyway, there were about a dozen tour buses idling around the mostly concrete plaza and groups of tourists snapping iPhone photos that they couldn't e-mail to anyone until they were out of Wi-Fi-less Cuba.

We'd all hoped to see public toilets, or vendors selling cold drinks in the plaza, as you'd see anywhere else in the world, but apparently cold drinks and toilets were not part of the new five-year economic plan.

A few of our group snuck onto the other buses to use the toilet, and some people got back on our bus to get out of the heat.
Our first few hours in Cuba were proving to be a challenge for the
less hardy souls, who probably wouldn't sign up for the Yale educational trip to Afghanistan.

One of the ugly buildings in the square had military vehicles
in front of it and dozens of armed soldiers around it. Tad said that
was the headquarters of the Communist Party. The Yalies took pictures.

The good news was that the plaza was filled with parked vintage American automobiles, and the drivers of these beautiful taxis
were hustling the tourists to have their picture taken next to the
cars, many of which had American flags flying from their antennas,
which was interesting.

The cars were all pre-1959, of course, the year that time stopped
here, and all of them were in mint condition, more lovingly restored
and maintained than the buildings around the square. Maybe I'd
buy a vintage Caddy when I was rich next month.

Meanwhile, I thought that one of these cars would make a good
photo for Dave Katz, so I picked a baby blue Buick convertible that
the owner said was a 1956 and I gave him my iPhone. Sara was
standing nearby and I asked her to pose with me, but she declined.
The Buick owner, who spoke good English, wouldn't take her no
for an answer—and lose two bucks—so he took Sara's hand and
led her to his car. The entrepreneurial and romantic gentleman
urged us to get closer and I put my sweaty arm around Sara.

"Beautiful! Smile!"

He took two shots and I said to Sara, "I'll text these to you. Can
I have your number?"

"Maybe later." As she walked away, I saw that a few of our group
had noticed my interest in the pretty single lady whom I'd assisted
at the airport. I gave the Buick driver an American five, though the
transaction was illegal for both of us.

On that subject, Alison announced that we had to get to the
bank to get CUCs because sometimes they ran out of money. We

all boarded the bus and Tad advised us that the bank tellers some-times slipped you counterfeit fifty- and hundred-CUC notes that they'd bought for half price, and they kept the real ones for them-selves. "Check for the watermarks," said Tad. Sara's grandfather was rolling over in his grave.

We got moving and headed north up a wide boulevard with a landscaped median flanked by art deco structures, most of which needed restoration. In fact, this whole city needed Cuban Ameri-can contractors from Florida.

The bus turned onto a side street and stopped in front of a small, shabbily constructed building that looked like a welfare of-fice, but was in fact a government bank. We filed out of the bus into the grimy building and stood in line to change our Yankee dollars into Cuban Convertible Currency.

Carlos had advised me not to change more than five hundred dollars at a time to avoid drawing attention to myself. According to Carlos, half the population of Havana were volunteer snoops called los vigilantes, or los chivatos—the finger pointers—members of the revolutionary watch committees who reported on their neighbors and also reported any suspicious activities of for-eigners. Okay, we definitely weren't in Switzerland, but I had the feeling that Carlos, like Eduardo, exaggerated the degeneration of Cuban society. Somewhere beyond the paranoia and the hate of the regime was a reality that was not easily understood.

I handed over five hundred greenbacks and my passport to an unsmiling teller and expected to get five hundred CUCs back at the official exchange rate of one for one, but there was a ten per-cent Screw You, Yanqui charge for American dollars, and they also Photostatted my passport.

After everyone was back on the bus—holding up their CUCs to find the watermark—Tad did a head count and off we went. Alison said our next stop was the Hotel Nacional, where lunch awaited us, then to the Hotel Parque Central, where hopefully our rooms would be ready.

I looked out the window as we made our way north toward the

Straits of Florida. *Havana. Mildewed magnificence,* said the guide book.

When you get to a place that you think you know because it's been in the news, or because it's been talked and written about so much, what you discover is that you know nothing about the place. As it said in my travel packet: *Put your prejudices aside and discover Cuba for yourself.*

Okay, but in the end it didn't matter much to me what the truth or the reality was of this place, and I didn't need to leave here wiser; I needed to leave here richer. And alive.

CHAPTER 15

Our tour bus pulled into a long, tree-lined drive that ended at the imposing Hotel Nacional, which according to Alison had been inspired by the Breakers in Palm Beach, where I'd actually stayed once, and when I got my bill I knew why they called it the Breakers. But that was in my carefree days before I sunk my small fortune into *The Maine*—which I actually didn't own anymore.

Alison also informed us that the Nacional had been opened in 1930, and that it had been the scene of many important events in Cuban history, including a takeover by a group of revolutionaries, many of whom were later executed—maybe for complaining about their bill. Also, according to Alison, the Nacional had hosted many rich, famous, and powerful people, including royalty, world leaders, and American movie stars. The infamous had also stayed here, including Meyer Lansky and Lucky Luciano, who in 1946 convened the largest meeting ever held of the American Mafia, which gathered in the Nacional under the cover of a Frank Sinatra concert. I wondered if Frank knew what was going on. In any case, I'd heard of the Nacional and it had come to mind as a good place to meet Jack.

We all got off the bus and marched through the ornate lobby, which showed signs of restoration, then out the back doors across a terrace and down the sloping lawn toward the Straits of Florida. We followed Tad and Alison to an open pavilion that was serving lunch to tourist groups.

There were two long tables in the pavilion reserved for the Yale group. We all seated ourselves, and I found myself between two couples who were trying to make conversation. Across from me was the bestselling author and his better-looking wife. Sara was at the other table.

I couldn't imagine sitting here through a family-style lunch—pass the beans, please—so I excused myself and walked down toward the water to what seemed to be fortifications overlooking the Straits of Florida.

A freelance guide offered me a history lesson for an American dollar, and I promised him two if he kept it under four minutes.

The guide, a university student named Pablo, told me that some of these fortifications were ancient, but that F.C. had ordered new fortifications built on the high ground of the Hotel Nacional during the 1962 Cuban Missile Crisis when the regime feared a U.S. invasion.

The so-called fortifications looked pretty pathetic, consisting of some bunkers and a few exposed gun emplacements. As a former military man I knew that these structures could be knocked out in about two minutes by a single salvo of 16-inch naval guns. But sometimes the optics are more important than the substance.

Pablo also thought the fortifications were a joke, and he confided to me that he wanted to go to the U.S. He looked at the Straits and said, "Over there."

"Good luck." I gave him an American ten, and he gave me his opinion on the Cuban economy. It sucked.

As I was contemplating heading for the bar, Sara appeared and said something in Spanish to Pablo, who laughed and replied in Spanish, then walked off with his half month's pay.

"What did you say to him?"

She smiled. "I asked if you were flirting with him, and if not, I'd give you a try."

"You could have just said, 'Adios, amigo.'"

"Conversation in Cuba has to be clever. That's all they have." She suggested, "Let's take a walk."

We walked along a park path that overlooked a four-lane road bordered by a seawall that ran along the shore. Sara said the road was called the Malecón, which meant the Breakwater. The Straits were calm, the sun was hot, and there was no sea breeze. Sara asked, "How are you enjoying your Cuba experience so far?"

"Too early to tell." I added the mandatory, "The people seem nice." Actually, they seemed listless and indifferent. "I need another day before I become an expert on Cuba."

She smiled, then said, "They're good people who've been badly served for five centuries by inept, corrupt, and despotic leaders. That's why Cuba has had so many revolutions."

They might have better luck picking a government out of the phone book. I asked, "How do you feel about being here?"

"I don't know." She confessed, "I feel some ancestral connection . . . but I don't feel that I'm home."

"How many Cubans in America would return if Cuba was free?"

"Fewer than those who say they would. But all of us would like to travel freely back and forth, to see family, and maybe to buy a vacation house—and to show our children and grandchildren where their parents and grandparents came from."

"That would be nice. But not on that airline we flew in on."

She smiled. "Within a year, there'll be regularly scheduled airline service from the U.S. And by next spring there'll be cruise ships at the Sierra Maestra Terminal filled with Americans."

"Two nations, one vacation."

"That's clever. Did you make that up?"

"I did."

We walked in silence awhile, me wondering why Sara skipped lunch to be with me, and she knowing why.

We reached the end of the park where a monument stood that Sara said was the Monumento a las Víctimas del Maine.

Well, that was ominous.

We turned and began walking back toward the hotel.

She asked, "How do you feel about the U.S. seeking improved relations with Cuba?"

"Well . . . I understand why it's time to do that. But we need to get something in return."

"We won't get anything from these bastards. Except lies. Nothing will change here until the regime changes."

"It's a process. Cuba needs a half million American tourists and business people with money and big mouths spreading the idea of freedom."

"Which is exactly what the regime is afraid of. There's nothing in it for them, and they'll pick some fight with the U.S., or . . . arrest some Americans on trumped-up charges in order to set back the process."

"Is that what you'd like to see?"

"Yes, to be honest."

"Well, as long as it isn't us who are arrested."

She didn't reply, so I changed the subject. "I'm not sure I'm understanding our supposed relationship."

"That's what I wanted to talk to you about. As you know, we need to look like we're having a holiday romance, so that when we disappear—"

"I understand. Happens to me on every vacation."

"Yes, I'm sure, but not with a tour group in a police state. So to keep Tad and Alison from panicking and calling the embassy, we'll leave them a note saying we've gone to the beach in Mayabeque Province—which is not where we're going, of course—and we'll be back in time for the return flight. As Carlos probably told you, we'll leave our luggage in our rooms as though we're coming back."

"Right."

She continued, "But even if Tad and Alison don't call the embassy, our Cuban tour guide will report our disappearance to the authorities, who may or may not consider this a serious issue, and may or may not circulate our names and our airport photos to the police in Mayabeque—or all the provinces."

"I'm listening."

"Europeans, Canadians, and South Americans are allowed to travel independently around the country, so we won't stick out in the countryside, and even if we're stopped by the police I can probably talk us out of getting arrested." She glanced at me. "We're just starry-eyed lovers, off on a romantic getaway."

"Hot as chili peppers."

She smiled, then said, "We'll probably be expelled, or possibly just returned to the group."

"Sort of like catch and release."

"I like your sense of humor."

"Thank you. Here's what's not funny—if we have the sixty million dollars on us when we're stopped—"

"Obviously that would be a problem. That's the critical period—between the cave and The Maine."

"Right. And if we get arrested with sixty million American dollars, you'll get your wish about an incident that would set back diplomatic relations."

"I don't think our arrest would be enough to refreeze the Cuban Thaw. We'd also have to be executed."

I saw she was smiling, but I didn't think that was actually funny.

She said, "We need to take it a step at a time, and worry about it a step at a time. We need to be smarter than the police. Very soon we will be on The Maine, with the money, heading for Key West. That's what I see in our future, and that's what you need to see."

"That's why I'm here."

"Good."

"And by the way," I asked, "do you know how we're going to get the money onboard The Maine?"

"I don't know at this time."

"And when do you think you'll know?"

She stayed silent a moment, then said, "Our contact in Havana will lead us to our contact in Camagüey Province, then my map will lead us to the cave, and a road will lead us to Cayo Guillermo."

"I got that. How do we get the last five yards over the goal line?"

"We'll find out when we get to Cayo Guillermo." She reminded me, "This is all compartmentalized. Fire walls."

Obviously there was a contact person in Cayo Guillermo, but

Sara wasn't sharing that at this time. So I returned to my more immediate concern and asked, "Am I supposed to romance you? Or vice versa?"

She glanced at me. "Let me fall all over you—as unbelievable as that may seem to our group."

Was I supposed to smile? I asked, "When do we begin our charade?"

"We start tonight at the cocktail reception. By day four, which is Sunday, when the Pescando Por la Paz fleet leaves Havana for Cayo Guillermo, we'll be having a romance."

"Let me make sure I understand—"

"We'll be sleeping together. Is that all right with you?"

"Let me think. Okay."

"Good."

And I get paid for this. There must be a catch.

She stayed silent a moment, then said, "I like you. So it *is* okay."

I didn't reply.

She glanced at me. "And you?"

"Just part of the job."

"That was going to be my line."

"You intrigue me."

"Good enough."

"And I like you."

We strolled on in silence, then against my better judgement I said, "I thought you had a boyfriend."

"I thought *you* had a boyfriend."

"Just kidding."

"Good. Then neither of us has a boyfriend."

We walked up the sloping grass toward the hotel and reached the pavilion. I said, "I'm lunching in the bar. Join me."

"We need to stay with the group."

"I'm grouped out. See you on the bus."

"Thank you for a nice walk." She entered the pavilion and I could hear Tad say, "There you are. Have you seen . . . what's his name?" *The roster-snatcher.*

I continued across the terrace, where a few dozen turistas were drinking mojitos.

I found the bar called the Hall of Fame and ordered a Corona but settled for a local brew called Bucanero. There was a pirate on the label, which was appropriate for the eight-CUC price. I gave the bartender a ten and sat in a club chair. The patrons were mostly cigar-smoking men, prosperous-looking, maybe South Americans. For sure no Cuban could afford this place, and if they could they wouldn't want to advertise it.

A young lady in fishnet stockings approached with a cigar tray. "Cigar, señor?"

"Sure." I picked out a Cohiba and the young lady clipped my tip and lit me up. Twenty CUCs. What the hell. I'd be lighting my cigars with fifties in a few weeks.

I sat back, drank my beer, and smoked my cigar, surveying the opulent room whose walls were covered with photos of the famous people who'd stayed here in happier times. I wish I'd been at that 1946 Sinatra concert.

But back to the present. Sara Ortega. That was a pleasant surprise.

CHAPTER 16

We arrived at our hotel, the Parque Central, which, as the name suggested, was across from a park in Central Havana.

We filed off the bus, collected our luggage, and entered the hotel, a fairly new building with an atrium lobby surrounded by a mezzanine level that could be reached by a sweeping staircase.

Most of the lobby was a cocktail lounge with a long bar off to the left. I saw that many of the tables were occupied by cigar smokers, filling the air with a not-unpleasant smell, though many of the Yalies seemed horrified. Hey, it's 1959. Deal with it.

We were checked in as a group by clerks who had never heard of the hospitality industry, but mojitos were handed out to make up for the inefficiency and indifference.

Tad and Alison bailed out, leaving their flock of poor little lambs to fend for themselves—but not before Tad reminded us, "Welcome cocktail party and dinner on the rooftop terrace at five-thirty."

That was where Sara was going to start falling all over me, so I should take a shower and get there on time.

Sara got her room key and wheeled her bag past me without a glance.

I got checked in and went up to the sixth floor and found my room.

The park-view room was clean and functional and had a queen-sized bed and a flat-screen TV. It also had its own safe, which I wouldn't trust to be safe from the policía. There was a minibar but it was empty.

The room was sweltering and I lowered the temperature, which didn't seem to do anything. I unpacked my few belongings, got out of my sweaty clothes, and hit the shower. I don't know why I expected hot water, but cold showers were what I needed to lower my libido until Sunday.

I got dressed in clean clothes, including my blue blazer, and went down to the lobby bar. They didn't have Corona, so I ordered a Bucanero. Six CUCs. A third of a month's wages. The only person I recognized from our group was Tad, who was reading a stack of papers at the end of the bar, sipping a bottled water. I sat next to him and asked, "What are you reading?"

He looked up at me. "Oh . . . Mr. . . . ."

"MacCormick. Call me Mac."

"Okay . . . these are my lecture notes." He put his hand on them, and I felt I owed him an explanation for my intemperate roster-snatching, but instead I bought him a Bucanero.

To make conversation as I kept my back to the bar, looking for Sara in the lobby, I told Tad, "My four-star room has no hot water, and the A/C has asthma."

"Sorry. It's intermittent." He gave me a tip. "There's actually hot water in the sink and the tub. The showers seem to be on a separate system." As for the A/C, he said, "Mine's out, too. Havana has power problems."

"What's going to happen when a half million spoiled Americans hit this city?"

"God only knows."

"At least the beer is cold."

"Usually."

We chatted a bit as I looked at people getting off the elevators. Tad was actually okay, but he took the opportunity to lecture me, "We missed you at lunch. It's important that you stay with the group."

"Why?"

"This is a group tour. If you go off on your own to someplace that we are not licensed to visit—like the beach, or on a boat, or any place that is not considered educational—then we risk losing our educational tour license from the State Department."

"How does the State Department classify bordellos?"

He actually smiled, then confided, "As a practical matter, you're free to do what you want after the group dinners."

"So no bed check?"

"Of course not." He suggested, "There are some good night-clubs in Havana. I'll mention them at my first lecture tomorrow night."

"Great. What's your lecture about?"

"The history of Cuban music."

"I don't want to miss that one."

"Actually, attendance at the lectures is required."

I guess TBA didn't mean what I thought it meant. "Can I see your notes? So I can ask intelligent questions."

"I'm sorry, but—"

"That's okay. Let me ask you something—there's a lady in our group, the one I helped with her luggage at the airport, Sara Ortega. Do you know anything about her?"

He shot me a look. "No. I don't know any of the people in our group."

"I hope you get to know Alison."

He ignored that and asked, "Is there anyone from your class in the group?"

"I'm not a Yalie. Can't you tell?"

He smiled politely.

I asked him, "Did anyone go off on their own last time you were here?"

"No . . . Well, a couple did go to a Havana beach."

"Did you have them arrested?"

He forced a smile. "I just spoke to them in private, and I also reiterated the rules to the group at my next lecture."

"Are you obligated to call the embassy if someone breaks the rules?"

"I . . . Well, last year the embassy wasn't open. But . . . why do you ask?"

"I was hoping I could go scuba diving while I'm here."

"Sorry, you can't." He added, "It would cause all of us trouble."

"But no problem with a bordello?"

He again forced a smile. "I don't think they exist here. But if you discover otherwise, let me know."

I smiled. Tad was really okay—just a little uptight and anxious about his responsibilities as a group leader in a police state. I hoped he handled it well when Sara and I disappeared. Bye-bye license.

We chatted a bit, and Tad asked me, "What do you do for a living?"

Good question. And that's what I was asked on my visa application. Carlos and I both knew that my cover story—my legend, in Intel parlance—should be close to the truth in case the Cuban authorities did a background check. You don't want to be caught in an unnecessary lie, so Carlos and I agreed that my occupation was "fisherman," and there was no way anyone would connect "fisherman" to the Pescando Por la Paz, especially now that I wasn't the registered owner of a boat in the tournament.

"Mister MacCormick?"

Also, Tad would have photocopies of everyone's Yale travel application, so I replied, "I'm a fisherman."

"I see. Well, I hate to say this to you, but Cuba is a fisherman's paradise. Though not for you."

"Maybe next time I'm here."

"Eventually Americans can come here as tourists with no restrictions."

"Can't wait."

Well, I had set the stage, delivered a few lines, and it was time to exit left. "See you at cocktails."

I took my beer to a cocktail table in the lobby and surveyed the lounge. A few of our group had drifted in, but not Sara.

Carlos, in his briefing, had told me that the hotels used by Americans were under surveillance by undercover agents from the Orwellian Ministry of the Interior. But because Cuban citizens were generally not allowed in the hotels for foreigners, these surveillance men tried to look like Latin American tourists or businessmen. I should be able to spot them, Carlos said, by their cheap clothing, bad manners, or by the fact that they never paid for their drinks. Sounded more like a scene from an Inspector Clouseau movie than Big Brother in Cuba. But maybe I should listen to Carlos.

As I was sitting there, it hit me—I was in Communist Cuba, where paranoia was a survival tool. And at some point in the next ten days, I was going to be either rich in America, or in jail here, or worse. Also, I was going to have sex with a woman I barely knew— not a first, but exciting nonetheless.

Regarding Sara, empathy is not one of my strong points, but I thought about the risks she was taking. She had much stronger motivations for being here than I did, but that didn't diminish her courage. In fact, to be less empathetic, her motivations could lead her into some risk-taking that I wouldn't approve of. Beware of people who are ready to die for a cause—especially if they're your team leader.

And finally, I knew, as Sara did, that sleeping with me was ac- tually not part of the job, and that our romance could easily be faked—and that was the original script that she and Carlos had probably worked out, thus the made-up boyfriend. But Sara had changed the script and changed her mind, and not only was she willing to die for her cause, she was also willing to . . . well, fuck for it. That's a dedicated woman.

And what Sara wanted from me in exchange for sex was loyalty, reliability, and commitment. Men in combat bond in other ways. Women in dangerous situations with a male partner have figured out that the sexual bond can usually keep the idiot in line.

Or maybe she actually liked me. As unbelievable as that seems. And that could lead to a whole different set of problems. Especially if the feeling was mutual.

I finished my beer and checked my watch. Cocktails in fifteen minutes.

As in a war zone, I had a sense of heightened awareness, coupled with a contradictory sense of unreality. Like, this can't be happening. But it was, and as I promised Sara on *The Maine*, if I got here I wouldn't go back on my word. I'm all in, as we used to say in the U.S. Army. Good to go.

Sex, money, and adventure. Does it get any better than that?

CHAPTER 17

The upscale open-air rooftop restaurant was in a new wing of the hotel, and it could have been in Miami Beach. The winds of change were blowing in Cuba, but not the trade winds, and it was still hot and humid.

I'm usually on time for cocktails and chicks, but about half our group had not yet arrived, including Sara. Tad, Alison, and Professor Nalebuff were standing near a potted palm, talking to a tall guy with long, swept-back hair and tight pants who I guessed was our Cuban guide.

Everyone looked refreshed after their long day of airports, bureaucratic bullshit, and tropical heat. Cold showers are invigorating. As per our Travel Tips, the men in our group wore sports jackets, but no ties. The ladies had repaired their makeup and seemed cool and comfortable in nice summer dresses.

A waiter came up to me with a tray of mojitos, which like the daiquiri had been invented in Cuba and probably should have stayed here. But to get some gas in the tank, I took one.

I noticed that Richard Neville was mopping his brow with a handkerchief and also downing a mojito while simultaneously grabbing hors d'oeuvres from passing waitresses and somehow managing to smoke a cigarette. Amazing. His pretty wife, Cindy, was alone, staring out over the parapet at the lighted city, sipping a mojito. Under other circumstances I would have joined her, but I was about to be swept off my feet by Sara Ortega.

I spotted a bar and walked over to it. Former combat infantry officers don't drink cocktails that come in primary colors with little umbrellas in them, so I gave my mojito to the bartender and ordered a vodka on the rocks.

Sara suddenly appeared beside me and said to the bartender, "May I have a Cuba Libre?" She added, "Por favor."

She seemed to notice me for the first time and said, "Excuse me, what did you order?"

"Vodka."

"You should be trying something local." She said to the bartender, "Please give this gentleman a Cuba Libre." She asked me, "Have you ever had one?" She smiled.

Playacting is fun. "Once. On my boat."

"Do you sail?"

"I'm a fisherman."

"What do you fish for?"

"Peace."

"That's good." She put out her hand. "Sara Ortega."

"Daniel MacCormick." We shook, and I reminded her, "We met at the airport and took a picture together in the plaza."

"Your arm was sweaty."

Sara was wearing a white, off-the-shoulder silk dress that reached down to the straps of her patrician sandals. Her lipstick was that frosty pink that used to drive me crazy when I was a teenager.

The bartender gave us our Cuba Libres and I raised my glass. "To new adventures."

We touched glasses. Here's looking at you, kid.

She asked, "What brings you to Cuba?"

"Curiosity. How about you?"

"I'm looking for something."

"I hope you find it."

"I will."

She walked to the parapet and gazed out over the city. "It's beautiful from up here. But down there, not everything is beautiful."

"I noticed."

"But still romantic in a strange way."

Sara pointed out some of the landmarks of the city, then drew my attention to the harbor. "You can see the Sierra Maestra Cruise Terminal on the far side of that plaza." She stepped out of character and said, "We saw this on Google Earth."

I nodded and asked, "Where is the Nacional?"

She pointed to the tall building, silhouetted against the sea, then pointed out the wide boulevard that snaked along the seashore. "That's the Malecón, where half of Havana gathers on hot nights."

"To do what?"

"To walk and talk. It is a place for lovers, poets, musicians, philosophers, and fishermen . . . and those who gaze toward Florida."

Well, I thought, if you don't have air-conditioning, television, money, or hope, the Malecón might be better for the soul than church. I was actually beginning to feel sorry for these people, though I almost envied their simple lives. As for Sara, she was more Cuban than she knew.

Sara said we should be sociable, and she took my arm and led me around the rooftop to meet our fellow travelers, introducing me as Mac, though I was Daniel when she picked me up at the bar. She told a few people that I wasn't a Yalie, but that everyone should be nice to me anyway. That got some polite chuckles.

We circulated a bit, and Sara did most of the talking. I was starting to feel like a hooked tuna, so I joined in the dumb cocktail conversations. I remembered an old Bowdoin joke and said to a group of people, "I hear Yale is going co-ed. They're going to let men in." That didn't go over well.

Anyway, about half the group seemed normal and the other half needed more mojitos, or an enema.

I used to be good at cocktail parties in Portland, college, the Officers' Club, and Wall Street. But four years at sea and too many Key West dive bars had apparently taken the shine off my silver tongue. Not that I gave a shit.

Sara, on the other hand, was good with tight-assed strangers, poised and charming. Her eyes sparkled. What was more impressive was that she knew she was possibly facing death, and she was handling that well for a rookie.

My own face-offs with death had made me see death differently. Death had become not a possibility, but a probability, so I made peace with that dark horseman, and that peace has stayed with me on my borrowed time.

I looked at Sara, who was engaged in a conversation with four men who obviously found her to be the life of an otherwise dull and awkward icebreaker party. It would be ironic, I thought, if I finally found the love of my life on the eve of . . . whatever.

I found myself in a conversation with two of the younger and better-looking women in our group—Alexandra Mancusi and Ashleigh Arote. Alexandra and Ashleigh were wearing wedding rings, but I couldn't remember if their husbands were on the group roster. Nametags would have been helpful for me tonight, indicating marital status and where the spouse was. But then I remembered that my dance card was filled. Old bachelor habits die hard.

Ashleigh said, "You look familiar. Were you TD?"

I wasn't sure what that meant. "If you mean totally drunk, yes."

Both ladies laughed.

I confessed, "I'm not Yale."

Ashleigh explained that TD was Timothy Dwight, the name of one of the twelve residential colleges that made up Yale.

Alexandra was JE—Jonathan Edwards—and they were both Class of '02, which was my class at Bowdoin, but somehow I felt older. The Army will do that to you.

A young man joined us, maybe thinking I needed reinforcements, and introduced himself to me as Scott Mero. I asked him, "Are you TD?"

"No, JE."

Who's on first?

Anyway, I was hoping that Sara noticed that I was talking to these attractive young ladies, but she either didn't notice or didn't care. The mating game is TD—Totally Dumb.

Scott Mero, as it turned out, was married to Alexandra Mancusi, who'd kept her maiden name, she told me, and only married Scott Mero because she didn't have to change her monogramed towels. Funny. I needed another drink and was about to excuse myself and go to the bar, but Tad called for our attention and the group obliged, except for Richard Neville, who couldn't tear himself away from Sara.

Tad officially welcomed us to the Yale alumni educational tour of Cuba. He kept it short, ending with, "Put your prejudices aside and discover Cuba for yourself," which seemed to be the theme of this trip—though we had to stay with the group to discover Cuba for ourselves.

Tad introduced Alison, who also kept it short and counseled us, "There will be some challenges ahead in the coming days, but when you get home you'll be glad you came." Alison introduced our Cuban tour guide, Antonio, who she said was the best guide in Cuba. Certainly he had the tightest pants.

Antonio was about thirty-five, not bad-looking and he knew it. He gazed out at the group, smiled, spread his arms, and shouted, "Buenas noches!"

A few people returned the greeting, but not enough people, apparently, because Antonio shouted again, "Buenas noches!"

The response was better and Antonio flashed his pearly whites. "Bienvenido. Welcome to Cuba. Welcome to Havana." He let us know, "This is a beautiful group. And intelligent, I am sure."

I asked Sara, "What is the Spanish word for bullshit?"

She gave me an elbow in the ribs.

Antonio continued, "This will be the most amazing experience for you. And you are so lucky to have Tad and the beautiful Alison to be your group leaders, and I am sure we will all make your experience beautiful."

Antonio was not only full of shit, he was enthusiastic about it.

Carlos had advised me—and I'm sure Sara also knew—to be wary of the tour guides, because most of them were informants who had the secret police on their speed dial. Antonio looked more like a gigolo than a chivato, but I'd keep Carlos' warning in mind.

Antonio concluded, "I am keeping you from a beautiful dinner, and you will not forgive me, so I will close my big mouth and open it only to eat."

Laughter from the Americanos who wanted to show their love to the ethnically different bullshit artist.

There were four round tables set up for dinner and it was open seating, and when that happens there's usually some hesitation and confusion. You don't want to wind up next to assholes. Sara sat and patted the seat next to her. "Sit here, Mac."

I sat, and as the table of ten filled up I saw that Richard Neville had planted his butt on the other side of Sara. The other seven people included Cindy Neville, Professor Nalebuff, the two couples who hadn't laughed at my Yale joke, and unfortunately, Antonio, who said, "We will have a beautiful dinner."

A waiter took drink orders and I ordered a double vodka, straight up.

Shrimp tartare was the appetizer, and Professor Nalebuff, a bearded gentleman of about sixty, said he'd been to Cuba twice, and advised us, "This may be the best meal you'll get in Cuba."

Antonio disagreed, saying, "I have booked eight beautiful paladares—you know this? Privately owned restaurants which are a new thing to Cuba."

Nalebuff said dryly, "We also have privately owned restaurants in America."

"Yes, good. But they are expensive. Here, not so much. And everyone should try a government restaurant. Where the people eat very cheaply."

The two middle-aged couples across from me thought that was a swell idea.

Antonio did not keep his mouth shut as promised, and he held court as I knew he would. He sounded like a dyed-in-the-wool Commie, or he was just trying to provoke a response from the privileged Americans as he shoved shrimp tartare in his mouth. The two couples seemed to be getting instantly brainwashed, agreeing with Antonio about the justice and humanity of socialism. If they spent an hour in a kennel, they'd probably come out barking. So much for an Ivy League education.

Neville had little to say except, "Pass the wine," and his wife began a tête-à-tête with Nalebuff.

Antonio looked at Sara for a few long seconds, then said to her, "So you are Cuban."

"I am an American."

"Yes. But a Cuban. Do you speak Spanish?"

"Poco."

"We will practice. You should speak your native tongue."

I thought he was going to ask her if she was born in Cuba, or how her parents or grandparents had come to America. But then I realized this was a loaded subject for those who left and those who stayed.

Antonio said to her, "Welcome home."

Sara didn't reply.

Antonio had apparently gotten tired of his own voice, so he began asking each of us to say something about ourselves, starting with the two middle-aged couples, but he was not a good listener and his dark eyes went dead.

Barry Nalebuff told us he was a history professor at Yale and he had two lectures scheduled, the topic of which was Cuban-American relations since the Spanish-American War. He assured us, "I'll keep them short, and the takeaway is that it's a love-hate relationship, like a troubled marriage, and both sides need serious anger management counseling."

Antonio said reflexively, "America has always treated Cuba as a colony. Until the revolution."

Nalebuff replied, "I address that in my lecture. Please come."

Antonio didn't commit, though the lecture might do him some good. He looked at me. "And you? Why have you come to Cuba?"

"I thought the brochure said Cayman Islands."

That got a laugh. Even Antonio smiled. He looked at Sara again, then said to Neville, "So Tad tells me you are a famous author. Tomorrow we go to Hemingway's house. You will be inspired."

"I don't like Hemingway."

His wife, of course, contradicted him. "You *love* Hemingway, darling."

Antonio didn't know what to say to that, so he called the waiter over for another bottle of wine. Antonio had a good gig.

The fish course was served and Sara asked me, "What is this?"

I can identify a hundred kinds of fish on the line, but not on the plate. I actually don't eat fish. "It's a henway."

"What's a henway?"

"About three pounds."

"Stupid joke."

Have we already had sex?

The multi-course meal continued as the sun set. The two middle-aged couples, whose names I couldn't remember, asked Antonio lots of questions about the itinerary, which, on paper, seemed like a cultural version of the Bataan Death March.

Sara saw an opportunity to plant a red herring and asked Antonio, "Why can't we go to the beach?"

He shrugged. "My government would allow this. But it is your State Department which prohibits it. You should ask them."

Professor Nalebuff provided an answer. "Because of the embargo, Americans are not allowed to travel to Cuba for vacations. But we can come here for people-to-people exchanges, family reunions, art, education, and culture."

I inquired, "Are the nightclubs considered art, education, or culture?"

Nalebuff smiled and agreed, "It all seems very illogical, but the purpose is to limit the amount of dollars that flow into Cuba."

Antonio said, "The embargo has caused suffering among the people."

Nalebuff had apparently had enough of Antonio and replied, "You can trade with ninety-five percent of the rest of the world. Stop blaming the American embargo for all your problems. Your problems are made in Cuba."

Antonio didn't like that, and I think he would have moved to another table, but Nalebuff beat him to it. "Excuse me. I need to circulate." He got up and found an empty seat at Tad's table.

The two middle-aged couples looked embarrassed and I'm sure they would have smoothed Antonio's ruffled feathers, but Sara returned to her topic, "If we were allowed to go to a beach, where would you recommend?"

Antonio still seemed pissed at Nalebuff, maybe thinking about reporting him, but he smiled and replied, "There are beautiful beaches all over Cuba, but the closest are in the province called Mayabeque, which surrounds Havana." He named half a dozen playas, then reminded her, "But this is forbidden for you. However . . ." He then said something to her in Spanish, which seemed to embarrass Sara. In fact, I heard the words "desnudo" and "playa," which I translated as "nude beach." Antonio was a pigalo.

After dessert was served, Tad announced that we were free to go and explore Havana by night, assuring us it was a safe city. "But be in the lobby at eight A.M. for the bus to Hemingway's house and other stops on our itinerary. Breakfast at seven."

About half the group stood and drifted toward the elevators, and I asked Sara if she wanted to hit a nightclub.

"It's been a long day. I need to turn in."

"Let's have a nightcap in the lobby. We need to talk."

She glanced at me and nodded.

Sara said a few good-byes and we crowded into an elevator. On the way down, she locked arms with me, and I knew I was hooked.

CHAPTER 18

We found a table for two in the lobby near the piano. The pianist, dressed in a dark suit, was playing Broadway show tunes, and I said to Sara, "I'm not having an authentic Cuban experience yet."

"You will when we're trying to outrun the police."

You'd think she had served in combat, where we made jokes about death every day.

A disinterested waitress came to our table and we ordered brandies.

Sara asked, "Did you enjoy the evening?"

"I enjoyed being with you."

She smiled. "You're an easy pickup."

"I'm following your script." I changed the subject and said, "Antonio is an asshole."

"You were giving him some competition."

Definitely a bit sassy. Maybe I bring that out in women. I advised her, "Be careful of him."

"I know that. And I assume Carlos briefed you about the chivatos—the police informants?"

"He did."

"And about the undercover agents from the Ministry of the Interior who hang around the hotels?"

"He did."

"Cuba looks deceptively like any Caribbean tropical paradise, and the police state is not always apparent, so some people let their guard down."

"I hear you."

We checked our cell phones, but we had no service, though we exchanged phone numbers in case Verizon put a cell tower on the roof this week. "I'll send you the photos of us in front of the Buick."

She smiled.

I said, "Good question about the beach."

"Thank you."

"What was that about desnudo and playa?"

She smiled again. "So you recognize important words in Spanish." She translated, "He said there was a nude beach in Maya-beque, for foreigners only, but he would be allowed to go as my private guide." She added, "He has a car."

"Pig."

"I hope you're not the jealous type."

I didn't think I was, but I had my moments. More to the point, when Sara and I went missing, Antonio would report the beach conversation to the police, which would hopefully lead them on a wild-goose chase.

Our brandy came, and we sat in silence, listening to a medley from "South Pacific."

She looked at me. "Now that you're here, are you having second thoughts?"

"I'm here at least until Sunday."

She forced a smile.

A few other people from our group drifted into the lounge looking for either a hostess or the No Smoking section, neither of which existed. I scanned the tables, trying to spot an undercover agent, but everyone looked like an American tourist.

Carlos had also told me that some of the rooms were bugged, and that those rooms were usually given to journalists, foreign govern-ment officials, and others who had come to the attention of Cuban state security. That might include Sara Ortega, so this was a good time and place to talk about something more important than An-tonio and nude beaches. I asked Sara, "Where is your hiking map?"

She patted her shoulder bag. "And the pesos."

"Don't leave the map or the money in your room safe or the hotel safe. And be careful of what you say in your room."

"I know that."

"Good. Do you have any idea of how, where, or when our man in Havana will contact us?"

She put down her brandy glass. "Well, not here. But last time I was in Havana, a man just came up to me one night on the Malecón and said, 'Would you be interested in some historical artifacts?'" She added, unnecessarily, "That was the sign—the identification phrase."

Unless he was really selling historical artifacts. "Were you supposed to be walking on the Malecón that night?"

"No. It was just an impulse." She explained, "It was after a group dinner in the Riviera Hotel. I needed a walk."

"So this guy must have known that you'd be at the Riviera, and what you looked like."

"Our friends in Miami were able to get him a photo of me and the Yale itinerary."

"How?"

"Through a Cuban American tourist."

"Okay . . . and what was the purpose of making this contact?"

"Just to see if it worked. A sort of dry run for the next time I came to Havana. I was also here to familiarize myself with the city. Also, we were still exploring ways to get the money out of the country." She looked at me. "Now we have you and your boat."

"I sold the boat to Carlos. It's now Fishy Business."

"I know that." She assured me, "Carlos thinks of everything."

"He thinks he does." I returned to the subject and asked, "Did you meet your second contact in the countryside?"

"I wish I could have. But as you can see, no one can leave the group, even for a day—"

"Right. So this guy came up to you on the Malecón—"

"Marcelo. We walked along the seawall, just talking . . . to see if we were being followed—or got arrested."

"Sounds romantic."

"He was nice. He gave me some tips on Cuban slang, local customs, and how the police operate."

"Did you buy any historical artifacts?"

"No, but I bought him a drink in the Nacional, slipped him two hundred thousand pesos, and took a taxi back to the Parque Central." She added, "I wasn't arrested, but for all I know, he was."

"If he was, you would have been."

"Unless they were just following him to see if we made contact again."

I looked at her. "Do you have any formal training in this sort of thing?"

"No . . . not formal. But I was briefed."

"By whom?"

"By a retired CIA officer. A Cuban American." She asked, "What is *your* training?"

"You tell me."

She hesitated, then said, "We know you took some Defense Intelligence Agency courses."

"You'll be happy to know I passed one of them."

She smiled.

"What else do you know about me?"

"Everything that's in the public record. School, Army, bad credit score." She smiled again.

I continued, "Rented house, old van, credit card debt."

"But no bank loan on The Maine."

"Right."

"You could leave here tomorrow and start a new life."

"I could. But that's not what I promised you."

She smiled. "At least I know you'll be here until Sunday."

I returned the smile, then reminded her, "I'm in Cuba to make three million dollars."

"But you thought you were going to the Cayman Islands."

Funny.

She asked, "What do you know about me?"

"Virtually nothing. But I like your smile."

"Did you see my work on my website?"

"I did. You have talent."

"And you have good taste."

And don't forget balls. I returned to the subject and asked, "Could Marcelo be our contact again?"

"I have no idea."

"What is the ID this time?"

"It's 'Are you interested in Cuban pottery?'"

"Spanish or English?"

"English."

"Do you have a countersign?"

"No."

"Then your contact is sure of who you are."

"Obviously, or he wouldn't be approaching me."

"Unless he was just a guy struck by your beauty."

"Then he'd have a better line than that."

"Right. Okay, do you or your contact have a code word for, 'I am under duress—being followed, wearing a wire, and being made to do this'?"

"No . . ."

"You should. Does the contact know my name or what I look like?"

"No name or photo. Just a description." She looked at me and smiled. "Tall, dark, and handsome."

We made eye contact. "And following you around like a puppy dog."

"That's right. In any case, it's me, not you, who he—or she—will contact."

"Okay." It seemed to me that these people knew what they were doing, up to a point. I asked, "What is our contact in Havana going to do for us to earn his pesos?"

"Two things. First, give us the name and location of our contact in Camagüey Province. Then give us a means of getting there."

"Such as?"

"Travel in Cuba is difficult—but our contact will get us to Camagüey. Safely."

"All right. Then we meet our Camagüey contact. What is he or she going to do for us?"

"He or she will give us a safe house, and a truck to transport the goods to Cayo Guillermo. And some tools to get into the cave."

"Good. And you trust these people?"

"They are Cuban patriots. They hate the regime."

"And I assume they have no idea that we're looking for sixty million in cash."

"They have been told that I'm recovering a box of important documents—property deeds, bank records, and other paperwork that has no intrinsic value."

"Right. You don't want to tempt them to double-cross us."

Sara had no reply to that, but said, "In fact, there is a trunk of such paperwork that we need to take with us." She explained, "In my grandfather's bank vault there were land grants going back to the Spanish kings and queens, property deeds for houses, factories, plantations, hotels, and apartment buildings—all potentially worth more than sixty million dollars. Much more."

That was exciting. Except for the word "potentially." I'll take the sixty million in American dollars.

She continued, "Carlos and other attorneys will present all this documentation to an appropriate court and file a claim for this stolen property on behalf of their clients."

"That won't make the Cuban government very happy."

"The hell with them." She added, "It will make the Cuban exiles happy."

"Right. Okay, and I assume the deed to your grandfather's house is in the cave?"

"Actually, he smuggled it out. I have it in Miami."

Maybe she should have brought it with her for when we visited the house. Along with an eviction notice. But I sensed this was an emotional subject for Sara Ortega, so I left that alone.

I thought about all she'd said regarding our contacts and what they were going to do for us. There was some obvious danger in making these contacts, but that came with the territory. I gave this mission a 50/50 chance of success.

Sara put her hand on mine. "It will go well." She assured me, "The secret police are not as efficient as they'd like you to think."

"Famous last words."

"They are good at one thing—instilling fear. And fear paralyzes the people." She looked at me. "I am not afraid."

"It's okay to be afraid."

"And you? Now that you're here—do you feel fear?"

"Yes. A nice healthy fear."

"You're honest."

"We need to be."

She nodded.

Sara looked tired, so I suggested, "Go get some sleep."

She stood. "You too."

"I'm right behind you. Room 615 if you need to call me."

"I'm 535. See you at breakfast." She walked to the elevators.

The piano player was playing the theme from "Phantom of the Opera."

Hard to believe I was in Miami this morning, annoyed that they'd under-toasted my bagel.

CHAPTER 19

I walked into the breakfast room at 7:30 A.M., wearing khakis, a short-sleeved shirt, and running shoes. I spotted a few people from our group, but not Sara. The buffet was American with some Cuban touches, including beans, to propel us through the day. I got a cup of coffee, sat, and waited for Sara.

I'd gotten back to my room at a reasonable hour, but I couldn't get to sleep so I'd checked out Cuban TV. There were five channels: Tele Rebelde, which was a news channel, CubaVision, an entertainment channel, and two educational channels to put you to sleep. The fifth channel told you to turn off the TV. Actually, there was CNN, in English, and according to my guide book, the satellite signal was pirated by the Cuban government and available only in select hotels and to the Communist elite, leaving the other eleven million news-hungry people on this island dependent on Tele Rebelde—which meant Rebellious, but could be translated as Government Bullshit.

I'd watched a little CNN, which reminded me of why I don't watch TV news, then I watched a news cycle on Tele Rebelde, looking for a mention of Pescando Por la Paz, but I didn't see anything. Maybe the regime was trying to decide if this was the kind of event they wanted to cover with reporters and a brass band, or wanted to ignore. If Sara was right, the Cuban government was not enthusiastic about the Cuban Thaw.

I intended to buy a newspaper, but there was no newsstand in the hotel, and no newspapers in the breakfast room, not even *Granma*, the Communist Party newspaper, which I could pretend to read instead of looking at the door. Where the hell was she? Maybe I should ring her room.

I had the daily itinerary in my pocket and I unfolded it on the table. I read: *Hemingway's house is just as he left it in 1960.* Probably because the Commies wouldn't let Ernest take anything with him when he left.

After Hemingway's house, we'd go to lunch, then a visit to Vivero Alamar, a co-operative research farm where we'd learn about growing organic food. I wondered what sadist put this together.

"Is this seat taken?"

Before I could reply, Sara sat.

"Good morning," I said. She was wearing jeans and a white Polo shirt and looked good.

"Have you had breakfast?" she asked.

"I was waiting for you."

"If you do that, you'll starve to death."

"Right. Did you sleep well?"

"No. Did you?"

"I watched Tele Rebelde all night."

"You should have watched the Cuban soaps on CubaVision. Margaretta is cheating on Francisco again, same as when I was here last year. I don't know why he doesn't leave her."

I smiled, then asked, "Were you here alone?"

"I was." She stood. "Let's get something before the bus comes."

We went to the buffet table, where Richard Neville was cleaning out the breakfast sausage, but he left a strip of bacon for me. Sara piled her plate with fruit and a glob of yogurt.

We sat and she said, "You'll never see fresh fruit in the countryside."

"Actually, we will at the organic food farm."

"That's all show, and what you see in the hotels is all imported." She explained, "The farms are government-owned and mostly deserted because the work is backbreaking, still done with animals and human labor. Farmers get the same twenty dollars a month that they'd get pushing a broom in the city, so there's no incentive to stay on the farm."

Sorry I mentioned it.

"Ninety percent of the Cuban diet is beans and rice, imported from Vietnam, and even that is rationed."

I stared at my strip of bacon and my scrambled eggs.

"Sorry. Didn't mean to make you feel guilty. Eat up."

I sensed a change in Sara, maybe as a result of her being here, and she was getting herself worked up, like Eduardo. I tried to imagine me returning to an America that had gone into the crapper because of government stupidity . . . Well, maybe that wasn't so hard to imagine.

Sara said, "The important thing regarding the Cuban countryside is that most people have moved to the towns and cities. That could be good for us, but maybe bad if we're the only people driving a vehicle on a lonely road."

"Right." I asked her, "Do you know how big this haul is going to be?"

"My grandfather told me it was all packed in steamer trunks."

"Good. How many trunks?"

She glanced at the nearby tables, which were empty. "A typical steamer trunk filled with hundred-dollar bills will hold about fifteen million dollars, and weigh about four hundred pounds."

"Okay . . . one in each hand, two people, that's sixty million."

She ignored my math and said, "But there are also fifty-dollar bills, and twenties, so there are more than four trunks."

"How many?"

"My grandfather said ten."

"Each weighing four hundred pounds?"

"Yes. A twenty-dollar bill weighs the same as a hundred-dollar bill."

"Right. That's four thousand pounds of steamer trunks."

"Give or take."

If I'd known this in Key West I would have gone to the gym. "How about the gold and jewels?"

"The gold may be too heavy to take. But there are four valises of jewelry which we'll take."

"Always room for jewelry. And how about the property deeds that you mentioned?"

"That's another steamer trunk."

I pointed out, "This could be a bit of a logistical problem. You know, getting the trunks out of the cave, onto a truck, then to the boat."

"Carlos has a plan."

"Well, thank God. Would you like another cup of coffee?"

She stared at me. "We wouldn't be doing this if we didn't think we could do it."

"Right."

A pretty waitress cleared our plates and smiled at me.

It was almost 8 A.M. and people from various tour groups were making their way toward the lobby. We stood and I left two CUCs on the table, and Sara said, "That's three days' pay."

"She worked hard."

"And she had a nice butt."

"Really?"

The Yale group was already boarding and Sara and I got on the bus together, said good morning to José, Tad, Alison, Professor Nalebuff, and our travel mates as we made our way toward the rear and found a seat together.

The efficient Tad did a head count and announced, "We're all here."

Antonio hopped aboard and called out, "Buenos días!"

Everyone returned the greeting so we could get moving.

"We will have a beautiful day!" said Antonio.

Sí, camarada.

CHAPTER 20

The bus wound its way out of Havana and again I had the impression of a once vibrant city that was suffocating under the weight of a rotting corpse.

Hemingway's house, Finca Vigía, was a handsome Spanish Colonial located about fifteen kilometers from Havana, and we got there in half an hour.

The house was well-maintained, according to Alison, because of a rare partnership between the U.S. and Cuban governments. Art and culture bring people together, said Alison, and that was why we were here; we were ambassadors of goodwill.

Even as ambassadors, we weren't allowed inside, but dozens of tourists were peering through the open doors and windows into the rooms that had been left exactly as they were when Hemingway left Cuba after the revolution.

Antonio told us that Señor Hemingway had given Finca Vigía and all its contents to the Cuban people. Professor Nalebuff, however, told us that Hemingway had willed Finca Vigía to his fourth wife, but when Hemingway took his own life in 1961, the Cuban government forced his widow to sign over the property to them.

It occurred to me that Antonio wasn't lying to thirty educated people; he lived in a time warp and an information desert like everyone else here and he had no idea of the truth. But reality was on the way. Unless the regime could stop it.

Anyway, Ernest had a nice swimming pool, and his boat, *Pilar*, was displayed in an open pavilion. Nice boat, but not as nice as mine—the one I used to own. On *Pilar*'s fantail were the words KEY WEST, which was where I'd rather be.

Neville's wife, Cindy, was insisting that her bestselling husband pose for photos. He complied, but he wasn't smiling, maybe thinking that people never took photos of themselves in front of *his* house, wherever that was. But maybe they would if he blew his brains out like Hemingway did. Just saying.

We left the grounds of Finca Vigía, and Antonio led us to a row of souvenir stalls where Sara bought me a Hemingway T-shirt, made in China.

We reboarded our air-conditioned Chinese magic carpet and went to lunch at an open-air restaurant. Lunch consisted of black beans, rice, fried plantains, and what appeared to be chicken that had been cut up by Jack the Ripper.

Then to the organic farm. A nice older gentleman explained, in Spanish, all the strides they were making in organic agriculture. Antonio translated, and Sara said to me, "All the farms in Cuba are organic because they can't afford chemical fertilizer." She added, "Most of this food goes directly to the Communist Party comemierdas—the shit eaters."

Antonio overheard that, and he shot her a nasty look.

After two hours in the hot sun, looking at beanstalks, bugs, and plants that I'd never heard of, we staggered back to the bus.

Sara, sensing I may not have enjoyed smelling manure all afternoon, said, "Tomorrow morning is the walking tour of the Old Town. We'll see my grandparents' house, and my grandfather's bank."

"I look forward to that."

"I have mixed feelings."

"Maybe someday you can buy the house."

"Maybe someday I can legally claim what was stolen."

"Don't hold your breath. Meanwhile, we can make a cash withdrawal from Grandpa's bank vault."

She took my hand and squeezed it. Don't hurt the hand. I need it to carry steamer trunks.

As the bus approached the Parque Central, Tad reminded us that he was giving a lecture on the history of Cuban music at 5:30, and please be on time.

Alison reminded everyone that the bus left for the Riviera Hotel right after Tad's lecture, so please be dressed for dinner. Also, there was a swimming pool on the roof if we were so inclined.

We got off the bus and I invited Sara to join me for a swim or for a cold beer at the bar.

"I need a nap and a shower."

"Am I invited?"

"I'll see you at the lecture."

So I went to the bar. I didn't recognize anyone from our group, but soon after I sat and ordered a Bucanero, Antonio sidled up next to me. He asked, "Did you enjoy your day?"

"I enjoyed the Hemingway house."

"Good. Most Americans do." He asked, "Did your companion enjoy her day?"

"She's actually not my companion."

"I see . . . So will she be joining you here?"

"No. She went to the nude swimming pool."

Antonio had no comment on that and took a seat next to me. He had a bottled water that he stole from the bus, and he lit a cigarette, saying, "I am supposed to ask you if you mind if I smoke."

"It's your country."

"It is."

Antonio appeared to have dropped his tour guide persona and he seemed slightly less of a clown, though I didn't know why he wanted my company *sin* Sara.

He asked, "Do you read Hemingway?"

"I did. How about you?"

"Yes, in Spanish and English. There is . . . how do you say . . . ? A cult of Hemingway in Cuba."

"Really?"

"Yes. In the Hotel Ambos Mundos, which we see tomorrow,

there is the room where he lived and wrote before he purchased Finca Vigía. The room is now a museum."

My beer came and Antonio continued his unpaid lecture. "Some of his novels are what we call his Cuban novels. Many of his books have a socialist theme."

"I missed that."

"But it is true. His books show people acting in a . . . a way that is for humanity . . . not for the individual."

"Most of his characters were selfish and self-centered, like me. That's why I liked them."

Antonio continued, "Fidel said, 'All the works of Hemingway are a defense of human rights.'" He added, without irony, "This is a socialist belief."

There's no point in arguing with brainwashed people, and Antonio was intruding on my quiet beer, so I said, "Well, thanks for the company. I'll see you at dinner."

But he didn't leave and continued, "Fidel also said that For Whom the Bell Tolls inspired his guerrilla tactics in the Sierra Maestra." He continued, "They met only once—F.C. and Hemingway. At the fishing tournament named for Hemingway. F.C. was to present the trophy to the winner. But it was F.C. himself who caught the biggest marlin and won the prize."

"Whose scale did they use?"

"What are you suggesting?"

I didn't want to get arrested on day two, so I didn't reply.

Antonio sipped his water thoughtfully, then got my attention by saying, "I understand from Tad that you are a fisherman."

"That's right." And why are you discussing me with Tad?

"So you understand the passion of this sport."

"I do."

"Do you know that there is a new tournament? The Pescando Por la Paz. It arrives in Havana from Key West tomorrow. You live in Key West. Correct?"

"Correct."

"This tournament did not interest you?"

"No."

He asked, "Have you read Islands in the Stream?"

"Have you?"

"Yes, of course. It is a very good book. It speaks of Cayo Guillermo—where the tournament will be held after they leave Havana."

I sipped my beer.

"There is a very prophetic line in the book . . . written before the revolution." He quoted without notes, "'The Cubans double-cross each other. They sell each other out. They got what they deserve. The hell with their revolutions.'" He said, "I will see you at dinner," and left.

What the hell was that all about?

CHAPTER 21

Tad's 5:30 lecture was being held in a meeting room on the mezzanine level, and everyone came dressed for dinner as instructed because the bus was departing right after Tad did the cha-cha or whatever he was going to do. Sara and I sat together. She was wearing a red lacy dress and sandals, and her perfume smelled good.

I noticed that Antonio was not in the room to monitor Tad's lecture for subversive material, so maybe he was busy reporting me to the secret police for questioning the weight of F.C.'s marlin. My mouth sometimes gets me into trouble, which makes life interesting.

Anyway, attendance was taken and three people were absent, though they'd sent word that they were in their rooms, not feeling well, which was understandable after a long day in the hot sun listening to Antonio's bullshit. Thinking ahead, Sara and I should go on sick call to give us a running start before we were reported as AWOL.

Tad began his lecture by playing Cuban music on a compact disc player while images of hot dancers flashed on a projector screen. This turned out to be the highlight of the lecture.

Tad then spoke from his notes, and I actually found the lecture interesting. I learned about *Son* music, salsa, rhumba, reggaeton, and the African origins of a lot of Cuban music and dance. There was no time for Q&A, but Tad remembered to give us the names of some good nightclubs, including Floridita, the birthplace of the daiquiri, and where Hemingway used to hang out. Tad said, "His record was eighteen double daiquiris in one sitting. Don't try to match that."

I said to Sara, "We used to do that before breakfast at Bowdoin."

On our way down the sweeping staircase to the lobby, Sara asked, "Did you enjoy that?"

"I did."

"Cuban music and dance are one of the few things that the regime hasn't changed or censored."

So even the Commies like to see boobs and butts shaking. In some ways, Cuba was still Cuba. I said, "I'm a little Hemingwayed out, but we can go to Floridita after dinner if you'd like."

"I think we should take a walk on the Malecón."

"You're a cheap date."

We boarded the bus. José was still on duty and Antonio had reappeared in time for a free dinner.

On our drive to the Riviera, Antonio gave us some background on the hotel to make our dining experience more meaningful and beautiful. The Riviera, he told us, was built by the notorious American gangster Meyer Lansky, and opened in time for Christmas 1957. "But on New Year's Day 1959," said Antonio, "the Communist Party crashed Mr. Lansky's New Year's Eve party."

That got a laugh from the Yalies—who had all seen Godfather II—and Antonio, who'd probably used that line a hundred times, smiled.

So, I thought, Meyer Lansky and his Las Vegas partners had made a bad bet on the Riviera Hotel and Casino and lost everything in one day. I wondered if any Mafia money was in the cave. I pictured bundles of cash labeled "Lansky" or "Luciano." Maybe that's where my cut was coming from. I'll take it.

We pulled up to the Riviera, which overlooked the Malecón and the Straits of Florida but looked like it belonged on the Las Vegas Strip.

We got off the bus and entered the huge marble lobby, which was eerily deserted. Antonio gave us a peek inside the empty Copa Nightclub, a Fifties time capsule. I could picture that New Year's Eve party, men and women in evening dress, smoking and drinking at the tables, and people dancing to a twenty-piece orchestra, while Fidel Castro and his ragtag army headed toward Havana. And the party was over.

Someone asked, "Will the casino reopen?"

"Never," replied Antonio. "It was completely destroyed with axes and hammers on the first day of liberation by the revolutionary army and the people of Havana." He added, "We will see a news film of this in the Museum of the Revolution."

I didn't think I could watch that.

Anyway, it was time for a beautiful dinner. We were dining in the original restaurant, called L'Aiglon, and Antonio escorted us in. The spacious room had a plush carpet, red ceiling, and crystal chandeliers that were once gaudy but are now mid-century antiques.

Only a few other guests occupied the tables, and Sara claimed a table for two so we could be alone. I looked at Antonio sitting with Tad and caught him looking at me and Sara. Clearly he was interested in us, and my encounter with him in the bar had put me on guard.

A bow-tied waiter took our drink orders, and Sara ordered an expensive bottle of Veuve Clicquot and said to me, "Get used to being rich."

Service was slow, so the Yalies used the time to take pictures. I could imagine the slide show conversation back in the States. "And those two hot tamales ran off together, and we all got questioned by the police and missed our day at the tobacco farm."

The drinks arrived and everyone sat.

The restaurant was French, but the cuisine was something else, and the service was what you get from waiters making twenty bucks a month. Reality check: The rest of the country carried food ration cards.

I filled Sara in on my bar chat with Antonio and said, "We can draw one of two conclusions—that his interest in you is personal, or that his interest in you is something else."

She nodded. "What is his interest in you?"

"Sizing up his competition."

She forced a smile, then asked, "Why was he discussing you with Tad?"

"Don't know."

"And I don't like that he mentioned the fishing tournament."

"In context, it seemed like small talk. Out of context . . . I'm not sure."

Sara seemed a bit concerned, so I changed the subject and told her that I had questioned F.C.'s marlin trophy in the Hemingway Tournament, and that I'd suggested to Antonio that it had to do with a rigged scale. I said, "I'm in big trouble."

She laughed. "That's a famous story. The Cubans in Miami say it was a scuba diver who put the fish on F.C.'s hook—with lead weights in its belly."

We both got a laugh at that.

Well, if this was our second date, it was going well. In the real world I should be thinking that I might score tonight, or next date latest. But Sara Ortega had put me on the itinerary for day four. Why? I don't know, but I thought I could fast-track this romance. Maybe another bottle of bubbly.

I emptied the first bottle into our flutes and said, "Your eyes sparkle like this champagne."

"Worst. Line. Ever."

"I've been at sea too long."

"Apparently."

A few more people drifted into the restaurant, and I could hear British accents and German being spoken.

Sara remarked, "This hotel seems like a lifeless parody of its former self."

"In the right hands, the Riviera could be a gold mine."

"This hotel is actually owned by the military, who are the biggest property owners in Cuba." She added, "Nothing will change in Cuba until property is returned to its rightful owners."

"In this case, Meyer Lansky's heirs and partners."

"It can be complicated," she admitted. "Or easy if you steal what's yours."

That might not be so easy.

Dinner was included in the tour, but I needed to settle the bar bill, which I did for two hundred CUCs in cash. The Cuban military didn't take American credit cards.

Sara and I skipped dessert, and I reported in to Tad—and Antonio—that we were going to take a taxi to Floridita.

"Have fun," said Tad.

Antonio advised, "It's a tourist trap. You should walk on the Malecón instead."

Which was where we were actually going, but I said, "That's too close to the beach. Tad will turn us in to the State Department."

Tad forced a smile but didn't reply. I didn't think he'd miss me when I was gone.

But Antonio would.

CHAPTER 22

We left the Riviera Hotel and began walking east toward the Nacional, which was about two miles farther down the Malecón. The night was warm, breezeless, and humid, and a bright moon illuminated the water, reminding me of Sara on my boat. Same moon, same water, different planet.

The wide sidewalk that ran along the seawall was a river of humanity, including multi-generational families dining al fresco. A few salsa and rhumba bands played and people danced. Others strolled, drank rum and beer, smoked, and gathered in groups to talk or read poetry.

Sara commented, "This is Havana's living room and dining room, and the poor people's cabaret. And this is the authentic Cuban experience you wanted."

"Including the secret police?"

"Marcelo said no. They would be easy for the people to spot." She added, "But there are always the chivatos."

I noticed that there were enough Americans and Europeans strolling that we didn't stick out, and I could also see that this was a good place for a chance encounter with a Cuban selling pottery—and Sara was certainly easy to spot in her red dress.

I asked, "Do you have your pesos with you?"

She tapped her shoulder bag.

We stopped near a salsa group, and, inspired by the hot music, Sara handed me her bag and joined a few people who were dancing. She had some good moves and she was really shaking it. She hiked up her dress and the crowd whistled and clapped, and I felt my pepino stirring.

Sara blew a kiss to the band and we moved on. I returned her bag with a compliment. "Not bad for an architect."

"I'll teach you Cuban dance when we get back to Miami."

I would have said "if," but I liked her optimism.

We stopped and looked out over the seawall at the beach and the Straits of Florida. People were fishing or wading in the water, maybe thinking about those ninety miles to Key West.

On that subject, Sara said, "You'll notice there are no boats out there."

"Right."

"There are virtually no private watercraft allowed in Cuba, for obvious reasons."

"They should just let people go."

"Sometimes they do. As with the Mariel Boatlift. The regime understands it needs a safety valve—an unofficial method of getting rid of people who could cause problems. But Cuba loses many of its best and brightest."

"I assume there are patrol boats out there."

"There are. The Guarda Frontera—the border guards. They keep an eye on the commercial fishing fleet and also look for the rafters. But they can't patrol hundreds of miles of coastline." She added, "About five or six thousand rafters a year try to escape, and fewer than half are caught."

Not bad odds. I asked, "Do the border guards have helicopters or seaplanes?"

"A few of each, but not many."

"It only takes one."

"It will go well."

"Okay."

We continued our walk, but no one approached us except artists selling their sketches or kids looking for a few coins.

I spotted a few ladies of the night, and Sara noticed. "Prostitution was one of the first things outlawed by the regime, and it carries a four-year prison sentence for both parties."

"I'll let Tad know."

She smiled and put her arm through mine. "But you don't need to buy sex."

"Right." Meanwhile, I'm not getting any for free.

"Cuba is a very promiscuous society, and casual sex is rampant. The Cubans say that sex is the only thing that Castro hasn't rationed."

Funny. But all this sex talk was getting me cranked. I could see the Nacional ahead and said, "Let's have a nightcap."

"We should keep walking."

"No one's selling Cuban pottery tonight."

She didn't reply.

"But that needs to happen soon. Our window will start closing in two or three days."

"Would you be willing to come with me to Camagüey Province even if our Havana contact doesn't show up?"

Actually, I'd prefer to do that and not have any Cubans involved. If Cuba was anything like Afghanistan, every time we relied on the locals to assist us we'd get double-crossed, ambushed, or at best screwed out of money.

"Mac?"

"Well . . . if I say no, would you go without me?"

"I would."

The lady had balls. "Let's give it a few days, then if our window of time is closing and we haven't met our contact here, we can make that decision."

"All right. And you understand that if we don't meet our contact in Havana, we won't know how to meet our contact in Camagüey, and we won't have a vehicle or a safe house."

I assured her, "I know how to hot-wire most vehicles, and the best safe house is under the stars."

She stopped walking and faced me. "I told Carlos and Eduardo you were the right man for this job."

Before I could think of a response, she threw her arms around my neck and we were locking lips on the Malecón.

She let go and we continued our walk. She asked, "Was that a gun in your pocket?"

"That was my Cuban Missile Crisis."

She laughed, then said seriously, "It would be good if we had a gun."

"We'll have guns on The Maine if we need them to get out of Cuba."

"We could need a gun much sooner."

"As I understand it, getting caught with a gun in Cuba could be a death sentence."

"I would rather die in a gunfight than be captured."

"I think it's time for a drink."

We walked in silence, then Sara pointed out a modern six-story building off to the right. "That's the U.S. Embassy."

The windows were dark, except for a corner office on the sixth floor. Someone was working late, maybe trying to catch up after being out of the office for fifty years. The area around the building was bathed in security lights, and I could see the Great Seal of the United States over the front door.

Sara said, "We have no ambassador yet, but we have a Chargé d'Affaires, Jeffrey DeLaurentis, who runs the embassy. His boss, the Secretary of State, John Kerry, is a Yalie, and I met him once. So if we wind up in a Cuban prison, I can play the Yale card."

Based on what I saw of her Yale alum group, neither the State Department nor the embassy would be taking that call.

Anyway, there was a small plaza in front of the embassy that Sara said was called the Anti-Imperialist Forum. "It's where crowds gather spontaneously to protest against America. Except nothing in Cuba is spontaneous."

"Except dancing." And sex, which is unrationed.

Well, our primary objective didn't go too well on the Malecón, but I had a secondary objective that might go better at the Nacional.

CHAPTER 23

We reached the tree-lined drive of the Nacional and entered the hotel lobby, which, unlike the Riviera, was hopping and crowded with what looked like an international clientele. I hoped Jack didn't show up here tomorrow in one of his inappropriate T-shirts.

Cocktails on the terrace appealed to me, and we went out the back door.

The terrace was crowded, but for five CUCs the hostess found us two comfortable chairs that looked out at the Straits. A waitress appeared and Sara ordered a daiquiri and I got a Bucanero, por favor. A three-piece steel band played Caribbean Island music.

A soft breeze came off the moonlit water, stirring the palms, and the air was sweet with tropical flowers. The combo was playing "Guantanamera," one of my favorites. Out over the water a jetliner was climbing out of José Martí Airport.

This would be the perfect end of a nice evening if I was going to get spontaneously laid.

On a different but somewhat related subject, Sara said, "This is romantic."

Our drinks came and we clinked. "To a new friendship," she said.

"And to you," I replied.

We stared out at the water, and I could see the silhouettes of the old and new fortifications along the beach. People have a way of screwing things up, even in a tropical paradise.

She said, "I never asked you—do you have a woman?"

The best and shortest answer was, "No."

"Why not?"

"I was married to my boat."

"Be serious."

"I never found the right woman." I added, "But I'm open to that possibility."

"Sounds like bullshit. That's okay. When we leave here, we go our separate ways."

I hate these kinds of conversations. "Let's focus on getting out of here."

"And if we don't, we'll always have this time together."

I had the feeling I was being manipulated, but I also felt that Sara honestly liked me. If we actually got out of this place alive, we could sort it out. Meanwhile, the clock was ticking—two more days until sex on Sunday, then a few more days after that until we had to make some big decisions. Regarding the first subject, I spontaneously suggested, "Let's get a room here."

She didn't reply.

"We could get arrested tonight and executed in the morning."

She laughed but it was a nervous laugh. Clearly she wasn't ready.

I was about to drop the subject but she said, "Get the check."

"And a taxi?"

"And a room."

"Wait right here."

I moved quickly to the front desk and inquired about a room. The clerk sensed that I was on a pepino mission, and he said that only luxury rooms were available, and I had my choice of four— the Errol Flynn room, which sounded exciting, the Ava Gardner and Frank Sinatra room, where I could also get laid, the Walt Disney room, which might be a little weird, or the Johnny Weissmuller Tarzan room, which sounded like a winner, for five hundred CUCs—more than I had in my wallet. But the clerk wanted me to get laid—or he wanted to pocket some cash—so he said he'd take part of the payment in American dollars, plus ten percent. Why is free sex so expensive?

I had to show him my passport and visa, and I signed in as

"Dan MacDick," which was either a Freudian slip or good trade-craft. He handed over a big brass key whose tag said: <u>232, Tarzan</u>. That's me.

I returned to the terrace, where Sara was downing another daiquiri. I asked, "Do you need a few more to do this?"

"It relaxes me."

I put an American fifty on the cocktail table. "Ready?"

She nodded and stood.

We walked into the lobby and got on the elevator, neither of us saying anything.

On the second floor, we followed the hall sign to 232. The brass plaque on the door read: <u>JOHNNY WEISSMULLER, TARZAN</u>.

Sara either didn't notice or had no comment. I unlocked the door and we went into the room. I turned on a light, which revealed a big space whose décor was sort of eclectic, with a few tacky touches such as the leopard skin on the floor and the tiger-striped bedspread. Maybe I should have asked for the Walt Disney room.

Anyway, there was a bar, thank God, and I said, "What would you like to drink?"

Sara seemed to have zoned out and was staring out at the water.

I opened the bar fridge and found a split of Moët and popped the cork, then filled two flutes and handed one to her.

She took it and stared at the bubbles.

I'm not pushy, but Major Johnson was in command now, so I had to strike the right balance between romance and sex. I turned on the radio and found some soft *Son* guitar music, which was sort of romantic.

Sara seemed to come out of her zone and I raised my glass. "To us."

We clinked and drank. I asked her to dance, and we danced to the rhythmic guitars. Her body felt good against mine.

She said softly, "I don't just jump into bed with any man."

"Me neither."

Anyway, the clothes came off as we danced and drank champagne, and we wound up in the shower together. I saw that Sara had a bikini cut and she sunbathed topless. You can learn a lot about people in the shower.

She ran her finger over the scars on my chest. "This makes me sad."

"Could have been worse."

She explored further, one hand cupping my bolas and the other wrapped around my pepino.

"It's all there," I assured her.

"Put it in a safe place."

I grasped her buttocks and slid inside her.

She put her hands on my shoulders then arched her back, and the water ran over her face and breasts as I got into the slow, rhythmic beat of "Chan Chan" coming from the radio.

Olé!

———

Later, in bed, Sara wrapped her arms and legs around me and whispered, "I'm happy, but now I'm also . . . frightened."

"That's okay."

"Last week, I lived for the day I could return to Cuba and steal the money from under their ugly noses . . . Now, I have . . . maybe something else to live for."

"I had the same thought."

"Were you frightened when you were there?"

"Every day."

She stayed quiet awhile, then said, "I don't want them to capture me."

"I understand." Same in Afghanistan. If you fell into the hands of the Taliban, you'd wish you were dead. I also remembered what Carlos had said about Villa Marista prison, and I was sure conditions there hadn't improved much.

She cuddled up to me. "It would be nice to be rich in Miami with you. But it would also be nice to just be in Miami with you."

"That *would* be nice."

She rolled out of bed, went to the bar, and poured two more glasses of champagne. She noticed the key on the bar and asked, "Why is this called the Tarzan room?"

"Come here and I'll show you."

CHAPTER 24

If you fell into the hands of the Taliban, you'd wish you were dead.

They'd cut off your balls, then slice off your face with razor knives. And they'd hold your head and make you look in a mirror at your own faceless red skull. And you couldn't close your eyes, because you'd have no eyelids. And then they'd make you watch the dogs eat your face and your balls. Then they'd give you a pat on the back and let you go.

And that was why you'd blow your brains out before you let yourself get captured by them.

It was my first tour, before I got promoted to captain, and I was leading my motorized platoon, about forty men from the 5th Stryker Brigade Combat Team in Maiwand, operating out of FOB Ramrod, into a moonscape of dust, dirt, and rocks, under a blazing sun.

The lead vehicle, a Bradley recon, got hit by an IED, then all hell broke loose and we were taking RPGs and automatic weapons fire from the piles of rock on both sides of the road. We dismounted quickly and moved away from the vehicles that were getting hit. I took a round in my body armor but kept moving, and we got flat and began returning fire.

There was very little cover or concealment, and it took me about ten seconds to realize we'd been caught in a well-planned ambush by a large enemy force, and there was the distinct possibility that we were all going to die. *Kill the wounded first, then yourself.*

Half our eight armored vehicles and Humvees were ablaze, and one exploded and I could feel the heat on my back.

They tell you in tactics class that the only way out of an ambush is to charge into the ambush. This is bullshit.

I got on the horn and ordered the platoon to move north along the road and begin flanking the ambush.

The Taliban are tough and sometimes fearless, but rarely smart, and never very good marksmen. They fire their AK-47s on full automatic like kids playing with toy guns. Their hits are lucky, but hits are hits, and a few of my men went down, but the medic reported light wounds.

The desert wind was from the south and we fired and maneuvered north, under the cover of black diesel smoke and smoke marker grenades until we were about a hundred meters out of the kill zone. Then we began flanking the ambush positions, moving from rock pile to rock pile, getting around them until they realized we'd turned the tables on them.

The crews of the undamaged Bradley Fighting Vehicles had remounted and were providing supporting fire with their 7.62mm machine guns and 25mm rapid-fire cannons.

The Taliban began withdrawing, dashing among the rock piles. I could see that they outnumbered us, but I ordered the platoon to pursue, though I knew that the turned-around ambush could easily turn into a secondary ambush, a.k.a. a trap. It's a game. No rules, but lots of strategy. Offense is the best defense, so we pushed on across the desert valley into thickening piles of rock that had rolled down from the nearby mountains.

My platoon sergeant strongly suggested we break off the pursuit and wait for the helicopter gunships to even the odds. But I was full of adrenaline and all pissed off, and I'd led a charge into the rock field, totally oblivious to the horseshoe-shaped ambush that awaited us.

The Taliban took the higher ground at the base of the mountain, and they'd also taken up positions in two parallel wadis to complete the horseshoe that we'd run into.

We formed a tight perimeter and returned the fire while the Bradleys continued supporting fire from the road about four hundred meters away.

The bad guys had the manpower, but we had the firepower, and it was sort of a standoff until a group of Taliban moved out of one of the brush-filled wadis and turned the horseshoe into a box. We were surrounded and starting to run low on ammunition.

My sergeant, a big black guy named Simpson, said to me, "You make life interesting, Lieutenant."

"You ain't seen nothing yet."

The closest wadi was about a hundred meters to our west, and the Taliban were strung out in the dry streambed, popping off bursts of AK-47 fire that mostly ricocheted off the rockfalls around us.

We were trapped, but relatively safe where we were, and we could have waited for the gunships, but in a situation like this, the Taliban sometimes start moving and maneuvering close to you, so the gunships can't fire their stuff without the risk of hitting friendlies.

So, when your ass is in a sling, you do the unexpected. I got on the horn and ordered the Bradleys to direct all their fire on the wadi to the west, then lift their fire after three minutes, and shift it to targets of opportunity.

I assembled the two squads that were with me, waited out the barrage on the wadi, then charged toward it just as the Bradleys lifted their fire.

We reached the dry streambed within a minute and found it unoccupied except for a dozen dead and wounded Taliban lying in the dried mud.

Their dead are often booby-trapped, and the wounded are ready to pull the pin on a grenade or pull a gun as soon as you come near them. So Sergeant Simpson and I drew our Glocks and did the dirty work while the rest of the men took up defensive positions.

The last wounded Taliban I came to was staring at me, his eyes following me as I moved closer to him. His legs were chewed up, like a 25mm round had exploded at his feet. He never looked at the gun in my hand, but kept staring into my eyes. I kept eye contact with him, and I hesitated, because maybe it would be good to take a prisoner for Intel. The wounded guy raised his arms and clasped his hands in prayer. In the distance I heard the sound of choppers coming toward us.

I lowered my gun and moved toward the Taliban, who suddenly reached out and grabbed my ankle. I didn't know if it was a sign of thanks, or an act of aggression, and I fired a 9mm round into his face. I still don't know what he was trying to tell me.

———

I was awakened by a foot rubbing against mine, and someone was saying, "Good morning."

I felt sweat on my face. It was still dark outside. She asked, "Did you sleep well?"

"No." I asked, "Would you like coffee?"

She yawned. "Let's get back to our hotel."

But we lay there, then she said, "I promised Carlos I wouldn't get emotionally involved with you . . . wouldn't have sex with you. And now we've had sex three times."

"Three?"

"You're going to do it again, aren't you?"

Funny. I got on top of her and we made love again.

Afterward, we lay side by side, and she took my hand. "I have a confession to make."

"There's a church down the street."

"Listen. I do have a . . . sort of boyfriend . . . but . . ."

That didn't completely surprise me. "That's for you to work out."

"Are you angry with me?"

"I have more pressing issues to worry about."

"I think you're angry."

"I'm not."

"Are you jealous?"

"No. Do you think he'd be jealous?"

"He's Cuban. They get jealous."

"Just explain that it was part of the job."

"I'll . . . just explain that it's over."

"That's your call."

"Can you at least give me some encouragement?"

"What do you want me to say?"

She didn't reply, so I said, "I like you very much."

"And I like you very much." She squeezed my hand.

Well, nobody was using the four-letter L-word. But it was out there. And I knew from the Army that hurried wartime romances lead to what seems like love, and half the men and women I knew in the Army who returned to duty from a pre-deployment leave had gotten married—or engaged, as I did. Then when you returned from overseas, reality set in.

Sara asked, "Do you have a confession to make?"

"I'm unattached, as I said."

"But you have women."

"Not for awhile."

"Why have you never married?"

I sat up in bed and glanced at the bedside clock: 5:34.

"Mac?"

"I've had a complicated life."

"Engaged?"

"Once. How about you?"

She sat up. "I've never found the right man."

I didn't reply.

"Would you like to change the subject?"

"I would."

She turned on the lamp. "What would you like to talk about?"

Coffee. But there was something else on my mind. "While we're being honest with each other, I want you to tell me if there's more to this trip to Cuba than I've been told."

"What do you mean?"

"More than the money."

She hesitated a second, then replied, "There is." She added, "You're very smart."

"Okay. And?"

"And I will tell you when you need to know."

"I need to know now."

"The less you know now, the better."

"No, the more I know—"

"What you don't know you can't reveal under torture."

That was a little jarring at 5:30. I almost wanted to return to the subject of love. "Okay, but—"

"I'll tell you this—you'll be very pleased with the other reason we're here. And that's all I'm saying."

"Okay . . . breakfast in bed?"

"We need to get back to our hotel." She got out of bed, went to the bar, and opened her shoulder bag, pulling out a wad of pesos.

I said, "That's okay. No charge."

She smiled and took out a piece of paper and gave it to me. "I made a photocopy of the map in the hotel business office." She looked at me. "If anything happens to me, you should be able to follow that to the cave."

I turned on my lamp and glanced at the map, which was like a child's drawing of a pirate treasure map. But the directions written on the bottom in English seemed clear if you started in the right place. The map was titled, "A great hike through the Camagüey Mountains."

"As I told you, I've altered it slightly, and I'll explain it to you later."

"Okay."

"Also, our Havana contact will give us a good road map for Camagüey. I assume that as a former infantry officer, you have good map skills."

"That's what I got paid for."

"Good. I trust you, Mac. I know you'll do the right thing, even without me."

I looked at her, standing naked in the lamplight. "I will do my best."

I got out of bed, went to the window, and looked out at the starlit Straits of Florida. Sara came up behind me, wrapped her arms around my chest, and put her chin on my shoulder. She said, "Just as I saw the green flash, I can also see our boat, sailing across the water, with Jack and Felipe in the cabin, and you and I sitting on the bow, looking at the horizon as Key West comes into sight. The sun is coming up. Can you see that?"

I could, and I couldn't. But I said, "Yes, I can see that."

"Our mission is blessed. You are blessed. Just as you returned twice from Afghanistan, you will return home from Cuba."

Unless God was getting tired of covering my ass.

————————

Sara ran a comb through her damp hair and put on a little lip gloss. Low maintenance. We got dressed, left the room, and rode down in the elevator. I dropped the key off at the desk, and the same clerk glanced at Sara, then asked me, "How was your stay, señor?"

Should I beat my chest? Or let out a Tarzan scream? "Fine."

"Breakfast is being served in the Veranda."

"Thank you, I've eaten."

Sara and I left the hotel. The sun was up and the air was already steamy. I suggested we walk to our hotel—or swing from tree to tree—but Sara said it was more than a mile to the Parque Central, and we should take a taxi so we'd get there before our group started coming down for breakfast.

"But I want everyone to see us staggering into the hotel together."

"I'm sure you do." She said to the doorman, "Taxi, por favor."

The only transportation available was a Coco cab, an open, three-wheeled Lambretta-type vehicle that reminded me of the ones in Kabul. We got into the rear seat, and off we went through the quiet streets of Havana. Sara said, "This is romantic."

I could see the pavement through the rusted floorboards.

There wasn't much traffic on this Saturday morning, but there were a lot of people walking, and the city looked spectral in the morning mist. This place totally sucked, but it was starting to grow on me.

Sara put her arm through mine and said, "I'm sorry I lied to you about the boyfriend. But I'll never lie to you again."

"And don't lie to him."

"I'll try to call him from the hotel phone."

"It can wait until you get back to Miami."

"I want to do it now . . . in case I don't get back."

"In that case, it doesn't matter."

"Yes . . . but . . . it's the right thing to do. Even if you cheat, you shouldn't lie."

Really? I thought lying and cheating went together. But maybe Catholics needed to confess. "Let's decide tomorrow."

We got to the Parque Central and entered together. The breakfast room was just opening, but I didn't see anyone from our group. "Coffee?"

"No. I don't want to be seen with you wearing the same dress I wore last night."

"Who cares?"

"I do. And you need to change."

"I need coffee."

"I'll see you later." She went to the elevators.

I walked into the breakfast room and ran into Antonio at the coffee bar. "Buenos días," he said. "I was looking for you and Miss Ortega last night in Floridita."

Really? Why? "We took your advice and walked on the Malecón."

"Ah, good. Did you enjoy that?"

"I did." I scanned the tables and saw an empty one near a sunny window. "See you later."

"Yes, for the walking tour. But you don't need a sports jacket."

"Actually, we just got back to the hotel."

"Yes, I saw you come in. I hope your evening was beautiful."

"It was, and now I'm going to have a beautiful cup of coffee."

"Don't let me keep you."

"I won't."

I got a cup of coffee and sat at the table near the window.

Antonio also sat by himself and made a cell phone call. I was annoyed that he had service and I didn't. Antonio hung up and took some papers from his shoulder bag. Today's itinerary? Or his police informant's report? The man was an asshole. Maybe worse—a chivato.

But the world looked a little different this morning, and I was as close to happy as I'd been in awhile.

My heart said that Sara and I should just get a flight out of here and go live happily ever after.

But my head said I'd regret it if I let three million dollars slip through my fingers. *I'd rather regret the things I did than the things I didn't do.* Also, I'd made a commitment to do this.

This was getting complicated, as I knew it would.

And what was she keeping from me? Something that would please me. I could not possibly imagine what that was. But if we pressed on, I'd find out.

CHAPTER 25

Back in my room, I changed into jeans and my new Hemingway T-shirt, then stuck two bottles of water in my backpack along with my Swiss Army knife, my binoculars, and my new treasure map. I was ready for my Havana recon.

I joined our group in the hotel lobby at 8 A.M. where Tad was taking attendance.

Sara was looking good in white shorts, a Miami Dolphins T-shirt, and a baseball cap. She had her big shoulder bag, which I assumed was filled with pesos and her map.

Sara and I held hands, and the Yale group, to the extent that they cared, understood that we were having a holiday romance. Antonio, too, noticed.

Antonio led us across the street to the small park, where he began by telling us that downtown Havana was divided into three areas: Habana Vieja, the Old Town, where we were going to walk this morning, Centro Habana, where we were standing, and the area called Vedado, the newer section of Havana where the Riviera and Nacional were located and that was once controlled by the American Mafia and their Cuban underlings.

Antonio went on a bit about the Mafia, which seemed to be an obsession of his. Antonio had probably seen Godfather II a dozen times.

Finally he said, "We will have lunch in a beautiful paladar, then we return to Centro to continue our walking tour."

I thought Antonio was finished, but he asked, "Who has been to Havana before?"

A middle-aged couple—who looked otherwise normal—raised their hands.

"Ah, good. So you can have my job today."

The Yalies, who were mostly humorless with each other, made an exception for the charming Cuban and laughed.

Antonio asked, "Anyone else?" He looked at Sara, who had not raised her hand. "Miss Ortega, weren't you here last year?"

"Why do you ask?"

He kept looking at her, but didn't reply. "So, we will begin our walk." He began walking east toward the harbor.

The streets and sidewalks got narrower as we entered the Old Town and the group was strung out for fifty meters as Antonio stayed in the lead and gave his talk, which, happily, I couldn't hear, but Sara gave me and the Yalies around us a commentary on the historic architecture.

Habana Vieja, some of it over three hundred years old, was very picturesque, but also hot, airless, claustrophobic, and aromatic. It was Saturday, so the cobblestoned streets were mostly free of traffic but filled with locals bartering for scarce goods and food, as senior citizens hung out their windows and watched the world go by. For people who had nothing, they seemed happy enough. Or maybe it was my outlook that had changed. Getting laid will do that.

Another thing that struck me was the number of buildings that had totally or partially collapsed. You could actually see the interiors of the rooms where the front walls had fallen away and vegetation sprouted from rotting stucco. Maybe my landlord wasn't such an asshole.

We came to a small square where Antonio began a commentary on the Catedral de San Cristóbal de la Habana, which, he said, was almost three hundred years old and had once held the remains of Christopher Columbus. But when the Spanish were defeated in the War of 1898, they stole Christopher and took him to Spain. "We want him back!" shouted Antonio. "He will be good for tourism!"

The Yalies laughed on cue, and I said to Sara, "Spain and Cuba should just divvy up the bones. They could flip a coin for the skull."

She glanced at me and said, "Yes, the bones need to come home . . . There are answers in the bones."

I had no idea what she meant, but she seemed suddenly far away. I took a bottled water from my backpack and made her drink.

Antonio was still talking and I tuned out. Tonight I was going to meet Jack at the Nacional, and I hadn't mentioned that to Sara, and I didn't think I needed to explain my being AWOL to her. But that was before we became lovers. Now I needed to say something. That's what happens when you sleep with someone.

Antonio said we could go inside the Catedral if we wanted. Ten minutes.

Sara said, "Let's go."

"Yes, dear."

There were a number of tourists inside the dark cathedral and a few locals were on their knees in front of the baroque altar. Sara, of course, wanted to pray.

I haven't prayed since Afghanistan, and then only when there was incoming, but Sara was insistent, and I followed her to the altar rail. This whole day would have played out differently if I'd kept my pepino in my chinos. On the other hand, if I hadn't yet scored, I'd now be on my knees, praying for it.

Sara knelt, made the sign of the cross, and prayed silently. Out of respect, I clasped my hands and bowed my head. And while I was at it, I prayed that we'd both get out of here alive—and that one of us would not get pregnant.

She crossed herself again, stood, turned, and took my hand. We walked down the side aisle, past racks of flickering votive candles. She stopped and lit one, then continued on.

Outside in the bright sunlight she said, "I prayed for our success here and lit a candle for the soul of my grandfather."

"That's very nice."

Antonio told us that we would visit three more plazas in the Old Town before lunch.

Dios mío.

We walked to a harbor fort, the ancient Castillo de la Real Fuerza, which was uphill all the way, and we ascended a rampart lined with ancient cannons from which we could see the harbor channel. We were alone, and Sara pointed to a building about four hundred meters away. "That's the Sierra Maestra Terminal, and that's the pier where the fishing fleet is going to dock. But I don't see any boats, and I don't see any activity in the plaza that looks like a welcoming ceremony."

I didn't need my binoculars to confirm that.

She said, "I hope it hasn't been cancelled." She reminded me, unnecessarily, "Everything depends on the Pescando Por la Paz."

Actually, everything depended on a chain of events that we had little or no control over. I reassured her, "Even if the fleet left Key West at first light, and maintained a fleet speed of twenty knots, they wouldn't reach Havana until about eleven, earliest." I looked at my watch. "It's just past ten now."

"All right . . . Carlos said if we didn't see it on the news, we needed to verify the fleet's arrival ourselves." She added, "He also said he'd try to get a phone or fax message to me at the hotel if the tournament was delayed or cancelled."

Carlos never told me that, but there were lots of things that Carlos hadn't told me, as I was finding out from Sara. In any case, it was time for me to share something, so I told her, "I'm actually meeting Jack tonight."

She looked at me. "Carlos didn't want—"

"Carlos didn't want you to sleep with me. We don't care what Carlos wants."

"You agreed to follow orders, Captain. I'm not going to let you compromise the mission."

I had a flashback to the ops bunker. Everyone who gave orders from the rear seemed to think they knew what was going on at the front. Well, if you're not standing next to me when the shit is flying, you don't know what's going on. "I agreed to do the job. My way."

"There's no reason for you to meet him."

"There are lots of reasons."

"What?"

"To be sure they've arrived, as you just said."

"If I don't hear from Carlos, we can find out by coming to the pier later."

"I need to exchange info with Jack. And have a beer." I added, "We may never see each other again."

She thought about that, then asked, "Where are you meeting him?"

"At a prearranged place. It's safe."

"What time?"

"Six."

"I'll come with you."

"No."

She looked at me and we locked eyeballs. Finally, she said, "All right . . . do what you have to do. But make sure you're not followed, and make sure he wasn't followed. There can't be a connection between—"

"I passed that class."

She seemed a bit miffed. Glad I got laid last night.

In fact, she seemed to be thinking the same thing and said, "That's what happens when you sleep with a man. They step all over you."

"Not if they want an encore."

"I should have waited until Sunday."

"I'm free Sunday."

"I should have listened to Carlos."

"You have to listen to your heart. Not your lawyer."

"And what organ are *you* listening to, señor?"

"My heart." Dick, too.

She looked at me. "I believe you."

We kissed and made up. Sex changes the rules and the dynamics. You get some control, but you lose some control. That's life.

I scanned the horizon with my binoculars, but there were no boats heading for the harbor.

I had a few other things on my mind and I asked her, "How well do you know Felipe?"

"I've met him. Carlos and Eduardo know him."

"Can we assume that Carlos or Eduardo have vetted him?"

"Felipe is actually the grandnephew of Eduardo." She added, "We try to keep these things in the family. Like the Mafia does. If you can't trust family, you can't trust anyone."

She hasn't met my family. But maybe she would. That should be interesting. I said, "I would have worried less about Felipe if someone had told me who he was."

She stayed silent awhile, then said, "We rarely include . . . outsiders in our business. And when we do, we don't say more than we have to about . . . anything."

People who know the Scots say we're clannish, and the MacCormicks, who are of the Clan Campbell, can be that way. But I suspect that the Cubans make the Scots look inclusive.

Sara took my hand and said, "We have a special relationship now." She smiled. "You're practically one of the family. You'll see when we get back to Miami and we have a big party to celebrate."

I pictured myself partying in Miami wearing a guayabera and my clan kilt. More to the point, this mission was like an onion that needed to be peeled away, layer by layer. There had to be an easier way to get laid and make three million dollars.

CHAPTER 26

At the base of the old fort was the Plaza de Armas, which was lined with royal palms, and the group took cover from the sun while Antonio gave a history lesson. I didn't want to bring up the subject of Antonio again, but I asked Sara, "How did Antonio know you were here before?"

"I don't know . . . I mentioned it to Alison, and she must have said something to him."

Or Antonio had some info from the police, who would have copies of our visa applications, which were filled with information.

Sara looked at Antonio, who was now texting. "Why is he asking about us?"

"We don't know that he is."

"And why did he quote those Hemingway lines to you? 'The Cubans double-cross each other. They sell each other out.'"

"Don't know."

"I'll be happy when we get out of Havana."

Out of the frying pan and into the fire.

Antonio led us to a pedestrian street called Calle Obispo—the Street of the Bishop—lined with old shops and some new, trendy stores, art galleries, and cafés. Creeping capitalism.

Sara stopped and we let the Yalies go on. She looked across the street at a large neo-classical stone and stucco building with a white portal that was decorated with carved four-leaved clovers for some reason. The building seemed derelict, though there were official-looking signs and revolutionary posters in the grimy windows. I knew this was her grandfather's bank.

She said, "I can picture him walking to work every morning,

dressed in his dark suit and tie." She added, "The Habaneros dressed well in those days. Well . . . the gentlemen and ladies did. Despite the heat, and no air-conditioning. It was important to look good."

I was feeling a bit inadequate in my Hemingway T-shirt.

"If Batista hadn't been such a corrupt thug, kept in power by the American Mafia, American corporations, and the American government . . . the Communists would never have won."

"And you would have been born here in luxury and we'd never have met."

She forced a smile. "We would have met. It's in our stars."

"That's a nice thought."

She kept looking at the former American bank, now a government office where people signed for their libretas—their ration books. She said, "Maybe this building will be returned to the American bank as part of the negotiations."

"Maybe. But we're not returning the money to the vault."

"No. But we'll return it to the rightful owners."

"That's why we're here."

She took my hand and we caught up to the group.

As Antonio promised, we stopped at the Hotel Ambos Mundos, a pastel-pink edifice whose façade had been restored to its pre-revolution glory.

Antonio said, "You can use the baño here, visit the bar where Hemingway drank each night, and have a daiquiri or mojito if it is not too early for you. For two CUCs you can see his room where he wrote Death in the Afternoon. Fifteen minutes."

The Yalies filed into the hotel, including Richard Neville, who looked like he was going in for a root canal. I was thinking about a cold beer, followed by a leak in the same urinal that Ernest Hemingway used, but Sara said, "I'll show you my grandparents' house. It's close."

"Okay." I followed her down Calle Obispo, then we turned onto a cobblestoned side street of old baroque mansions. As we walked I could see that a few of the grand houses had been restored, and

Sara said they had been turned into luxury apartment houses for non-Cubans by foreign developers in a joint partnership with the Cuban government. Sounded like a nice deal for everyone except the former owners. It struck me that the issues of legal ownership and compensation could drag on for half a century, which again made a good case for stealing what was stolen from you.

I saw that a number of the old houses seemed to be in a state of limbo—condemned but inhabited. Sara pointed to one of these balconied baroque mansions across the street. "That is my grand-parents' home—where my father and uncles were born."

I looked at the four-story house of faded blue stucco, most of which had fallen away, revealing the stone core. Some of the windows were gone, as were most of the louvered shutters. The house had an imposing entrance flanked by red granite pillars, and it wasn't difficult to imagine this huge house as it had once been. And it also wasn't difficult to understand why the socialist government thought it was too big for a family of five. Plus servants, of course.

I could see people through some of the big windows, and an elderly couple sat on a balcony that looked like it was held up by the Holy Spirit.

Sara told me, "I went inside when I was here. All the plumbing leaks, and there are only two working bathrooms. The kitchen is in the basement and it's communal, and the house is filled with mildew and vermin. When the rent is free, as it is in Cuba, you get what you pay for." She asked me, "Would you like to go inside?"

"Only with a hazmat suit."

She assured me, "The people were very nice to me."

"Did you tell them you inherited the deed to the house and you wanted it back?"

"I told them that I was an architect, and that if I could reclaim the house, I would restore it for them, top to bottom, and take a small apartment for myself."

"Did they believe that you would let them stay?"

"I mentioned a rent of five dollars a month."

"How'd that go over?"

"Not very well." She added, "They have a long way to go here. They're frightened of the future."

"Who isn't?"

She kept staring at the house, then said, "My grandmother's piano is still in the music room. I took a picture of it for her . . . She didn't want to see it."

I glanced at my watch. "You want a daiquiri?"

"No."

"You want a picture?"

She nodded and handed me her cell phone.

I took a few photos of her standing across the street from her former family mansion, then a few close-ups under the pillared portico while I listened for the sounds of imminent collapse.

We began walking back to the Ambos Mundos. I understood the emotional attachment and the sense of loss that Sara Ortega must be feeling, but you really can't go home again. Unless you're just there to pick up what you left behind.

CHAPTER 27

We got back to the Ambos Mundos as our group was exiting the hotel, and Antonio led us to the nearby Plaza de San Francisco de Asís. On one side of the plaza was the newly restored Spanish-style Sierra Maestra Cruise Terminal, which Antonio pointed to and said, "Today, at some hour, an invasion fleet is arriving from America."

The Yalies chuckled tentatively, waiting for a further explanation.

"It is actually a fishing fleet which has sailed out of Key West. This is a new tournament called Pescando Por la Paz—" He translated, "Fishing for Peace. A . . . how do you say, a double entendre. Very clever. Yes?"

The clever Yalies seemed to think so.

Antonio continued, "The fishermen will come through this terminal and walk directly into this beautiful plaza, and be welcomed by the people. And then they will find the good bars and get drunk like sailors." He laughed at his own lame joke.

I looked around the plaza, but there were still no signs of the fleet's arrival—no dignitaries, no reporters, no banners or bands.

The arrival of the fishing fleet from America was not exactly world-shaking news, but it was news in the wider context of the Cuban Thaw, so it should be marked by some sort of official ceremony and appropriate news coverage. Unless, of course, the regime wanted to ignore it or downplay it. Or cancel it.

Sara said, "I'm getting worried."

"Let's assume Antonio has the latest update."

Antonio fixed his gaze on me. "Mister Mac is a fisherman in

Key West, so perhaps he will want to drink with his fellow fishermen tonight."

I didn't respond, and Antonio moved on to other points of interest.

Our next and last plaza of the morning was Plaza Vieja—the Old Square—and on our way there Sara asked me, "Why did he say that?"

"I'm not reading anything into it."

"He practically said that he knows you're going to meet someone."

"There are only three people in the world who know that—me and Jack, and now you as of an hour ago."

She seemed frustrated with me. "He's made the connection between you—a Key West fisherman—and the Pescando Por la Paz."

"There is no connection. Only a coincidence which anyone would comment on."

We reached the Plaza Vieja and Antonio talked as he walked. "This square was laid out in 1559 for the private residences of Havana's wealthiest families, who in former times would gather here to watch the public executions." He added, "Now, of course, those wealthy families are gone."

Having attended their own public executions. But Antonio didn't say that. He said, "Please look around. Ten minutes. Then to lunch."

Half the group headed toward the fountain in the center of the plaza to get their fountain photos, and some headed for the shade, as did Antonio, who retreated under a tree, lit a cigarette, and made a cell phone call. I said to Sara, "He's calling for a firing squad."

"You deserve one."

Funny. I said, "You need to calm down—"

"And you need to ask yourself if this mission has been compromised."

"If it has, you should thank Antonio for letting us know." I added, "He may be reporting to the police, but he knows nothing. And if he's fishing for something, he's not using the right bait."

"But why is he fishing?"

Good question, and I'd thought about that. "Well, it could be that you came to his attention as a Cuban American, and he's trying to be a good chivato, making himself sound important to the police."

She didn't seem satisfied with my explanation, so I continued, "It's also possible that the immigration or customs people at the airport notified the police about you, and the police checked to see who the tour guide was for this group and told the guide—Antonio—to keep an eye on Sara Ortega." I reminded her, "You're supposed to be giving your three hundred thousand pesos to charities. And maybe that's why you're on their radar." Or there was a leak in Miami, and if that was the case, the game was over.

She looked at me. "You're either very cool, or you have your head up your ass."

Which reminded me of an old Army saying—"If you're taking intense fire and you're keeping cool while everyone around you is scared shitless, then you're not fully understanding the situation." I didn't think that was the case here.

"Do you think Antonio believes we just met?"

"We did just meet. You need to believe your cover story." Recalling my unpleasant hours in a mock interrogation cell, I added, "We'd be questioned in separate rooms and our stories need to match."

"I know that."

Our ten minutes of architectural appreciation were up, and Antonio called the group together. "Now to lunch."

We followed Antonio out of the plaza and into a street that led back to Centro.

Something had changed in Sara's positive attitude, and it probably had to do with last night. That's what happens when you have something to live for.

————

We walked in silence awhile, then Sara asked me, "Is it at all possible that the police have made a connection between you and Fishy Business?"

"Anything is possible. But let's trust Carlos on this."

"I do. But . . ."

"Even if the police somehow discover that I once owned one of the tournament boats, that's all they know. They may find it curious, or suspicious, but that doesn't lead them to any conclusions about why I'm in Cuba."

"No . . . but it could lead them to questioning you about that coincidence."

"You can be sure I've already thought of the right answers."

Clearly Sara was worried, so I let her know, "I don't see, hear, or sense anything that endangers us or the mission. If I do, I'll let you know."

We stood facing each other. She said, "This is Cuba, Mac. Not Afghanistan. The first sign of danger here is usually a midnight knock on your door."

"You're the one who said that the only thing the secret police are good at is instilling fear."

"Well . . . sometimes they get lucky." She thought a moment and said, "Maybe the money is not worth our lives—"

"It's not all about the money. It's also about stealing something from under their ugly noses. Remember? It's about finishing what your grandfather started. And, as I just discovered, it's also about something that's going to please me, whatever that is."

"All right . . . let me think about this."

"Let me know before I meet Jack so I can tell him if you and I are leaving Cuba early."

"All right . . . and if the tournament has been cancelled, then the decision has already been made for us."

Borrowing from her book, I said, "It will be a sign from God."

"No, it will be a decision made by the Cuban or American government."

"That too."

We looked up the street but the group had disappeared. "We lost them. Let's find a place for a cold beer."

She took her itinerary out of her bag. "Lunch is at Los Nardos. I know where that is."

"That's too bad."

"Come on. Tad will be in a panic if he thinks we're missing."

"Good training for him when we do go missing."

We took our time walking, and on the way I ran all this through my mind. I couldn't get a tight grip on Antonio, but if I had ten minutes alone with him in one of these back alleys, I'd have some answers. But as Sara pointed out, this was not Afghanistan, where I could be very insistent with the locals about answering my questions.

Anyway, it was easy to make a good case for abandoning this mission and getting out of Cuba. But I told Sara that if I came here, I wouldn't back out. So this was her decision. And if she was influenced by my assurances and we got arrested, it wouldn't be the first time I miscalculated.

She took my hand as we walked and said, "I'm not afraid of death, Mac. I'm afraid that the police will arrest us—here or in Camagüey—find the map, and . . . make us confess . . . I don't want to fail. I don't want to let everyone down."

"You won't."

"Also . . . I feel responsible for getting you into this."

"I understand the responsibility of command. But I knew what I was getting into." Well, not all of it. There are always surprises.

"In the Army . . . if you gave an order that . . . caused a death . . ."

"Shit happens." I added, "I wasn't back in the rear phoning in orders, I was right there at the front, and that's where you're at now."

She glanced at me, then said, "All right . . . if I say we leave, it's my decision. If I say we go forward . . ."

"I promise I won't blame you if we wind up dead or in jail. But I won't be happy."

She forced a smile, then said, "Most men in this situation would jump at the chance to go home, collect fifty thousand dollars, and tell their friends they slept with a woman in Havana who paid for their vacation."

"Don't tempt me."

"Well, thank you for listening. I'll let you know before you meet Jack."

"Okay, and if we're not going to Camagüey, I do not want to spend another week with the Yale educational tour."

"It won't kill you."

"It might."

She understood that I wasn't making a joke and agreed, "If we're being watched, it would be good to get out of here as quickly as possible."

"Correct."

"But it's difficult . . . There are no commercial flights to the U.S. . . . but maybe we can get a ticket to Mexico or Canada."

"Even if we do, we may be on a watch list at the airport."

"We seem to be running out of options," she said.

"We never had many options. And when that happens, you just push on."

"To Camagüey."

"Correct."

"With or without meeting our contact here."

"Correct."

"We're back to where we started," she concluded.

"When we got on that plane in Miami, there was no turning back."

"No, there wasn't," she agreed.

"The road home goes through Camagüey Province, the cave, Cayo Guillermo, and The Maine."

CHAPTER 28

We arrived late for lunch at Los Nardos, a small restaurant on the edge of the Old Town. Our group was already seated, filling up most of the tables, but Antonio had thoughtfully saved two seats for us at his small table, and we sat opposite the Nevilles.

Pretty Cindy Neville said to me, "I like your T-shirt."

Well, Richard did not. Nor did he like me—once he realized he had no chance with Sara Ortega. Plus he'd had to see where Hemingway drank at the Ambos Mundos hotel. He was having a bad day. He should only know what kind of day I was having.

Cindy said, "Richard wouldn't let me buy him a Hemingway T-shirt at Finca Vigía or Ambos Mundos."

I assured her, "There'll be many more opportunities." I suggested, "Make it a surprise."

Neville frowned, so to have a happy lunch, I said to him, "I've read a few of your books."

Well, you'd have thought I just handed him a carton of cigarettes and a Pulitzer Prize.

"I hope you liked them."

Of course you do. "Of course I did."

Frozen daiquiris were part of the package, and everyone got one put in front of them. Antonio proposed a table toast. "To a great novelist—Ernest Hemingway—a true Cuban soul and a beautiful writer of the people."

Neville's face got frostier than his daiquiri.

The menus came, and Antonio made a few suggestions to the Nevilles, who looked like Hamburger Helper people, so Antonio ordered family-style for all of us.

Cindy asked Sara and me, "Where are you from?"

"Miami."

"Key West."

"Oh . . . are you . . . ?"

I said, "We just met." I further explained, "We're discovering that we have a lot in common." We're both horny.

"That's nice." She said to Sara, "You mentioned at the welcome dinner that you are Cuban."

"Cuban American."

"So this trip must be very special for you."

"It is. And why have you come here?"

Cindy replied, "Richard wants to set his next novel in Cuba."

Antonio said to Neville, "Please put me in your book—as the hero."

Neville was definitely thinking: *Not after that toast, asshole.*

Cindy continued, "He's gotten a lot of material already."

I couldn't resist saying, "Don't ask too many questions in Cuba."

Cindy confided to us, "Richard says if he gets arrested, that will be good publicity."

Antonio assured her, "That can be arranged."

We all got a good laugh at that. This was fun. Like making jokes about blood while you're dining with a vampire. I was feeling reckless and said to the Nevilles, "Be careful of the chivatos."

"Who?"

"Ask Antonio."

Antonio looked at me, then at the Nevilles. "This is a . . . derogatory term . . . for the citizens who volunteer for the revolutionary watch committees. In America you would call them neighborhood watch groups. They assist the police in combating crime." He added, "They have nothing to do with foreigners."

Sara asked Antonio, "So if a chivato sees a foreigner who appears suspicious, they won't call the police?"

"Well . . . like any good citizen, they would, of course." He thought of something and said, "In America, where you have terrorism, the police say, 'If you see something, say something.' It is no different here."

Sara replied, "In America we don't report our neighbors to the police because of their political views."

Well, they used to in Maine.

Cindy changed the subject and said to me, "So you're a fisherman."

"I am."

"Will you go meet the fishermen coming in for this tournament?"

"I don't know them."

Richard remarked, "I'd like to go to the terminal and take pictures of the fleet's arrival." He looked at Antonio.

Antonio reminded Neville, "You must stay with the group. It is your State Department which does not allow you to go where you wish in Cuba."

It *was* ironic, I thought, that it was my government, not Antonio's, that restricted our movements in Antonio's police state. But soon Sara and I would have a unique opportunity to fulfill the stated goal of this trip—Discover Cuba for Yourself.

Antonio, however, had some good news. "There is no group dinner tonight, and you are all free to go to the Plaza de San Francisco and perhaps find some of the fishermen and crew from the tournament." He looked at me.

I wanted to get away from that subject, so I asked Neville, "Where do you get your ideas?"

He didn't seem to know.

Antonio dropped the subject and said to me and Sara, "We missed you at Ambos Mundos."

I let Sara reply and she said, truthfully, "I showed Mac my grandparents' home."

That seemed to interest him. "So you knew where it was?"

"I have the property deed, which goes back to 1895."

"Well," he joked, "hold on to it for another hundred years. You never know."

Sara, of course, didn't think that was funny and said, "It's now a crumbling tenement."

"It is a home for the people."

"It's not fit for animals."

Antonio looked at Sara. "You speak your mind."

"It's an American habit."

"Yes, I know." He asked her, "And what did your grandfather do to afford a large house in Havana?"

"He was an honest businessman. And he had the good fortune to escape to America before he was arrested for no reason."

Antonio had no reply.

I was wishing that Sara wouldn't provoke Antonio, but it seemed to be in the DNA of the exile community to bug the Commies. I get it, but it's safer to do it in Miami. Having said that, I, too, needed to control my mouth.

The Nevilles seemed to be feeling left out or uncomfortable, and Richard announced that he was going outside for a cigarette. I hoped Antonio would join him, but he didn't. Cindy asked where the baño was and Antonio told her.

So now we were three.

Antonio looked at Sara. "Do you still have family in Cuba?"

"I do not."

"May I ask—why have you come back a second time?"

"Obviously I enjoyed my first visit."

"Good. Cuba is like a mother who welcomes the return of her sons and daughters."

"Some of whom have been arrested on trumped-up charges."

Antonio had no reply, and Sara asked him, "How do you know this is my second visit?"

"Someone mentioned it to me."

"Why are you asking about me?"

He smiled. "I thought you were . . . unattached." He looked at me. "I congratulate you, señor."

Hey, no contest, señor.

Antonio looked over his shoulder at the front door, then

looked toward the baños, and I thought he was trying to decide if he needed a cigarette or a pee, but he leaned toward us and said, "Perhaps we can have a drink tonight."

Neither Sara nor I replied.

He continued, "Tonight is your free night. I can meet you both at seven at a bar called Rolando in Vedado." He smiled. "No tourists. No Hemingway."

Sara glanced at me, and I said to Antonio, "Thank you, but we've made other plans."

"Then tomorrow night. Same time and place. You will excuse yourselves from the group dinner."

This was not sounding like a friendly invitation anymore. I thought his next line was going to be, "You can meet me at the bar, or you can meet me at police headquarters." But he said, "This will be worth your time and trouble. And your money."

"Excuse me?"

"Five hundred dollars."

"For what?"

Richard Neville was returning from his nicotine break and Cindy was making her way back to the table.

As they both reached the table, Antonio said, "As Hemingway wrote, the Cubans double-cross each other. They sell each other out."

Which may have been the answer to my question.

The Nevilles sat and Richard asked, "Still Hemingway?"

No one responded, and the apps came.

Antonio said, "I hope everyone likes octopus."

What the hell was this guy up to?

CHAPTER 29

After lunch, Antonio led us on a short walk to the Museum of the Revolution, a neo-classical building that was once Cuba's Presidential Palace. In front of the former palace was a Soviet-made tank that Antonio said was used by Castro's forces to help repel the U.S.-backed Bay of Pigs Invasion. "The invasion failed," said Antonio, "so we invaded Miami with a million Cubans."

Sara said to me, "He won't find it so funny when the exiles start returning and buying up Cuba."

And round it goes.

As for the Yalies, they didn't know that their proudly patriotic Cuban guide was just another guy on the take. Five hundred bucks. Two years' salary for Antonio. But for what? Information? A shakedown? One way to find out.

Sara, however, on our walk to the museum told me she didn't want us to meet Antonio. She was in charge, but my instincts said we should meet him. It was possible, of course, that the meeting was some kind of entrapment and we'd get arrested. But in Cuba you could get arrested for no reason, so we may as well get arrested while having a drink. I needed to talk to Sara.

We went inside the huge palacio. Antonio was excited about showing us something, so we followed him to a lobby space near the grand marble staircase. He said, "This is the Rincón de los Cretinos—the Corner of the Cretins."

And who were the cretins in the corner? Well, they were cartoonish murals of ex-President Batista, plus George Bush and Ronald Reagan in cowboy clothes, looking like characters out of *Mad* magazine. In fact, George looked like Alfred E. Neuman.

Even the Yalies thought this was a little over the top, and I didn't think Cretin Corner would help improve relations.

We climbed the sweeping staircase and moved on to other rooms, all of which glorified La Revolución, though many of the exhibits were in bad taste, including grisly photos of revolutionaries being tortured and executed by former Cuban regimes. Also on display were blood-stained military uniforms that looked unsanitary. Unfortunately, there were a number of school-aged groups viewing all of this. That's probably how Antonio got his little head screwed up.

We entered the former executive office of the late President Batista, and Antonio pointed out a gold-plated rotary-dial phone that AT&T had given to their important customer, then he launched into a diatribe about American imperialism. Sara thankfully kept her mouth shut.

Tad, to his credit, said to Antonio, "We should move on."

So we checked out more of the Museum of the Revolution, which was deteriorating like most of Havana, and like the revolution itself.

Antonio showed us a secret staircase that Batista had used to save himself when a group of university students stormed the palace and tried to kill him. Antonio said, "Many of the students were arrested, tortured, and executed."

Apparently they take student protests seriously here. The group moved on without us and I said to Sara, "Let's escape down the secret staircase."

"Try to learn something while you're here."

"Okay. I learned from Antonio at lunch that his interest in you was personal."

"It was never personal. You know that."

"Don't be modest. Also, you shouldn't have pressed him on why he was asking about you."

"Sometimes, Mac, you just have to confront people who are causing you anxiety."

"Right. Well, I think you smoked him out. Now he wants to talk to us."

"We're not talking to him."

"You and I need to talk about that."

"Later. Maybe."

We caught up to our group, and Antonio escorted us into a room that had been turned into a stand-up movie theater, and we watched film clips of La Revolución in color and black and white, narrated in Spanish. I saw on the screen a young Fidel and a young Che Guevara, and a lot of other bearded guys moving through the bush carrying rifles. They looked like Taliban.

The scene shifted to Havana, New Year's Day 1959, and a convoy of rebel fighters in trucks and Jeeps was moving through the city, and crowds of Habaneros were cheering in the streets. Next was a scene at the Hotel Nacional and I looked for Michael Corleone and Hyman Roth jumping into their getaway cars, but they must have left already.

The Riviera Hotel appeared on the screen and, as Antonio promised, there was a newsreel of guerrilla fighters and civilians smashing up the casino, including the bar. This was a sad ending, so I left the theater.

Sara joined me and said, "My father told me that was the most frightening day of his life."

I guess it would be if you were a young boy waking up in a mansion on New Year's Day, wondering why the servants hadn't brought you your breakfast. I pointed out, "Everyone else looked happy."

"Yes . . . It started out with high hopes for the Cuban people . . . but then it turned into a nightmare."

"Right."

The Yale group filed out of the theater, and Antonio led us outside to what was once the back garden, and was now the Granma Memorial—a massive glass structure that preserved the yacht, named *Granma*, that had brought Castro and his small band of revolutionaries from Mexico to Cuba in 1956. The rest, as they say, is history.

Sara informed me, "When Cuba is free, this is all coming down, and this garden is where my memorial to the martyrs will be built."

And Eduardo could use the garden walls to shoot all the Commies. I said, "Good location." I was really feeling like an outsider now, caught in a family feud that went back to Christopher Columbus.

Anyway, around the Granma Memorial were some bullet-riddled military vehicles and a jet engine that Antonio said was from an American U-2 spy plane that had been shot down during the 1962 Cuban Missile Crisis. I wasn't born then, but I knew that this crisis had taken us to the brink of nuclear war with the Soviet Union. And if that had happened, I wouldn't be standing here. It occurred to me that Cuba had always been a thorn in America's ass, and that America had always tried sticking it up Cuba's ass.

This was not a happy garden, so Sara and I left the group and walked out to the street. Our next stop was the nearby National School of Ballet, where we were scheduled to see a rehearsal, and we headed that way.

As we walked, I said to Sara, "We need to meet Antonio."

"If we meet him, that's an admission that we're not innocent tourists."

"I follow that logic, but if you're at the craps table you have to throw the dice."

"No, you can pass."

"Let's try another cliché—you can't ignore the eight-hundred-pound gorilla in the room."

She stayed silent as we walked, then said, "I've already agreed that you can meet Jack tonight. I'm not agreeing to meet Antonio."

"Aren't you curious about what he has to say?"

"I know what he has to say. He wants five hundred dollars. It's just another shakedown of a Cuban American tourist."

"You know there's more to it."

"Yes. It could also be a sting. We give him five hundred American dollars, and the police appear and arrest us for bribery and currency violations—or, worse, trying to recruit a spy." She added, "That's happened before. And espionage is a capital offense here."

"I can go alone."

"You will not."

"All right . . . but—"

"You don't understand the Cubans, Mac."

"Compared to the Afghans, the Cubans are Boy Scouts."

"If we ever go to Afghanistan, you're in charge."

"Sí, comandante."

"Not funny."

We reached the National School of Ballet and sat on the front steps sharing a bottled water and waiting for our group. I said to Sara, "Antonio wants to tell you what interest the police have in you."

No reply.

"He's a Mafia wannabe. He wants to live the good life. He wants two years' salary. It's as simple as that."

"All right, I'll think about meeting Antonio. Meanwhile, there's no group dinner tonight. What am I supposed to do while you're out drinking with Jack?"

"I'll meet you at Floridita at . . . nine o'clock. I'm going to break Hemingway's daiquiri record."

She smiled. "I'll take pictures."

Our group arrived and Antonio invited everyone to enter the ballet school with Tad and Alison, then he came over to us and asked, "Are you joining us?"

"We're thinking about it."

"And have you thought about my offer of a drink?"

"Are you buying?"

"No. I'm selling."

I glanced at Sara. Still sitting, she looked Antonio in the eye. "We'll be there."

"Good. It will be worth your time and money."

"We'll be the judge of that."

He nodded, then hopped up the steps like he'd just made two years' pay—which he had.

Sara looked at me. "I'm trusting your judgement on this."

"Trust my instincts."

She stood. "We'll see." She asked, "Do you want to see sweaty young girls in leotards?"

Yes, but . . . "How far is it to the Parque Central?"

"About three blocks, right down this road."

"Let's go." I stood.

"We'll miss the Museum of the Firefighters."

"I'll show you my hose. Come on."

She smiled and took my hand. "If we're playing hooky, we first need to go see if the fleet has arrived."

"If we're being watched, we don't want to go anywhere near that terminal." I said, "We can check out CNN or Tele-whatever in the room."

So hand in hand we hurried to the Parque Central for a sponta-neous afternooner.

CHAPTER 30

On our way to the Parque Central, we passed one of the old men who hawked the Communist Party newspaper, *Granma*, and Sara gave him ten pesos from her stash and took a copy.

We entered the hotel and stopped at the front desk, but there was no fax or phone message from Carlos, and I said, "No news from Carlos is good news."

The elevator came and I asked, "My place or yours?"

"I think I was assigned a bugged room."

We rode up to my room, and I put the DO NOT DISTURB sign out and double-locked the door.

Sara turned on the TV and sat cross-legged on the bed, dividing her attention between Tele Rebelde and *Granma*.

"See if you can find the Mets score."

The minibar was stocked and I opened two Bucaneros and gave one to Sara, then sat in a chair with my beer and watched the news. The anchor guy and his female sidekick sounded like they were reading an eye chart in Spanish.

Sara used the remote to switch to CNN, but there was no signal so she turned back to Tele Rebelde, sipped her beer, and flipped through *Granma* again. "I can't believe there's not one word in here or on TV about Pescando Por la Paz."

"If the tournament was cancelled, the regime would be happy to report that and lay the blame on some American treachery." I repeated, "No news is good news."

She nodded. "You may be right." She said, "We need to discuss a few things about tonight. But first bring your map here and I'll decipher it for you."

I looked at my watch. It was almost 5 P.M. and I didn't want to be late for my six o'clock with Jack, so I suggested we talk in the shower, and we got out of our sweaty clothes.

The shower was freezing, but I left the water running in case my room was bugged, and I turned on the water in the bathtub, which, as per Tad, was warm. We climbed into the tub, facing each other.

Sara leaned toward me and said, "On your way to where you're meeting Jack, I want you to swing by the cruise terminal. If the fleet isn't in, you'll come directly back here."

"No, I go see if Jack shows up at our meeting place."

"Why—?"

"Because the fleet could have been delayed. Or if the government wants to low-key the arrival, it could have been diverted to someplace out of town, like the Hemingway Marina."

"All right . . . but when you get to where you're meeting Jack, call me from a pay phone and leave a message at the front desk. The message will be either, 'We're having a drink,' or, 'He's not here yet.'"

I watched the water rising above my periscope.

"Are you listening to me?"

"I am."

"If he's there, I'll know that the fleet is in. But if he hasn't shown up by seven, you'll leave and meet me here in the lounge. And on the way back here, you'll swing by the cruise terminal again."

I was going to wait for Jack at the Nacional, but I said, "Sí, co-mandante," so I could get laid.

"And make sure you're not followed." She informed me, "The best way to do that in Havana is to take a Coco cab." She explained, "You have clear visibility all around, and the Coco cabs take short-cuts through back alleys and narrow streets that cars can't use."

Same in Kabul.

"And I don't have to tell you not to give your driver your actual destination, and get out a few blocks before."

"Right." The water was now starting to float Sara's tub toys, so I turned it off, but the running shower provided some background noise.

She reminded me, unnecessarily, "If The Maine—Fishy Business—is not in Cuba, then we have no way to get the money out of here."

I pointed out, "We don't have the money yet." I asked her, "Aside from the money, how about the other thing that will please me? Is it bigger than a bread box? And can we get it out of Cuba without a truck and a boat?"

"I shouldn't have told you about that."

"You should tell me what it is."

"I can't." We made eye contact and she said, "The important thing tonight is to see if the fleet is in."

"Right. And if the fleet is in, and Jack confirms to me that they're going to Cayo Guillermo, then we're in business—and then we need to think about if we're going to wait in Havana for our contact, or head off on our own to Camagüey. We also need to meet Antonio to see what he's selling."

She thought about all that, then said, "Carlos, Eduardo, and I were very confident that we had a perfect plan . . ."

"It's a wonderful plan," I assured her. "That's why I agreed to it. Unfortunately, none of it has gone right. And, by the way, it never does. So we have to make it go right."

"I like your can-do attitude."

And I liked that she was back on track. "We make a good team," I agreed. "And that's why you hired me."

I lay back and closed my eyes. This was a pleasant moment, and I enjoyed sharing the warm tub with a friend and teammate.

I felt Sara's fingers fondling my bolas and I smiled.

My teammate said, "Now that I have you by the balls, where are you meeting Jack?"

Funny. I think. I reminded her, "The less you know—"

"I need to know in case I need to get hold of you."

"You've already got hold—don't squeeze. The Nacional. Hall of Fame bar."

She released my bolas and said, "If Jack doesn't show up and you don't see the fleet at the Sierra Maestra Terminal, we'll take a taxi to the Hemingway Marina."

"Okay."

"Have we covered all contingencies?"

"And some."

I don't recall life without cell phones, voice mail, texting, and the Internet, but in the good old days—according to my parents— all plans, contingencies, and meeting places had to be discussed and understood before people parted or hung up the phone, and my generation was spoiled, they said, and lazy, irresponsible, and too dependent on technology, including electric toothbrushes, and if anyone moved my dinner plate six inches to the left, I'd starve to death.

Well, my five years in the Army proved my parents wrong. I could survive without my iPhone.

"What are you thinking about?"

"I'm thinking that if we have Plan B and Plan C, we now need Plan A."

"Which is . . . ?"

"Insert Tab A into Slot B."

"I fell right into that one."

"You did."

So we made love in the tub. Good meeting.

———

Sara sat in bed wearing one of my clean T-shirts, with the TV tuned to Tele Rebelde and the volume turned up to cover our words. As I got dressed in slacks and a sports jacket, she said, "Be careful, and don't forget to call."

I looked at her. "If I don't call by seven—or if my message is, 'Don't wait up for me'—that means I'm in the company of the police."

She didn't reply.

"Go directly to the U.S. Embassy and get yourself inside—one way or the other. Meanwhile, go find some company in the lounge so you don't get that knock on the door." I added, "That's the last contingency."

She nodded.

I assured her, "All will go well tonight. See you at Floridita at nine."

"Say hello to Jack."

"You'll see him in Cayo Guillermo."

"Come here."

I went to the bed and we kissed. She said to me, "I'm going to call my friend in Miami now."

"Use the phone in the business center." And keep it short.

I went down to the lobby, where I exchanged five hundred dollars for CUCs at the cashier's desk, then I went outside and found a Coco cab. "Malecón, por favor."

And off I went in the little motorized tricycle.

Well, next time I get bored with life I'll try hang gliding.

CHAPTER 31

My little Coco cab was weaving through traffic, so there was no way anyone could have been following me unless he was the Lone Ranger mounted on Silver. Nevertheless, I did not swing by the Sierra Maestra Cruise Terminal. If Jack was in Havana, I'd know soon enough. Plus, I was running late.

It was still daylight but the Malecón was already hopping on this steamy Saturday evening and the seawall looked like the world's longest pickup bar.

I told the driver to pull over, gave him ten CUCs, and began walking, past beggars, poets and drunks, and a group of Americans who looked like the cyclone had just blown them in from Kansas.

I turned onto a side street, and continued to the long drive that led to the front of the hotel. I checked my watch: 6:15 P.M.

I entered the Nacional for the third time in as many days and stopped at the front desk to see if Jack—or Sara—had left a message, but they hadn't. I walked into the high-ceilinged Hall of Fame bar, which was filled with a haze of cigar smoke. I scanned the crowded room but I didn't see Jack.

I asked the maître d' for a table, and for ten CUCs he remembered a cancellation and escorted me to a small table under a photo of Mickey Mantle.

I optimistically ordered two Bucaneros from a waitress and asked for the cigar lady, who arrived with her tray, and I bought two Monte Cristos, which I left on the table.

My beers came and I drank alone. It was now 6:30.

So where was Jack? Maybe drunk in a waterfront bar, or getting laid, lost in space, arrested, or still in Key West. And if that was the case, I was going home without three million dollars.

Out of habit, I checked my phone for a text or voice mail. Still no service, so I went to the bar to see if Jack had left a message with the bartender, but there was nothing for me.

Sara must be worried by now, so before she called here I asked the bartender to dial the Parque Central from the bar phone and he handed it to me.

As the phone was ringing, a hand grabbed my forearm. "You are under arrest."

I turned and looked at Jack, who was smiling. "Did you piss your pants?"

"You're fired."

"Again?"

The call connected and I said to the operator, "Message for Sara Ortega in Room 535. We're having a drink. See you at nine." I asked her to repeat the message and hung up.

Jack asked, "You banging her yet?"

"She sends her regards."

I led Jack to the far end of the lounge and we sat.

Jack was wearing a decent pair of khakis and a white Polo shirt that I recognized as the one I kept on *The Maine* for formal occasions. He also had a fanny pack around his waist, something I'd never seen him wear before. "What's in there?"

"Condoms." He raised his beer bottle and we clinked. "Good to see you."

"Same here."

There were a few tables of well-dressed men around us speaking Spanish, and no one seemed interested in our conversation. I asked Jack, "How did you get here?"

"Fifty-seven Chevy convertible. My old man had a fifty-eight Chevy—"

"Were you paying attention to being followed?"

"Followed?" He thought about that and said, "I gave the guy an American ten to let me drive." He smiled. "I was all excited, but the guy'd put a fucking Toyota four-cylinder in the car and it was like two hamsters on a treadmill—"

"Jack, were you *followed*?"

"No." He added, "I don't think so."

Well, neither did I. Or if he was followed it was because the police already knew there was a connection between Jack Colby, Daniel MacCormick, and the newly renamed *Fishy Business*, and if they knew that, they'd want to know more. So we may as well have another beer. "Why are you late?"

Jack was looking around the Hall of Fame bar. "This is some high-class place."

"It's older than you."

"Yeah? Hey, there's a picture of Sinatra. And Churchill . . . Marlon Brando, John Wayne . . . There's Mickey Mantle—"

"They're all dead, Jack, like you're going to be if you don't tell me why you're late."

Jack looked at me. "I had a few beers with our three fishermen. Couldn't tell them I had to meet you, and couldn't think of an excuse to ditch them. I tried to call you but there's no service." He observed, "This place is fucked up." He asked, "How's it going here?"

"So far, okay." I asked, "What time did the fleet get in?"

"About noon."

"Any problems?"

"Nope. I navigated right into the harbor. Piece of cake."

"I assume you just followed the boat in front of you."

"Yeah. But it was tricky."

"How is Felipe?"

"He seems okay." Jack thought of something and said, "He knows Sara."

"Right."

"You fuck her?"

"She has a boyfriend."

"So what? You got to use the old 'We could be dead tomorrow' line."

"How are the three fishermen?"

"Regular guys. Can't even tell they're Cuban."

"I hope you complimented them on that."

He got that I was mocking him and laughed. Clearly he'd already had a few, but even when Jack's half in the bag he can be coherent if I'm up his butt. "How did it go after you docked?"

"Okay. A couple of Commie assholes went from boat to boat to check passports and stuff, and collect a fifty-dollar arrival fee—twenty-five for Fidel, twenty-five for them. Felipe gave them a couple bags of food and a bag of stuff from Walgreens—toothpaste, vitamins, and stuff—and they stamped our visas and went di-di mau."

Jack sometimes uses Vietnamese expressions, especially when he's had a few. I said, "I hope some of the crew stayed behind to secure the boats."

"You think we're stupid?" I didn't answer so he continued, "Felipe stayed onboard, and each of the boats left somebody onboard. Otherwise, there'd be nothing left when we got back."

Or there'd be ten fishing boats headed to Key West with five hundred Cubans onboard. "Was there any security on the pier?"

"Yeah. About ten military types with AKs. Haven't been that close to one of those since I took one off a dead gook."

"Did you tell them that?"

Jack laughed, then continued, "These bastards shook us down for twenty bucks from each boat—to help us keep an eye on the boats."

"You got off easy."

"If they didn't have guns, I'd've kicked them in the nuts and told them to do their fucking jobs."

"Right." But negotiations tend to favor the guy with the submachine gun, as Jack and I learned long ago when we held the guns. I asked him, "When you left the terminal, did you get a brass band?"

"No. But there was a film crew and, like, maybe a few hundred people in this plaza."

"Friendly?"

"Most of them. They were yelling, 'Welcome, Americanos,' and stuff. But there was another group yelling, 'Yankee, go home,' and 'Cuba sí, Yankee no.' Shit like that. So we got stuck there in front of the terminal." He took a swig of beer. "Fuck them."

I could picture this on Cuban TV with some creative film editing. The anti-American demonstration would look like half of Havana. The friendly group—who had somehow gotten word of the fleet's arrival—wouldn't be seen on Tele Rebelde. I asked, "Any police? Military?"

"A few cop cars. But the cops just sat there, then a loudspeaker blasted something in Spanish and everybody left."

End of spontaneous demonstration.

Jack said, "Tell your lady friend this wasn't the big welcome she talked about."

Nor the welcome that Antonio had talked about. And that made me wonder how Antonio knew so much about the arrival of the American fleet if it hadn't been reported on the news. Maybe the same way that the anti-American group knew about it—from the police.

In any case, the news blackout and the staged anti-American protest was a peek into the regime's mind-set about the Thaw. No big deal, unless the tournament was going to be cancelled. I asked, "Any word about your sail to Cayo Guillermo?"

"We leave at first light."

"Okay. Before you sail, I want you to get to a pay phone, or borrow a cell phone from a local, and call the Parque Central Hotel." I gave him my cashier's receipt that had the hotel phone number on it. "You'll leave a message for Mr. MacCormick in Room 615. If you're sailing for Cayo, your message is, 'My flight is on time.' If the tournament has been cancelled, your message is, 'My flight has been cancelled.' And your name is . . ." I looked at the cigars. "Cristo." I asked him, "How copy?"

He smiled at the Army radio lingo. "Solid copy." He asked, "Why do you think the tournament—?"

"I don't think anything. But I have no way of knowing if the

Commie assholes are going to find an excuse to cancel the tournament."

"If they do, you might as well go home."

Easier said than done. On the subject of the Commie assholes finding an excuse to cancel the tournament, I asked, "Did the crews or the fishermen have any trouble on shore with the police or the locals?"

"Not that I know of. We all started out together—maybe fifty of us, and three women fishermen, two not bad-looking—and we hit the bars. We all had these Pescando Por la Paz baseball caps, but I gave mine to a Cuban broad. Everybody in the bars and on the streets was friendly, and we bought lots of drinks for everyone."

"And a few for yourselves."

He smiled. "We spread goodwill. Then some of us split up." He showed me a piece of paper and said, "This is our visitors' pass or something. We all have to be back on the boats by midnight."

"Make sure you are."

"No problem." Jack was checking out the cigar lady in the fishnet stockings and asked, "Where does a sailor get laid around here?"

Recalling Sara's lecture on that subject, I informed him, "Being with a prostitute will get you four years in the slammer."

"That sucks. But how much do they charge?"

"Jack, you're on an important mission. Keep your dick in your pants." I should talk. Jack looked unhappy, so I said, "I'm sure you can charm the pants off a señorita after a few drinks and dinner."

He smiled. "I need a wingman."

"I have a date."

"Yeah? Your girlfriend has you on a short leash?"

I ordered two more beers. Jack had his Zippo and we fired up the Monte Cristos.

I asked him, "Did the customs guys search the boat?"

"No. They didn't even go below. They were happy with their gifts and welcomed us to Cuba."

"Did you declare the guns?"

"They were stowed in the locker and I forgot them."

"Okay . . . Did you remember the extra ammo and the Kevlar vests?"

"Cost me a fortune." He asked, "Did you find out how we're getting the money onboard?"

"No, but I'll find out when Sara and I get to Cayo Guillermo."

"And how am I supposed to find out?"

"Did you ask Felipe if he knows anything?"

"Yeah. I asked. And he said, no comprende."

And he could be telling the truth. But not the whole truth. I said to Jack, "I'm sure someone will get word to you—or to Felipe— while you're in Cayo."

"How much money is this?"

"Let's just say we'll have some heavy lifting to do."

"What do I do if you don't show up by the time the fleet sails for home?"

"You and The Maine sail home with the fleet."

He looked at me. "I can't do that."

"That's an order."

He watched the smoke rising from his cigar.

"Jack, don't worry about what you can't control. You just go and have a nice tournament." I added, "As for getting me, Sara, and the money onboard, as you saw at the pier, everyone in this country is on the take."

He reminded me, "You and me spent some time in fucked-up countries like this. You ever been double-crossed by the locals?"

"At least once a week."

"Me too. So—"

"So if we get double-crossed, we do what we did then. Shoot our way out."

"You got a gun?"

"No. You do. Four of them."

"You need a gun before you get to Cayo Guillermo." He looked at me.

Well, I knew where this was going, and I knew that Jack didn't have condoms in his fanny pack. "How did you get it past customs?"

"Easier than I thought." He explained, "The two Cuban guys who came aboard gave us customs forms that we filled out and signed. Nothing to declare. They took the forms and their loot and left."

I informed Jack, "Having a gun in Cuba is not your constitutional right—it's your death sentence."

"Well, sonny, in my country, gun control means using both hands." He added, "Your Glock will increase the chances of you—and my money—getting to The Maine."

"And increase my chances of getting arrested if I get stopped and searched on my way out of this bar."

Jack quoted from one of his T-shirts. "Better to have a gun and not need it than to need a gun and not have it."

"Right. Okay . . . thanks."

"You don't mean that now, but you might later." Jack drank his beer and commented, "This shit isn't half bad. We need this in the States. I can use my million to open a U.S. franchise when the embargo is lifted."

I reminded him, "Half a million for deployment and half a mil for combat pay if we get shot at." I also reminded him, "They don't have to hit you."

He looked at me through his cigar smoke. "I forgot to tell you—the Glock is costing you half a million."

"It's actually my gun."

"I risked my life getting it to you."

"I didn't ask for it."

"Tell you what, Captain, if you don't want the gun, I'll take it back to the boat."

"I'm surprised you're not a millionaire already."

"Me too."

"But you are an asshole."

"Don't piss me off. I got a gun. And you don't." He thought that was funny.

We sat in silence awhile, enjoying our beers and cigars. A D.J.

set up his electronics and played a Sinatra album. Jack was hungry and we got a bar menu and ordered Cuban sandwiches. Frank sang "That's Life."

On that subject, I asked Jack, "What happened to the lady you married?"

"She got sick."

"Children?"

"No."

"Who are your next of kin?"

"I got a sister in New Jersey."

"You have a will?"

"Nope."

"If you don't make it, how can I find your sister?"

"If I don't make it, neither will you."

"Let's say I make it home, Jack, with the money. How do I get your money to your sister?"

"If you get that lucky, you keep it."

"Okay. How do I find your sister to let her know you're dead?"

"You sound like an officer."

"I'm trying to sound like a friend."

He finished his beer, then looked off into space.

I changed the subject and asked, "How's the weather look this week?"

"Next couple of days look okay for fishing. But there's a tropical depression brewing out in the Atlantic."

It was the end of the hurricane season, but the Caribbean had been unusually hot for October. "Keep an eye on that."

"We all are." He asked, "Why is Havana so much fucking hotter than Key West?"

"Must be the women."

He laughed. "Yeah. Felipe said if you stick a candle in a Mexican woman it comes out melted. Stick a candle in a Cuban woman and it comes out lit."

Glad to hear they were bonding. I asked, "Any mechanical issues with the boat?"

"Nope."

"When are your three fishermen flying to Mexico?"

"They go to Havana Airport right after the last day of fishing. They miss the awards dinner and all that shit."

"When does the fleet sail for home?"

"About nine the next morning." He looked at me. "I can develop a mechanical problem and wait for you past nine."

I had no idea what time or even what day Sara and I would get to Cayo Guillermo, or what the security situation was at the marina, or who'd been bribed, or who might need to be taken out, or who, if anyone, was in Cayo to assist us. As a tactical matter it wasn't important for me to know any of this right now, but from a psychological point of view it's always good to visualize the path home.

"Mac?"

"You sail with the fleet. But thanks."

"Hey, this has nothing to do with you or your girlfriend. This has to do with my money."

"So if I show up in Cayo without the money—"

"I leave you on the dock." He did a finger wave and smiled. "Adios, amigo."

"You're a tough guy, Jack."

"Don't take it personally. And by the way, asshole, you promised the boat to me if you got killed, and then you sold it to fucking Carlos."

"If you make it back, he'll be happy to sign it over to you in exchange for you keeping your mouth shut. And if we both get killed, there's nothing to worry about."

Jack had no response to that and knocked the ash off his cigar.

Sinatra was singing "New York, New York," which was where I'd like to be right now.

Well, the time had come to move from future problems to present problems. "Listen to me." I looked around to be sure no one else was listening. "It's possible that the police are interested in me and Sara."

He looked at me.

"If the police question you, here or in Cayo Guillermo, you can say you've heard of me in Key West, but you don't know anything about me being in Cuba, and you don't know anything about me selling my boat. You never heard of Sara Ortega and you're just a hired hand. And if they tell you they've got me or Sara in jail and we told them otherwise, you stick to your story, 'cause that's all you got."

He nodded.

"If you get questioned in Havana, demand a call to the embassy. If you're in Cayo Guillermo and something smells fishier than the fish, you can tell Felipe what I just told you—if he hasn't already told you the same thing—and you and Felipe go out fishing with your customers and keep going."

Jack looked at me. "Why do you think the police are interested in you and Sara?"

I wanted to be honest with Jack, but I honestly didn't know if this mission was coming apart, or if Sara and I were overreacting, or misinterpreting Antonio's bullshit. And I wouldn't know until we met him tomorrow night, and by that time Jack would be in Cayo Guillermo. I asked him, "You remember getting paranoid five hours into a patrol when nothing was happening?"

"Yeah."

"That's God's way of saying this isn't a walk in the park. Keep your head out of your ass."

"Okay. But that don't answer the question."

"Right." So I briefed him about Sara's problems at the airport, and about our Cuban tour guide, Antonio, and Antonio's interest in Sara. "It could be a personal interest, but maybe something else."

"Sounds like he just wants to fuck her."

"Right. But it's also possible that this guy is a police informant."

"Yeah?"

I explained that tour guides in Cuba sometimes reported to the police, and I also told Jack, "Antonio mentioned the Pescando Por la Paz a few times. And he knows I'm a Key West fisherman."

"How'd he know that?"

"He asked our American tour guide about me."

"Yeah? So this guy's a snoop and a stoolie."

"And a lousy tour guide."

Jack thought about all this and concluded, "You should kill Antonio."

"He's not that bad of a tour guide." I told Jack, "I'm meeting this guy in a bar tomorrow night. I think he's playing a double game. He wants five hundred dollars to tell me what the game is."

"Okay. Then follow him home and shoot him in the head. End of game."

"I think it might be easier for me and Sara to just get out of Havana and head out to where the money is stashed."

"Maybe tomorrow night is a trap."

"The secret police in Cuba don't have to waste time with traps."

"I told you this place was fucked up." He also reminded me, "It would be easier to rob a bank in Miami for three million dollars."

"That's illegal. This is not. This is fun."

Jack laughed. "You're fucked up."

"Me? You just told me to blow a guy's brains out."

"Just a suggestion. Do what you think you gotta do."

"Thank you."

The D.J. was playing Dean Martin now, and we sat in silence awhile, then I asked, "Did the security people who came aboard ask to see the boat's registration?"

"Yeah . . . One of them checked it against the hull numbers."

The registration certificate didn't show the previous owner—me—though that information was available from the state of Florida if you were someone in law enforcement who had a legitimate need to see it. But that didn't include the Cuban secret police. That was the good news.

Jack, however, had some other news. "A few of the crew on the other boats are from Key West, and they know you just sold The Maine, which is now Fishy Business."

"Let's just assume the police are not asking questions about any of this. But ask the other crews to give you a heads-up if they are." I added, "And tell them: Don't remember The Maine."

Jack leaned toward me. "Maybe you and Sara should think about getting out of Cuba."

"And you should think about becoming a millionaire."

"I don't think that's gonna happen."

"You'll never know if I go home."

"Okay. If you got the balls for this, I'll see you in Cayo Guillermo."

"Trust my instincts."

"Your instincts are as fucked up as your judgement."

"They must be if I hired you."

The sandwiches came, but we weren't hungry and we ordered two more beers. Dino was singing, "When the moon hits your eye, like a big pizza pie, that's amore . . ."

On that subject, Jack said, "I hope you're not just showing off for your girlfriend."

There's always a little of that. But . . . "I'm here for the money. Same as you."

"If you say so."

I looked at my watch. It was early for my rendezvous with Sara, but I said, "I have to go."

"One more thing."

"What?"

"The old man—Eduardo."

I already knew what he was going to say.

"He's onboard. Got himself a phony passport. Says he wants to see Cuba one last time before he dies."

"Shit." I asked, "Did he come ashore with you?"

"No, and Felipe is sitting on him."

Well, Eduardo wouldn't see much of Cuba from a docked boat. So by now he could have given Felipe the slip, and he could be wandering around Havana, drunk, yelling, "Down with the revolution!" False passport or not, Eduardo Valazquez in Cuba was a massive security breach, making my security breach in meeting

Jack look like a minor lapse of judgement. "Why did you let him onboard?"

"You think I let him onboard? He stowed away in a stateroom. Squeezed his skinny ass under a bunk. Nobody knew he was onboard until we got into Havana Harbor."

I wondered if Carlos knew. Carlos wasn't stupid enough to okay this, but Eduardo was the client and Eduardo had the money and called the shots. I was pissed.

I asked, "Did the Cubans who came onboard see him?"

"No. Like I said, they didn't even go below."

"Okay. When you left the pier, was there any passport control?"

"Yeah. Just one guy."

"Did he have a passport scanner?"

"Just his eyeballs." He added, "The place don't look open for business yet."

"All right . . ." I suspected that Eduardo's passport was a gift from the people he called "our friends in American intelligence," and I assumed it was a very good passport that would withstand scrutiny. But if Eduardo wound up in an interrogation room, he would not withstand a good beating, and he'd tell them he'd arrived on *Fishy Business*. Damn it.

I looked at Jack. "Okay . . . When you get to Cayo, make sure the old man doesn't step foot off the boat."

Jack suggested, "I can throw him overboard on the way if you want."

"Just keep him below." I let Jack know, "He's Felipe's granduncle or something."

"Yeah? Nobody told me that."

"Now you know. So don't feed him to the sharks."

"Okay."

I wondered if Sara knew that Eduardo had a nostalgic yearning to see Cuba one last time. Maybe. And maybe that was why she didn't want me to meet up with Jack. Same with Carlos. Though to be fair and rational, neither Sara nor Carlos would put the mission at risk for something so stupid as Eduardo's homesickness, so neither of them could have known. On the other hand . . . well, if I was Cuban, I might understand this.

I checked my watch. It was 8:30. I asked Jack, "Anything else?"

"Just the gun."

"Okay. You leave first and leave the fanny pack on your seat."

"You buyin' the gun?"

"It's my gun."

"I'll give you a deal. Four hundred thousand and that includes three magazines, one locked and loaded, ready to rock and roll."

"Okay, asshole, I'll buy the gun. But you're not getting combat pay."

"Okay. Sold." Jack finished his beer and looked at me. "Here's what else I'll throw in. There's an old waterfront bar called Dos Hermanos a few blocks from the pier. All the crews and fishermen are gonna meet up there at eleven. If you and your lady have nothing to do, meet me there at eleven-thirty—with your passports and money, no luggage. I bought a few blank visitor passes from the security guys—to get women onboard. They're stamped and signed. So I'll be able to get her—and maybe you—onboard The Maine." He added, "When the fleet sails for Cayo at first light, The Maine is gonna sail for Key West."

"I'll see you in Cayo Guillermo."

"You should ask Sara."

"Okay. But if we're not at Dos Hermanos at eleven-thirty, have a drink for us."

"You got balls, Mac."

"You gotta die someplace."

He unhooked his fanny pack and stood. "My sister's name is Betty. Elizabeth. Lives in Hoboken. Last name Kuwalski. Married a Polack. He's an asshole. Two kids, Derek and Sophie, both grown up and on their own. See if you can find them. They could use the money."

"Okay."

"And if I make it and you don't—?"

"Go see my parents in Portland and say good things about me."

"I'll try to think of something."

"You know the drill, Jack—'died quickly with no pain or suffer-ing.' Last words were 'God bless America' or something."

"I know the drill. Okay, see you later."

I stood and we shook. "This is your last fishing trip, Jack. Good luck."

"You too." He turned and left.

I called for the check, sat in Jack's chair, and buckled the fanny pack under my sports jacket. I paid the check in cash and headed toward the lobby, half expecting to hear, "Stop where you are, señor. You are under arrest. For real this time."

I moved through the lobby, exited the hotel, and the doorman signaled to a white Pontiac convertible.

I got in and said to the driver, "Floridita, por favor."

The cabbie, who spoke English said, "Yes. We go to Florida." He laughed.

Everyone's a comedian.

So off we went in the mid-century American convertible.

Not only was this place a time warp, it was an alternate universe where the past and the present fought to become the future. And I thought Key West was fucked up.

CHAPTER 32

Floridita, a pink stucco place on Calle Obispo, looked like a dive bar in a seedy Miami neighborhood, complete with a neon sign. I passed under a white awning that said <u>ERNEST HEMINGWAY</u>, and inside, Señor Hemingway was at the bar, captured in a life-sized bronze, sitting precariously at the edge of a stool with his elbow on the polished mahogany. I would have bought him a drink, but he was already ossified.

On the wall behind Hemingway was a black-and-white photograph of E.H. and F.C. sharing a moment, and I deduced that the occasion was the Hemingway Tournament before or after F.C. won the trophy with his lead-belly marlin.

The inside of Floridita looked better than the outside, more 1890s than 1950s. There was a large mural behind the handsome bar, depicting what looked like Havana Harbor in some past era of square-riggers. The long open room had a blue ceiling and mottled beige walls, and a staircase that led to an upper floor. The café tables were littered with guide books, and the chairs were filled with American tourists, half of whom were badly dressed in shorts and T-shirts. The other half were badly dressed. The waitstaff wore nice red jackets and bow ties. Lined up on the bar were five electric blenders beating rum into glucose tolerance test cocktails.

The maître d' sized me up as an Americano—who else would come here?—and asked in English, "Table or bar, señor?"

"Table for two, por favor."

He showed me to a table against the wall, and a waiter came by for my order.

The drink menu listed half a dozen kinds of overpriced daiquiris, including a Papa Hemingway—but no Fidel Castro. I actually wanted a beer, but to get into the spirit I ordered a Daiquiri
Rebelde—a rebellious daiquiri.

"Excellent. Will someone be joining you?"

Well, you never know in a police state. I checked my watch:
8:55. "Make it two."

So I sat there listening to American accents and the clatter of
electric blenders.

The A/C was trying to keep up, but the place was warm. I
would have taken off my jacket, but . . . well, the other thing about
a police state is that you're not supposed to be carrying a loaded
9mm Glock in your fanny pack. I mean, this wasn't Florida, where
a gun permit was easier to get than a fishing license.

Anyway, Floridita was a tourist trap, but a nice enough one,
though Richard Neville might not agree.

The daiquiris came and I sipped one. These things should come
with insulin. I checked my watch: 9:05. I checked my cell phone:
no service. Maybe next year.

A guy walked in wearing a light green shirt with military epau-
lets, a black beret, and a gun belt and holster.

The crowd got a little quieter as the guy walked toward the bar,
and before he got there the bartender squirted a seltzer siphon into
a glass and handed it to him with a forced smile. So the guy—cop
or military—was a regular on a break, not on a mission. That was
the good news. The bad news was that he put his back to the bar
and scanned the crowd as he lit a cigarette and sipped his seltzer.
Half the tourists looked away and the other half looked excited.
What a great picture this would be. A real Commie with a gun. In
Floridita! *Shit.*

The guy's gaze settled on me, sitting by myself, wearing the only
blue blazer in the place, not to mention the only fanny pack that
hid criminal evidence. Stop-and-frisk was not a debatable issue
here. Thanks, Jack.

The cop—or soldier, or whatever he was—gave me a final look, then shifted his attention to a table of two young ladies in shorts. They had good legs.

I looked at my watch: 9:15.

I would have used the bar phone to call the Parque Central, but that could be an invitation for this guy to engage me in conversation. *It is warm in here, señor. Take off your jacket.*

Señor Beret put his seltzer on the bar, then started toward me. I buttoned my jacket to hide the fanny strap. The baños were in the back, and I stood, evaluating my chances of getting to the crapper and doing a Michael Corleone with the gun.

Just then, Sara came through the door and the guy gave her a glance, then stopped at the table with the four pretty legs.

Sara noticed the guy, frowned, then saw me and smiled. She came over to me and gave me a kiss on the cheek. I pulled out her chair and she sat. "Sorry I'm late."

I gave the guy another glance. He was smiling as he chatted up the two American señoritas.

I sat. Sara was wearing black pants and a white silk blouse. "You look beautiful."

"Thank you." She said, "You're sweating."

"It's warm in here."

"Take off your jacket."

"I'm okay."

Sara looked at me. "I'm late because I had trouble finding a Coco cab. Not because I was on the phone."

"You don't have to explain."

"I actually didn't make that call to Miami. I decided to take your advice and do it in person."

Also known as keeping your options open.

"That gives us time to . . . make sure . . ."

I thought we already had this conversation. "If you still want me after you hear me snoring tonight, I'm yours."

She smiled and we held hands. She looked at the drinks. "What is this?"

"Daiquiri Rebelde."

She sipped her drink. "Not bad." We clinked glasses.

Sara informed me, "Long before Hemingway came here, ex-pats from Florida used to gather here, so the locals called this place Floridita—Little Florida—and the name stuck."

"I thought it meant 'tourist trap.'"

She smiled. "If you're in Havana, you have to come here at least once."

"Right. I'll cross it off my bucket list." In fact, I'll cross this whole country off my list of places to see before I die.

I was keeping my eye on the man with the gun, and Sara glanced over her shoulder, then turned back to me. "He's BE—Brigada Especial—part of the PNR, the Policía Nacional Revolucionaria. A branch of the Ministry of the Interior." She added, "They have an eye for the foreign girls. The blonder the better."

"That leaves you out."

"They're thugs."

The BE guy gave me another glance—or he was checking out Sara.

She said, "If he asks us for our passports, just show them to him without comment—though I doubt he'd do that in here."

Or he'd ask us to step outside. I glanced at her shoulder bag filled with pesos, plus her map—a copy of which I had in my jacket. Was that suspicious? Not as suspicious as the gun. I knew that if I got busted, Sara was going down with me. Not good.

She said, "The PNR have a scam where a street peddler will accuse a tourist of underpaying for something, and a PNR or BE guy suddenly appears and settles the dispute for money. And if a tourist gets into a car accident and one of them shows up, you've got a problem. And if you report that your passport was stolen, they'll actually arrest you for not having a passport."

"Well, there's a certain logic to that."

"They're comemierdas. Shit eaters. That's what the people call them and call the Communist Party officials. Shit eaters."

"Sounds better in Spanish." It also sounded like the revolution had taken a bad turn.

"They're actually trained to be paranoid about foreigners. They work closely with the chivatos."

"Maybe Eduardo was right. When you overthrow the regime, shoot them all. Or better yet, torture them with a job in the hospitality industry."

Sara smiled. "Let's talk about something more pleasant." She leaned toward me. "So the fleet is in."

"Yes. Jack sends his regards."

"Did he ask if you were sleeping with me?"

"It was written all over my face."

"I hope he doesn't say anything to Felipe."

I reminded her, "No one knows that Jack and I were meeting." Though I forgot to tell him to keep his mouth shut.

The BE guy was now posing with the two young ladies, and a waiter took a picture with the guy's cell phone, but not with the ladies' phones.

Sara said, "You're not allowed to take pictures of them. But they collect pictures of themselves posing with"—she nodded toward the girls—"dumb blondes."

"He was giving you the eye."

"He won't come over here because I'm with you. But when I was here last year, if I strayed even twenty feet from the tour group, I got pestered by the police and every jinetero on the street."

"Every . . . ?"

"Hustler. Gigolo. Asshole. Havana is full of them. Women are fair game here."

"I see now why you wanted me along."

"I can take care of myself. In Spanish and English. I just needed your boat."

"I also carry steamer trunks."

"The perfect man."

The BE guy seemed to be finished with his seltzer and señoritas and he headed for the door, then glanced back at Sara before he exited.

Sara seemed happy he was gone, and so was I.

She asked, "So tell me what happened with Jack."

"It went well. Are you ready for another?"

"I am."

I signaled to the waiter and ordered another Daiquiri Rebelde for Sara. I switched to Bucanero.

Sara also ordered two cheroots. "We have something to celebrate." She said, "So I assume the fleet is sailing to Cayo Guillermo tomorrow."

"As of now. I told Jack to leave a message for me at the hotel either way."

"Good thinking. But let's think positive." She asked, "Did Jack say if there were any problems at the pier?"

"Nothing that greenbacks couldn't solve."

"Good . . . Was there any official welcoming ceremony in the plaza?"

"Not exactly." I related Jack's description of what happened.

Sara nodded and said, "The anti-American demonstrators were the BRR—the Brigadas de Respuesta Rápida. The Rapid Response Brigades."

"What do they rapidly respond to?"

"To whatever the government tells them to respond to." She explained, "They're officially sanctioned civilian volunteers who are supposed to look like spontaneous demonstrators. But as I told you, nothing here is spontaneous."

"Except . . . love."

She smiled.

I asked, "Does the BRR turnout mean that the government may cancel the tournament?"

She thought about that, and replied, "The regime is like someone who agreed to host a house party, then changed their mind too late. And we'll see more of that in the months ahead." She added, "They've been isolated so long that they can't make decisions. Also, there are pro- and anti-Thaw factions within the regime."

"So is that a yes or no?"

"If they're looking for an excuse to cancel the tournament,

they'll find one. But they may be satisfied with the propaganda value of the anti-American demonstration. And they may have another one planned for Cayo Guillermo."

"Right." I asked, "How did all the pro-American Cubans know about the fleet's arrival?"

"Word of mouth, which is bigger than texting here. Or Radio Martí, broadcast from the States if it isn't being jammed."

"So Antonio could have heard about Pescando Por la Paz from Radio Martí."

"Or from the Rapid Response Brigades, whose members include los vigilantes—the chivatos who in turn report to the PNR—the National Revolutionary Police."

"Sorry I asked."

"This is a police state, Mac. That's all you have to remember."

"Right. Okay, we'll find out tomorrow night where Antonio gets his information."

"You still want to meet him?"

"When a local offers to sell you information, you never say no. Even bullshit has some Intel value."

"All right . . . What else did you learn from your unauthorized meeting with Jack?"

Well, I'm glad you asked. Where do I start? With the gun? Or with Eduardo? I should save the gun for last. I said to her, "Eduardo has stowed away on the boat." I looked at her.

She kept eye contact and said, "I was afraid of that."

"Well, if you—or Carlos—knew that Eduardo might pull a fast one, you should have had someone sit on him in Miami."

She stayed silent, then explained, "Eduardo is . . . a powerful man."

"Right. He pays the bills."

"It goes beyond that. No one says no to Eduardo."

"So we're talking about the Cuban godfather?"

"Sort of." She forced a smile. "But a nice godfather."

"Well, if I knew what Don Eduardo was up to, I damn sure wouldn't have said yes to you about this trip."

"I don't blame you for being angry. But I didn't think he was going to—"

"Well, he did. And if the police get hold of him, we could have a serious problem."

"He would never—"

"I've seen the Afghan police reduce Taliban fighters to whimpering children."

She had no reply.

"All right. If Eduardo wasn't Felipe's . . . whatever, I would have told Jack to throw him overboard."

"No you would not—"

"I will protect this mission—and my life and yours and Jack's—at any cost."

Sara did not look happy, but she looked convinced.

"Meanwhile, Felipe is watching Eduardo on the boat." I added, unnecessarily, "I don't want him running around Havana."

"He . . . he wants to walk from Cayo Guillermo to his family home, through the countryside. And to visit the cemetery where his family is buried. On All Souls' Day—the Day of the Dead. That's what we do." She looked at me. "Then he wants to die in Cuba."

Well, that should be easy. I softened a bit and said, "All right. I get it."

Thinking back to the sundowners on my boat, and my subsequent meetings with Carlos in Miami and Key West, I'd identified a number of things that could go wrong with this mission, and one of them was Eduardo coming along for the ride. Another was Sara coming to the attention of the authorities, and then there was the problem of me getting involved with Ms. Ortega. Well, that all happened. And now there were new problems, like Antonio, and also the gun, which was a problem only if I got caught with it. But if I followed Jack's advice, the gun could solve the Antonio problem—though I saw no reason for that. Yet.

To add to these concerns was the possibility that the tournament would be cancelled, and/or we wouldn't meet our contact. But were those problems? Or safe passes home?

Bottom line, we weren't even out of Havana yet, and as my Scottish ancestors used to say, "The best-laid schemes o' mice an' men gang aft agley," meaning, "This shit's not working." Next was Camagüey, the cave, and Cayo, which were going to be a challenge—if we could get out of Havana.

"What are you thinking about?" she asked.

"The road ahead."

"I'm feeling more confident about that."

·It must be the daiquiris. I also told her, "I briefed Jack about Antonio and our possible problems with the authorities, and about Antonio mentioning Pescando Por la Paz."

"All right . . . and did that spook him?"

"It raised his awareness. If it needed raising."

"I assume he's still in."

"He's in if I'm in."

"And you're in."

"If you're in."

"So we're all in."

And all crazy. I finished my beer and she finished her daiquiri, then asked, "Did Jack say anything about Felipe?"

"No . . . just that Felipe was not happy to find Eduardo under the bed."

"Felipe can handle his uncle."

"I hope you're right. And does Felipe know anything about what's going to happen in Cayo Guillermo that he's supposed to pass on to Jack?"

"I don't know what Felipe knows," she replied.

"How about Eduardo?"

"Eduardo did not want to know any of the operational details about the mission. His only mission is to go home."

"He's going back to Miami on The Maine."

"Let him—"

"Subject closed."

She called the waiter over, ordered another round, and asked for a light. I limit myself to a cigar a week in Key West. But here, as in Afghanistan, tobacco was not the primary health issue in terms of life expectancy.

Three guitarists appeared and began strolling around the room, strumming and singing. I recognized a few of the songs from Tad's lecture. I was really getting my money's worth on this tour.

Sara leaned toward me. "Are the guns onboard?"

Well, three of them are. One was sitting on my fanny. But I didn't want to upset her—or excite her—with that news until the right moment. I replied, "They are. And Jack also has four bulletproof vests onboard. Hopefully, we will not need them, or the guns."

She nodded.

The strolling guitarists arrived at our table and asked for a request. Sara, who I noticed didn't reveal her fluency in Spanish, said in English, "Please play 'Dos Gardenias' from the Buena Vista Social Club."

The three guitarists seemed happy with that and began playing and singing in Spanish. Not bad.

I looked at my watch: 10:35. We had an hour to get to Dos Hermanos if we wanted to go there. Next stop, Key West.

I looked at Sara smoking her cheroot and she saw me looking at her and winked. I tried to picture us together in Miami, or Key West, or even Maine. The picture looked better if we were in a red Porsche convertible.

The guitarists finished, and I gave them a ten and they gave us a happy smile. So if anyone was watching us, we looked more like dumb tourists than enemies of the state.

Floridita was getting more crowded and Sara said, "There's a floor show later. Do you want to stay and drink sixteen double daiquiris?"

Or do I want to go to Key West and drink sixteen Coronas? Sara didn't know she had that option.

"Mac?"

I looked at her. "The crews and fishermen are meeting at a place called Dos Hermanos at eleven."

"That's a famous old seafarers' bar."

"Jack asked if we'd like to meet them there."

"We can't do that."

I leaned toward her. "Jack says he can get us onboard The Maine tonight."

Sara looked at me.

"The fleet sails for Cayo Guillermo at first light. The Maine will sail for Key West."

She stayed silent awhile, processing that, then asked, "What did you tell Jack?"

"I told him not to expect us. But he said I should ask you. So I'm asking."

"I thought we made the decision to push on."

"We did."

"All right . . . what has changed?"

"Someone offered us a ride home."

She seemed to be considering this and asked, "How do you know we can get on the boat?"

I explained about the blank visitor passes. I added, "Sort of like the letters of transit that Bogie gave Bergman and her husband. Just fill in the names."

She nodded absently.

I continued, "We have everything we need with us—passport, visa, and bribe money." To give her all the info she needed to make a decision I also told her, "Jack gave me my Glock, which I'll ditch before we go through security. And let me remind you that Eduardo is on the boat, and he needs to go back to Miami." And finally, I reminded her, "If the tournament gets cancelled, the fleet will be heading home in the morning and we'll be in Cuba without a boat."

The guitarists were serenading a young couple who were holding hands, gazing into each other's eyes. I looked at my watch, then at Sara. "We need a decision."

"I'm . . . weighing the pros and cons."

"The reasons for scrubbing this mission far outweigh the reasons for going ahead. But that's not how you're going to make this decision."

"Call for the check."

I signaled the waiter for the check, paid in cash, and we left Little Florida, perhaps to go to Big Florida.

She asked me, "Where is the gun?"

"In a fanny pack around my waist."

"Is that why you wanted to meet Jack?"

"No. But maybe it's why he wanted to meet me. And maybe Eduardo being onboard is why you didn't want me to meet Jack."

"I was as surprised as you were."

"Life is full of surprises."

"It is," she agreed. "Some pleasant, some not."

"Indeed. Where are we going now?"

"It's a surprise."

Calle Obispo was a pedestrian street and we walked past her grandfather's bank, where this all started fifty-five years ago, and came to the corner where a few cabs waited for tourists. We climbed into a Coco cab and the driver asked, "A dónde vas?"

Good question.

Sara replied, "Hotel Parque Central, por favor."

"Good decision," I said.

"And the right one."

That remained to be seen.

CHAPTER 33

Sunday was not a day of rest nor a day of worship unless you worship an air-conditioned Chinese bus.

Our itinerary had us on a road trip to a city called Matanzas, a hundred kilometers east of Havana, and Sara and I sat together as the bus pulled away from the Parque Central, our home away from home.

The morning had started off with two messages: a phone message from Jack, a.k.a. Cristo, saying, "My flight is on time," and an announcement from Tad saying, "Antonio won't be joining us today."

Regarding Jack's message, Sara saw this as a sign that she'd made the right decision last night and that the mission was back on track. I wasn't sure Jack would agree. In any case, I hope he got laid last night.

Regarding the news that Antonio was AWOL today, Sara asked, rhetorically, "Where do you think he is?"

Well, hopefully he got run over by a Coco cab. Or shot by a jealous boyfriend, thereby saving me the trouble. On the other hand, be careful what you wish for. I wasn't exactly looking forward to meeting Antonio tonight, but neither did I want him dead before I heard what he had to say.

Sara, however, said, "I don't think we should go to that bar tonight."

Well, if we were on *The Maine* now, heading to Key West, she wouldn't have to worry about that.

"Mac?"

"That's how we left it with him."

"I'm wondering why he didn't tell us he had today off."

"Ask him when you see him."

"I think tonight is a trap and he didn't want to . . . interact with us today."

"Interesting logic. But you could make the opposite case. If tonight is a trap, Antonio would be on this bus reminding us about cocktails at seven."

She had no reply.

In fact, though, she could be right. Antonio seemed like a guy who didn't have the cojones to look you in the eye before he gave you the kiss of death. Judas had more balls.

Also missing today was José, our driver, and a guy named Lope was subbing for him. If I were paranoid, I'd say Lope was actually subbing for Antonio. Another week in this place and I'll start to think my dick is reporting to the police.

The bus rolled through the quiet Sunday streets of Havana and Sara put her head on my shoulder and closed her eyes.

We'd slept together in my room, and this morning I gave her a quick tutorial on how to fire the Glock. Pull the trigger. The Army women I'd dated considered a gun a fashion accessory, but with most civilian women it was best to keep the gun out of sight when you dressed or undressed. Sara, however, was happy that I was armed, though she understood that the gun totally blew our cover as innocent tourists.

There was no safe place to stash the Glock except on my person—or Sara's—so I had it with me now in Jack's fanny pack along with the three loaded magazines. Hopefully, there'd be no occasion today for the policía to inquire about the contents of my butt bag.

Sara had advised me last night, "You can't take the gun to our meeting with Antonio. If it's a trap, the gun is all the evidence the police need to turn us over to a military tribunal."

Right. You can bullshit your way out of a lot of things, but getting caught with a gun wasn't one of them in Cuba.

Also last night, while we were discussing evidence of our crimes against the state, Sara explained to me the alterations she'd made to the treasure map. They were fairly simple, basically reversing a few double-digit numbers, and as a former infantry officer well-trained in map reading, I was sure that I—if I was on my own—could follow this map to where X marked the cave.

We were on the coastal road now, heading east toward Matanzas. The countryside was very pristine—no gas stations or outlet malls, no motels, and no billboards advertising a pick-your-own-mango farm. Also, the countryside seemed sparsely populated and many of the farm houses appeared abandoned, as were the fields around them. Off in the distance I saw a field being plowed by a farmer with two oxen.

Antonio wasn't onboard to tell us about the new five-year agriculture plan, so Tad stood and gave the group some uncensored info, telling us that agriculture in Cuba had regressed to the nineteenth century, validating my opinion that the organic farm we'd visited was a pile of bullshit.

Professor Nalebuff was onboard, and he offered more subversive information. "Cuba's last financial lifeline was Venezuela, whose socialist government kept Cuba afloat with oil money. But the price of oil has fallen, and Venezuela, like Cuba, is an economic basket case." He added, "Ironically, Cuba's last real hope is U.S. tourism and trade."

Don't forget fishing tournaments.

Tad and Alison, who'd been holding back on their criticism of the regime, thought they could speak freely without Antonio around, but Lope, who said he spoke no English, seemed to be listening.

The highway ran close to the coast and I gazed out at the Straits of Florida. Somewhere out there, running on a parallel course with us, was the tournament fleet, and *The Maine*, which, if we'd gotten aboard last night, would now be heading for Key West. As Yogi Berra wisely said, "When you come to a fork in the road, take it."

———

As we reached the outskirts of Matanzas, Alison told us, "Before the revolution, Matanzas was home to a large number of artists, writers, musicians, and intellectuals, and was called the Athens of Cuba."

And now it looked like Pompeii.

We got off the bus into the heat and humidity of a large plaza, and we followed Tad and Alison to a nineteenth-century pharmacy that had been turned into a pharmaceutical museum, housed in a grand mansion once owned by the family who'd also owned the pharmacy. Then came La Revolución.

The old pharmacy was sort of interesting, especially the big apothecary jars of belladonna and cannabis. The opium looked good, too. They don't have this in Walgreens.

We then walked through the narrow streets of the town, jostling for sidewalk space with the natives, who probably thought our tour bus had taken a wrong turn. I said to Sara, "Now you know why Antonio took the day off."

"Stop complaining."

Tad advised us that these provincial towns were safer than Havana with regard to pickpockets and purse snatchers, but we should safeguard our valuables as we walked. I didn't think he was referring to my Glock, but I'd already moved my fanny pack to my front and covered it with my Polo shirt, giving me a nice beer belly.

As we walked through the town, I spotted a few PNR guys, who looked us over as we passed by, but there is safety in numbers, and as long as Sara and I stayed in the herd we wouldn't be picked off by a wolf asking to see our passports and visas. *Señor, are you pregnant?*

Sara, however, might be too pretty for the wolves to ignore, so I told her, "If you're stopped, I can't come to your assistance. That's Tad and Alison's job. And if I'm stopped, you don't know me."

"Everyone knows we're together."

"The police don't." And I was happy Antonio wasn't there to rat us out. I reminded her, "We just met. And sleeping together doesn't mean we have to get arrested together—or even walk to-gether."

"All right . . . I understand." She offered, "I can carry the gun."

"It's my gun."

On the plus side, the natives seemed friendly, though there didn't seem to be any reason for this town's existence.

After a few hours of trying to figure out why we were here, the heat-exhausted herd returned to the plaza and boarded the bus. Sara and I sat together and shared a bottle of water.

Maybe because it was Sunday, our next stop was lunch at the Matanzas Seminary, located on a hill above the city. Alison told us that the seminary was not Catholic—it was Methodist, Presbyterian, and Episcopal—with forty students of both sexes, half of whom, said Alison, would probably leave Cuba at the first opportunity. Me too.

We pulled into the seminary grounds, which were nicely land-scaped, and the buildings were in better repair than any I'd seen in Matanzas. I was fairly certain they didn't have stop-and-frisk here, and I relaxed for the first time today.

As we got off the bus, Sara said, "Religion will save Cuba."

"Right. Look what it did for Afghanistan."

"Don't be a cynic. I never asked—what religion are you?"

"You've been sleeping with a Presbyterian. But when I'm get-ting shot at, I pray to everyone."

"Would you consider converting to Catholicism?"

Were we talking about a wedding? Or Last Rites?

"Mac?"

"Yes, I'd consider that."

She took my hand and squeezed it.

We were greeted by a pleasant middle-aged lady who escorted us into a refectory with long tables and benches, and Sara and I found ourselves sitting with Tad and Alison, who didn't appear to have hooked up yet. Also at our table were Alexandra and Ash-leigh, whom I'd chatted up at the welcome dinner before I fell in love with Sara Ortega. At the end of the table was our driver, Lope, who hadn't picked his table at random.

There were pitchers of iced tea on the table, hopefully wait-ing to be turned into wine. Nice-looking young men and women, alight with the Holy Spirit, brought out platters of food. I'd ex-pected loaves and fishes, but we got rice and beans, and poultry that had come in second in a cockfight.

We all made small talk, then Tad asked me, "How are you en-joying yourself so far?"

"This has been an eye-opening experience."

"And there's more to come."

Right. But not with you. I asked, "Where's Antonio today?"

"I'm not sure. He was scheduled to be with us."

"I hope he's not sick."

"He left word that he'd be joining us tomorrow."

"But not tonight for dinner?"

"Apparently not."

Correct. Sara and I were having drinks with Antonio tonight.

Alison said, "We're having dinner tonight at La Guarida, one of the best restaurants in Havana, housed in a huge old mansion. If you've seen the movie Fresa y Chocolate, you'll recognize scenes that were shot there." She added, "La Guarida was favorably re-viewed in the New York Times."

"So was Fidel Castro," I said.

Everyone thought that was funny. Even Lope, who smiled.

Alison asked us all where we'd wound up having dinner on our own last night, and everyone at our table had a culinary adventure tale, some good, some not so good. I admitted, "Sara and I drank dinner at Floridita."

That got a few chuckles. We were really bonding. In another week we'd be calling one another by our first names.

Tad took the opportunity to chide me and Sara. "We missed you at the ballet rehearsal and the visit to the firefighter museum."

Sara responded, "I wasn't feeling well and Mac walked me back to the hotel."

Alison advised, "Stay hydrated."

This wasn't a good time to tell Tad and Alison that we were

blowing off the group dinner tonight, but I set it up by asking, "What are the first symptoms of malaria?"

No one seemed to know.

Anyway, before lunch was finished, Sara looked at her watch and made an announcement. "I have an appointment with Dr. Mendez, who is the rector here."

Really?

She explained, "I'm involved with an ecumenical charity in Miami, and I've brought cash donations for several religious institutions in Cuba." She stood. "I'll meet up with the group shortly." She left, carrying her purse of pesos.

Alison said, "That's very nice."

And also consistent with her cover story.

Our next stop was the chapel to hear the chamber choir perform. I wasn't looking forward to this, but the young men and women in the choir had angelic voices, singing some great oldies like "Rock of Ages" and "Amazing Grace," and for a few minutes I was a kid wearing my Sunday suit, sitting in First Pres in Portland. Meanwhile, Sara was still MIA.

We next went to an outdoor lecture given by a theologian who told us that there was a religious revival occurring in Cuba, but it was mostly driven by Evangelical Protestants, not the Catholic Church. I was sure the Pope would be back.

Sara appeared at the end of the lecture and we all boarded the bus for the trip back to Havana.

I asked her, "How much did you give them?"

"Thirty thousand pesos. About twelve hundred dollars, which is a lot of money."

"Are we good with God now?"

"We'll find out tonight."

Indeed we would.

CHAPTER 34

Before the revolution, the Vedado district of Havana was controlled by Cuban mobsters and the American Mafia in a profitable joint business venture that might be a good model for the future.

Our taxi, a dilapidated Soviet Lada whose upholstery smelled like bleu cheese, traveled along the Malecón toward the far western edge of Vedado, where we were to meet Antonio in a bar called Rolando.

Parts of Vedado, according to Sara, still retained some of its pre-revolutionary flavor, and remained home to a number of unauthorized activities, including black marketeering, midnight auto sales, rooms by the hour, and unlicensed rum joints, to name just a few of Vedado's private enterprises. Every city needs a Vedado.

Our driver, who spoke a little English, had never heard of Rolando's, and our hotel concierge couldn't find it listed anywhere, but our driver made a few cell phone calls to his colleagues and thought he had an address. If this was a trap, Antonio wasn't making it easy for us to fall into it.

I'd left a note at the hotel for Tad and Alison saying that Sara and I had been stricken with Fidel's revenge and would not be joining the group for dinner. P.S.: Gotta run now.

We continued along the Malecón, and Sara didn't have much to say, except things like, "This is a mistake," and "This was your idea."

Sara and I were casually dressed in jeans and T-shirts, and we both wore our running shoes in case the evening included a sprint to the American Embassy.

I'd left my treasure map in my room, stuck in my backpack with my Cuba guide, but my Glock and the three loaded magazines were now in Sara's backpack, buried under wads of Cuban pesos, along with her map and all my American dollars. Now all we had to do was find a place to stash this before we met Antonio.

The driver turned off the Malecón and traveled south along a dark residential street of shabby multi-family housing units, almost invisible behind overgrown vegetation.

The driver slowed down and we all looked out the windows, trying to find the address or a sign, but most of the street lights were out and the landscapers hadn't been here since 1959.

Sara told the driver to pull over and said to me, "We'll walk."

I paid the driver, and we began walking. The only sounds on this dark, quiet street were tree frogs croaking in the hot night air. I wasn't concerned about being followed, because if this was a trap the police were already at Rolando having a beer with Antonio while they waited for us. I checked my watch: 7:16.

Up ahead I could see a small bridge over a narrow river that Sara ID'd as the Río Almendares, and on the opposite bank was a well-lighted area that she said was Miramar, Havana's wealthy and clubby suburb, now occupied by foreign businessmen, embassy people, and the Communist elite. So we had come to the end of Vedado and the literal end of the road where Rolando's was supposed to be.

Just as I was wondering how to call Uber, I spotted a pink two-story building near the river, set back from the road. There were lights in the windows, and a high hedge ran around the building. I didn't see any cars parked out front, but I could see a few bicycles leaning against the hedge.

Sara said, "That has to be it."

As we walked toward the pink building, we came to a shoulder-high wall running along the sidewalk, and on the other side of the wall was the shell of an abandoned house, nearly invisible in the middle of an overgrown lot. I suggested, "Good place to lose your backpack."

She nodded and we both looked up and down the dark street. And though we hadn't seen a car or a person since we began walking, I knew that every street in Havana had los vigilantes—the kind of people who peeked through the window blinds.

Sara looked over the wall, then dropped her backpack into a thick growth of vines.

I asked, "Did you remove all your ID?"

"No, Mac, I left my passport so the police could track us down and return your gun."

"Good thinking." She didn't seem to be in a good mood. "Okay, let's have a drink."

We continued to the end of the street and stood at the gated opening in the hedge, through which we could see a patio and a half dozen tables whose chairs were filled with tough-looking hombres, smoking, drinking, and playing cards.

I took her arm and we walked onto the patio of what I hoped was Rolando's.

The customers gave us the once-over, but no one said anything. I saw this scene in a movie once, but I don't remember how it ended.

Over the entrance door was a hand-painted sign that said: ROLANDO—AQUÍ JAMÁS ESTUVO HEMINGWAY. Sara translated, "'Hemingway was never here,'" which was funny, and which was also what Antonio promised. I should give this address to the Nevilles.

I entered first, with Sara right behind me.

The front room looked like a grocery store with shelves along the dingy stucco walls displaying canned food. The only person in the room was an old man sitting behind a counter, reading a newspaper. He glanced at us, and before I could say, "Antonio sent us," he cocked his head toward a curtain in the wall.

I led the way, and we passed through the curtain into a stairwell where steps led to the upper floor.

I could hear recorded music at the top of the stairs—"Empire State of Mind"—and we ascended into a dimly lit room with louvered windows, unadorned red walls, and floor fans.

Men and women sat on ratty upholstered furniture that was

scattered haphazardly around the concrete floor, and a few couples were dancing. Everyone seemed to have a drink and a cigarette, and a few of the couples were working up to the main event. There must be rooms available. Or maybe a broom closet.

I didn't see Antonio, but a guy got up from a chair and motioned us to follow him. He led us to a door that went out to a small rooftop terrace dimly lit by oil lamps on the four tables. The only customer was Antonio, sitting by himself, drinking a beer, smoking a cigarette, and talking on his cell phone.

He saw us, hung up, stood, and smiled. "Bienvenidos."

CHAPTER 35

Antonio was wearing his tight black pants and a tight black T-shirt, which looked kind of ridiculous. We didn't shake hands, but he invited us to sit.

He asked, "Did you have difficulties finding this place?"

"It wasn't in my Michelin guide."

He looked at us. "Do you think you were followed here?"

That was a funny question coming from a police informant. "You tell me."

He shrugged. "It's not important. I have taken American tourists here before. To show them how the people relax after work."

Right. Those twenty-dollar-a-month jobs can be stressful. "You live around here?"

"Yes. This is my neighborhood bar."

Jack would advise me to get Antonio's address, follow him home, and shoot him in the head. Sara might second that.

He also let us know, "We have this terrace to ourselves until we are done."

Sara said, "That could be two minutes."

Antonio looked at her, but didn't reply.

I could hear Black Eyed Peas singing "I Gotta Feeling."

A young waiter wearing an Atlanta Braves T-shirt came out to the terrace. Rolando's cocktail menu was limited to rum and beer, and because everyone here made twenty bucks a month, all drinks were ten pesos—forty cents. Well, the price was right. Antonio was drinking Bucanero, but Sara and I ordered colas. I told the waiter, "Unopened bottles. No glasses."

Antonio didn't look offended that I was suggesting the place was dirty, or that he was going to drug us. Also, Antonio could be wearing a wire, but his pants and shirt were so tight he'd have to have the transmitter up his ass.

I said to him, "We told a few people in our group that we were having drinks with you here."

"So if you disappear, the police will consider me a suspect. Except the police don't care if you disappear."

Right. In fact, the police would be the prime suspects in our disappearance.

Antonio asked, "What did you tell Tad and Alison about your absence tonight?"

"I told them we had Fidel's revenge."

He looked at Sara. "Que?"

"Diarrhoea."

He smiled. "That's why I was absent today. From eating an American apple."

Asshole.

The waiter brought our drinks, and I opened the bottles myself. No one proposed a toast.

The sunlight had faded from the western sky, replaced by the lights of Miramar, and ninety miles north, across the Straits, was Key West, where Fantasy Fest was in full swing. Life takes some interesting turns.

Antonio got down to business and asked us, "Do you have the money?"

Sara replied, "It is against Cuban law for us to give you American dollars, and we have no reason to give you anything."

Antonio turned to me, the voice of reason. "Most of my tip money is in American dollars. It is of no consequence."

"We have no American dollars with us, but if we're interested in what you say, I'll put your tip in an envelope and leave it for you at the hotel."

"I think you don't trust me."

"What was your first clue?"

"I'm taking a big risk to meet you."

"Same here."

"You are already at risk."

"Can you be more specific?"

"I can." He looked at Sara. "I have information that the police are interested in you."

Well, that was no surprise, and that didn't seem to include me. Unless Antonio was saving the best for last.

Sara looked Antonio in the eye. "There are not many scams or entrapments that I haven't heard of in Cuba, including this one."

Antonio informed us, "If this was a police trap, both of you would already be under arrest. And if you think this is a scam, you will be making a big mistake. Your problem is not me—it is the police."

"You work for the police," said Sara.

"Everyone in Cuba has two jobs and two lives." He added, "And two souls. That is how we survive." He reminded us, "The Cubans double-cross each other. They sell each other out. In the end, we all work for ourselves."

Right. Also, Antonio had a serious case of multiple personality disorder, and I wasn't sure which Antonio had shown up tonight. "Okay, so tonight you sell out your police friends for money, and tomorrow you double-cross us."

"That is a chance you will have to take."

"No. I can pass."

"You can. But that could cost you your freedom."

Sara said to him, "Look at me."

He looked at her.

Sara spoke to him in Spanish, and I could hear the words "los vigilantes," "chivatos," and "Policía Nacional Revolucionaria," but not the word for "shit eaters," so she was controlling herself. I mean, not to engage in ethnic stereotyping, but Miss Ortega had a Cuban temper, especially when speaking to someone she believed was a Commie shit eater who had destroyed Cuba.

Antonio listened impassively, then said, "Your Spanish is more than 'un poco.'"

Sara said to me, "Let's go." She stood.

I said to Sara, "Let's let Antonio tell us why he thinks the police are interested in you."

She hesitated, then sat and shot me a very annoyed look.

I said to Antonio, "You're on, amigo."

He lit another cigarette and said to me—not Sara—"She had a problem at the airport."

Did he get that info from Alison? Or the police? "I didn't see any problem at the airport, and she never mentioned a problem to me."

"She had three hundred thousand pesos with her."

Well, he could have only gotten that from the police. "That's not illegal."

"It is suspicious."

"If you'd been with us today—or if you've spoken to Lope— you'd know that Miss Ortega made a donation, in pesos, to the Matanzas Seminary."

"Yes, and very kind of her. But the police are interested in the remainder of the money."

"It's all for Cuban charities. But let's back up. Explain how you know what happened at the airport."

"I thought you understood this. My job puts me in contact with tourists—mostly American. The police find this useful, so they ask me to tell them if I see or hear anything that seems suspicious. In some cases they ask me to watch a certain person"—he glanced at Sara—"who they already suspect of criminal or political activities."

"And why would the police suspect Sara Ortega of anything?"

"They don't tell me everything. But in addition to the problem at the airport, they also told me she has been to Cuba once before. And she is Cuban."

Sara interjected, "Cuban American."

I asked, "Have you done this before? Telling American tourists—Cuban Americans—that the police were interested in them? And then asking for money?"

"You have asked enough questions."

"Sorry, I've got more. What are you telling the police about Miss Ortega?"

"I am telling them the truth—that she has made some insulting remarks about Cuban socialism."

"Did you also tell the police you had a personal interest in Miss Ortega?"

He smiled. "I don't tell them everything. But I told them she is having a holiday romance."

"Is that why you invited me to come along?"

"I invited you to come along because the police are now interested in you."

He must have told the police that I had questioned F.C.'s marlin trophy. Also, he knew that Sara would not meet him alone. "Why are they interested in me?"

"Because you and Miss Ortega have disappeared together for lengths of time. You said you were going to Floridita after the Riviera Hotel, but you were not there, as I discovered, and you spent the night out of your assigned hotel. You also left the group after the Museum of the Revolution. All of that is suspicious, and that is what I told the police."

"Did you also tell them that Miss Ortega and I just met on this trip?"

"So you say."

Antonio was probably very selective about what he told the police, which is what police informants do to curry favor. It's also what assholes do.

He continued, "I also told the police that Miss Ortega was inquiring about an unauthorized visit to the beach."

"And you told them, of course, that you offered to drive her to a nude beach."

He looked at Sara, perhaps thinking about what could have been—if I hadn't entered the picture. In fact, Antonio had probably pictured a different meeting here with Sara Ortega, and without me. He would have let her know that the police were interested in her, and told her how he could help her and what she could do

for him to return the favor. Good fantasy, but at some point Antonio realized that Sara Ortega wasn't the kind of woman to be
frightened out of her clothes. Then I entered the picture and his
fantasy of taking her home morphed into the more realistic possibility of taking five hundred dollars home. Well, ironically, he was
onto something, but he hadn't mentioned Pescando Por la Paz, or
my meeting Jack Colby at the Nacional, so my guilt seemed to be
by association with Miss Ortega, whose guilt was a result of her
birth.

I said to Antonio, "You haven't told us anything we haven't already figured out. So . . . I'll buy the drinks and contribute to your
group tip at the end of the tour."

"The end of the tour for you is closer than you think."

Why did I know he was going to say that? "Does that mean
we're going to be expelled?"

"Unfortunately it means something else."

I wonder what that could be.

Antonio chain-lit another cigarette and told us, "As you know,
there are those in America and in Cuba who are not in favor of
normalizing relations. The regime itself is ambivalent about normalization. Perhaps frightened of what it means."

Neither Sara nor I replied, and he went on, "You may have
heard that there was an anti-American demonstration at the pier
when the fishing fleet arrived."

As a matter of fact I did hear that, but I replied, "That's not good
for improving relations."

"No, and this was not a spontaneous demonstration. It was . . ."

"Staged?"

"Yes. Staged. By the Ministry of the Interior." He looked at Sara.
"As I'm sure Miss Ortega knows, they are a very powerful ministry
in Cuba, responsible for internal security, the border guard, and
the police. They are also very much opposed to normalizing relations. They are afraid of"—he pointed north—"what is over there."

"The Conch Republic?"

He seemed confused. "America. That is the reality that is coming.

But the Ministry of the Interior is looking for an incident that will refreeze the Cuban Thaw and keep the Americans away—and the incident, unfortunately, will be the arrest of Miss Ortega. And you."

I wasn't sure if Antonio was telling the truth, or if he was trying to frighten us into a big tip. "There is absolutely nothing in my background that has anything to do with Cuba."

"So you say. But I know the police are investigating your background. Through the Internet. And through sources in Key West. And they are also investigating Miss Ortega's activities in Miami."

That sucked. Well, I had taken down my website when I sold *The Maine*, but the police might still be able to find something to connect me to *Fishy Business*. As for Sara, she'd told me she kept a low profile in Miami. I glanced at her and she seemed cool and composed.

Antonio continued, "I'm not sure when this arrest will happen. But you will probably get a late-night knock on your doors . . . or one door if you are sleeping together." He added, "They like to do these things when you are most vulnerable—in your beds—and when everyone else is asleep." He looked at Sara, then at me, waiting for a reaction.

I asked him, "If the police don't tell you much, why did they tell you all this?"

I think Antonio expected a more agitated response from us, and he stayed silent, then replied, "They told me to make myself available for the police interrogation, where I will denounce both of you and write a statement."

"Okay, if we buy all that—for five hundred dollars—what are we supposed to do with this information?"

"You need to get out of Cuba."

"If we do that, the police will suspect that you tipped us off."

"And if they arrest you, you will tell them that I betrayed them."

"We wouldn't do that to you, amigo."

"Of course you would. I am playing a very dangerous game. So it is as important for me as it is for you that you get out of the country."

My bullshit detector was beeping, but I said, "Okay, so how do we get out of Cuba?"

He didn't take that as a rhetorical question, and answered, "I have made inquiries and I can get you both on a British cruise ship leaving Havana in two days. It is sailing to Bridgetown, Barbados."

Well, that was the second boat ride out of here that I was offered this week. This one sounded too good to be true, but I asked, "How much?"

He seemed to be thinking about that, then replied, "Whatever is left of Miss Ortega's three hundred thousand pesos, and an additional thousand American dollars—which I will need for bribes at the pier."

Antonio was good at upselling. Five hundred for the advertised special, but for another thousand, plus all our pesos, he'll throw in a cruise to Barbados.

Sara said, "We need to think about this."

"There is not much to think about. And I will need your answer tomorrow, by noon. I will also need the thousand dollars tomorrow to make the travel arrangements, and then the three hundred thousand pesos when I can assure you of your passage on the ship."

Neither Sara nor I replied, so Antonio continued his sales pitch. "Because of the American embargo, no ship of any nation that comes to Cuba may enter a U.S. port for six months after visiting Cuba, so there are not many cruise ships in Cuban ports, but fortunately, this British ship—The Braemar—never enters American waters and is now in Havana." He continued, "Many Americans come to Cuba by flying to Bridgetown, which is the home port of The Braemar, so there should be no difficulties in getting you onboard for the return voyage to Bridgetown."

"Then why do we need you?"

"To get you through security and passport control—where your names are now on a watch list."

Thanks for that, asshole.

"This is your only opportunity to leave this island."

"We understand. And you'll have our answer tomorrow."

Antonio also advised us, "Calling your embassy will put your State Department in a difficult position at this time of sensitive diplomatic negotiations."

Should I tell him that Sara Ortega and the Secretary of State were practically classmates at Yale?

"And if you try to get into the embassy, the police will stop you and discover that you are on the watch list, and arrest you."

Should I remind Antonio that Richard Neville *wanted* to be arrested? He'd get more out of it than me or Sara.

Antonio also told us, "If you were to be arrested—or if you were to somehow escape from Cuba—your tour group will be expelled. This has happened before. Also, as in the past, to increase tensions, the regime will cancel many goodwill exchanges, including, for instance, the Fishing for Peace tournament."

And why did he mention that? To see if I reacted? This was not good news, but I didn't comment and said, "You understand that Miss Ortega and I are tourists who have just met. We are here with a licensed group to experience Cuban culture, not to overthrow the regime."

He smiled, then said patiently, "In Cuba, guilt or innocence is not important. Politics are important. Let me remind you that your compatriot Alan Gross received a fifteen-year sentence for spying and spent five years in prison, and he was innocent."

"Apparently he didn't have someone like you to tip him off."

"You are fortunate to have me."

"In America we say, with friends like you I don't need enemies."

He seemed uncertain if that was an insult or a compliment. He looked at us. "Despite our differences, I actually like you both, and I'm happy to be in a position to help you out of your difficulties."

"Which you helped get us into." I asked, "Anything else?"

"My five hundred dollars—which, you will agree, I have earned."

"It will be in an envelope at the front desk tomorrow morning."

"And the thousand dollars for bribes."

"Same envelope."

I was about to stand, but then Antonio said, "You understand that I am giving you your life—your freedom." He looked at Sara and they made eye contact.

He said something to her in Spanish, and though I don't understand Spanish, I knew exactly what he was saying.

She took a breath, and I thought she was going to unload on him, but she controlled her voice and spoke to him in an almost meek tone, and shook her head. Antonio said something else to her and she nodded and replied.

He looked at me, maybe trying to see if I got what the deal was. I glanced at Sara and she said, "It's okay."

She stood and looked at me. "It's time to go."

I stood, but Antonio remained seated and said to Sara, "You should not have come back."

She nodded.

"But I will get you out of here."

Again, she nodded.

I took her arm and we left. Pharrell was singing, "Because I'm happy . . ."

CHAPTER 36

We stood in the dark, quiet street. I asked, "Did I hear what I think I heard?"

She nodded. "He told me there were rooms available there. But I told him I couldn't do that with you sitting there while I was with him."

"How long do you think it would have taken?"

"This isn't funny."

"Sorry."

"But we agreed he'd come to my room tomorrow night—at about midnight."

"Okay. And he thinks he has a deal?"

"He thinks I'm frightened. And he thinks I will enjoy myself."

"I can't believe that slimeball actually did that—even in Spanish—with me sitting there."

She looked back at Rolando. "He thinks I'm just a loose woman, and that you and I are just casual lovers. He also thinks that you'd agree I could sleep with him if it was a choice between imprisonment or escape from Cuba." She added, "I said I'd speak to you, and I was sure you'd agree with that."

"I guess we should have seen that coming."

"I did. From day one." She said, "We need to leave tomorrow night."

"Right." I didn't think we were being watched, but to be safe I said, "We shouldn't retrieve your backpack tonight."

She glanced down the street at the abandoned house, then looked at the bridge over the river. "All right. Let's walk to Miramar and get a taxi."

We walked onto the footpath of the narrow bridge that spanned the Río Almendares, and from here Miramar looked like a pleasant 1950s Florida suburb. I could see why the international community and the Communist elite would want to live here, away from the two million less fortunate souls who were crowded into the decay of Havana.

We came off the bridge and turned into a palm-lined street of pastel-colored houses. The streets of Miramar were laid out in a grid, and Sara seemed to know the area. We turned north and she said, "The main thoroughfare, Avenida Quinta, is up here and we can find a taxi."

We continued and I said, "You noticed that Antonio again mentioned the Pescando Por la Paz."

Sara had no response.

"It's possible that the police may suspect my connection or they may discover the connection through their background investigation. And if they do, they'll be waiting for us when we get to Cayo Guillermo."

"We'll worry about that when we get there."

That strategy wasn't in my training manual, but the problems with this mission—including Eduardo running down memory lane—were piling up so fast that it wasn't worth arguing about.

Sara looked at the well-kept houses along the road. "These Communist pigs have beach clubs, good food, and access to foreign goods that the Cuban people can only dream about."

"I'm sure they're wracked with guilt."

"They're hypocritical shit eaters."

And if the regime was overthrown, the exiles would be back, living in Miramar. I could see Carlos opening a branch office here. "You need to focus on the mission. Not the residents of Miramar."

"Don't lecture me. You're not Cuban."

"I'm not lecturing you. I'm telling you—put the hate on hold and think about why we're here and how to get the hell out of here."

She didn't reply.

I took my own advice and thought about all the curve balls that had been thrown at us since we stepped off the plane. God was trying to tell us something. And I thought I knew what it was. I asked, "How long would it take us to drive from here directly to Cayo Guillermo?"

Sara didn't reply.

"How long?"

"Maybe eight hours."

"For a few hundred bucks we can find a taxi to take us to Cayo tonight, and we could be there before dawn, get onboard The Maine before they go fishing, and be in Key West in time for happy hour."

She took my hand as we walked. "You said the road home goes through Camagüey."

"I did say that. But that was before Antonio told us that the police were coming for us—or that the fleet could be ordered to leave."

"Why would you believe any of that?"

"Because it could be true." I also reminded her, "You have a date with him tomorrow night, so tonight is a good time to leave Havana."

She let go of my hand and didn't reply.

We came to Avenida Quinta, which was divided by a median and flanked with tropical trees and lined with mansions. A few taxis slowed, then drove on. "So, do we want a taxi to the hotel, or a taxi to Cayo?"

"We leave tomorrow night for Camagüey Province."

"Listen to me. Even if Antonio is wrong about the fleet being ordered to leave, or even if he's lying about the police arresting us, or us being on a watch list, let's assume he wasn't lying about the police investigating our backgrounds. And if the police discover the connection between me and Fishy Business, and if we leave for Camagüey tomorrow, by the time we get to Cayo Guillermo they'll be waiting there for us. And not only will they get us, they'll get the money. And the property deeds, and . . . whatever the other thing is." I asked, "Do you understand all of that? And do you understand what they will do to you in a Cuban prison?"

She stayed silent, then said, "You can go to Cayo Guillermo if you want. And when you get there, you can either wait for me, or you, Jack, and Felipe can sail off with my transportation home."

Well, whatever was driving her was too powerful to stop with logic, facts, or even fear. "All right . . . you've shamed me into keeping my promise."

"This will go well." She took my hand. "I feel safe with you."

I wish I could say the same.

She pointed up the avenue. "Over there is the Museum of the Ministry of the Interior, which is on our tour. The museum pokes fun at all the CIA's attempts to kill Castro."

"I'm surprised the exploding cigars didn't work."

"The history of American intervention in Cuba is a history of failure."

I had the same thought back in Key West.

"But we—you and I—are going to turn that around."

"Right. Taxi?"

She nodded.

I stepped into the street and hailed a passing cab, a nice late-model Toyota that didn't smell like bleu cheese.

I said to the driver, "Hotel Parque Central."

Sara said something to him and they had a brief conversation in Spanish. She said into my ear, "I asked him to take us to a casa particular in Vedado—a private house that rents rooms, usually with no questions asked." She added, "We don't want to risk a knock on the door tonight. And I don't want an early visit from Antonio." She took my hand. "We'll go back to the hotel in the morning and join the group. Then, after the group dinner, we retrieve my backpack and go to Camagüey."

"Okay."

The driver took the tunnel that went under the Río Almendares and drove into Vedado. Sara exchanged a few words with him, then said to me, "I told him—Tomás—that we were Canadian Embassy staff, married to other people, and we needed a very discreet casa that didn't ask for passports."

"I think you've done this before."

Well, to look the part, Sara put her arms around me and we started making out like caribou in heat. I glanced at Tomás, who was adjusting his rearview mirror. He didn't know Canadians were so hot.

Within a few minutes we pulled up to a small stucco house, nearly hidden by vegetation. Tomás got out and knocked on the door. The way our luck was running, this was probably Antonio's house.

An elderly lady came to the door, and she and Tomás exchanged words, then Tomás motioned for us to join them. We got out of the taxi and Sara and the old lady—Camila—chatted for a minute, and Sara said to me, "This is good. Give him a twenty."

I gave Tomás a month's pay, and he gave me a wink and wished us buenas noches. Camila didn't ask about luggage or passports and she invited us inside as she scanned the block, then closed the door and locked it.

The casa's front room was small and shabby, but neat and clean. On the wall was a nice black-and-white photograph of a young Fidel Castro. Camila showed us the baño and the small kitchen where, said Sara, we could have coffee in the morning, no charge. The price for the room was five CUCs, up front, and I gave Camila a ten, which made her happy, and she offered us some leftover rice and beans if we were hungry.

"Ask her if she has any Canadian Club."

Sara said something to her, and Camila poured us two glasses of rum, compliments of the house.

Camila showed us to our room, a tiny space filled with a double bed and a wooden bench. A small barred window let hot, humid air into the room. On the wall facing the bed—where the flat-screen TV should be—was a crucifix.

Camila smiled and wished us buenas noches and I bolted the door behind our hostess.

I asked, "Are we safe here?"

She motioned toward the crucifix. "He's watching over us."

But look what happened to him.

We clinked glasses and sipped our rum. "What would you like to do?" I asked.

"Get out of my clothes and have sex."

Just what I was thinking.

————

We lay in the dark room, naked and sweaty. "Aside from the money, what is it that we're here for?"

"The deeds and titles to the stolen properties."

"What else?"

"It's something that you will understand as soon as you see it."

"Is it worth risking our lives for?"

"Trust me, Mac."

"I do."

"Do you love me?"

"I came for money, but I'm staying for love."

She rolled on top of me. "We're going to have it all. Money, love, and . . . justice."

And hopefully a long life to enjoy it all.

CHAPTER 37

We rose before dawn, got dressed, and slipped quietly out of Señora Camila's four-star casa.

Sara said we weren't far from the Plaza of the Revolution, and we walked there to look for a taxi. There weren't many cars or people on the dark street, but a Policía Nacional Revolucionaria car slowed down, and the driver gave us the once-over. I was glad we didn't have the Glock.

We walked into the plaza and I could see the building that sported the metallic outline of Che Guevara, lit with spotlights. HASTA LA VICTORIA SIEMPRE.

Sara said, "That's the Ministry of the Interior—the ministry of torture and repression." She told me, "That's coming down when the regime falls. I've designed a beautiful building for that space."

"Good. That one's ugly."

"Uglier on the inside. And if you ever see the inside of that place, you'll never see the outside again."

I didn't doubt that. It seemed like a long time since my first day in Havana, when I'd had my picture taken in this plaza with Sara Ortega. If I'd known then what I know now . . . who knows?

Sara spotted a black Cadillac, maybe 1957, parked in the square, and we walked toward it.

I asked, "How do you want to handle Antonio's offer?"

"I have about fifteen hundred American dollars in the hotel safe that I'll give him this morning. I'll agree to give him three hundred thousand pesos tonight when he assures me . . . in my room . . . that we can get on the ship to Barbados." She added, "We just need to get through this day."

Antonio must be very pleased with himself. Getting laid and getting paid.

The Caddy driver was asleep, and we woke him and he took us to the Parque Central.

————

The breakfast room wasn't serving yet, but I snagged two cups of coffee and we took them up to my room.

There was no sign that the room had been entered or searched, and my travel guide and treasure map were still in my backpack.

Sara turned on the TV to Tele Rebelde and said, "I have a strong feeling that today is the day we meet our contact."

"Well, it's today or never."

"And if we don't . . . we have the map. That's all we need."

Well, a ride to Camagüey might help. But why mention it?

She finished her coffee. "I'll meet you in the breakfast room."

"Be nice to Antonio today."

"He doesn't expect me to be nice. He expects me to be good."

She left and I undressed and got into the shower, which was warm today. A sign from God.

————

I sat in the breakfast room with my coffee, waiting for Sara. Antonio was not there, but Tad was, and he got up from his table and came over. "How are you feeling?"

"I wish that toilet on the bus was working."

"We can stop at a farmacia and get you something."

"I just need some gummy rice. But thanks."

"Will Sara be joining us?"

"She will."

Tad sat, uninvited. "May I be honest with you?"

"Sure."

"You and Sara have missed a lot of this trip."

You ain't seen nothing yet.

"I need to file a final report with the Office of Foreign Assets Control, and your and Sara's absences, if they continue, can cause

the Yale educational travel group—and both of you—some problems."

"Sorry, Tad. I certainly don't want any problems with the Office
of Foreign Assets Control. But you understand that we're having
a ... sort of romance, and she—we—want some time alone."

"I understand that, but—"

"How are you doing with Alison?"

"But you've agreed to the conditions—"

"I promise that you won't have to worry about us for the rest
of the trip."

"All right. Thank you." He hesitated, then said, "Antonio has
asked me and Alison about both of you."

"Really?"

"Is there ... any problem I should know about?"

"That's very kind of you to ask."

"Well ... ?"

Well, this might be an opportunity to cover our tracks and also
cover our asses. "This is Cuba, Tad. And Sara Ortega is anti-Castro,
and Antonio is a chivato. Do you know what that is?"

"I do."

"So next time he asks about us, tell him to go fuck himself."

"I ..."

I leaned toward him. "If Sara and I should fail to appear one
morning, do us a favor and call the embassy."

Tad seemed speechless. And a bit pale. Finally, he said, "Maybe
you should leave the country."

"We're thinking about it."

"All right ... can I help?"

Tad was really okay. And I knew he'd call the embassy when
Sara and I didn't show up tomorrow morning. And the embassy
would call the Ministry of the Interior, who would deny having us
in their custody—which might be true, but maybe not. In any case,
I think I covered most of the bases, and gave Tad two plausible
reasons for our disappearance—prisoners of love or prisoners of
the state.

"Maybe you should visit the embassy today," he suggested.

That wasn't possible if Antonio was telling the truth about Sara and me being on a watch list, and in any case the embassy was only a Hail Mary option. Camagüey was the next stop. I said, "Maybe I'm just being paranoid."

"Well . . . this is Cuba . . ."

"Right. Do me a favor and don't mention this to anyone. You and I and Sara can talk tomorrow."

"All right."

"I hope my and Sara's problems don't get the group kicked out of the country."

He seemed distraught.

"I'm going to get some gummy rice. Would you like some?"

He looked at me. "No . . ." He stood. "I'm sorry about all this."

"Not your fault. And by the way, Lope is also a chivato and he understands English."

Tad looked a bit paler. He nodded and went back to his table and sat with Alison. I really didn't understand why he hadn't nailed her yet. Maybe he lacked self-confidence.

Sara came into the breakfast room, looking refreshed and pretty in tight white jeans, a blue Polo shirt, and a baseball cap—the same outfit she'd worn when she stepped onto my boat a million years ago. I recalled thinking how great it would be if we had sex.

She sat. "I'm starving."

"Let's get some gummy rice."

"Some . . . what?"

"Tad asked how we were feeling."

"Oh."

I filled her in about my conversation with Tad. I concluded, "Tad is aware that because of your bad attitude toward the regime, you and I may be in the crosshairs of the police."

"I'm not sure you should have told him that."

"When we don't show up for roll call tomorrow morning, he'll contact the embassy and tell them what I just told him."

"I like the original plan of leaving him a note saying we went to the beach and we'll be back in time for the return flight."

"That's Plan A. Plan B covers the possibility that we might become guests of the Ministry of the Interior."

She stayed silent awhile, then said, "You're either very smart,
or . . . you're outsmarting yourself."

"I know the answer to that."

"You need to consult me before you change the plan."

"Tactics and strategy need to change in quick response to bat-
tlefield realities. That's why you hired me."

She nodded.

"Did you leave an envelope for Antonio?"

"I did. My last dollars."

"I know where there's more."

She stood. "Are you getting breakfast?"

"Just bring me some gummy rice. And get some for yourself."

Sara went to the buffet.

I sipped my coffee. In the civilian world, we say that life is about
choices. In the military, we use the word "decisions," which seem
to have more weight, and more consequences, than choices. In the
case of choices, the right ones will eventually make you healthy,
wealthy, and happy. With decisions, the wrong ones have a way of
being instantly unforgiving.

Well, if I was going to die here, it wouldn't be because I got
blindsided by some asshole with a rocket-propelled grenade; it
would be because I made a few bad decisions, the first being to let
Sara Ortega make bad choices.

And yet . . . Sara had that one thing that was indispensable for
success in life and in battle—self-confidence. And also a belief that
God and justice were on her side. So how could I go wrong following her to the end of the rainbow, where sixty million dollars sat in
a cave waiting for us? Teamwork makes the dream work.

CHAPTER 38

Sara and I sat in the middle of the bus. José was our driver again, and Antonio hopped aboard with a new spring in his step and six years' pay in his pocket, with visions of more in his head. Not to mention his date with the insolent and beautiful Sara Ortega. He'd show the Miami Beach Bitch who was boss.

"Today," said Antonio, "we go to the Forbidden Zone." He explained, "Vedado means 'Forbidden Zone,' and in the old days Vedado was a hunting preserve outside the city walls of Havana, reserved exclusively for the upper classes."

Who gives a shit?

Antonio prattled on as the bus made its way along the Malecón into the Vedado district. Now and then he would try to make eye contact with me, maybe to assure himself that we had a deal. Or maybe to let me know that when he was fucking Sara, he was also fucking me. He barely looked at Sara. Asshole.

Tad sat quietly and seemed to be still distraught. He glanced at Antonio a few times, seeing him in a different light. Tad had discovered Cuba for himself—and it wasn't all about the rhumba.

Sara took my hand. "We're halfway home."

So was Amelia Earhart.

We drove past the Monument to the Victims of The Maine, and Antonio said, "After the failed Bay of Pigs Invasion, the people of Havana ripped the American eagle from the monument, and there is now a plaque there that reads: 'To the victims of The Maine, who were sacrificed by imperialist greed in its eagerness to seize the island of Cuba.'"

Must be something lost in the translation.

We passed by the Plaza of Dignity, which included the Anti-Imperialist Forum, and this inspired Antonio to go into an anti-imperialist spiel.

Antonio, as I always suspected, was a Commie for convenience, an opportunistic chivato, an enthusiastic scammer, and a full-time amoral pig. I would have no problem putting a bullet in his head.

We drove past the American Embassy and I noticed the Cuban police who were posted outside the gates. Quite possibly they had my and Sara's names on a list, and our photos from the airport. We weren't exactly on the lam yet, or on the most wanted list, but if we believed Antonio, we weren't getting into our embassy—or out of this country—without his help.

"And now," said Antonio, "on your right you will see the statue of Lenin," which turned out to be John Lennon, not Vladimir Lenin. The Yalies laughed and Antonio smiled. He was in a good mood this morning.

The bus zigzagged through the streets of Vedado so that we could see and appreciate the accomplishments of Cuban socialism, and we stopped at a memorial to the American Communist spies Julius and Ethel Rosenberg, which I had always wanted to see.

The bus drove through the gates of a huge cemetery, the Necrópolis Cristóbal Colón, a.k.a. Christopher Columbus, which held, said Antonio, over five hundred major mausoleums, chapels, vaults, and galleries, and thousands of tombstones. If I had my Glock, this would be a good place to whack Antonio. Not that it would solve any problems. But it would make me feel good.

"The rich and famous, the colonial aristocrats, the war heroes, the merchants, the artists and writers—they all rest here alongside the martyrs of the revolution," said Antonio as though he were trying to sell us a plot. "In the end, death is the great equalizer."

Indeed it is.

The bus continued slowly through the vast marble orchard, past Greco-Roman temples, miniature castles, and mausoleums embellished with cherubs and angels, and even an Egyptian pyramid. It occurred to me that the dead of Havana had better housing than the living.

The bus stopped in a plaza near a Byzantine-styled church, and we all got off.

Antonio gave us his cemetery lecture, peppered with Marxist observations about the extravagance of the rich, even in death. Turns out you *can* take it with you.

Antonio said, "You may explore on your own. Please be back on the bus in thirty minutes." He added, "Miss Ortega, I don't want to come looking for you." He smiled, and a few of the Yalies laughed.

Sara did not reply to Antonio, but said to me, "I'd actually like to meet him in my room tonight."

I pictured Antonio in Sara's bed with the lamp cord wrapped around his nuts and the other end plugged into the socket. I said, "The best revenge is leaving him standing at your door with a deflated ego and an inflated pepino."

She smiled.

The Yale group separated into smaller groups and began wandering through the cemetery, which was laid out in a grid with wide avenidas, calles, and plazas, the city of the dead.

Sara took my arm and led me past an imposing mausoleum of the Spanish royal family to a smaller burial vault whose inscription read: <u>AMELIA GOYRI DE LA HOZ</u>. Carved in marble was the figure of a woman with a baby in her arms. About a dozen people stood or knelt around the tomb, which was piled with hundreds of fresh flowers.

Sara said, "This is the tomb of La Milagrosa—the Miraculous One."

"Right."

"She died in childbirth on May 3, 1901, and was buried here with her stillborn child at her feet. For many years after her death her grieving husband visited the grave several times a day. He would always take hold of one of those brass rings on the tomb and knock when he arrived, then back away as he left so he could see her resting place for as long as possible."

In fact, a number of people who approached the tomb were doing just that.

Sara stood silently, looking at the tomb, then said, "After her husband died, Amelia's sarcophagus was opened and her body was found to be incorrupt—a sign of sanctity in the Catholic faith. And the baby that had been laid at her feet was now found cradled in her arms."

Okay.

"Since then, she has been called La Milagrosa, and if you pray to her for a miracle, it will be granted."

We should have come here sooner.

Sara approached the tomb, knocked three times with the brass ring, then knelt with a dozen others, mostly women. She prayed, made the sign of the cross, then stood and walked away backward, still facing the tomb.

She took my arm and we strolled down a tree-shaded lane between the tombs and statues. She said, "Many childless women pray at Señora Goyri's tomb for a pregnancy."

"Excuse me, but that's not a miracle I would have prayed for."

She smiled. "Relax. I prayed for a successful mission and a safe journey home."

That would be a miracle.

We wandered around the necropolis, which was filled with tour groups, and every time we passed some of our Yale group, I said to Sara, "I see dead people."

She didn't think that was funny, but she seemed in a better mood than last night after Antonio's proposition. In fact, she said, "I'm happy to put Havana behind us and get on the road to Camagüey."

"Assuming we don't meet our Havana contact in the next few hours, how do we get to Camagüey?"

"Carlos had a contingency plan."

"Which is?"

"A livery service in Miramar used by foreign business people that will take us anywhere we want to go in Cuba. Cash, no questions asked, and no record of the trip."

I wish I'd known this last night, when I was trying to talk her into taking a taxi to Cayo Guillermo.

Sara added, "When we get to Camagüey, we become backpackers—and cave explorers."

"Okay. And how do we get the dozen steamer trunks to Cayo Guillermo?"

"You steal a truck."

"Right."

"From Camagüey to Cayo is about a hundred and eighty miles. We can make that in three or four hours."

"And what do we do when we get to Cayo Guillermo?"

She stayed silent a moment, then replied, "We go to a resort hotel called the Melia and sit in the lobby bar."

Well, I knew that *someone* must know what Sara and I were supposed to do in Cayo Guillermo. Turns out it's Sara.

"At seven P.M. each day, starting last night, there will be someone in the lobby bar who knows what we look like and who will approach us."

"ID phrase?"

"He—or she—will say, 'It's good to see you here.'"

Indeed it would be.

"He or she will tell us the plan to get the goods onboard The Maine."

"Okay."

Sara continued, "The Melia Hotel's clientele are mostly European and Canadian tourists, so we'll fit in."

"And where do we park the truck with sixty million dollars while we're having a drink?"

"I'm told we can see the hotel parking area from the lobby bar. Or you can stay in the truck with your gun."

"Can I get a roadie?"

"We'll play this by ear when we get to the hotel."

I had more questions, but she'd told me enough—the last piece of this plan—to carry on without her, which was why she was telling me this. "Okay. I get it."

She took my hand and we continued through the quiet cemetery, then turned back toward where the bus was parked.

Aside from the tomb of La Milagrosa, there weren't many locals visiting graves on this Monday morning, and we were alone on the path except for a guy in a black shirt coming toward us. He was about thirty, tall and lean, and he wore wraparound sunglasses. I said to Sara, "I saw that guy near the bus."

She looked at him as he approached, then let go of my hand and we slowed our pace.

As the guy got within ten feet of us, he looked around, then stopped.

Well, I didn't want my back to this guy, so we, too, stopped, about five feet from him. The three of us stood there, then Sara said to him, "Buenos días."

He returned the greeting, then said to her in English, "Are you interested in Cuban pottery?"

CHAPTER 39

As the bus made its way from the cemetery to the Parque Central, Tad reminded us that our afternoon was on our own—for meaningful independent cultural experiences—until our 5 P.M. lecture given by Professor Nalebuff. Then to dinner at 6:30 at Mama Inés.

"Chef Erasmo," said Antonio, "has cooked for Fidel Castro and Hugo Chávez. Also Jane Fonda, Jack Nicholson, and Jimmy Carter."

All of whom got the senior citizen discount.

Well, our much-anticipated meeting with our man in Havana wasn't as interesting as Sara's meeting with Marcelo on the Malecón. Our guy just handed Sara a flyer advertising a nightclub called Cabaret Las Vegas. This is the kind of thing you toss in the next trash can, but the man said the magic words, so Sara scanned the flyer as we walked toward the bus, then handed it to me.

Written in pencil on the flyer was an address: *Calle 37 No 570, El Vedado.* And a time, *22 h,* which five years in the Army taught me meant 10 P.M.

Sara said that this would be where we would meet our Havana contact, who would give us our instructions for meeting our contact in Camagüey, and provide our means of transportation.

Or sell us pottery. I asked, "Should we thank La Milagrosa for this timely miracle?"

"I already have."

"Right."

We committed the address to memory and Sara made confetti

out of the flyer and dropped it into a storm drain on our way to the bus. As we boarded, Antonio said to Sara and me, "We will meet in the rear of the lobby."

My dance card was filling up.

———

Our tour bus pulled up to the Hotel Parque Central and Alison advised, "Dress at Mama Inés is casual."

Which was good, because we'd be living and sleeping in the same clothes for awhile.

We filed off the bus and Sara and I walked to the rear of the lobby, where Antonio joined us. Tad noticed, and he hesitated before he got on the elevator. I was sure this was going to be his last trip to Cuba. Mine, too.

Antonio looked at Sara. "Thank you for the envelope." He patted the side pocket of his tight black pants. "And I have good news for you. I made calls last night and you will be expected at the Sierra Maestra Cruise Terminal tomorrow morning at seven." He glanced around and said in a conspiratorial voice, "A man named Ramón will meet you at the entrance and walk you through passport control and onto the British cruise ship The Braemar, which sails at nine for Bridgetown in Barbados." He looked at Sara. "I assume you wish to be on that ship?"

She nodded. "We do."

"Good. You will be ticketed onboard and pay for your passage with a credit card." He smiled. "I am your travel agent. And your guardian angel who will give Ramón a thousand dollars to pay people who will get you through security."

The only possible response to all that bullshit was, "Muchas gracias."

"De nada." He continued, "It's a two-day cruise to Bridgetown, and when you arrive there"—he smiled again—"you can continue your Caribbean holiday in Barbados."

Nothing could top my Cuba vacation.

He advised us, "You should leave a message for Tad and Alison tomorrow morning that you are not feeling well and will remain in your rooms."

"We know that."

"Also, it would not be good for you to be seen leaving the hotel with your luggage, so you will leave it in your rooms, as though you are going out for a morning walk."

"Good thinking."

"You can buy what you need on the ship."

Actually, we'll be on our way to Camagüey Province to find sixty million dollars. And Antonio would be explaining to his police pals that the two Americanos disappeared during the night. Maybe they'd beat him up.

"Ramón has a description of you both. He is a short man, about sixty years old, and he will be wearing the green uniform of the security guards."

But he's actually an undercover agent for the Ministry of the Interior, and he has our photos from the airport.

"All you will need are your passports and your exit visas." He asked, "Do you have any questions?"

"No."

He looked at us and said, insincerely, "I'm sorry about this, but you have been caught up in historical events—a chess game played in Havana and Washington—and you are the innocent pawns."

No, we're actually guilty of something, but you don't know what it is, asshole.

He informed us, "I need to see Ramón tonight, so I will not be at the dinner, but . . ." He glanced at me, then said to Sara, "I think I will see you later for the three hundred thousand pesos."

What a deal. He gets laid, gets paid, and walks away, leaving us to get arrested.

Sara said to him, "I will see you later." Then she said something to him in Spanish.

Antonio nodded, then looked at me. "I don't think I should apologize. Do you?"

"I think you should leave."

But he didn't and said, "This is Cuba. My country. And you are lucky I am getting you out of here. So instead of your arrogance, I think perhaps you should thank me."

Well, since he wasn't going to fuck Sara, and since we were going to fuck him, I said, "Thank you." I added, "Gracias."

"De nada." He smiled, then said to Sara, "I look forward to tonight," and left.

She said softly, "I hate him."

"Put the hate on hold." Though, to be honest, if I had him alone I'd probably snap his neck. I asked her, "What time are you entertaining Antonio?"

"I confirmed midnight."

Well, that would give us a little head start in getting out of Havana.

I asked her, "What other meaningful Cuban cultural experience would you like to have now?"

"We need to get my backpack."

"Right. And we need to recon Calle 37."

We went out into the heat of the city and took a Coco cab to the Vedado district, then walked to Calle 37, which was a street of nondescript buildings that looked like warehouses or auto repair shops. Number 570 was a ramshackle stucco building with an old wooden barn-like garage door, barred windows, and a rusty steel entrance door.

Sara said, "This looks like a place where there'd be a vehicle for us."

I was reminded of the garage where the St. Valentine's Day Massacre took place, but I didn't share that thought with her.

There was no possibility that we were being watched or followed, so we headed toward Rolando's to retrieve her backpack.

It was a fifteen-minute walk to the residential district, which appeared different in the daylight but no less deserted, and we still looked like we didn't belong there. It was possible, I thought, that we'd been seen last night by the ubiquitous neighborhood vigilantes and chivatos, and that the police were staking out the area and waiting for us behind the wall. *So, señor and señorita, are you looking for this backpack with the gun and the pesos?* I mentioned this to Sara and she replied, "Chivatos turn in their friends and neighbors to the police, but they'd never turn in any evidence of a crime if it was worth more than two dollars."

Right. In other words, if you see something, say something—unless you see that it's worth money. Patriotism doesn't buy the beans.

The low wall came into view and Sara suddenly picked up her pace, vaulted over the wall, then reappeared a few seconds later with the backpack, scrambled onto the sidewalk, and kept walking. The police did not pop out of the bushes.

As we headed for the bridge over the Río Almendares, I pulled the Glock out of her backpack and stuck it in my belt under my Polo shirt. We were traveling hot again.

As we crossed the bridge, I wrestled with the idea of dropping the hot gun in the cool river. But then I thought about our meeting tonight in the St. Valentine's Day Massacre garage, and our road trip into the Cuban heart of darkness, and our rendezvous in Cayo—and I recalled Jack's wise T-shirt words, "Better to have a gun and not need it than to need a gun and not have it."

We looked less conspicuous in Miramar, and we retraced our path to Avenida Quinta and hailed a taxi. We were back at the hotel by four o'clock, hot, sweaty, and tired, but happy in the way that a successful but uneventful recon patrol makes you feel.

———

Sara went to her room to shower and change into clothes that would be appropriate for both the Mama Inés restaurant and what could be a week in the boondocks, trying to look like a backpacker. I did the same, saying adios to my discount luggage and dirty clothes except for my sweat-stained Hemingway T-shirt, which I put in a plastic bag and stuffed in my backpack.

I strapped on my fanny pack containing the Glock and the extra magazines and left the room with a DO NOT DISTURB sign on the door, then went down to the meeting room where the Yalies were assembling for Professor Nalebuff's lecture on Cuban-

American relations. On his next trip here Nalebuff could add a footnote about Dan MacCormick and Sara Ortega. Arrested and executed? Or escaped with the Batista-era loot and living happily ever after? I took a seat and waited for Sara.

Professor Nalebuff took the podium and began, "This is the story of David and Goliath, Cuba and America. It is the story of a long love-hate relationship that spans the centuries, a story that is both heartbreaking and hopeful."

I noticed that Richard Neville was taking notes, and I had no doubt that Professor Nalebuff's eloquent words would find their way into Neville's next novel. Plagiarism is the sincerest form of flattery.

Sara appeared at the door with her backpack, wearing black jeans, a dark green T-shirt, and hiking boots, and she had her shoulder bag, presumably packed with pesos. I was similarly dressed in blue jeans, a gray gym shirt, and boots. Our backpacks didn't draw any attention because some of our group carried their packs on the bus, day and night.

Sara sat next to me and I asked, "Did you pack a bathing suit?"

So we listened to Professor Nalebuff tell us, in scholarly language, what I'd concluded before I even got here—Cuba and America had been fucking each other so long that we both must be getting something out of it.

Professor Nalebuff concluded, "If both sides act with goodwill, and if neither country causes or exploits a diplomatic incident, the future looks promising."

Should I tell him that the diplomatic incident was sitting in front of him?

———

As Sara and I descended the sweeping staircase into the lobby, she said, "Since we're not coming back tonight, we need to leave a note now for Tad and Alison to get in the morning."

"No note. Let them think we may have been detained by the police." I added, "Which may be true."

She didn't reply.

As the Yalies filed out of the hotel to board the bus, I stopped at the front desk, took the plastic bag out of my backpack, and gave it to the desk clerk. "This is for Señor Neville. Please have it delivered to his room tonight." I gave the clerk a five.

"Si, señor." He made a note of it and asked, "Your name?"

"He'll know who it's from."

Sara and I exited the hotel, and she asked me, "What was that?"

"My Hemingway T-shirt."

"This is no time for jokes."

"It's good for my head."

"You need to grow up."

"I'm sorry I didn't have an exploding cigar to leave for Antonio." I asked her, "Did you leave a note in your room for him?"

"I left a 'Do Not Disturb' sign on the door."

I pictured Antonio arriving at midnight with a smile and a stiffy. Sorry, amigo. Go fuck yourself.

We boarded the bus and I saw that the driver was now Lope— Antonio's eyes and ears when he was absent. Well, that could be a problem when Sara and I didn't return to the bus after dinner. But I had a new teammate—Tad—who would cover for us. Or at least give us a head start.

Tad did a head count and the bus pulled away.

Within ten minutes we were in the Old Town, and we pulled up to Mama Inés restaurant, which was located in a colonial building a few blocks from the Sierra Maestra Cruise Terminal where Sara and I were expected at 7 in the morning. But we had other travel plans—if all went well at Calle 37.

The restaurant was dark and crowded, and the Yale group was assigned several tables. Sara and I found ourselves sitting with two young couples who should have been wearing T-shirts that said: "Clueless." We made small talk and I was surprised to discover that these college-educated Americans didn't completely comprehend that Cuba was a police state.

I changed the subject to sports, and as we waited for our drinks,

Sara commented that she and I were going to take a walk along the Malecón after dinner and share a bottle of wine on the beach—which accounted for our backpacks if anyone wondered.

Mama Inés' clientele, aside from the Yale group, looked like Europeans and some Latin Americans with money. The last Cuban who could afford this place was probably Fidel Castro. More importantly, I didn't see anyone who looked like they were interested in us.

Dinner was good and our four tablemates got smarter with rum, and one of them told us that Cuba was a Communist country.

Sara glanced at her watch and said in my ear, "Let's leave."

"It's early for our ten o'clock."

"I want to take a last walk through the Old Town."

"Okay."

We stood, wished everyone a good evening, and collected our backpacks. I went to Tad's table where he was sitting with Professor Nalebuff, the Nevilles, and Alison. I was actually going to miss them. I congratulated the professor on an informative lecture and told Tad and Alison, "Sara and I are going to take a walk on the Malecón, so we won't be on the bus."

Tad looked at me with concern. "Be careful."

I reminded him, "Havana is a safe city."

He had no reply, but Alison, who I was sure had been briefed by Tad, said to us, "Don't stay out too late."

"We'll stay hydrated," I assured her. I said to the Nevilles, "You should try a place called Rolando's tonight, in the Vedado district. Very authentic. Forty-cent drinks and no Hemingway."

Cindy Neville gave me a nice smile. Richard grunted.

I asked Tad, "What's on the agenda tomorrow?"

"It's in your itinerary. The Museo de Bellas Artes, then a tobacco farm in the afternoon."

We were getting out of here none too soon. "See you in the morning." I really hoped Alison and Tad hooked up. Life is short.

We left Mama Inés, and also left behind our new alum chums,

who, without their knowing, had provided us with some laughs, good cover, and even some degree of safety in the herd.

So, I'd had my last lecture in Havana, my last meeting with Antonio, and my last supper. We were now on the road to Camagüey, Cayo, and home. Hopefully richer and definitely wiser.

Our bus was parked down the street, and we turned in the opposite direction and began walking through the Old Town, toward the Forbidden Zone.

CHAPTER 40

We walked down Calle Obispo, past the Last National Bank of Grandpa, then past Sara's ancestral home for what was most likely the last time in either of our lives. We also passed by Floridita, the scene of one of our many fateful—and probably stupid—decisions that had brought us to this moment.

I had no sense that we were being followed, but outside of Floridita were two black-bereted policemen who gave us the once-over as we passed by, reminding me that Sara attracted attention and that I was carrying a gun that would put me away for a decade or two.

Sara, too, realized we were shiny fish among sharks and said, "We need a taxi."

"Right." I spotted a blue Chevy Impala, circa 1958, cruising the street and I waved him down.

She said to me, "There's actually something I wanted you to see before we leave Havana."

There was really nothing in this city that I wanted to see except 570 Calle 37, but we had time. "Okay."

We got into the plush rear seat of the big old Impala and Sara exchanged a few words with the young driver, Paco, then said to me, "I told him we want to sightsee. He gets thirty dollars an hour."

"How much does he charge to outrun the police?"

"With or without a shoot-out?"

Funny. I liked Sara Ortega.

Sara spoke to Paco and we drove out of the Old Town, onto Avenida Salvador Allende, then toward the Plaza of the Revolution. I was starting to get to know the city, and when that happens in a screwed-up place, it's time to leave. Also, there were so many streets named for revolutionary dates—Avenida 20 de Mayo, Calle 19 de Mayo—that you needed a calendar instead of a road map.

Anyway, we cruised past the Plaza of the Revolution and headed south, toward the airport. "Where are we going?"

"You'll see."

We continued south and within fifteen minutes were in a district of the city called 10 October, another date that will live in obscurity.

Paco seemed as mystified as I was about why we were in this nondescript suburb, but Sara was directing him through the dark streets, and she said to him, "Calle La Vibora," then to me, "The Street of the Viper."

I'll bet this isn't on the Yale tour.

We came to a long iron fence on our right, and beyond the fence I could see a complex of tan-colored buildings set among palm trees and open lawns, which looked like a college campus.

Paco seemed to recognize the complex and he glanced quizzically at Sara, who said, "Dobla a la derecha." He turned right, and she said, "Detente," but Paco kept going, and Sara said, "Detente!" and he stopped.

She told him to wait, then took her shoulder bag and backpack and got out of the car. I did the same and we stood near the front gates, where four uniformed men stood with submachine guns. The sign out front said: MINISTERIO DEL INTERIOR, and DPTO. SEGURIDAD DEL ESTADO, which I translated as Department of State Security.

I asked, "What is this place?"

"Villa Marista prison."

She crossed the Street of the Viper and I followed her to the other side, putting some distance between ourselves and the guards.

Paco was still stopped near the main gate, close to the guards, but he suddenly took off like he was wanted for something. He drove down the street, but then did a U-turn and stopped a few hundred feet from us and shut off his lights.

Sara was staring at the prison, and I inquired, "Why are we here?"

"I wanted you to see this."

"Okay. I see it. Let's go."

But she stood where she was and said, "This is where we could wind up—if we ever made it out of the Ministry of the Interior in Revolution Plaza."

"Actually, we could wind up here now if those guards come across the street and ask what we're doing here and what's in our backpacks."

"Fuck them."

Sara was going into her Fuck Them I Hate Them mode. Not good.

She said, "Villa Marista was originally a Catholic boys' school, run by the Marist Brothers."

Now it's run by the Castro Brothers.

"The regime expropriated the school and kicked out the Marists and the students, and turned this campus into a hell on earth."

Which it may have already been when it was a Catholic boys' school.

"It's a pleasant-looking place, so you wouldn't know what goes on in there." So she told me, "Physical and psychological torture . . . things that destroy the soul before the bullet is fired into the back of your head."

I glanced at the four armed guards, who were looking at us, then glanced at the Chevy to make sure it was still there.

"The State Security Police are headquartered here, and the prison holds no criminals—only political prisoners. Enemies of the state. There are no visitors allowed, and the few prisoners who are released from here are the walking dead. Examples to others who might dare to oppose the regime."

I put my hand on Sara's shoulder and said, "Paco is waiting."

But she continued, "In the early 1960s, Castro invited the Soviet KGB to Villa Marista to teach the State Security Police the finer points of psychological torture and interrogation using psychoactive drugs. Then the Cuban torturers were sent to Vietnam to continue their practice on American prisoners of war in the Hanoi Hilton and other North Vietnamese prisons. The torturers then came back to Cuba."

I recalled what Carlos said on my boat about Villa Marista and I knew what Sara was going to say.

"They brought with them seventeen American POWs who were secretly imprisoned in Villa Marista for advanced experiments with drugs."

It was hard to imagine being taken prisoner in Vietnam, tortured there, then being shipped to Cuba for more of the same. And these men must have known they were less than a hundred miles from America. And that they would never go home.

Sara continued, "Most of these seventeen men died, or were as good as dead, and those who survived were shot here in 1973 when the Vietnam War ended. The American POWs in Vietnam were returned home, but these seventeen soldiers and airmen in Villa Marista were listed by the Pentagon as missing in action, though there is solid evidence that they had once been prisoners in North Vietnam—one of them was even identified in a photograph that showed Fidel Castro visiting a prisoner-of-war camp in North Vietnam. And now we know, from Cuban prison guards who have defected to the U.S., that these missing American POWs were *here*, died here, or were murdered here, and were buried in an unmarked common grave on the grounds of Villa Marista."

If I actually had post-traumatic stress disorder, something like this could spark an episode. In fact, I had a brief flashback to a moment when . . . if one or two things had gone differently, I'd have been in the hands of the Taliban . . . or . . . I'd have put a bullet in my head.

Sara glanced at me. "I thought that you, as a veteran, would want to say a prayer for the souls of these seventeen American prisoners of war who died here, alone and with no one knowing their fate."

She took my hand and we bowed our heads. We didn't have

many missing men in the Afghan war, but I thought of the nearly two thousand men who were still missing in Vietnam, and I thought of Jack, and my father, and the other men I knew who'd served in that war. And I prayed for all of them. Which I had never done before.

One of the prison guards began shouting at us and making menacing motions with his rifle.

Sara said softly, "Amen," then, "Fuck him." She retrieved her cell phone from her shoulder bag and took a photo of me with Villa Marista prison in the background. "So you'll remember."

The guard was not happy.

We turned and walked down the street toward our waiting car.

She asked, "Do you understand why we came here?"

"To honor the dead."

She didn't reply, and as we walked, I recalled what she had said outside the Catedral de San Cristóbal: *The bones need to come home . . .* , which, now that I was here, made more sense if it was *these* bones, not Christopher Columbus' bones, that she was referring to. I recalled again Carlos' words on my boat about Villa Marista, which I'd thought was just an offhand remark. And Sara's words in bed. *You'll be very pleased with the other reason we're here.* And what I concluded from all this was that the Cuban exile groups who were opposed to the Thaw had plans to rekindle these unconfirmed stories about American POWs being tortured and murdered in Cuba, and to demand the return of the bodies—and to fire up the American public and the politicians and upset the ongoing diplomatic negotiations.

"Do you understand?"

"I think I do. But . . ."

"More later."

There always is.

CHAPTER 41

Sara told Paco to take us to Bollywood, an Indian restaurant on Calle 35, which she'd chosen for the location, not the cuisine.

Paco dropped us off and I gave him a hundred CUCs, which he had earned for not abandoning us at Villa Marista. And if he was a rat and called the police, they'd be looking for us at Bollywood. Staying ahead of the police in a police state was an intellectual challenge. And a bit of twisted fun.

Paco pulled away and I looked at my watch. We had ten minutes to walk to Calle 37, Number 570. If this was a Cuban Monopoly game, we'd just gotten out of jail free, and I hoped the next card we drew at Calle 37 said *Go to Camagüey and Collect Sixty Million Dollars.*

Sara and I walked in silence through the dark streets, then she said, "I went to Villa Marista the last time I was here . . . It is the evil heart of an evil monster." She added, "The world needs to know."

"Right." But does the world—or the American public or the politicians—care enough to cause a major rift in the ongoing diplomatic negotiations? If we actually had the names of those seventeen men, then, yes, it would be big news. Well, more later, as Sara said.

We reached Calle 37 and began walking toward 570 at the end of the dimly lit block. I took the Glock out of my fanny pack and stuck it under my shirt.

As we approached the garage I noticed a movement in the shadows under the flickering streetlight, and as we got closer I saw a man sitting in a chair near the steel door. Sara and I continued at the same pace and now I could hear music—"Dos Gardenias"— coming from somewhere.

We stopped a few feet from the man in the chair, who was smoking a cigar, drinking a Bucanero, and listening to an old tape player that sat on the sidewalk. He seemed lost in the music, and Sara said, "Buenas noches."

He turned his head toward us. "Buenas noches."

The guy was old, with white hair and white stubble on his face, and he wore a tank top that was wet with sweat or beer. A walking cane leaned against the wall.

He drew on his cigar and asked in English, "What are you looking for?"

Sara replied, "Pottery."

He nodded. "You have come to the right place."

That's always good to hear when you're in a foreign city, walking at night to an address that a strange man handed to you in a cemetery.

The old man—obviously the lookout—grabbed the walking cane and smacked it hard three times against the steel door, then said, "Go in. They are waiting for you."

High-tech security. I led the way, and as I passed the old man he tapped my stomach with his cane and said, "You don't need that," referring to my gun, not my gut. Well, I liked the Glock where it was and I opened the rusty door, which creaked on cue. Sara was right behind me and I heard the old man say, "Bolt the door."

Sara bolted the door as I peered into the dimly lit space, and as my eyes adjusted to the darkness I could see that this was indeed a garage, or an auto repair shop. Car parts—mufflers, exhaust pipes, hoods, and doors—lay strewn on the floor, and acetylene torches sat on a work bench. An engine hung from the ceiling on chains, reminding me for some reason of the Texas Chainsaw Massacre. If it wasn't for my Glock, this could be a scary place.

I spotted a movement at the far end of the shop and saw two men coming toward us. One of them said in English, "Welcome to Chico's Chop Shop." The other man said nothing.

Sara strode toward them—getting in the way of my line of fire—and they all shook hands and chatted in Spanish as I covered the rear and checked out the dark corners in the cavernous space. I noticed a few motorcycles, which might be our transportation to Camagüey.

Sara and her new friends came toward me and she introduced me to Chico, a scruffily dressed man of about fifty with recently degreased hands, and a younger guy named Flavio, who was neatly dressed, handsome, and clearly nervous about something. Nervous people make me nervous.

Chico said to me, in nearly perfect English, "I have a car for you. Do you have a hundred and fifty thousand pesos for me?"

Recalling that Cubans liked clever conversation, I replied, "Is this an authorized dealership?"

He laughed. "He told me you had a sense of humor."

"Who told you?"

He didn't reply and led me and Sara across the shop to an old Buick station wagon. Flavio stayed behind.

"This is a beauty," said Chico, sounding like he'd once worked in a used car lot in Miami. "A real cream puff. A piece of history."

Actually, it looked like a piece of shit.

"It's a fifty-three Roadmaster Estate Wagon. I got it from a little old lady in Miramar who only drove it on weekends since her husband was arrested in 1959." He laughed.

Did I just enter the Twilight Zone?

I asked, "Does this thing run?"

"Like a rabbit. Take a look."

Sara and I slipped off our backpacks and moved closer to the Buick wagon, which had recently been spray-painted in black, except for the original wood paneling that looked like it might have termites. The iconic Buick chromework was pitted, but none of the windows were broken and the headlights and taillights were intact. I asked, "Who are these plates registered to?"

"The little old lady." He added, "They're not hot."

I didn't reply.

He assured me, "This is not the U.S., señor. The police don't have computers in their cars to check plates." He also assured me, "You won't get stopped."

Famous last words.

I glanced around the shop. "You got anything newer? Like a red Porsche convertible?"

"For another hundred thousand pesos, I got a ten-year-old Honda Civic. But they told me you needed a wagon, or a van or an SUV."

"Who told you—?"

"Because you got some stuff to haul."

Obviously this station wagon couldn't haul a dozen steamer trunks. "What stuff?"

"How do I know?" He opened the Buick's hood and said, "Take a look at this motor. You know what this is?"

I peered under the hood. "No. Do you?"

"It's a Perkins ninety-horsepower boat motor. Completely rebuilt." Chico smiled. "I got the suspension from a Russian military jeep, and I rebuilt the steering with some Kia parts. The transmission is from a Hyundai, five years old, the shocks are from a Renault truck, and the disc brakes are from a Mercedes." He informed me, "This is what we call a Frankenstein car."

"Because it kills people?"

He laughed and said to Sara, "He's funny."

She had no response.

I looked at the tires. "How's the rubber?"

"Tires are something you can buy new in Cuba. You got four Goodyears imported from Mexico. Cost me a fortune. Don't kick them."

"Spare?"

"Don't get a flat."

Chico opened the driver's door. "The interior is original."

"I see that."

"Sorry, the interior lights don't work." He slid behind the wheel and hit the brakes. "See the brake lights?"

"I do."

He demonstrated that the turn signals and headlights also worked, then started the engine, which sounded good, though I wasn't sure the 90-horsepower could move this monster.

Chico called out over the sound of the engine, "Purrs like a kitten."

"Can I take it for a test drive?"

"Sure. After you buy it." He turned on the windshield wipers, then blasted the horn and shouted, "Get that donkey outta my way!"

The man was obviously nuts, but he seemed like the happiest man I'd seen in Havana. And I guess that was because Chico worked for Chico.

He shut off the engine and slid out of the car. "Okay, keys are in there. You got a full tank of gas, but the gauge reads empty. None of the instruments work, but you don't need them. Radio works, but the tubes are a little loose, so it might cut out when you hit a bump. Give it a whack. It has a cigarette lighter that still works."

"Where is the air-conditioner control?"

"In the Honda." He laughed.

Well, we could do this all night, but we were both running out of one-liners. I looked at Sara, who nodded.

I asked Chico, "Can you do better than one-fifty?"

"If I restored her, I could sell her for five hundred thousand. Only six hundred of these babies made in Detroit. As is, she's yours for one-fifty." He added, "That includes sales tax and dealer prep." He laughed.

"Okay . . . sold."

"You got a beauty there."

"Right." Bride of Frankenstein.

"Come into my office."

Sara and I followed Chico to a table in the rear of his man cave. Flavio seemed to have disappeared.

Chico slid some beer bottles and coffee cups to the side. "Hundred and fifty. Gas is on me."

Sara pulled a wad of five-hundred-peso notes from her shoulder bag and she and Chico began counting.

Well, we had a vehicle that could hopefully get us to Camagüey, but we didn't have a name or address in Camagüey, and I didn't think Chico had that for us. Maybe Flavio. This wasn't playing out as I'd imagined, but nothing had so far—including us needing a station wagon to haul something. Maybe pickaxes for the cave.

Sara and Chico re-counted the equivalent of about six thousand dollars, leaving us enough, I guess, to give to our contact in Camagüey for the truck we'd need to transport the dozen steamer trunks to Cayo Guillermo. Which, now that I saw Chico's sub rosa chop shop, raised the question of why Chico wasn't told we needed a truck. I mean, this guy could build a sixteen-wheeler out of Legos. There was something missing here. Like who told Chico I had a sense of humor.

The recount was done and we all shook hands as Chico stuffed the pesos in his pockets.

I asked him, "Does this vehicle have a registration?"

"The only paperwork, señor, is the pesos."

"Right." No use asking about insurance or an inspection sticker. The good news was that there was no paper trail here—no car rental agency and no limo or taxi driver who might have the police on their speed dial. There was only Chico. And Flavio. And I guess we trusted them.

Chico found three clean glasses and poured us all a little white rum. We clinked. "Salud!"

He looked at the bulge in my shirt and said, "I don't know who you are, or why you need a car, or where you're going. And I don't want to know. But I was told you could be trusted to forget where you got this car if you're stopped by the police."

"And I don't know who you are, señor, but if you don't tell, I won't tell."

He looked at Sara, and she said something to him in Spanish and he nodded.

Chico wished us buenas noches, walked over to an old Harley, kick-started it, and headed for the garage door. Flavio reappeared from the shadows and opened one side of the barn door just in time for Chico to exit his unnamed dealership. If it *was* his. Flavio closed and bolted the door.

I glanced at Sara, who hadn't said much since we'd gotten here. I was anxious to get on the road, but first we needed the contact info for our person in Camagüey, and I assumed we'd get it from Flavio, but he came over to us and said, "Someone will meet you here."

No use asking who, so I asked, "When?"

"Soon. And I wish you good luck."

I guess he was leaving. He looked like he needed a drink.

Sara said to him, "Thank you for being here."

"Marcelo wishes it could have been him. But they are watching him."

"Perhaps next time."

"He sends his regards."

"And mine to him."

He bid us good evening, turned, and walked toward the door.

Well, I was getting that outsider feeling again, like you get when a woman invites you to meet her family and they're all talking about people you don't know, and not talking about the crazy uncle in the attic.

I asked, "Who is he? And why was he here?"

"He was here to make sure everything went well with Chico." She added, "He's new to our organization. Unknown to the police."

"He looked like he'd crack like an egg if the police got hold of him."

She didn't reply.

I looked at my watch. We'd been here about forty minutes. My training emphasized leaving a meeting place as soon as you've done a deal with the locals. But now we were waiting for someone. Maybe the local police.

Meanwhile, I scanned the shop to see if there were any side or back doors, then I went to the front door, opened it, and con-firmed that our beer-guzzling lookout was still there—the tape was playing a nice guitar solo—and I closed and bolted the door.

Not that the bolts or the old man were going to keep out the police, but they would give us a few seconds to react. I walked back to Sara, who was now looking at our new car. I asked her, "What's going on here?"

"We're waiting for someone."

"Who?"

"I don't know."

"And who told Chico we needed a station wagon, and that I had a sense of humor?"

"Eduardo."

But it wasn't Sara who said that. It was Eduardo.

CHAPTER 42

So, Eduardo Valazquez was our man in Havana.

I had no idea where he'd been lurking—maybe the baño—and I looked at Sara, who didn't seem overly surprised to see him. In fact, I wasn't completely surprised myself.

He was wearing the same outfit I'd last seen him wearing on my boat—sandals, black pants, and a white guayabera shirt, but no gold cross, which would attract attention in Cuba.

He went to Sara and they embraced. "You look well," he said to her. "Are you well?"

"Sí."

Eduardo looked at me. "Have you been taking good care of her?"

"Sí."

Eduardo walked over to the Buick and put his hand on the fender. "Beautiful. My father had an Oldsmobile."

Those were the days. Well, Eduardo was beginning his walk down memory lane in Chico's Chop Shop. He had apparently given Felipe the slip—or more likely, he just told Felipe to go sit in a corner. Eduardo was the boss. And, I guess, the brains behind all of this.

He lifted the wagon's rear window and looked into the storage space. "This will be good."

"For what?"

He didn't reply.

I had the impression I wasn't supposed to speak unless spoken to, and Sara, too, wasn't saying anything. I get impatient with old people, especially if they're screwing up my schedule and my life. It was almost 11 P.M., and about midnight Antonio would be knocking on Sara's door with his woody, then he'd probably use the house phone to call her room and probably my room, then he'd get a manager to open Ms. Ortega's door. Then he might call his police comandante. Or maybe he'd wait for Sara in the lobby, not believing she'd jilted him after all he'd done for her to get her out of Cuba. In any case, we needed to get on the road before we were the subjects of a police search.

Eduardo walked over to Chico's all-purpose table and bar and poured himself a white rum, inviting us to join him. Sara and I declined. He then produced three Cohibas in aluminum tubes and gave one to me and one to Sara.

He took a lighter out of his pocket—a Zippo—and held it in the palm of his hand. He looked at me and said, "This is a gift to you from Señor Colby." He handed it to me and I looked at the lighter. It was indeed Jack's Zippo. *Yea, though I walk through the valley of the shadow of death, I fear no evil . . .*

Well, apparently Jack—like Felipe—couldn't keep Eduardo from jumping ship, and apparently, too, Eduardo told both of them he was going to meet us. I wasn't happy when I'd learned he'd stowed away on *The Maine*, and I wasn't sure I should be thrilled to discover he was our contact.

Eduardo said, "Perhaps not a gift, but a good-luck charm. He wants it returned to him when you meet in Cayo Guillermo."

"I'll be there." *. . . for I am the meanest motherfucker in the valley.*

Eduardo uncased his cigar, but Sara and I said we'd save ours for the road. I lit Eduardo up with the Zippo. Just like old times on my boat.

He let out a stream of white smoke and said, "They taste better here."

Actually, they tasted better in the U.S., where the cigars were illegal and we were legal. On that subject, I let him know, "I'd like to get moving."

He stared off into space, then said, "Havana does not look as

I remember her . . . She has gotten . . . shabby. And the people . . . Where is the joy I remember in Old Havana?"

I took that as a rhetorical question, but Sara replied, "It is gone. But the people's hearts will come to life again."

I had the impression they'd had conversations like this before. Not that I cared, but Sara and Eduardo, like all exiles and the children of exiles, romanticized the old days and the old country, which in the case of Cuba had been run by the most corrupt thugs in the Western Hemisphere. The current regime was long past its expiration date, but the damage had been done, and I couldn't imagine what was next for this unblessed island. Nor did I care. Well, maybe I did.

Eduardo contemplated his cigar, then asked us, "How are things?"

I beat Sara to a response and said, "We had a little problem."

He nodded. "Yes, I heard this from Señor Colby."

So Señor Colby couldn't keep his mouth shut about our meeting, or what was said there. Wait until I get my hands on his skinny neck.

Eduardo looked at me. "But you were not supposed to meet him."

"Why not?"

"For reasons of security."

"Excuse me, but you are the biggest security problem so far."

He ignored that and continued, "But I'm happy he gave you—" He tapped my belly bulge, which must be a Cuban custom. "I was going to bring that to you."

"He saved you the trouble."

"So you had this problem with . . . your tour guide."

"We've put that problem behind us and now we need to get on the road." I added, "I assume you have the Camagüey contact information for us."

He didn't reply, and he was annoying me, so I said, "I hope you don't think you're coming with us."

"I am walking home."

"Well, good luck with that. And if you get picked up by the police—"

"I have a cyanide capsule with me."

That's good news.

"They will never take me alive."

Bite hard.

Sara said to Eduardo, "Please come with us. We will all go home together."

"I am home." He refilled his glass and drew on his cigar, then looked at me, then at Sara—and I knew that look. He asked, "Are you . . . working well together?"

Yes, I'm fucking her.

Sara replied, "Mac has been extraordinary."

"Good. We made a good choice." He added, "I admire the American Army. Excellent training. Men who are trustworthy and keep their word."

"Thank you."

"Men like Mr. Colby." He looked me in the eye. "Mister Colby seems to think you and Sara have formed a romantic attachment."

Thanks, Jack. Asshole. Or was the old fox just baiting me?

Sara didn't help the situation by turning red. She blushes too easily.

Eduardo looked at her. "You are committed to a man in Miami."

This isn't Miami, señor. I couldn't believe the old boy was hung up on this. I mean, we're on the lam in an f-ing police state with our lives on the line and . . . Well, officer and gentleman that I am, I said, "Señor Valazquez, I assure you that Sara has been faithful to . . . whoever."

"Do you both swear to this?"

"I do."

Sara hesitated, but said, "I swear."

I didn't think he believed us, but he had the answer he wanted, so now we could talk about sixty million dollars.

He changed the subject and asked Sara, "Do you understand how you are to make your contact in Cayo Guillermo?"

Sara replied, "The Melia Hotel lobby bar, any night after seven P.M."

"Correct. And your contact will say, 'It is good to see you here.'" He stared at Sara for some reason, as though she'd once forgotten an ID phrase.

She nodded.

He let us know, "The three fishermen are staying at the Melia. Felipe and Señor Colby are sleeping on the boat. So when you make your escape in the darkness, the fishermen will not be onboard—they will be in their beds."

Innocent as sleeping babies. But with some explaining to do to the police about their missing tournament boat. Hopefully, they'd just be allowed to fly to Mexico City. But if they were jailed, Eduardo and his amigos would have their diplomatic incident, and the fishermen would just be collateral damage. Señor Valazquez and his amigos played rough. And I'd keep that in mind.

He looked at me. "Do I have your word that you will continue this mission even if . . . something should happen to Sara?"

"If I'm alive and able, I will be at the Melia Hotel in Cayo Guillermo."

"Good."

I seemed to be the only one who understood that we needed to get out of here, and I said, "If there's nothing else, we're ready to go. We need the contact information for Camagüey."

He ignored me again and asked, "Do you think the police have made any connection between you and the boat?"

Sara replied, "We don't think so. But it's possible they'll discover something if they're making inquiries."

Eduardo nodded. "This was always a concern."

I asked him, "Do you have any way to contact our person in Cayo?"

"No." He added, "I don't know who he is."

Then how do you know it's a he? "Do you have any way to contact Felipe?"

"I have no way to contact anyone. Including you. So when we part, this is all in the hands of God."

I prefer Verizon to keep me in touch. But this was one of those unguided missions, like a rocket that you have no command or control of, and no communication with after it's launched. It would be good to know what was going on in Cayo Guillermo—like if the tournament had been cancelled and the fleet was gone, or if the police were waiting there for us—but we weren't going to know anything until we got to the Melia Hotel. If we made it that far.

Eduardo returned to the subject of Antonio and said, "Mister Colby told me you were to meet this man—this tour guide."

Jeez, Jack. Did Eduardo waterboard him? Or get him drunk? Or was Jack trying to get this mission scrubbed?

"What did you learn at this meeting?"

Sara replied, "We learned we were on a police watch list." She added, "But this man is a liar and a scammer. He wanted money."

And some love. But not worth mentioning.

Eduardo nodded, but didn't reply.

I wondered if Eduardo was thinking about aborting this mission. Sara and I had talked ourselves into pressing on, but Eduardo might now be thinking otherwise. In fact, he said, "Perhaps the money is not that important."

I assured him, "It is to me."

"There are things more important than money."

"I agree. And money can buy all those things."

He looked at me. "We are motivated by something greater than money."

"I'm not."

"Our life's goal is to destroy this regime."

"That takes money."

Sara said to Eduardo, "I have taken Mac to Villa Marista."

He nodded and looked at me. "So you understand."

Something was getting lost in the translation, but in the back of my mind maybe I did understand.

Eduardo changed the subject again and asked Sara, "Did you see your grandfather's bank?"

"I did. I showed it to Mac."

Three times.

"And your home?"

"Yes."

"I, too, walked to see it." He shook his head. "Very sad. It made me unhappy." Eduardo Valazquez walking around Havana made *me* unhappy. And standing here made me unhappy. I looked at Sara and tapped my watch.

She nodded.

Eduardo said to me, "Another of our goals is to return the property that was stolen by the Communists to the rightful owners."

"Sara has mentioned that."

Eduardo walked over to a work bench where a tarp covered something big. Sara joined him, and I followed.

Eduardo said, "Flavio has delivered something here for you." He pulled away the tarp, revealing two medium-sized steamer trunks. They'd fit nicely in the Buick wagon.

He stuck his cigar in his mouth, took a key out of his pocket, and opened the padlock on one of the trunks, then lifted the lid. The trunk was crammed with paper, but not the green kind.

Eduardo said, "This is worth hundreds of millions of dollars."

I knew what this was, and so did Sara, but Eduardo told us, "Land deeds, property titles . . . records of the true ownership of houses, plantations, farms, factories, apartment buildings . . . banks . . . all nationalized—stolen—by the regime."

I said, "I thought this stuff was in the cave in Camagüey."

"It never left Havana." He looked at Sara. "Your grandfather chose to hide it separately from the money." He smiled. "He was a careful man who believed that one should not put all of one's assets in one basket."

She nodded.

He also explained to me, "Almost all Cubans believed that the Castro regime would not last more than a year. That the Americans would not allow a Communist country to exist off its shores."

Why not? We've got California and Vermont.

"Cubans who escaped to Miami thought they would be back in a year." He looked at Sara. "As did your grandfather. So he gave this trunk to his trusted priest, who hid it in a burial vault beneath his church in the Old Town, where it has remained until this morning."

I guess there was no room in the burial vault for twelve steamer trunks filled with money. Which would have made our job a little easier. Assuming the Catholic Church had no use for the money.

In any case, we now had to haul these two trunks of paper to Camagüey, in a sixty-year-old station wagon. No big deal, but . . . I wish they had FedEx here.

Eduardo took a wad of tri-folded paper out of the trunk. The paper was yellowed, maybe brittle, and it was bound with a green ribbon, which he untied, then opened the papers and spread them carefully on the work bench. "Ah . . . yes. This is a título de propiedad . . . a property deed which shows that Señor Alfredo Xavier Gomez is the legal owner of an apartamento . . . an apartment building on Calle San Rafael, in Vedado."

Lucky man. Though he was probably dead by now. I hoped we weren't going to go through all of this.

Eduardo refolded the deed, tied it, and put it back in the trunk, then stared at the mass of legal documents. "Who knows what is in here? Historical land grants. Deeds to entire factories, mansions, plantations . . . all stolen."

Goes to show you what a piece of paper is worth. Unless it's a U.S. Treasury note. "Okay, so—"

"You—" He pointed to me. "You and Sara will bring all this to America on your boat."

"Right."

"The exile organizations have kept lists of people and families who claim property in Cuba. These deeds will be returned to the rightful owners and heirs."

This might be a bad analogy, but it was like telling people you'd found their Confederate war bonds.

But hope springs eternal and Eduardo said to us, or to himself, "There will come a day when the owners and their heirs can claim their property." He reminded us, "It has happened when the Communists were overthrown in Eastern Europe. And with property stolen by the Nazis. It will happen in Cuba."

Possible. But I wouldn't buy those deeds even at a ninety percent discount with my American dollars from the cave. "Okay, so let's load this up—"

He looked at me. "We will need you—and Sara—to publicly verify how you came into possession of these two trunks."

I was hoping to keep a low profile with my—and Jack's—three million dollars. "What do you mean?"

"We are planning a big press conference in Miami. We have good friends in the Miami media."

"I'm sort of modest—"

"There will be attorneys at the press conference who represent the families whose property was stolen. Now that we have legal proof of ownership, we will file claims in Federal court."

"Right." Carlos would be busy for the next decade. "Sounds good. But I'll take a pass on the press conference—"

"This is an important story—an exciting story. You and Sara traveling to Cuba—"

"Hold on, amigo. No one told me about this."

"You will be famous."

"I want to be rich."

"You will be good on television. You are an attractive couple."

No argument there. But I had this vision of being shot at the press conference by her jealous Cuban boyfriend. I glanced at her again and she looked away. I didn't think this relationship was going to travel well.

Eduardo was caught up in his excitement. "We will tell the story of the Pescando Por la Paz, The Maine, Fishy Business—"

"I'll bet the regime doesn't renew that fishing license." Or the Yale educational travel license.

"I have spoken to Jack about this, and he has agreed to interviews."

Really? Well, Jack missed his three minutes of fame when he

came ashore in Havana looking for the brass band and the TV cameras and found instead an anti-American demonstration. Also, I wondered *when* Eduardo had spoken to Jack about this. After I met Jack? Or before? Jack never mentioned this to me at the Nacional.

More importantly, these documents had less to do with returning the property to the owners and more to do with creating legal issues that could derail the diplomatic negotiations now taking place. I would have mentioned this, but we all understood that.

Meanwhile, I was still in Chico's Chop Shop, along with Sara, Eduardo, two trunks of títulos, and my new Buick. And it was a long way to Camagüey and Cayo Guillermo. I said to Eduardo, "I need the contact information in Camagüey." I looked at him. "Now, por favor."

"I hope you will agree to be part of this story."

"Sure, I'm in. Let's go."

"You have what is called credibility as an American with no ties to the anti-Castro organizations."

"Don't forget photogenic."

"And a man who is a wounded combat veteran. An officer who has received many medals."

I wasn't sure what that had to do with anything. "Look, Eduardo, with or without me at the press conference, or me appearing on the morning news, what you have here"—I motioned to the trunks—"speaks for itself. Don't oversell it."

He didn't reply, and I continued, "My concern is the sixty million dollars. First, getting it, second, getting it and us out of Cuba, third, getting my cut, and fourth, we should all shut our mouths about the money or we could get it taken away by the U.S. government, who could put it in escrow while the negotiations go on for the next fifty years."

Again, he didn't reply, and I looked at Sara, who had been uncharacteristically quiet during Eduardo's monologues. "Do you agree?"

Apparently she didn't. I looked at Eduardo. "What's happening?"

He got right to the point for a change and said, "You are not going to Camagüey."

Did I see that coming? "Why not?"

"Because it is dangerous."

"It was dangerous yesterday. And last week."

"It could be more dangerous today. Or tomorrow."

"You don't know that. That's for me and Sara to determine."

"It is for me to determine. And as you said yourself, the money could compromise our efforts to publicize this—" He motioned toward the trunks. "It would distract from our main objective."

Well, I guess a dozen trunks filled with sixty million dollars would be more interesting to the American public than worthless paper. "That's why we shouldn't advertise the money—"

"And as you know—as you said to Mr. Colby—there is a possibility that the Cuban government will cancel the fishing tournament and send the boats away."

Was there anything Jack forgot to tell him?

"So time is of the essence."

I looked at Sara again. Apparently Eduardo's arguments for scrubbing the mission were more convincing than the ones I or she had already discussed. Though they were the same arguments. But, to be fair, the situation had changed.

In fact, Eduardo said, "We cannot risk losing these documents on a dangerous journey to the cave."

"All right . . . but I just lost three million dollars."

"You will be compensated."

"How?"

"The fifty thousand dollars you were promised if the mission was aborted. And the title to your half-million-dollar boat, free and clear."

Which I could rename *The Albatross.* I would have negotiated with him, but he was sort of a dead man. And maybe I was, too.

Eduardo also told me, "Mister Colby knows he will be compensated for his time and his cooperation in helping us publicize this great legal and moral victory over the regime."

Jack and I had some talking to do. I looked at Sara. "Did you know we weren't going to Camagüey?"

"I . . . knew there was a possibility."

"Thanks for letting me know."

She looked at me. "Mac . . . it's better this way. It's safer. It's less than an eight-hour drive to Cayo, with only two trunks. We'll meet our contact at the Melia tomorrow night, get onboard The Maine, and sail for Key West."

Right. What was I going to do with three million dollars anyway?

Eduardo said, "Sara did not know what would happen. This decision depended on getting these trunks in our possession before you left for Camagüey. We have the trunks, so you are not going to Camagüey for the money." He added, "The money has sat there for fifty years. It will be there when we return."

Right. I couldn't wait to do this all over again. In fact, count me out. I said, "It's your show."

"It is." Eduardo said to Sara, "The map."

She walked over to where we'd laid our backpacks and retrieved her map and mine. I hoped she didn't notice I had packed only one pair of clean underwear.

She brought the maps to us, and Eduardo said, "I see you made a copy."

"For Mac."

"Are there any more copies?"

"The original—my grandfather's—in my possession in Miami."

Eduardo nodded, and said to me, "Your lighter, please."

I fired up the Zippo and Sara held both maps to the flame, watched them burn, then dropped them on the floor. They smelled like money burning.

Eduardo advised me, "You will forget the existence of this map."

"I won't mention it at the press conference." I looked at Eduardo, then at Sara. "Are we ready to get out of here?"

Apparently not.

Sara put her hand on my arm, then realized that Eduardo would not like that and drew it away as she said, "You asked me if there was more to this mission than the money."

"Right . . . where did I ask you that?" Oh, in bed.

"And there is."

"Right. The property deeds. The press conference . . ." I thought back to what Eduardo had said when Sara told him we'd gone to Villa Marista. *So you understand.* And Eduardo's mention of my military service. And I now understood that Captain Daniel MacCormick was going to raise the issue of the missing American POWs at that press conference. I hope Sara's photograph came out good.

She looked at Eduardo and nodded toward the trunk that hadn't been opened. I assumed it was also filled with property deeds, but Eduardo hesitated and Sara said, "He needs to see this now."

Eduardo nodded, produced another key, and opened the padlock of the second trunk.

It was Sara who took hold of the lid and said, "Something that will please you more than money." She raised the lid. "The bones are going home."

Lying in the trunk were rows of neatly piled skulls, their empty eye sockets staring at eternity, staring at me, and I knew without a doubt that these mortal remains had come from Villa Marista, and that the answers to what happened to seventeen missing Americans were in the DNA of those bones.

PART III

CHAPTER 43

Eduardo's last words to us were, "Vayan con Dios," and mine to him were, "Have a safe journey home." And I meant it.

Eduardo and Sara had a more emotional good-bye, mostly in Spanish, and Sara—now sitting next to me as I drove the Buick station wagon through the quiet streets of Vedado—was still upset. But not as upset as I was about Eduardo cancelling my payday—or me being the last to know what was going on.

Anyway, Eduardo had given us a road map with instructions to head south and look for signs for the Autopista Nacional, the A-1, which I was doing.

It was just before midnight, and very shortly Antonio would be knocking on Sara's door. I hope he had the decency to bring flowers and a bottle of rum. In any case, he would discover that there was no love or money in Room 535 for him. And he'd be furious. But what would he do? Call his police comandante? Or wait to see if Sara showed up? I hoped he waited. We needed to get clear of Havana before the police started looking for us.

I concentrated on the road and my driving. I'd never sat behind the wheel of a vintage American car, and it took some getting used to, especially with Chico's modifications. It was hot in the wagon, but I had to leave the windows up so that we weren't so visible. There were, however, little butterfly windows that let in some air. They should bring those back.

Also, as Chico said, the fuel gauge didn't work, but I'd take his word that the gas tank was full.

The 90-horsepower Perkins boat engine didn't give the same performance as the Buick's original 300-horsepower V-8, even with Chico's newly installed Hyundai manual transmission. But the gas mileage would be better, and maybe we'd have to stop only once for gas. On the other hand, we weren't going to outrun any police cars.

Sara came out of her funk and said, "He's like a grandfather to me . . . This is sad."

"He's where he wants to be," though I wished he was where he was supposed to be—in Miami. And I wished I was where he'd arrived from—Key West.

She asked, "How are you doing?"

"Okay. You see any signs for the Autopista?"

She looked out the windshield. "No, but we're heading in the right direction." She added, "We're in the district of 10 October— near Villa Marista."

I had a vision of my Villa Marista photo on a screen at the press conference, and maybe all over the news and the Internet. The surprises on this mission never seemed to end. The biggest surprise so far had been the skulls. I could still see them staring at me . . . as though pleading, "Take me home."

I continued on through the dark streets of 10 October. The Autopista was south of Havana and it ran east, according to the road map, in the direction of Cayo Guillermo, though it went through the interior of the island, far from the coast. The Soviet-built highway hadn't existed when Eduardo fled Cuba, but Eduardo and Sara agreed that the Autopista would be faster than the more direct coastal road that the tour bus had taken to Matanzas. And it would be safer—no towns to pass through and no local police. You could legally do a hundred K—60 mph—on the Autopista, and with luck, said Sara, we might never see a police car. Sounded too good to be true.

Sara and I and Eduardo had loaded the two steamer trunks into the rear, and I was surprised how heavy the legal documents were, and how light the skulls were. We'd covered the trunks with the tarp, and Eduardo had given Sara the padlock keys and said, "The next time these trunks are opened will be in Miami."

Or when the police ordered us to open them.

Before we'd closed the lids on the trunks, I'd looked at the soil-stained skulls more closely. Some of the lower jaws were missing, but all of them had their upper teeth, mostly intact—and through dental records and DNA they could be identified and matched against the Department of Defense's list of missing in action. And then we would have names. And those names would have families . . .

About half the skulls had the distinctive round hole of a bullet entry wound, but one of the skulls looked like it had been crushed with a blunt instrument. The rest were free of trauma, and I assumed those men had died from . . . who knows? In any case, these skulls would be a powerful visual image, and very strong evidence of imprisonment and murder in Castro's Cuba. What I—and Sara—had to do was tell the world how we'd gotten them.

Sara asked, "What are you thinking about?"

"Our cargo."

She nodded. "It's fitting that it's you who are bringing the bones home, and that it's me who's returning the deeds to the stolen property."

That sounded like a talking point for the press conference.

I had asked Eduardo about the rest of the remains—the skeletons—and he'd told me and Sara that the bodies had been exhumed from their common grave on the grounds of Villa Marista about a year ago, and the purpose of the exhumation was to burn the bones in order to obliterate any evidence of the American POWs. And this was done, Eduardo said, in advance of the diplomatic talks, and in anticipation of demands from the Americans—politicians, MIA groups, and veterans' organizations—that a U.S. military body recovery and identification team be allowed to visit Villa Marista to investigate the rumors and accusations that seventeen American servicemen had been murdered there.

And how had the skulls survived the bonfire? According to what Eduardo had been told, the skulls, and especially the teeth, were difficult to burn, so they were to be pulverized before burning. And according to Eduardo, this presented an opportunity and an incentive to someone—maybe a worker or a guard or someone who opposed the regime and recognized the potential value and importance of these skulls—to smuggle them out of Villa Marista. For money. Or for truth and justice. Or both.

I saw signs for José Martí Airport, which brought back memories of my arrival when I stepped off the plane a virgin, hoping to make my fortune in Cuba. And hoping to get laid. One out of two ain't bad.

Sara said, "Turn here."

I turned left where a sign pointed to A-1, and we came to a ramp that took us to the eastbound lanes of the Autopista. If we drove through the night, we'd be in Cayo Guillermo at about 7 or 8 A.M. And at about 7 P.M., we'd meet our contact in the lobby bar of the Melia Hotel, then sometime in the night we'd get this cargo aboard *The Maine* and set sail for Key West. What could possibly go wrong?

The divided highway had four lanes in both directions and the pavement was good, though the road lighting was not—which was also good; the darker the better. There wasn't much traffic heading away from Havana, but enough so that we didn't look like the only vehicle on the road. But later, as we got farther into the interior, and into the early-morning hours, we might actually be the only vehicle on the highway—certainly the only '53 Buick Roadmaster Estate Wagon, which, even in a country of vintage American cars, would attract almost as much attention as Sara Ortega in a tight dress walking down Calle Obispo at two in the morning.

I mentioned my concern to Sara—without the analogy—and she assured me, "According to Marcelo, the Tráficos—the highway patrol—are underfunded, and they don't want to burn gas or put miles on their cars if they don't have to."

Good that Sara learned so much from Marcelo last year. But all it takes is one Tráfico waking up from his backseat siesta to cause a problem.

She reminded me, "You have a gun."

"Right." And I'd use it if I had to.

I pushed the wagon up to what I estimated as sixty miles an hour and it handled okay, despite its ethnically diverse body parts. Which made me think again of our cargo, and do some fact checking.

I wasn't sure how Eduardo knew that those property deeds were hidden in a church in Havana, and not in the cave at Camagüey as Sara had told me. I could assume that Eduardo knew Sara's father and/or grandfather, though he didn't say that, and neither did Sara. Eduardo also didn't tell me or Sara how the skulls from Villa Marista came into his possession, though the less we knew about that the better. Bottom line, there was a lot of dark matter that held this universe together.

In any case, those exhumed skulls were now sitting next to a trunk of exhumed documents that were to be reunited with the families who'd lost their property, and the skulls were to be reunited with the families who'd lost and loved these men in life. There was something in this for everyone. Mostly loss, unfortunately, but also maybe hope and closure.

We continued on the straight highway, and I hadn't seen a police car yet, though I'd seen military vehicles in the oncoming lanes. The Buick dashboard had lots of old gauges and instruments, but none of them were working, so for all I knew the engine was overheating, the oil pressure was dropping, and the generator had stopped working. A mechanical problem on the road was basically a survival problem.

"You're not saying much."

"I'm thinking."

"Are you angry?"

"No. I'm saving that for when we're on the boat."

She put her hand on my arm. "I'm sorry I lied to you."

Didn't we have this conversation?

"Mac? You understand why I had to lie."

"I can answer that question if you can answer the question of what you actually knew and when you actually knew it."

"I honestly wasn't sure that Eduardo would be here . . . or that we weren't going to Camagüey. Or that either of those trunks would be waiting for us in Havana . . ."

I didn't reply.

"I really thought we'd be able to fulfill my grandfather's promise to his clients."

Not to mention her promise to me of three million dollars. I thought back to my boat, to when she was pitching this to me. It was, as I suspected, a story too well told, but . . . "I can believe that Carlos and Eduardo were not completely honest with you. And we both know that you weren't completely honest with me."

She didn't respond directly but said, "What we're doing . . . it's important . . . and sometimes the ends justify the means."

I had a flashback to some bad days in Kandahar Province, and I advised her, "Don't become what you're fighting."

She nodded.

"Are there any new surprises in Cayo Guillermo that I should know about?"

She stayed silent for a few seconds, then replied, "When you ask a question like that, you know the answer."

"Then why would I ask?"

"The answers are all there. I told you, you're very smart. You just need to take what you know and come to a conclusion."

This was sounding like Cuban Zen. "Is it something that will please me more than the money?"

"No."

So that ruled out me killing time on a nude beach in Cayo Guillermo before our 7 P.M. rendezvous at the hotel. Well, I didn't want to ruin my surprise, so I dropped the subject.

We drove in silence, then Sara said, "I *am* sorry about the money."

Not as sorry as I am. But right from the beginning the money seemed more illusion than reality; like El Dorado, the City of Gold, shimmering in the distant hills. How many men died looking for that?

I said, "I'm sure that the exiles and their families will be even sorrier to hear that their money is still in Cuba."

"We're going to come back for the money someday. Soon." She asked, "Will you come with me?"

"No."

"Think about it."

"Okay. No."

"Think again."

"Maybe."

"You have adventure in your soul."

And rocks in my head.

CHAPTER 44

It was 1 A.M., and the traffic was thinning, and there were fewer signs of human habitation along the highway. The terrain was getting hilly and I noticed that the engine strained on the uphill. Was it ironic that this wagon was powered by a boat engine? Was it Karma? Or was it just Chico's cheapest option? Well, you get what you pay for. Except in Cuba.

Sara said, "Two things have made this trip more important than money."

"The day at the organic farm, and—?"

"*Us*, Mac. We found each other."

"Right." With some complications.

"And we are bringing home the remains of those men."

No argument there. But like everything else in this country, there was undoubtedly a price tag on those skulls, and that made me think of a nation of people who were so desperate that they had become accomplished scammers to survive. Like Antonio. And it occurred to me that maybe those skulls weren't those of American POWs murdered in Villa Marista prison; that some con artists had capitalized on the story and sold Eduardo and his friends a bill of goods and seventeen random skulls. There was no shortage of executed prisoners in Cuba, and no shortage of Cuban American exiles who'd believe anything that would help topple the regime. But would Eduardo be so gullible? Well, when—or if—we got those skulls out of Cuba, we'd find out, scientifically, what we'd risked our lives for.

And while I was not taking anything at face value, what about those twelve steamer trunks filled with money and hidden in a cave in Camagüey? Did they really exist? And if they did, were they still there?

This country was like an elaborate magic show, a grand illusion, a game of three-card monte, and a Hogwarts for con artists. And I thought the Afghanis were slippery.

Well, the property deeds seemed real enough.

I glanced at Sara. She was real. And she had confessed all her lies. What more could I want?

"What are you thinking about?"

"I'm thinking about Antonio coming to your room at midnight and seeing the 'Do Not Disturb' sign."

"Do you think he'll notify the police?"

"That depends on whether or not he wants to tell them he had a date with you, and that you jilted him."

She nodded.

"I myself would be embarrassed, and probably not tell the police that I'd been scammed. But if he's a good police informant, he might make that call and give the police a heads-up, and by seven A.M., when we don't show up at the pier, there'll be no question that we're gone."

She thought about all that and replied, "We didn't get much of a head start."

"No." And we were already on a police watch list, thanks to Antonio. And we had a few other problems with this road trip. Like if the police had already made the connection between me and *Fishy Business*, which would lead them straight to Cayo Guillermo. And we wouldn't know we had that problem until we got to Cayo, and by that time . . . Well, as they say, you should never travel faster than your guardian angel can fly.

Another problem with this Misión Imposible was us arriving in Cayo and discovering that the fleet had been booted out of the country. And the third possible problem was Eduardo, wandering around Havana, or beginning his cross-country walk home.

Eduardo was the only person in Cuba—except for Jack and Felipe—who knew where Dan MacCormick and Sara Ortega

were going, and he even knew what we were driving. And if the
police picked him up, and ID'd him as Eduardo Valazquez, the notorious anti-Castro enemy of the state, they'd ask him why he was
in Cuba as they were electrifying his nuts. Eduardo had assured us
he would take the poison—but you never know.

And then there was Chico and Flavio, both of whom knew a
little more than I wanted them to know. And I shouldn't forget
the old man with the cane. I was sure that Eduardo's amigos in
Miami and Havana had vetted all three of them, but . . . everyone
in Cuba, as Antonio said, had a second job. And everyone sold
each other out.

Sara said, "Someday, Antonio and everyone like him in Cuba
will face a day of judgement."

Actually, I would've liked to have been in Sara's room at midnight to deliver my own judgement to Antonio's nuts. But the mission comes first.

Sara was looking in her sideview mirror, and now and then she
glanced over her shoulder.

I asked her, "Do the Tráficos use unmarked cars?"

"They do." She added, "They drive mostly Toyota SUVs."

Sara was a wealth of information. Some of it obtained from
Marcelo last year. Some of it obtained from her briefing officer,
the retired CIA guy. And some information had come to her from
Eduardo, Carlos, and their amigos in the exile community. I wasn't
as well-informed as she was, but I noticed that if I asked, sometimes I got an answer. So I asked, "Did Eduardo know your father
or grandfather?"

"He knew both."

"Right. So one or both of them must have told Eduardo that
those property deeds were hidden in a church, not in the cave."

"I guess."

"But you didn't know that."

"I . . . may have known. But forgot."

"Or those deeds *were* in the cave, and someone has already
been to the cave and cleaned it out."

"What are you suggesting?"

"I'm suggesting that Eduardo has been playing this game long before you or I were even born."

"This is not a game."

"It is. But who's calling the plays?"

"Not you."

"Right. I'm just the running back. You're the quarterback, and Eduardo is the coach."

"Good analogy." She advised me, "Don't think about this too much."

"Okay." But I was thinking about who owned the team. And I concluded that the Company owned the team.

It occurred to me that cyanide is not that easy to come by. They don't sell it in Walgreens. I thought, too, about Eduardo's forged passport, and about his friends in American intelligence. And the more I thought about all this, the more I saw the hand of the Company in some of this mission—the CIA. I mean, any normal American boy raised on conspiracy theories sees the hand of the CIA in everything. Even my father, who blames his bad golf game on CIA mind control. I had worked with the CIA in Afghanistan, and seen them at their best in Special Ops. Cuba, however, was another story. The CIA had been intimately, obsessively, and unhappily involved in Cuban affairs even before Castro took over. The careers of CIA officers had been made and broken in Cuba— mostly broken. That was a long time ago, but the pain and institutional embarrassment of those failures lingered on. I mean, the exploding cigars had become a joke, but the Bay of Pigs Invasion was a historic catastrophe.

I assumed, therefore, that the CIA wanted a win. And I suspected that the CIA was no fan of the Cuban Thaw, which would legitimize the regime and help keep the Castros and the Communists in power. And to allow the Thaw to go forward would be a betrayal of all the dissidents risking their lives in Cuba, and all the exile groups in America who still had a relationship with the CIA—people like Eduardo Valazquez and his amigos. So, yes, I could see the hand of the CIA in this mission, and if true, it never was about the money in the cave; it was always about recovering the skulls and the stolen property in the back of this Buick, and stirring up a shit storm that would send the diplomats home, or at least give them more to argue about.

And if all this was true, what was also true was that my three million dollars was just bait—and not even a real hunk of meat; just a shiny lure. Well, as Sara said, I shouldn't think about this too much. But it explained some of the bullshit. And maybe prepared me for my surprise in Cayo.

Bottom line, though, I felt good about getting out of Havana and sitting behind the wheel of my own car with a loaded Glock in my belt. It was still a long way to Key West, but we were heading in the right direction, and I was in the driver's seat for a change. The Havana bullshit was behind me. From here it was all balls, all the way.

Sara had retrieved a bottle of water from her backpack and we shared it. She said, "I've been thinking about the Yale alum group."

"Who's that?"

"Be serious, Mac. I hope we don't cause them any problems."

"That's nice of you to think about them." While we're running for our lives. "Any problems they have will be caused by the Cuban government. Not us."

"I feel that we used them."

"We did." I reminded her, "That was your plan." Or maybe the CIA's.

"They may be questioned by the police."

"The highlight of their trip."

"And kicked out of the country."

"Or worse. Another week with Antonio. Unless the police beat him up."

"Be a little sympathetic."

"Okay, I liked Tad," I admitted. "And Alison, and Professor Nalebuff, and some of the others, like . . ." Pretty Cindy Neville. I reminded Sara, "I left my Hemingway T-shirt for Richard."

She ignored that and said, "I wonder what Tad is going to do when he discovers we're missing."

That was the more important issue. "Hopefully, he'll alert the embassy, who will call the Ministry of the Interior, who will deny we are in their custody but will be put on notice that the U.S. Embassy is aware of our absence and concerned."

She nodded.

"Unfortunately, before Tad makes that call, Antonio will have made his call to the police sometime before dawn, and the Ministry of the Interior will e-mail our airport photos to every police station, military installation, airport, and seaport in the country, including Cayo Guillermo."

She stayed silent, then asked, "Do you think we're going to make it?"

"We are going to give it our best shot."

She nodded. "Do you remember what I told you in our room at the Nacional?"

"About . . . ?"

"About us sitting on the bow of your boat, with Jack and Felipe in the cabin, looking at the horizon as Key West comes into view."

"Right."

"And I said that our mission is blessed. And that just as you returned home from Afghanistan, you will return home from Cuba."

"I remember that."

"You need to believe that. *That* is what got you home from the war." She put her hand on my shoulder. "When you are blessed, and when your cause is just, God is with you, and you are strong."

I nodded. And I recalled something handwritten on a piece of paper that had made the rounds among the troops: *Fate whispered to the warrior, "You cannot withstand the coming storm." And the warrior whispered back, "I am the storm."*

"We're going home. Jack and Felipe are going home. And the warriors are going home."

CHAPTER 45

It was about 2:30 A.M., and we were almost three hours out of Havana. I hadn't seen another vehicle for awhile, and I was feeling conspicuous by their absence.

On another issue, if I was getting about fifteen miles to the gallon, we had, theoretically, enough fuel to drive a few more hours. But that was based on two assumptions: that Chico had topped off the tank, and that he hadn't swapped the standard twenty- or twenty-five-gallon tank for something smaller.

Also, without a working speedometer or odometer, the math had too many unknowns. But based on my estimated speed of 60 mph, and three hours on the road, I figured we were about one hundred and eighty miles out of Havana—about three hundred kilometers. It was about another three hundred kilometers to Cayo Guillermo, though a lot of that was on secondary roads, and that could take over four hours.

But my main concern at the moment was hearing the engine sputter. Then having a Tráfico stop to see what our problem was.

The interior lights didn't work, so Sara was reading the road map by the light of her otherwise useless cell phone. "We should be approaching Santa Clara—a fairly big town."

"Will they have all-night gas stations?"

"Yes. But . . . us pulling into a gas station at three in the morning might not be a good idea."

"Right. But I'm not sure of our fuel situation."

She thought about that and said, "I think we need to get off the road and continue at dawn when we won't be the only car on the highway."

We probably had more gas than I thought, but the real issue now was a police car pulling up behind us. "Okay."

The signage on the Autopista was either nonexistent or unlit, but we looked for the Santa Clara exit.

Meanwhile, Mama Inés' ropa vieja was just a distant memory and my stomach was growling. "Did you pack anything to eat?"

"I have some chocolate from the minibar that I might share with you."

"I'll give you a hundred thousand pesos."

She retrieved a Kit Kat from her backpack and we split it. I wondered who was going to pick up our minibar charges at the Parque Central. Well, they had our luggage and all our clothes. My suitcase alone was worth at least fifty dollars.

We drove on, and we were definitely pushing our luck regarding police cars. I would have gotten off the road anywhere, but there were deep drainage ditches along the shoulders and we were basically stuck on the limited-access highway until the next exit.

Meanwhile, I was listening for the sputter of the engine, and looking for headlights in my rearview mirror.

And sure enough, I saw headlights cresting the hill behind us. Sara also saw them in her sideview mirror, but didn't say anything.

The 90-horse engine didn't have much more in it, so I maintained my speed, and the headlights got closer. Sara had said the Tráficos used mostly Toyota SUVs, and some of them were unmarked, but I couldn't make out what was behind us.

She was staring at her sideview mirror. "I can't tell."

The vehicle got closer and it was in the right-hand lane, about fifty feet behind me, and now I could see that it was a small SUV. I tried to see if there was anyone riding with the driver, but his headlights were glaring and I couldn't see through his windshield. "How many cops ride in a car?"

"Usually two. But sometimes one."

I could take out one guy easily enough, but a second guy could be a problem.

The vehicle was less than thirty feet behind us now. He had three other lanes to use but he wasn't using them.

I didn't know who this was, but what I knew for sure was that if it was a cop, he was going to pull us over. And he didn't need any reason other than to see who was driving the American car at three in the morning.

Sara said, optimistically, "If it's a police car and he pulls us over, I'll speak to him and offer to pay a fine for speeding. That usually does it."

Actually, I would speak to him. A Glock 9mm speaks every language.

"Mac?"

"What if he asks to see what's in the rear?"

She didn't reply.

I had no idea if Antonio had alerted the police that Sara was missing, or if he was sitting in the lobby bar of the Parque Central at 2:30 A.M., waiting for his date, torn between his duty and his dick. Hopefully his dick said be patient. But there were a lot of other things that could have gone wrong in Havana—like Chico or Flavio selling us out, or Eduardo singing in the hot seat—and if the police were looking for two Americanos in a Buick wagon, these guys behind us could be waiting for other police cars to arrive, or there could be a roadblock ahead. So I needed to deal with this now. "I assume they have radios."

"Yes . . . but they're not always reliable . . . They rely on their cell phones."

The headlights were even closer now and I knew I had to force the situation, so I slowed down and veered toward the shoulder.

"What are you doing?"

"I'm seeing what he does."

"Mac . . ."

I came to a stop on the shoulder, drew my Glock, and cranked down my window. "Get down." But she sat there.

The headlights were less than twenty feet away, and the vehicle was slowing to a stop on the deserted highway.

My instincts said that the police in Cuba were not used to approaching a car driven by armed desperados, and they probably sauntered over to you with a shitty attitude and their gun in the holster. If so, I should be able to take care of this. But if they were looking specifically for us, they'd have guns in hand.

The vehicle came to a stop on the highway, and its hazard lights began flashing. I looked over my shoulder and saw that it was definitely an SUV, but its headlights were glaring and I couldn't see if it had police markings, or how many people were in the vehicle. And no one was getting out. Was he waiting for reinforcements?

Sara said in almost a whisper, "You're supposed to get out of your car and go over to them."

That would actually make it easier. I stuck the Glock under my shirt and was about to exit the wagon when the SUV suddenly pulled abreast of us, and I drew the Glock as its passenger window rolled down.

Before I had to make the decision to fire first and answer questions later, a middle-aged lady with a British accent asked, "Are you all right?"

I took a deep breath. "We're fine. How about you?"

"Oh . . . Are you American?"

"Canadians, actually." I glanced at Sara, who was sitting with her eyes closed, breathing hard.

There was a man in the driver's seat and he leaned past the lady and said, "We're trying to get to Santa Clara. No bloody road signs. I think we missed it."

"It's up ahead."

Sara leaned over. "It can't be more than five or ten kilometers."

"Thank you." He asked, "Are you having trouble?"

"Just stopped for a wee pee," I replied.

"Oh . . . All right, then. Carry on."

The lady said, "I love your car."

And off they went, to discover Cuba for themselves.

Sara opened the door and I asked, "Where are you going?"

"For a wee pee."

"I think I'll join you."

We finished our business and got back on the road. I could see the taillights of the British couple up ahead and I closed the distance.

Sara said, "That was the most frightening five minutes of my life."

I wished I could say the same. "You were very cool," I assured her.

She stayed silent, then asked, "If they were police, what would you have done?"

"Killed them."

She had no reply.

I kept a few hundred yards behind our fellow tourists, and I saw now that the terrain was getting more hilly and the countryside was very dark.

Sara took Eduardo's cigar from her pocket, lit it with Jack's Zippo, then took a long drag and passed it to me.

We shared the cigar as we drove in silence. She said, "We might not be so lucky next time."

"Let's avoid a next time."

Sara was looking at the map. "The exit should be coming up."

In fact, I could see the brake lights of our British friends, then their right-hand turn signal.

I closed the gap and followed them onto the exit, which was marked but unlit. At the end of the exit ramp was a T-intersection, but no sign. The Brits turned left.

Sara looked up from her map. "Santa Clara is to the left. The middle of nowhere is to the right."

I ditched the cigar and turned right onto a dark, narrow road and drove slowly down a hill. There was a small lake to my left, but if there were any houses along this road, they weren't lit or visible, and there wasn't a single light in the distance.

Sara said, "The area around Santa Clara was once known for its tobacco. I think most of the farms are abandoned, so maybe we can find an empty house or barn."

"Right."

My head beams illuminated the potholed road, but the glare reduced my night vision, so I turned off the headlights, and the moonlight now revealed bare fields, surrounded by low hills.

Sara checked her map. "Nothing on this road until a place called Osvaldo Herrera, about ten kilometers."

"Okay." I continued slowly with my headlights off, looking for cover and concealment, just like in my Humvee in Allfuckedupistan.

We went another few hundred yards, and over the next rise Sara spotted a large building up ahead.

As we got closer, we could see that it was a wooden barn-like structure with a partially collapsed roof. There was a dirt path leading to it and I turned onto the path and drove into the building through a doorless opening. I shut off the engine and the night became very quiet.

Sara got out, leaving her door open, and I did the same and looked around. I could see the sky through the holes in the roof, but I couldn't see any window openings. I smelled the faint odor of tobacco, and Sara said, "This was a tobacco-drying shed."

"Wasn't there a tobacco farm on the Yale itinerary for today?"

"Yes."

Coincidence? Or a great cosmic joke? "Check it off."

As Sara inspected our accommodations, I went outside and reconned the surrounding terrain. I still couldn't see a single light in the distance, and I was fairly sure that no one had seen us drive in, and that no one would be calling the police tonight. There might, however, be some activity here in the morning, so we had to get back on the highway at the crack of dawn.

I came around to the open doorway and noticed my tire marks on the dirt path, so I looked for some fallen vegetation to cover my tracks. There wasn't much around, but the moon would set soon, and darkness was the best concealment.

Sara came out of the barn and asked in a whisper, "What are you doing?"

"Earning my pay."

"Come inside." She took my arm and led me back into the barn.

It was past 3 A.M., so we had less than four hours until dawn, then we could get back on the road.

Sara said, "Let's get some sleep. You want the front seat or back?"

Obviously she had never camped out in a combat zone. "I'll stand watch for the next two hours, then wake you to relieve me, and give you the gun. You'll wake me at first light, and we'll leave here as soon as we don't need to use our headlights."

She stayed quiet a moment, then said, "All right." She asked, "Can I have a kiss?"

I don't normally kiss the guards that I post, but I made an exception and we kissed good-night. She climbed into the rear seat of the Buick Roadmaster and shut the door without making a noise.

The barn door was missing, so I sat on the dirt floor with my back resting against the Buick's rear bumper, and drew my Glock, facing the open doorway.

Well, it had already been a long day and a longer night and I should be tired, and I probably was, but I was fully alert. I remember this feeling in Cantstandthishit Province.

The moon was setting and the sky was dark, and there was no breeze. Tree frogs croaked nearby and a night bird sang in the distance.

I stared out the open doorway into the darkness, watching for a movement, listening for the sound of a motor or a footstep, or the sound of too much silence.

It's always good to visualize the path home, so I did. If we could get through this night and get to Cayo Guillermo in the morning without getting stopped by the police, we were a boat ride from home.

———

An hour passed, then another, and a false dawn lit up the eastern sky, then sunlight peeked over a distant hill and spread over the empty fields.

Sara came out of the wagon. "I thought you were going to wake me."

"I wanted to see this sunrise."

She nodded. "Our next sunrise will be on the water. We'll see it together."

"We will." I stood. "Time to go."

CHAPTER 46

We found a servicentro on the outskirts of Santa Clara. You don't pump your own in Cuba, so an attendant filled us up with petróleo especial at about six bucks a gallon, which is pricey if you make twenty dollars a month.

Sara got out of the wagon and spoke with the young attendant as he pumped, and he seemed more interested in her than the vintage Buick or me sitting behind the wheel with my face in the road map. More importantly, the guy seemed at ease, joking and laughing, and not looking at us like he'd seen our photographs somewhere.

Sara paid with pesos and got back in the wagon. The pump showed we took fifty-eight liters, about fifteen gallons, and even though I didn't know how many gallons the tank held, I was sure we could make it to Cayo Guillermo on this tank.

I pulled away and Sara said, "I told him I was from Baracoa. That's on the remote eastern tip of the island, where the accents are very different."

I didn't think she could pass as a native, especially with her Teva hiking boots, but the young man seemed like he'd believe anything she said as he was pushing his nozzle into her tank and pumping her up with petróleo especial while thinking of something else.

She said, "I told him you were my older brother."

"Thanks."

"And we were taking the American car to Havana to sell it."

"Good thinking." Bullshit must come naturally here.

We found the entrance to the eastbound lanes of the Autopista, and within a few minutes we were cruising along at an estimated sixty miles an hour.

There was some early-morning traffic going in both directions, mostly trucks and vans, and though there were no vintage American cars on the highway, no one was gawking at us.

I noticed a group of people on the side of the highway, waving at us, and I said to Sara, "Friendly people here."

"They're hitchhikers, Mac. They're waving pesos at us."

"I see an opportunity to pay for our gas."

"Public transportation is a catastrophe. The people are so desperate that they rely on hitching a ride in anything that moves, and the government has set up botellas—hitching spots—where government workers are assigned to decide who gets to ride in any vehicles that stop." She added, "Life is very hard here."

Actually, it sucked.

We continued on the Autopista. The sky was clear, as it had been every day since we'd landed in Havana, but on the far horizon I saw black clouds gathering.

I said, "I hope they've had good weather for the tournament."

"Do you enjoy fishing?"

"I don't fish. My customers fish."

"But do you enjoy what you do?"

If I did, I wouldn't be on the Autopista. "I like being on the water."

"My condo overlooks the water."

"So does my boat."

"Tonight we go for a midnight cruise on The Maine."

"Looking forward to that."

We were making good time, but there was no hurry. We had time to kill. I thought about Jack and Felipe and the three fishermen who should be out on the water now, competing with the nine other boats. This was day four of the Pescando Por la Paz, but today was the last day for *Fishy Business*, one way or the other. Jack and Felipe had been waiting for us, but they didn't know when— or if—we'd show up. I wondered if Jack was worried about me—or worried about his money. Well, I had two surprises for him; I made it, and the money didn't. Actually we didn't even know if the fleet was still there. I said, "Turn on the radio. Maybe we can hear something about the tournament."

She turned on the vacuum tube radio and static filled the car. She figured out that the chrome dial tuned in the stations and she played with it for awhile, but all I heard was Cuban music, and a few excited people who Sara said were shit eaters spouting propaganda.

About twenty miles out of Santa Clara, we hit a bump and the radio went dead and Sara shut it off. "We'll try again later."

"No news is good news."

"Here's some bad news. I see a police car in my sideview mirror."

I looked in my rearview and saw the green-and-white Toyota SUV about a hundred yards behind us in the inside lane of the highway, which was now down to three lanes. I was in the middle lane, behind a big truck, and I moved into the outside lane, pushed the pedal to the metal, and slowly came abreast of the truck, blocking the Tráfico's view of me. I stayed next to the truck and saw the police car move ahead at a high speed in the inside lane. I dropped back and put the Buick behind the truck again.

Well, this was going to be a cat-and-mouse game for the next three or four hours. We actually had no reason to believe that the police were looking for a 1953 Buick Roadmaster wagon, but by now—8 A.M.—we had lots of reasons to believe they were looking for Sara Ortega and Daniel MacCormick, who had gone missing from the Parque Central. So I shouldn't play too much cat-and-mouse with my driving and draw attention to ourselves.

We were definitely in the hills now, and the 90-horsepower was straining on the upgrades. Sara looked at her map. "The next big town is Sancti Spíritus, another half hour or so, then about thirty kilometers farther, the Autopista ends."

"Sorry to hear that."

"The regime ran out of money when the Soviets pulled out.

But we have a few options to get us farther east, then north to the causeway that will take us to Cayo Coco and Cayo Guillermo." She looked at the map. "There's the old highway, called the Carretera Central, that continues east into Camagüey Province."

"We'll remember that for next time."

"Or this time."

I glanced at her and saw she had a piece of paper in her hand that she put in my lap. I looked at it and saw it was in fact our treasure map. Copy number three, which she forgot to tell me or Eduardo about.

"That's yours," she said. "For next time—or this time."

I didn't reply.

"It's your call."

"We don't have our contact info for Camagüey."

"We don't need that. We have the map."

"We need a truck."

"Steal one."

Well, the lady had balls. Or lots of bluff. "We don't know if the money is still in the cave."

"We'll find out when we get there."

"I guess the question is, do we take the risk?"

"We're already in a high-risk situation, Mac. You may have noticed."

"I did. But now I'm thinking about not putting our cargo at further risk."

"I'll let you answer that question."

"All right . . . well, life's a bitch, isn't it?"

She didn't reply.

I drove on, thinking about my three million dollars, which had suddenly reappeared. If we could get to Camagüey Province without getting caught, we could steal a truck, ditch this Buick, find the cave, and drive to Cayo Guillermo with twelve steamer trunks stuffed with cash, then meet our contact tomorrow night, if in fact he or she was at the Melia Hotel every night at 7, as instructed. This could be doable. "How far is it to Camagüey Province?"

She glanced at the map. "About a hundred fifty kilometers to the border of the province. Then . . . we follow your map to the cave."

"Okay . . ." So, putting aside the logistics and the suicidal nature of this detour, I had to consider the cargo we already had, and also wonder if Sara was bluffing or serious. Was she trying to make amends for the aborted mission? "I'll think about it."

"We'll be in a city called Ciego de Ávila in about an hour. That's where we need to head north toward the Cayo Coco causeway. Or continue east toward Camagüey."

So, causeway or Camagüey? The first option was easier and safer, but my monetary reward would be much smaller. The second option, if it worked, would be a clean sweep—the contents of the cave, plus what I already had in the back of the wagon, and whatever else I could squeeze out of Carlos in Miami. I said, "Eduardo voted no on this. How do you vote?"

"This is *your* decision, Mac. And if you decide to go for it, I'm with you. And if you decide not to, I don't want to hear about the three million dollars—ever."

Comprende? Well, I give her credit for clarity *and* balls.

"Whatever you decide, the map is yours. I trust you to let me know if you plan a future trip to Cuba."

"You know I wouldn't—"

"I said I trust you."

"Thank you. I'll make a decision before we get to Diego Devilla."

"Ciego de Ávila."

"Whichever comes first."

We continued on through the highlands of Santa Clara, which were starkly beautiful and which in no way resembled the mountains of Afghanistan, except for their quiet, brooding presence above the dangerous road.

We drove in silence and passed the exit for Sancti Spíritus. About ten minutes later the highway went to two lanes and Sara said, "The Autopista will end in a few kilometers. We need to get on the CC—the Carretera Central—and continue east to Ciego de Ávila."

"Okay."

The Autopista petered out and I followed the traffic to the CC, a badly paved road heading east, and joined a line of trucks and buses in the two slow-moving lanes. Hitchhikers lined the road, calling out to the passing vehicles, and a few of them looked like backpackers from somewhere else: blonde hair, young, fearless and clueless, on a great adventure. God bless them. And I hope they never see what I saw when I was their age.

Sara said, "About thirty minutes to Ciego de Ávila."

I glanced at her and asked, "If we go to Camagüey, what's in it for you?"

"Two things. The first is to make good on my grandfather's promise to his clients. The second is to make good on my promise to you."

That sounded very nice. But that wouldn't incentivize *me* to risk my life. "Tell you what—if we go to the cave and find the money, I'll split my share with you."

"Thank you. But I'm not doing this for money."

"Never turn down money you've earned."

"I'm also giving you this choice so I don't have to hear you complaining about losing three million dollars."

"That sounds like put up or shut up."

"Take your pick."

"Thanks."

The CC was moving at about forty miles an hour, and I shared the road with lumbering trucks and farm vehicles that were in no hurry. I spotted an old Ford sedan in the oncoming lane, which made me feel less like the only hot dog in a bowl of chili.

Sara glanced at her map. "There's a ring road around Ciego de Ávila. When we get on it, we can continue to Camagüey, or take the Carretera Norte to the coast."

I didn't reply, and we drove on in silence.

We came to the circular road and the moment of truth. The first exit road headed south, then we came to the exit road that continued east to Camagüey. I slowed down and glanced at her, but she had her head back and her eyes closed.

The road to Camagüey beckoned, like the road to El Dorado, and I hesitated, then waved good-bye to my three million dollars and turned onto the Carretera Norte, toward the sea.

I drove for a few minutes, then said, "I'll buy you a drink at the Melia Hotel."

She kept her eyes closed, but nodded.

Well . . . I would have risked it if it was only me. But I wasn't going to risk Sara's life, or risk losing the remains of the forgotten dead who had been waiting too long to go home to their families and their nation. Jack would agree. You never leave a body behind.

There wasn't as much traffic on the Carretera Norte, and the road was mostly downhill, and the highlands were flattening out as we headed to the coast. "How far?"

She opened her eyes and looked at the map. "About thirty kilometers to a town called Morón, then fifteen kilometers on a road that leads to the Cayo Coco causeway." She added, "The causeway looks about fifteen kilometers long."

So, to do the math, it was about sixty kilometers to Cayo Coco. Maybe another hour at this speed. I checked my watch. It was just past 11. We should be in Cayo Guillermo at about 12:30. I said, "I think we're going to make it."

"There was never any doubt in my mind."

"Me neither."

"Do you have any regrets?"

"About what?"

"The money."

"What money?"

She put her hand on my shoulder. "We'll come back someday."

"Give me a call. Or stop by the Green Parrot."

She didn't reply.

I took the treasure map off my lap and handed it to her. "Burn this."

"It's yours."

"Then I say burn it."

She looked at the map. "A great hike through the Camagüey Mountains." She fired up Jack's Zippo, touched the flame to the map, and let it fly out the window.

I took my cigar out of my pocket and handed it to her. "We're in the home stretch."

We shared our last cigar as we headed for Cayo Guillermo and our rendezvous with Jack, Felipe, *Fishy Business*, and fate. I wondered when I'd get my surprise.

CHAPTER 47

We drove through the picturesque town of Morón and took a two-lane road that skirted a lake and cut through an expanse of lush and pristine marshland. A flock of pink flamingos settled into the water, fishing for lunch.

There didn't seem to be anyone else on this road. "Where is everyone?"

Sara took her eyes off the flamingos and replied, "Most people arrive at the resort islands by boat or plane. There are actually direct commercial flights to the airport on Cayo Coco from Toronto and London, and charter flights from all over Europe."

"What's the draw?"

"It's warm and it's cheap."

"Right." The Europeans would go to hell if they could get a cheap charter package.

She continued, "Also, as you know, this is some of the greatest sports fishing in the world." She smiled. "In fact, I think there's a fishing tournament going on right now."

"I hope so."

"They're still here, Mac." She added, "Someday, maybe soon, Americans will be coming here in droves to fish."

Not if Eduardo and Carlos and their amigos had anything to say about it. But maybe—now that I needed to work for a living again—I could run charters to Cayo Guillermo from Key West. Two nations, one vacation. All I needed was my boat and a new identity.

The road continued through the wetlands, and up ahead I could see blue water, which Sara said was the Bahía de Perros—the Bay of Dogs—and a spit of land jutting out to the horizon.

She said, "That's the causeway."

We continued through the wetlands, which were now giving way to the deeper waters of the bay ahead.

She assured me, "Once we're over the causeway, we won't attract any attention."

"What do we do for the next six hours?"

"Whatever we do, we need to stay close to our cargo."

"I could use a wash. Are there any nude beaches?"

"What did it say in your guide book that you were supposed to read?"

"I didn't get that far because I didn't think we'd get this far."

"Well, let me brief you. First, there's not much of a Cuban population on the islands except for day workers at the resorts, so there are no neighborhood watch groups. That doesn't mean there are no chivatos among the hotel and restaurant workers, but almost all the foreigners on the islands are Europeans, Canadians, and Brits, whom the regime does not associate with suspicious activity."

I didn't think any of that was in the guide book. That came from someplace else. I suggested, "Let's be Canadians again." I got laid last time.

"There is a police presence on the islands, but I'm told it's light and soft."

"That's a nice change. But, as per what I did read in my guide book, Cayo Guillermo is an entry port, so there'll be port security and patrol boats." I added, "Getting in by car is easy. Getting out by boat, maybe not so."

"We'll find out tonight."

"And we'll find out very soon if the fleet is still here or back in Key West."

"They're here," she said.

"If not, is there a Plan B?"

"We'll find out when we meet our contact."

"What if he or she doesn't show up?"

"He'll be there, and the fleet will be there."

"We'll see. And last but not least, there's the possibility that the police have connected me to Fishy Business, and are waiting for us in Cayo Guillermo."

"No, they'll be waiting for us at the toll booth on the causeway where we have to show our passports."

"No one mentioned toll booths or passports."

"It was in the guide book that Carlos gave you."

"Is there a way around the toll booth?"

"No. But there's a way around showing our passports."

"Do I need my wallet or do I need my gun?"

"Neither." She pulled two blue passports out of her pocket and handed one to me.

I glanced at it and saw it was a Canadian passport, which was a lot more authentic-looking than my Conch Republic passport. I thumbed open the cover and looked at the photo, which was the same as my real passport photo. But my name was now Jonathan Richard Mills. The passport was issued in Toronto. I didn't even remember being there. "Where did you get this?"

"Amigos."

"Right." I looked at the passport pages and saw a few exit and entry stamps. I didn't know I'd been to London's Heathrow Airport.

She said, "These passports will withstand visual scrutiny at the toll booth, but not a passport scanner at an airport."

I reminded her, "We're sailing home." I also reminded her, "Our airport photos are probably being circulated, and mine looks a lot like this one."

"Hopefully, the Ministry of the Interior forgot the Cayo Coco causeway toll booth. And if not, just smile at the toll collector and say buenos días as he's glancing at your Canadian passport and taking your two CUCs."

"Okay." I looked at the solitary toll booth that was placed in the middle of the road so that the toll taker could collect from the drivers in either direction. "Do they have SunPass here?"

"Give him a sunny smile."

"Right." I asked, "What's your name?"

She handed me her Canadian passport. "Anna Teresa Mills. We're married."

"When did that happen?"

"That explains my Latina appearance if someone is thinking about the face matching the name."

"Right." And obviously someone back in the U.S. thought about it. "Do you speak Spanish?"

"Un poco."

"Is this going to work?"

"Mac, if you can't get past a toll booth, we should turn around."

I didn't know architects could be so cool and calm. But then I remembered she'd been briefed—or trained—by a retired CIA guy . . . or maybe not retired.

As we approached the toll booth, a pickup truck pulled in front of me from a side road, and in the bed of the truck were about a dozen men and women, joking and smoking.

Sara said, "Day workers."

I felt like I was home.

The toll booth guy waved the truck through, but I knew we had to stop.

Sara said, "Don't offer the passports. Let him ask."

I pulled up to the booth, smiled, and said to the uniformed toll taker, "Buenos días," as I handed the guy two CUCs.

"Buenos días, señor . . . y señorita." He hesitated, then said, "Pasaporte, por favor."

I gave him the two passports, which he flipped through, then glanced at me, then bent his head to get a look at Anna Teresa, who was leaning toward the window, smiling at him.

He said something in Spanish and handed me the passports. Adios.

I proceeded onto the causeway. "I'm glad he didn't ask to see what was in the back."

"This is not a border crossing." She added, "I was told this was easy."

I didn't ask who told her that, but I said, "Well, we can beat the toll when we leave here."

The two causeway lanes weren't much wider than a single lane, and there were no guardrails on the road, which was built on piles of rock. A truck came toward me, and we both had to squeeze to the side, and I thought one of us was going to wind up in the Bay of Dogs. An accident would not be good. "How long is this?"

"I told you. Fifteen kilometers." She suggested, "Enjoy it."

I kept my speed down and continued on the causeway, which reminded me of the Overseas Highway where I'd begun this vacation. Gulls and pelicans swept back and forth over the road, and the bay was alive with waterfowl.

Sara said, "I'd like to come back here someday."

I'd like to get out of here tonight.

The causeway continued in an almost straight line across the bay and I could now see the shoreline of Cayo Coco in the distance.

I thought back to the uniformed toll booth collector, which made me think back to the uniformed passport guy at José Martí Airport—the guy who called ahead and had Sara stopped. I said, "The police could be waiting for us on the other end."

"There's not much we can do about it now."

"Right." U-turns were not an option.

I could see a jetliner making its slow approach into the island airport, and as it got lower I saw the Air Canada maple leaf logo on its tail. And this brought home the fact that for the rest of the world, Cuba was just a holiday destination. For us, it was a legacy of the Cold War, a place where Americans were loved or hated, depending on who you ran into.

As we got closer to the end of the causeway, I could see what looked like mangrove swamps along the shore. The causeway curved left and I had a clear view of the road that went inland. I looked for police activity on the road, but it appeared to be clear. "I think we're okay."

Sara, who had seemed cool as a frozen daiquiri, now took a

deep breath. Then, out of the clear blue Cuban sky she asked me, "What did you mean when you said, 'Give me a call, or stop by the Green Parrot'?"

Well, I guess what I meant was that we were going our separate ways. Freudian slip?

"Mac?"

"Just a dumb joke."

"It wasn't funny."

"Right." Had she been brooding this whole time? I mean, we had more immediate problems.

She said, "If we get out of here alive—"

Like that problem.

"—we'll have a bond that can never be broken."

Did her boyfriend have a gun?

"Do you believe that?"

"I do." I let her know, "The bonds I formed in combat will be with me all my life." Though I wasn't having sex with those guys.

"Do you love me?"

"I do."

"That's what I needed to know . . . in case we get . . . separated."

"And you?"

"You don't have to ask."

We held hands as we drove off the causeway onto Cayo Coco and continued on a narrow tree-shaded road.

"Turn left for Cayo Guillermo."

Next stop, Key West, Florida, U.S.A.

CHAPTER 48

Cayo Coco, the largest of the islands in the archipelago, seemed to be in the midst of a construction boom, with hotels and cottages rising along the white beaches. This was a different Cuba, and I wondered if all this foreign investment was in anticipation of the arrival of the Americans. If so, the investors might have a longer wait than they thought.

Sara was looking at a map in her Cuba guide book. "Stay on this road for the Cayo Guillermo causeway."

"Okay." I spotted a few vintage American cars, which I assumed were taxis, and in fact, an older couple tried to wave me down. I waved back. "Dave Katz should come here."

"Who's that?"

"A taxi driver in Key West."

"*We* should come back here. On your boat."

Did she mean the same boat that we were going to use to escape from Cuba? "I think we'll be unwelcome here after our Miami press conference."

She didn't reply.

I drove onto the Cayo Guillermo causeway, which was lined with anglers, and I saw that one guy had caught a red snapper. "You like sushi?"

"Don't talk about food."

The sand banks and shallows along the causeway were pink with hundreds of swaying flamingos, and Sara said, "This is breathtaking."

"It is."

The short causeway ended and we were now in Cayo Guillermo—not the end of our journey, but maybe the beginning of the end. And that depended on the Pescando Por la Paz fleet still being here. And we'd know that in about ten minutes.

Sara said, "We made it."

Indeed we did. "Where's the marina?"

She glanced at her guide book. "Take a right."

Cayo Guillermo wasn't as developed as Cayo Coco, and there was almost no traffic on the narrow road, except for bicycles and Coco cabs. I saw a sign ahead that said: MARINA MARLIN, and I turned into a gravel parking area and stopped.

The marina was a collection of decent-looking buildings along the shoreline, including a big open shed where the fishermen brought their catch to be weighed and photographed while they told fish stories and had a brew. I noticed, off to the left, a shabbier structure flying the Cuban flag, and I assumed this was the government Port of Entry building. In fact, there were four olive drab military-type vehicles in front of the building, and I saw a wooden sign that said: GUARDA FRONTERA. And under that, it said, MINISTERO DEL INTERIOR—same as Villa Marista prison. These assholes were everywhere.

As I watched the building, a guy in an olive green uniform came out, got into one of the vehicles, and began driving toward us. I drove the wagon toward the main marina building, but I saw the guy give us a glance as he passed by.

Some of the docks were visible behind the marina and there weren't many boats tied. I looked at my watch. It was a little after 1 P.M., and the fleet should still be out. Unless it was in Florida. "I'll go see what I can find out. You stay with the cargo."

She said something to me in Spanish that I didn't understand, but I got her point. "Adios, and good luck."

She got out of the wagon, walked to the main marina building, and went inside.

Well, this was another one of those moments on which hung the fate of this mission and our own fate. If the fleet had been ordered out of Cuba, we'd be joining the balseros on a raft tonight.

I saw a boat anchored about a hundred yards from the marina—a 100-footer, painted gray, and though I couldn't see the markings, I saw a Cuban flag flying from its stern, and on its rear deck was a gun turret. That was not a fishing boat.

It occurred to me, again, that too much of this mission relied too heavily on a series of events over which we had little or no control. I would have liked a plan that didn't depend so much on vaya con Dios.

Another military guy came out of the government building, looked at the American station wagon, then got into his vehicle and drove off. Must be lunch time. And here we were parked right next to a Guarda Frontera and customs and immigration facility whose employees made a living asking for your passport. *Pasaporte, señor?* What was my name again?

Sara came out of the marina and I couldn't tell from her face if she had good news or if we were swimming home.

She got into the wagon and said, "Good news. Fishy Business is now in third place."

I never thought third place would be good news. "They'd catch up if they had a few more days. Okay, where to?"

"Melia Hotel. Down the road a few hundred yards."

I pulled out of the parking area and turned right on the sand-swept road.

The first hotel we came to was the Grand Carib, then a place called the Iberostar Daiquiri, which reminded me that I needed a drink.

"Turn here."

I pulled into the long palm-lined driveway of the Melia Hotel, a complex of pink stucco buildings with lush landscaping. This was where the three fishermen were staying while Jack and Felipe lived on the boat, and it was where Sara and I would meet our Cayo Guillermo contact tonight at 7. If he—or she— showed.

Sara, confirming what she'd been told about the Melia, said, "For a nice tip, we can park here tonight in the circular driveway and keep an eye on the wagon from those windows, which are the lobby bar."

Well, when I pictured this scene after my cemetery briefing, I saw me sitting here in a truck with sixty million dollars in the back. I suppose I should be grateful I got this far. But would I have accepted this job if I knew the sixty million was optional? No. But I might have if they'd told me about the Villa Marista bones.

"Mac? Let's go."

"Okay . . . but now that we're Canadians, we can get a room here right now and take turns showering and getting some sleep while one of us hangs out in the bar." Though I didn't know how we were going to have sex with that plan. "We'll pay cash."

"Sounds tempting, but we also need to show visas, and show our means of arrival and departure."

"Okay, then let's just go to the bar."

"We're not supposed to be here until seven and we'll follow the plan." She added, "I have a place we can go. Take a right on the road."

Sara had obviously been instructed on what to do here and what not to do. All I knew—from Sara in the cemetery—was Melia Hotel lobby bar, 7 P.M. And I guess that was all I needed to know until I needed to know more.

I pulled out of the Melia Hotel and turned right on the beach road. We passed a hotel called the Sol Club, which seemed to be the last hotel on the road. Ahead was an expanse of low tropical growth, punctuated by palm trees, and to our right was the white sand beach and the Atlantic Ocean, where I'd be tonight if everything went according to the plan we'd hear at 7.

We came to the end of the road and a wooden sign that said: PLAYA PILAR. Sara said, "Named after Hemingway's boat."

"I never would have guessed."

"He named his boat for his heroine in For Whom the Bell Tolls. Would you name a boat for me?"

"Of course." If I had a boat. Anna?

I pulled into the sandy parking area, which was hidden from

the road by high bushes, and stopped under a palm tree. There were a few other cars in the parking area, and closer to the water was a long blue building with a thatched roof that looked like a beach bar and restaurant.

Sara said, "We can kill some time here and still keep an eye on the wagon from the back deck."

Obviously someone had done a recon, which encouraged me to believe that someone knew what they were doing.

We got out of the wagon and retrieved our backpacks from the rear seat. I pulled the Glock out of my belt and shoved it in my pack.

We walked into the restaurant, called Ranchón Playa Pilar, and through a beach bar called Hemingway, which was no surprise. We went out back to a raised wooden deck where a few people sat at plastic tables, mostly couples in their thirties, and others ranging in age from old to young, and in color from pale to lobster red. I could smell french fries.

There was no waitstaff around, so we seated ourselves at a table with a good view of the beach and the Roadmaster. At the other end of the wooden deck was a couple with three children, and the kids were running around, being obnoxious.

Sara said, "I'd like to have children."

"I'll have the fries."

I looked out at the water, which was partially blocked by high sand dunes. There were wooden walkways going out to the beach, and someone had built a lookout tower where I saw people with binoculars and cameras. This was a nice piece of the world.

So we sat there, smelling the fries and salt air, and listening to the surf and the hyperactive children. We could have been anywhere on holiday in the Caribbean or South Florida. But we weren't. We were, in fact, in Cuba, where, as Sara once said, the police state is not always apparent.

I noticed that the dozen or so customers were dressed in casual beach attire, including bare feet, whereas Sara and I were dressed more like hikers, complete with boots. Also, I was fairly sure I was the only person on the deck with a gun in my backpack. Fitting into your environment is more a matter of state of mind than of attire, and trying to be inconspicuous draws attention.

A young waitress wearing black pants and a pink T-shirt came over to our table and wished us buenos días as she checked us out, maybe trying to determine our national origin. I'm Canadian.

Sara returned the greeting in Spanish, then said in English, "We'd like to see a lunch menu, por favor."

"Sí, señora."

I thought Sara was señorita. This trip must have aged her.

"Meanwhile," I said, "I'll have a beer. Do you have Corona?"

"Sí."

There is a God. I asked Sara, "Have you thought about what you would like, Anna?"

"Well, Jonathan, I'd like a daiquiri."

"Just like in Toronto." I said to the waitress, "A daiquiri for the señora, por favor—eh?"

"Sí, I will return." And she left.

Sara said, "You're an idiot."

"You have to immerse yourself in your cover story. Didn't they teach you that?"

She had no reply.

"Can we hang out here until seven?"

"This place closes at four-thirty." She looked at me. "Sometimes, before a clandestine rendezvous, it's best to be static. Sometimes it's best to be mobile."

"They taught you well."

"I read Richard Neville novels."

"Don't confuse fact with fiction." Which reminded me of something. "Do you have our group roster?"

"I do. I took it in case we could use it for cover. Why?"

"I want to get a Hemingway postcard from here and send it to Richard."

"Please focus on the mission."

"I have many missions in life."

"Not if you don't complete this one."

"Right."

I looked again at the beach. The sand was almost iridescent, with a touch of blue and pink, and the water was a deep aquamarine. But farther out, I could see whitecaps and wispy clouds scudding quickly from east to west. There was a weather system on the way.

The waitress returned with our drinks and two lunch menus, and I noticed the prices were in CUCs only, which effectively barred Cubans in their own people's republic. The waitress said she'd come back for our orders, but we didn't let her get away. We both ordered the specialty of the house, which was a lobster salad, and I ordered two bottles of water and papas fritas—french fries. I asked the waitress, "Do you know where I can buy postcards?"

"Sí. Inside you will find these."

"Gracias."

Sara asked, "Los baños?"

The waitress directed us to the baños, took our menus, and left.

I asked, "What are we going to do with all our Cuban pesos?"

"Save them for next time."

Send me a postcard.

Sara took her backpack and stood. "Keep an eye on our cargo."

"Find me a Hemingway postcard."

So I sat there, rehydrating with my Corona, which, though it came from Mexico, brought back memories of home. And I looked out at the sea in the same way that the Habaneros on the Malecón stared wistfully at the Straits of Florida. So near, yet so far.

Actually, Cayo Guillermo was about three hundred and fifty kilometers from Key West—about two hundred and fifty miles from Cayo to Key. That would be about a ten-hour cruise at twenty-five knots, depending on winds, waves, and tides. If we left here at midnight tonight, we should be at Charter Boat Row no later than 10 A.M., and at the Green Parrot in time for lunch. And Fantasy Fest was still in full swing.

More important, we should be in international waters an hour after leaving here, theoretically safe from Guarda Frontera patrol boats.

I wasn't sure what the plan was to transfer our cargo to *Fishy Business*, but we'd find out at 7 tonight, and I hoped the plan didn't rely too heavily on a prayer to the Virgin Mary. If it did, I, as captain, would change it.

One of the obnoxious kids ran over to me, a six- or seven-year-old porker wearing only a bathing suit. He had a paper cup of french fries in his hand that I would have broken his wrist for. He stuffed a handful of fries in his mouth and inquired, "Where are you from?"

"Canada. Can't you tell?"

"We're from Hamilton. Where are you from?"

"Toronto."

"You sound like an American."

"Go play in the riptide."

"You're an American."

"Are you a chivato?"

"What's that?"

"Give me a french fry and I'll tell you."

"You mean a chip."

Busted by a six-year-old. "Right."

He stuck the cup toward me and I grabbed a few fries—chips— before he pulled them away.

"What's a . . . chovi—"

"Comemierda. It's a smart person. In Spanish. Say it."

He got it right on the second try and I encouraged him to use the word with the waitstaff.

His mother called to him to stop bothering the nice man and he ran off with his chips, yelling, "They're Americans!"

Thanks, kid. Well, it wasn't a crime to be an American in Cayo Guillermo, but it was a crime to be Daniel MacCormick and Sara Ortega in Cuba. I should have shown the kid my Canadian passport. If it fooled him, it would fool the police.

Sara returned and I decided not to mention the kid. She didn't spook easily, but she might want to leave before I got my lobster salad.

She put a stack of postcards on the table. "Pick one. We'll keep the rest as souvenirs."

I was hoping for three million dollars to remember Cuba by, but I wasn't allowed to say that.

I flipped through the postcards and found one of a fishing boat that said, *Cayo Coco and Cayo Guillermo, Where Ernest Hemingway Loved to Fish.* Perfect. "Dear Richard, I hope you liked your T-shirt and I hope you and Cindy went to Rolando's."

"And I hope you get to mail that postcard from Key West."

"We will."

So we sat there and enjoyed the moment. I glanced at the Buick Roadmaster in the parking area. Almost as important as us getting out of Cuba alive was getting our cargo safely and secretly into the U.S. And that made me think ahead to the American Coast Guard cutters and the DEA intercept boats. But Jack and I and *The Maine*—now *Fishy Business*—were in the computer system and we were considered trusted boat owners and crew, and we knew some of the Coast Guard people by name and we'd chatted with them on the radio. Same with U.S. Customs in Key West. And that, I knew, was one of the many good reasons why Carlos and his amigos picked Jack and me for this interesting job.

Our lobster salads and fries came and we ate and drank in silence, dividing our attention between the sea and the parking area where the Buick wagon sat—and where the police would come if they were looking for us.

Well, we'd gotten to Cayo Guillermo, and we'd learned that the fleet was still here. That was the good news. The bad news was that Sara and I were by now the subject of a nationwide police hunt. But Cuba was a big island, and the police, as in most police states, were better at intimidation than police science. I was sure that most fugitives were found as a result of chivatos tipping off the police. So we were relatively safe here, in a chivato-free zone.

Unless, of course, the police had made the connection between me and *Fishy Business,* which could have happened an hour ago, or could happen an hour from now.

So that was my analysis of enemy strengths, weaknesses, and capabilities. Now for my friends.

First, there was Eduardo on the loose. I probably should have stuffed him in a car trunk in Chico's garage, but Sara would have been upset.

Next, I still hadn't gotten my surprise. It wasn't my birthday, so it had to be something else. Maybe the plan called for leaving me and Jack in Cayo Guillermo. Surprise! But they needed us for the press conference—unless that was all bullshit. But they also needed Jack and me to get the boat past the Coast Guard, and to avoid U.S. Customs. Also, now that we didn't have the sixty million dollars with us, the chances of Jack and I being double-crossed were greatly reduced. But not zero.

And finally, I couldn't help but think—for the last time, until next time—about the three million dollars. Two for me, one for Jack. That would have been a life changer. But maybe the money was still there, and maybe I'd come back for it with Sara—if we didn't have a life-changing experience here in the next few hours.

Meanwhile, our contact person at the Melia Hotel didn't know what night we'd show up, but I hoped he—or she—showed up at the lobby bar every night as instructed. *It's good to see you here.*

Sara asked, "Have you figured out your surprise?"

"I haven't thought about it."

"Well . . . then maybe I should tell you now."

"Now would be good."

She hesitated, then said, "Our contact at the Melia bar is Felipe."

That *was* a surprise. But not a big one. And it made sense from a security standpoint—fewer people involved, and someone with skin in the game. "That's good." But why did she think I wouldn't be pleased? Well . . . if I'm so smart, I should know.

I looked at her, and we made eye contact. "Okay . . ." I think I got it. "Okay . . . and . . . ?"

"I'm sorry, Mac. You needed to know before we met him."

Right. So I could act as though Sara and I were barely on a first-name basis after a week together. Well, these people really did keep it in the family.

She looked at me. "I . . . don't know what to say."

"Well . . . me neither. But what were you thinking?"

"I was thinking that we wouldn't get this far. So it didn't matter. I *wanted* you . . . and I guess I should have thought ahead."

Well, in truth, I myself don't often think farther than my dick, but . . . I had to admit I was . . . angry? No, more like surprised at my feelings. When the boyfriend was abstract and in Miami, it didn't bother me too much. But now that I could put a handsome face on the generic boyfriend, and a name, Felipe, it was starting to hit me—hard.

"Say something."

I looked at her and saw she was upset. I assured her, "When we meet Felipe, I will act as though nothing has happened between us." I saw Casablanca six times.

"He's already half crazy with jealously."

"Can't imagine why."

"He's Cuban."

And this was the guy I'd be on the boat with for ten hours. Well, I had a gun. But so did he. I thought back to when I'd asked her, "How well do you know Felipe?" And she'd replied, "I've met him." Well, I guess so. And I also thought back to Sara in Floridita, asking if Jack had asked me if I was sleeping with her. I recalled, too, that Jack had told me that Felipe knew Sara. Was Jack trying to tell me something? Also, Eduardo knew what was going on, maybe from Jack, or maybe from looking into Sara's eyes at Chico's garage, and I remembered that Eduardo reminded her that she was committed to a man in Miami. And he'd stared at her when he confirmed what the contact—Felipe—would say. *It's good to see you here.*

So, yes, I had all the clues I needed. Then why didn't I put them together? Because love is blind.

In any case, Eduardo had no way of contacting his nephew about his suspicions. And he never would. So I assured her again, "I will be an officer and a gentleman."

"Is that all you have to say."

"What do you want me to say?"

"I want you to say you *want* me."

She may have watched too many Cuban soap operas, which was what this was starting to sound like.

"You said you loved me."

"I do." And I really did. So I had to ask, "Do you love him?"

"I did. Not anymore. I wouldn't have had sex with you if I did."

"Okay. Does he love you?"

"He confuses jealousy with love."

I never had that problem, though I have confused sex with love. But not this time.

Well, I was feeling really crappy, and I'm not used to being one side of a triangle. "We'll stick to our story tonight, and when we get home, we can sort it out."

She nodded and took my hand. "When we get back, I'll tell him."

I thought she was going to do that in Havana. But Felipe was not reachable by phone because he was on the boat. She must have forgotten.

She forced a smile. "I love you even though you have no money."

Thanks for reminding me. But that was nice to hear, and I smiled.

She looked around for the waitress. "Let's have another drink."

"Not for me. But you have one." I stood and slung my backpack on my shoulder.

"Where are you going?"

"For a walk on the beach."

"I'll go with you."

"No. We should split up—for tactical security. If the police are looking for us, they won't get both of us, and one of us will be able to get to the hotel bar and meet our contact . . . Felipe."

She stood. "No—"

"I'm giving the orders now, as I will be when I'm captain of my ship tonight. So get used to taking orders."

"Mac . . . *no* . . ."

"You need to stay with the cargo." I threw the keys on the table. "I'll meet you at the Melia Hotel, lobby bar, at let's say six-thirty."

She looked really upset, and we were starting to attract attention, so I gave her a kiss and said, "It's okay. This is the way to do it. I'll see you in a few hours."

And off I went, down toward the beach with my backpack and Glock. I glanced back to see if she was following, but I didn't see her.

In love and war, you need to make hard decisions.

Well, this should be an interesting night. And hopefully the last surprise.

CHAPTER 49

I walked west along the nearly deserted beach, then came around to the tip of the island and continued along the southern shore, but I ran into a mangrove swamp and headed inland. Sometimes you need to recon the terrain, and sometimes you need to do a one-man recon of your head.

I made my way through the bush for awhile before I realized I was half asleep and still walking. I used to be good at sleepwalking on forced night marches, but I had no objective today except to be alone, so I found a patch of clear ground under a tall palm and sat.

I pulled my Glock from my pack, stuck it under my shirt, and leaned back against the tree trunk. It was hot inland, and buggy, so I didn't expect company.

Thinking back on all this, I should have suspected that Sara's boyfriend in Miami was none other than Felipe. The clues, as I said, were there, but I wasn't putting them together. And not because I'm dense, but because I didn't want to go there. My mother used to call this willful ignorance. She still does.

Well, I've been in situations like this before, but this was the first time the boyfriend was going to be onboard the boat we'd all have to share on our midnight run. Me, Jack, Felipe, and Sara. We'd have to figure out the sleeping arrangements. Could be awkward, even though we were all going to pretend that I'd been a perfect gentleman in Cuba.

I understood why Sara had lied, and I understood that she was conflicted, and that at some point she'd made up her mind about Felipe. But the only way this wasn't going to be a problem in Cayo

Guillermo was if she and I had never made it here, as she said. But here we were, against all odds.

Side two of this triangle was Felipe. I really didn't give a shit that he was half crazy with jealousy because his girlfriend was alone with me in Cuba. But as a guy, I could sympathize with him. I actually liked him when I met him in Key West. He seemed competent, assured, and trustworthy. But thinking back, I realized now that he was sizing me up, probably trying to guess if I was the kind of guy who'd try to pop his girlfriend. If I'd known what the situation was, I would have assured him that I wasn't that kind of guy. But no one told me, so I didn't have the chance to be noble. Instead, I had a chance to get laid.

And why, I wondered, did no one tell me that Sara and Felipe were an item? Maybe Sara *was* supposed to tell me. And if not her, why not Carlos or Eduardo? Well, maybe because they really wanted me to come onboard, to use a nautical term, and Sara Ortega was one of many shiny lures. Sara, though, did say she had a boyfriend. She just couldn't remember his name.

Bottom line, this mission was important to Eduardo, Carlos, and their amigos, and they'd do or say anything to make it happen. I could only imagine what they'd said to Felipe to make him agree to send his girlfriend on a dangerous mission with a handsome stranger. And what did Sara say to assure Felipe that she'd keep her legs crossed? I suspect there were promises made and talk of issues larger and more important than two people. And maybe a large cash payment to Felipe, to help him with his jealousy. And no one was really thinking about this moment when it all came together.

And then there was Sara, the object of many men's affection—me, Felipe, Eduardo, and of course Antonio. Carlos liked her, too, but Carlos was all business. Love is a subparagraph in the contract.

But Sara, I was sure, had thought all this out more than she let on—and maybe more than she knew. She'd teased and flirted a bit on my boat, and I understood what she was doing. And long before we got to Havana, she knew we'd wind up in bed. I mean, I wasn't sure, but she was. And she told me, matter-of-factly on day one in

Havana at the Hotel Nacional, that we had a date. So at least she wasn't pretending to me or to herself that she had been seduced. She was in fact, as I knew, making a deal with me: sex for reliability and commitment to the mission.

But when you make a deal like that, there are unintended consequences. Like falling in love. I think that's what happened.

Now we needed to come full circle, back to the mission, and make sure that hearts full of passion, jealousy, and hate didn't screw it up in the last act. Key West was in sight. Except it would be me at the helm with Jack. And Felipe and Sara would be sitting on the bow—or in a stateroom together. Should I make a captain's rule—no screwing onboard?

It should be an interesting cruise. But first, cocktails at 7. Then a midnight escape past Cuban gunboats.

I closed one eye and went into that half-sleep that I'd perfected in the Army, with one hand on my gun and one half of my brain awake and alert.

My last conscious thought was that Sara really believed she was in love with me in Cuba—palm trees, danger, daiquiris, moonlight, and love songs. We'd see how this played out in Key West and Miami. But first we had to get there.

CHAPTER 50

I woke from my afternoon siesta, stuck my Glock in my backpack, and made my way through the bush to the road that led to the Melia Hotel.

It was just past 6 P.M., the sun was low on the horizon, and the beach road was deserted. I guessed it was about two miles to the Melia, and I could make it in less than half an hour if I picked up my pace and if a police car didn't offer me a lift.

On that subject, I felt just a bit guilty about leaving Sara on her own, but she could take care of herself, and splitting up really was a good tactical move. Also, she'd pissed me off.

I'd had no startling revelations during my half-sleep, no subconscious insights or fuzzy feelings, and no epiphany when I woke up. I was actually still pissed off.

And what pisses me off is when people lie to me, and I was also pissed off at Carlos and Eduardo. Carlos had a lot of explaining to do when I got back. Eduardo was a dead man walking, so he got a pass.

If I thought about it, Felipe was the guy who'd been totally bull-shitted. And there was more bullshit to come for Felipe.

I passed the Sol Club, and I could see the Melia ahead, set back from the road. I checked my watch. It was 6:30. I noticed that the sun set a little earlier here than in Havana. I also noticed that the sky was dark with fast-moving clouds.

I picked up my pace and walked up the palm-lined driveway of the hotel, hot, sweaty, and looking for the Buick in the circular driveway—but I didn't see it. *Shit.*

I was about to ask a car park guy if he'd seen a beautiful lady in a beautiful American car, when I spotted the Buick pulling up. Sara saw me, but stayed in the wagon and spoke to one of the attendants in Spanish, then gave him some folding money and parked the car herself in the driveway. She got out with her backpack, locked the doors, kept the keys, and walked over to me.

I didn't know what to expect, but she said, "I was worried sick about you."

"I'm fine. How about you?"

"Do you care?"

This was going to be a long night. "Let's get a drink."

We walked into the hotel and found the lobby bar, a dimly lit place called Las Orquídeas, The Orchids, though there wasn't an orchid in sight. There were, however, lots of empty cocktail tables and chairs, and Sara asked the hostess, in English, to seat us by the window because she wanted a view of her Buick that had seventeen skulls and título de propiedades in the back, though she didn't explain all that.

We put our backpacks on the floor and sat in facing armchairs, leaving a seat for Felipe to form a triangle.

Sara said, "I was afraid you weren't going to show up."

"Where was I going to go?"

"I thought you were going to pick up a woman on the beach."

Why didn't I think of that?

"I was also worried you'd get stopped."

It occurred to me that this mission could proceed without me. "That would have solved at least one problem."

She leaned toward me. "If you didn't show up here, I would have searched every inch of this island for you."

"Same here."

She sat back in her seat and glanced at her watch, then looked around the lounge. "Most of the guests are in the outdoor bar at this hour, and it's usually empty here."

I wasn't overly impressed that Carlos—or someone—had sent an advance party to scout out the terrain. But I was again encouraged that there was a plan to get us out of here.

Regarding that, assuming Sara and I were the subjects of a police hunt, it wasn't entirely safe to be meeting Felipe in a public place. The original plan anticipated that our disappearance from the Yale group might trigger a police response, but it would have been a low-priority search for two hot tamales missing from their tour group, and the police would have had fun searching the nude beaches around Havana. But because of shithead Antonio, Sara Ortega and Daniel MacCormick were now suspected of . . . whatever. And here we were in the bar of the Melia Hotel, and I wondered if our airport photos were appearing on Tele Rebelde.

Well, the lounge lighting was romantically dim, and the last week had changed our appearance a bit, so I didn't think the waitress was going to start screaming, "Here are the Americanos they're looking for!" We'd see soon enough.

Sara was staring at me and I flashed a phony smile.

"Where did you go?" she asked accusingly.

"I took a walk. How about you?"

"I stayed where you left me until I got kicked out at five, then I sat in the wagon and cried and worried about you."

Daniel MacCormick, you are a true and total shit. "I just needed a walk."

"Don't do that again." She added, "You stuck me with the bill."

"I'll buy tonight." Unless Felipe is buying.

A waitress in a sort of sarong came by, wished us good evening, and didn't start screaming for the police. She asked, "Are you guests of the hotel?"

Sara replied, "We're at the Sol Club. We'll pay in CUCs."

"Sí, señora."

Sara ordered a daiquiri—just like in Toronto—and I ordered a diet Coke so I could keep a clear head.

Sara said to me, "You should be trying something local." She said to the waitress, "Please give this gentleman a Cuba Libre." She asked me, "Have you ever had one?"

I smiled. "Once. On my boat."

The waitress left to get our drinks and Sara asked, "Do you sail?"

"I'm a fisherman."

"What do you fish for?"

"Peace."

"That's good."

She looked at me. "I'm Sara Ortega. Do you love me?"

"I do."

She leaned toward me. "Can we start all over?"

Meaning, can I put all the bullshit behind me? Why not? Life is short. "Sure."

"The only lies you're going to hear from me tonight or ever again are what I say to Felipe."

I remembered a similar promise, but I replied, "Okay."

"Are we going to be together when we get back?"

"I'd like that . . . but . . . you know, sometimes when people are thrown into a dangerous situation together—"

"They see what the other person is made of. I like what I've seen." She looked at me.

"Me too." I've done a great job. Sara, too.

Our drinks came and we touched glasses. Here's looking at you, kid. Cue the soundtrack.

I said, "I assume I'm supposed to know that you and Felipe are an item."

She nodded. "I was supposed to tell you."

"When?"

"After we landed at the airport."

I seemed to recall that when we took a walk at the Nacional, on our first day in Havana, she'd told me she didn't have a boyfriend, which contradicted what she'd said on my boat when she told me she *did* have a boyfriend. But she later confessed—after sex—that, actually, she had a boyfriend. I should have written this down.

She reminded me, "I did tell you."

"I appreciate your honesty." I suggested, "Sometimes a name helps."

"Would it have made a difference?"

Good question. If I'd known I was cuckolding Felipe, a teammate, would I have gone to bed with her?

"Mac?"

"It's a moot question."

"You sound like Carlos. That's what lawyers say."

"I've never been so insulted."

"Let's change the subject."

That's what women say. But I didn't say that.

She sat back in her chair and confessed, "I'm a little nervous."

"Drink up."

"I think he's going to take one look at us—"

"He already knows. Or he thinks he knows. Or he's just pissed off that we've been together, day and night, for a week."

She nodded.

"Let's stick to business. And the business is getting the hell out of here without getting killed." I assured her, "He knows that, and that's his primary concern tonight. You are his secondary concern."

"You know how to make a woman feel special."

I agreed, "I'm a hopeless romantic."

I also mentioned my concern about being recognized if our photos were being circulated, or broadcast on TV.

Sara had obviously thought about that—or been briefed—and replied, "The average Cuban wants nothing to do with the police, and they would only be good citizens if the police were looking for a murderer or rapist. They don't care about enemies of the regime." She added, "Most Cubans like Americans."

"We're Canadians."

She continued, "The chivatos are another matter, but as you saw with Antonio, most chivatos would like to shake you down before they called the police." She also reminded me, "There are few if any chivatos in the resort islands."

"It only takes one." I asked her, "What if the Ministry of the Interior has offered an actual monetary reward for information leading to our arrest?"

She didn't reply immediately, then said, "Well . . . that would be a problem." She added, "But we won't be sitting here long after we meet our contact . . . Felipe." She explained, "The tournament has booked an extra room at the Melia and Felipe is supposed to have a key, and that's where we're going to hide out—and freshen up—until we're ready to leave here and get our cargo aboard the boat."

"Okay. And who stays here to watch our cargo, and who goes up to the room?"

"We can work that out when Felipe gets here."

That should be interesting. I know I don't want to shower with Felipe. I asked, "Am I fully briefed now?"

"Felipe has information that I don't have, such as how to get us and the cargo onboard."

"Right." Regarding our vehicle, if one of our amigos back in Havana was voluntarily or involuntarily talking to the police about a black '53 Buick Roadmaster station wagon, we'd have a major problem, second only to the problem of the police connecting me to *Fishy Business*. We needed to get the Buick out of sight as soon as possible. And the faster we got on the water, the better.

Sara had seated herself so she could see the station wagon through the window and also the lobby entrance. I had my back to both, so I wouldn't know when our contact—Felipe—arrived until I saw the happy and surprised expression on Sara's face. Or not so happy if it was the police.

She kept looking at her watch. "He's late."

"He's probably having a few drinks before he gets here."

"Is that what you would do?"

"I may have done that on similar occasions."

She looked at me. "You're cool without being too macho."

"It's okay to be honest. As long as you're fearless."

She smiled, then looked over my shoulder, and I knew Felipe had arrived.

Sara said to me, "Tell me you love me."

"I love you."

She stood, smiled, and said, "Well, look who's here."

I stood and turned around. It was Felipe. What a surprise.

CHAPTER 51

Felipe, wearing jeans, sandals, and a silly tropical shirt with a pineapple motif, walked up to us.

He glanced at me, then tried out his smile on Sara and said, "It's good to see you here." And he really did look happy. And relieved to see that his girlfriend was alive and well. He didn't seem as thrilled to see me alive.

This was supposed to look like a serendipitous meeting, so Felipe and Sara did a hug and double-cheek kiss, then he turned to me and put out his hand. We shook and he said, "I haven't seen you since Key West. How are you?"

I'm glad he didn't ask me what I've been up to. "I'm well. And you look well."

"Thank you. And you look . . ."

Unshaven, unkempt, and maybe a bit guilty.

"Mind if I join you?"

"Have a seat," I said.

He summoned the waitress, whom he seemed to know because he'd been coming here looking for us for the last few nights.

Felipe ordered a daiquiri, which is a close cousin to a pink squirrel, and I knew I could beat him up. Sara and I ordered another round. What the hell?

While the waitress was still there, he asked Sara, "So what brings you to Cayo Guillermo?"

"You."

He smiled, but clearly he was trying to figure out if I'd seen her naked.

Felipe was looking tan and fit. He was younger than me and

younger than Sara, and I wondered what she saw in him. I had no idea what Felipe did for a living when he wasn't the first mate on *Fishy Business*, but I had the impression he could have worked in retail. Maybe ladies' handbags.

He looked around to see if we were alone, then asked Sara, "How did you make out?"

"Good and bad."

"Tell me the bad."

"We didn't get to Camagüey."

He didn't look happy. "What happened?"

I didn't like his tone of voice to Sara, and I said nicely, "It doesn't matter what happened. It only matters that we didn't get to Camagüey." I asked him, "What did Eduardo tell you?"

He stared at me. "Eduardo, the last time I saw him, was undecided about Camagüey."

"Well, he decided." I asked him, "How's Jack?"

"He's good. And he'll be happy to hear you've made it."

Did he tell you I was probably fucking your girlfriend?

Felipe said, "You weren't supposed to meet Jack in Havana."

Felipe was a little more cocky than I remembered. "It was Eduardo who I wasn't supposed to meet in Havana."

He had no reply to that, but asked Sara, "How was my uncle when you saw him?"

"He was happy," Sara assured him. "He was ready to go home."

Felipe nodded. "He's walking with God."

I said, "He's walking with too much information."

Felipe informed me, "You don't understand."

I almost said, "Sara has been trying to make me understand," but I bit my cocktail stirrer.

Sara said, "I pray for him."

Felipe seconded that. I could see they had a lot in common.

Felipe asked me, "Do you still have the gun?"

"Why would I not?"

"I can take it if you're uncomfortable carrying it."

Sigmund Freud would say he wanted to take my dick off. I didn't reply.

The waitress brought our drinks, and Felipe asked us, for her benefit, "So are you staying here?"

Sara replied, "No. We're at the Sol Club."

"Just in from Toronto," I added.

The waitress left and Felipe told me, "This is where the tournament is staying, and there's an extra room that you can use to freshen up before our cruise."

"Sara said."

He looked at me as though I needed a bath. "I have the key. You can go first, and Sara and I will follow when you come back."

Really? I didn't think so. "We have a lot to talk about."

"We'll have time after Sara and I use the room." He smiled. "I need a real shower after five days on your boat."

I leaned toward him. "Let me make something clear. When we step on my boat, I am in charge. And let me make something else clear—there is no time when you are in charge."

So we locked eyeballs, and if we'd had horns we'd have locked them, too.

Felipe backed off and said, "The showers can wait."

Sara said, "Thank you."

She was obviously a little intimidated by her boyfriend—or feeling guilty. I asked him, "What time do we sail?"

"About eleven."

"Why eleven?"

"Two reasons. One is port security. The Guarda Frontera—the border guards—have two patrol boats, and Jack and I have watched them. One goes out at dusk, and returns at about three or four in the morning. The other, the faster one, goes out at about midnight and returns at dawn." He continued, "We want an hour head start on that one."

"Then let's leave earlier and get a two-hour start."

"We can't. The second reason is the tide. It'll be high tide at eleven-twelve and I'm going to take the boat into the mangrove swamp on the south side of the island, and I can only do that at high tide." He added, "I will meet you both there."

I'd thought we were going to load up and cast off at the marina, and I wasn't sure about *The Maine* in a mangrove swamp. "We have only two trunks to load. Why can't we leave from the marina?"

He explained, a bit impatiently, "Because the border guards want to know what you're doing, who and what you're bringing onboard, and if they don't recognize you, they check passports and tourist visas."

"They actually want a donation to their retirement fund."

Felipe nodded, but said, "I don't want you two to interact with them."

He sounded like he knew what he was doing. If he could stop thinking about me screwing his girlfriend, he should be able to concentrate on the great escape. "And we meet you in the mangrove swamp?"

He nodded. "This place was scouted a few months ago, and I checked it out and drew a map for you."

Apparently every Cuban thought he was Magellan.

He continued, "There's a dirt road that goes down to a floating dock in the mangrove swamp. Locals and tourists use the dock, usually during the day, and the road will support a heavy vehicle." He asked, "What are you driving?"

Sara replied, "A Buick station wagon."

He looked at her. "What's in the two trunks?"

I replied, "If your uncle didn't tell you, you don't need to know."

"I think I know."

"Then don't ask."

He started to say something, then thought better of it and finished his daiquiri, then signaled the waitress for another. I didn't want him drunk, so I said, "That's the last one." I asked, "Is there a problem for you and Jack getting the boat out of the marina at that hour?"

"I just need to have the Guarda Frontera sign a despacho for some night fishing, which I'll do when I get back to the marina. If it's just Jack and me, and if I don't have our three fishermen aboard, the Guarda won't think we're all trying to escape from Cuba for some paranoid reason."

"Will your fishermen be okay after we disappear?"

"They'll be as surprised as the border guards tomorrow morning. They should be okay under questioning." He added, "They have tickets to fly to Mexico City on the last day of the tournament."

Unless they were in jail. Well, every mission has collateral damage. "All right. And you're sure you can navigate through the mangrove swamp."

"No, I'm not sure, and neither is Jack. But my tide table says I have seven feet of water at that dock at high tide, and Jack says The Maine draws about five feet, depending on her weight, and we're light on fuel."

I wasn't sure he should put so much faith in the tide table. "Side clearance?"

"There's a path cut through the mangroves that the sightseeing boats use, from the dock to the Bahía de Perros—the Bay of Dogs."

I liked that he translated.

"I'll back it in, then we load up from the dock and off we go."

I was going to miss the Buick Roadmaster. But not as much as I was going to miss my red Porsche 911.

I didn't want to sit here too long, and the question of who was going to use the room and when was still not resolved. Would I let Felipe and Sara go to the room together? Would Sara go, and take one for the team and the mission? Stay tuned.

Well, when you're looking for something to talk about, the weather is a good subject. I asked Felipe, "What's the weather looking like?"

He sipped his daiquiri. "Not good." He glanced out the window. "There's a late tropical storm developing, and it's about sixty K east of here, moving west-northwest at ten or fifteen K. So it should hit"—he looked at his watch—"maybe midnight. Maybe earlier or later." He complained, "It's hard to get an accurate forecast here."

"What are the winds?"

"About thirty to forty knots. Waves are between five and ten."

I hoped he meant feet, not meters.

"We should be able to keep ahead of the storm," said Felipe with the phony nonchalance of all seafarers. "Depending on its speed and how it tracks."

Thanks for your insight into the obvious. Sara was looking a little concerned, so I said, "The Maine can handle much worse weather." With me at the helm. "In fact, a little weather will be good if the patrol boats are out and about."

Felipe agreed, and had some good news. "I'm told they don't usually go out in bad weather." He explained, "They're mostly out there to look for rafters, so they might not be out on a night when there'll be no one trying to escape this paradise." He smiled.

Sara returned the smile.

"Also," said Felipe, "they try to conserve fuel." He added, "The regime is broke."

This was sounding like an escape from the Swiss Navy. Unless the Cuban Ministry of the Interior was specifically looking for us. I asked Felipe, "What kind of patrol boats do they have?"

"They've got, like I said, two boats here. They used to have seven here, gifts from the Russians, but after the economic collapse they're running only two out of Cayo Guillermo. One is a Zhuk-class eighty-footer, which can make about twenty-five knots— same as The Maine." He glanced at Sara, hesitated, then said, "She mounts two sets of twin 12.7-millimeter machine guns, manually aimed, and she has a crew of eleven."

I didn't think he got all that from the Cuban crew or from a public information tour of the boat. So I concluded that Felipe had been briefed back in Miami by Eduardo's amigos.

Felipe sipped his daiquiri and continued, "That's the boat that goes out at dusk and returns about three or four in the morning. It runs west along the coast, looking for rafters, which it can't see on its radar. But its radar can see a small boat that may have been sto- len for an escape." He added, "If we're spotted visually or by radar, the Zhuk can't overtake us at his max speed, but he can stay with us, and if he's close enough, he can hail us and order us to stop, or . . ." He glanced at Sara again. ". . . Or fire warning shots."

Right. It's hard to ignore machine-gun fire.

Felipe looked at me. "I think, with our speed, we can avoid this guy."

I agreed. "And we have radar."

Felipe nodded. "Also, half the Russian electronics on these tubs don't work, and the crews aren't well-trained in electronics."

They must have gone to the same school as Jack. Well, this was sounding easier. I wondered what we could do to make it a fair fight.

Felipe finished his daiquiri and looked for the waitress.

I said, "Make it coffee."

He didn't like that but he didn't argue, and got back to business. "Okay, then there's the second boat, which is a Stenka-class patrol boat. The one that goes out about midnight. She's big, about a hundred and twenty feet, and can make thirty-eight to forty knots."

That was the patrol boat I saw anchored at the marina. I wouldn't want to see her on the high seas.

Felipe continued, "At that speed, she's a threat, and at that size she can go out in any weather." He drank the dregs of his daiquiri and continued, "She has a crew of thirty-four, but usually sails with half that. Her radar is sophisticated, but again, not always operational or well-manned."

"Armaments?"

"A few manually aimed machine guns, and two radar-controlled thirty-millimeter twin rapid-fire cannons—one in the bow, the other in the stern."

That's what I saw at the marina. And radar-controlled meant they could hit you in the dark, even with rough seas and fog. Not good. Maybe I should call for another round of drinks.

Felipe looked at Sara and assured her, "They're not supposed to fire at boats that are trying to flee Cuba." He looked at me. "You may remember an international incident about twenty years ago."

I was fifteen. And totally uninterested in international incidents. "Refresh my memory."

"There was a tugboat, named 13 de Marzo, stolen by Cubans

trying to escape. A Guarda Frontera boat fire-hosed it, but it wouldn't stop, so they rammed it and sunk it. Seventy-two people drowned, including twenty-three kids. There was a big international uproar, and since then the regime has promised not to fire on or use any force to stop a fleeing boat."

"What's the bad news?"

"The bad news is that they're full of shit. They may or may not fire warning shots that accidentally hit you, and they may or may not try to ram you, but they will definitely come alongside and board you."

Sort of like Pirates of the Caribbean. "All right, I think we understand the threat assessment, but we're not Cubans trying to flee the country. We're actually Americans, and Fishy Business is part of the Pescando fleet, and you've gotten permission to go night fishing."

"If they see us on radar, they don't know that. They'll try to call us on the radio, or hail us on their bullhorn and order us to stop. At that point, we can stop and explain on the radio who we are and hope they don't come aboard and start looking at passports and cargo, and looking for a donation. But—"

"They're not coming aboard," I assured him.

Felipe nodded.

Sara looked at her Cuban boyfriend and said, "I will not be taken alive."

Felipe didn't know how to reply to that, but said, "The choice may not be ours to make."

She looked at me.

I said, "If I can get into open water, The Maine can outmaneuver a bigger craft, even if it's capable of forty knots." Which was true. But we all knew I couldn't outrun radar-controlled rapid-fire cannons.

Felipe said, "We have another issue. Fuel." He explained, "We've been keeping the fuel light." He looked at me. "On your orders. But we always had enough to make it to Key West. Except tonight." He further explained, "We came in about four this afternoon, and as always we pulled up to the pumps to put a few hundred gallons of diesel in the tanks, but the pumps were closed." He added, "Probably out of fuel."

"What do we have?"

"We have less than three hundred gallons."

"Okay . . ." So, depending on winds and tides, at a speed of twenty-five knots we might have a cruise range of three hundred miles. It was about two hundred and fifty miles to Key West, but the rule of thumb is always to have one hundred and fifty percent of the fuel you think you need, particularly for a blue-water trip. But to radiate optimism I said, "We'll make it."

Felipe looked doubtful, thinking, I'm sure, about his side trip into the mangrove swamp, rough seas, winds, and maybe outmaneuvering a faster patrol boat.

"Or close enough," I said. "We'll be in international waters in less than an hour, and U.S. waters in about six hours."

He nodded, but we both knew we didn't want to be towed in by the Coast Guard. Not only was it embarrassing, but if they had to tow us they might also ask questions. Like, "Where were you and what do you have onboard?" Or, "Are those bullet holes in your hull?"

Well, that was a worry that wasn't worth worrying about. We should be so lucky as to get that far.

CHAPTER 52

I decided we could all actually use another drink, though I insisted it be beer. You can't get drunk on beer.

I glanced at my watch. We'd been here close to an hour, and though we weren't attracting attention, we should think about splitting up—Sara to the room, and me nursing a beer and keeping an eye on the Buick. Felipe needed to go back to the marina.

Our beers came—Coronas—and we clinked bottles and Sara said, "To a happy voyage home."

Anchors aweigh.

Felipe took a piece of folded paper from his pocket and handed it to Sara. "That's the map. It's easy. You go west on the beach road for about two miles and you'll see a sign on the left that says 'Swamp Tours.' It's about a half mile on the dirt road to the dock."

That sounded close to where I'd taken my siesta in the thick brush. "Anybody go there at night?"

"I checked it out two nights ago at eleven. No one there."

I had to admit that Felipe was competent. Or he was a jerk-off who was motivated. I mean, like Jack, Sara, and me, he was putting his life on the line, so he had motivation to keep his head out of his ass. And why, I wondered, had he volunteered for this? I'm sure for the money. And maybe for the cause. But also because he couldn't stay in Miami while his girlfriend was risking her life in Cuba. She might think less of him. Or even cheat on him.

I asked him, "How do you get around the island?"

"Everyone rented bicycles. That's how I got here."

"And Jack's with the boat now?"

He nodded. "Someone has to stay onboard." He explained, "The Cubans are not thieves, but they take things."

I could use that line at the Green Parrot. "Any problems with the guns onboard?"

"They're still there." He complained again, "We have to tip the Guarda Frontera every time we cast off and tie up, and we make donations to keep them off the tournament boats."

Fishing for peace was expensive. "Any mechanical issues?"

"I would have told you."

We were in a little bit of a pissing match, which we would not be in if Sara were named Steve. Men are assholes.

Felipe took a key card out of his pocket, gave it to Sara, and said, "You go first. Room 318. I'll be up shortly." He looked at me. "And you can watch the car. Then it's your turn to use the room." He asked, "Is that okay?"

Actually, no. "Let's finish our business here."

"What else do you need to know?"

"How was the fishing?"

"It's been excellent." He let me know, "We were in third place, but today we're in second."

"Congratulations." Jack has an uncanny knack for finding fish. "Too bad you can't stay a few more days."

He smiled, then looked at the key, which Sara had put on the table. He really wanted to get laid.

I glanced at her and saw she was . . . tense? I think, too, that Felipe was baiting us. Or running a test.

I asked him, "How was the Pescando Por la Paz received here?"

"There were a few government press photographers when we arrived. But no one is covering the tournament. Why?"

Sara replied, "We were worried that the fleet might be kicked out of Cuba."

Felipe nodded. "Well, that would have left you both high and dry." He asked, "What would you have done?"

Fucked our brains out until we figured out how to get out of Cuba. "I was thinking we could make it to Guantánamo by land."

He thought about that. "That's possible." He added, "But the question is now moot."

How could she love a man who said "moot"? I asked Felipe, "Did Jack mention my concern about the police connecting me to Fishy Business?"

Felipe looked at me. "He did, and we made sure that none of the other fishermen mentioned to anyone that Fishy Business used to be The Maine, and we asked all the crews to tell us if anyone came around asking questions."

"Okay." Glad Jack remembered. He, too, was motivated—by money and survival. The money wasn't there anymore, but survival is a good motivator by itself.

I said to Felipe, "You understand that the police in Havana could be making this connection right now, and calling the police in Cayo Guillermo as we speak."

Felipe had no reply, but I thought he went a little pale.

"Also, I have to tell you—if Jack didn't—that Sara and I came to the attention of the police in Havana."

He nodded, as though Jack had filled him in.

"And now that we've disappeared from our tour group, the police will be looking for us." I also told him, "And the Buick could be hot by now. So if there's any way we can move up the sail time, I suggest we do it."

He nodded. "I'll . . . check the tide table again . . . but . . ."

"Is there a public phone you can use at the marina?"

"There is . . ."

It was time to get rid of Felipe, and I said to him, "Okay, so you need to return to the boat now, brief Jack, then leave a message here at the front desk for Jonathan Mills. That's me. The message will be to meet for drinks at the Sol Club, at whatever time you think you can get The Maine into the mangrove swamp. Shoot for ten P.M. You have a depth finder. Also, if you are in the custody of the police, use the words 'coming storm' when you call. Meanwhile, get the boat out of the marina, ASAP. And if you see police cars at the marina, you can assume they're there for you, and you'll pedal your ass back here and we'll get in the Buick and try to get across the causeway." I added, "And make sure Jack is pedaling with you." My instructions to him were so chilling that I'd scared myself.

Felipe looked more pale and nodded.

"If I don't see you or hear from you in twenty minutes, tops, I'll assume you are in the custody of the police, and Sara and I will be heading for the causeway. And you—and Jack—will hold up well under police questioning, to give Sara and me time to get to the mainland." I looked at him. "Understand?"

He seemed to have zoned out, but then he looked at me and said, "Maybe we should all get on the boat now. I think I can get you onboard without—"

"We're really trying to avoid interaction with the authorities, Felipe. We and the car may be hot." I also reminded him, "We have cargo. And we can't have the border guards looking at it."

"Leave it."

Sara said sharply, "We will not leave it."

I stood. "Time to go. We'll see you—sooner or later." I added, "Vaya con Dios."

He stood, and we made eye contact. He definitely understood he wasn't going to have sex in Cuba with his girlfriend, and I think he knew why—and it wasn't for the reasons I'd just laid out.

He took a deep breath, glanced at Sara, then said to me, "I never liked this idea of me being on the boat and you being with Sara."

"Well, we all have different skill sets."

"I told Carlos I was best suited to go to Cuba with Sara and find the cave—and that he needed to find a different boat with a Cuban American captain and crew."

That may have actually worked better. And I'd be sleeping with Amber in Key West, blissfully unaware of the adventure I was missing. I assured Felipe, "Next time we'll try it your way. But for now, we do it my way." Regrets? I have a few.

Felipe needed to get the parting shot and said to me, "When we come back for the money, only those who speak Spanish and those who hate the regime need apply for the job."

Sara said, "Felipe, that's not—"

He shot her a look and she stopped talking.

Felipe needed some reality, so I said to him, "As you may know, I'm out three million dollars because of Eduardo. So I'm not in the best of moods, and when I step on that boat, I am in command, and I don't want anyone second-guessing me about the weather, the patrol boats, the fuel, or when or if we use the guns." I looked at Felipe. "Tell me you understand that. Or you can stay in Cuba."

Felipe was pissed, and embarrassed in front of his girlfriend. I would be, too. But as I learned the hard way in Afghanistan, there is only one top dog when the shit is flying. And you gotta get it straight who that dog is before it starts flying. "Comprende?"

He was *really* pissed. But he managed a smirk and said, "Sí, Capitán."

"Adios."

Sara was standing now, and she hesitated, then gave Felipe a brief hug and kiss and said something in Spanish. That pissed me off, but maybe she told him to man up and vamoose.

Felipe said, "I'll see you later," and removed himself from the triangle, forgetting the room key.

Sara and I stood there, looking at each other. Finally, she said, "You handled that . . . well."

"I did."

"And you saved me from having to . . . go to the room with him."

"That wasn't my purpose."

"Of course it was."

Maybe it was. "Have a seat. I'll tell the front desk I'm waiting for a message."

I went to the front desk, showed my Canadian passport, and said to both clerks, a man and a woman, "I'm in the lobby bar, with a young lady, waiting for a phone message. Please deliver it to me as soon as you get it." I incentivized them with ten CUCs each and they assured me they'd find me, even if I was in the baño.

I went back to the cocktail table, called the waitress over, and settled the bill.

Sara said, "We'll be out of Cuban territorial waters by midnight."

"We will." I thought back to my last days and hours in Afghanistan. The short-timers, who'd gone through hell without even a small pee in their pants, were all jittery that something was going to happen before they boarded the freedom bird home. I mean, after you've cheated death for so long, you become paranoid, sure that death had just remembered you were leaving.

Sara said, "I think he knows."

If he did, we might be waiting in that mangrove swamp for awhile. And Jack would be treading water while Felipe was in the cabin opening up the throttle as he took a direct heading for Miami, ahead of the storm and the Cuban gunboats. I mean, the money was still in Camagüey, his girlfriend was screwing around with the captain, and the police were closing in. Felipe would like to say adios to all that shit.

Sara and I sat in silence and waited for the desk clerk or Felipe to appear. Or the police.

I looked at my watch, stood, and said, "Time to go."

"Where?"

"Let's find out."

Sara stood, and we collected our backpacks and walked to the lobby. I checked with the desk, and a phone message had just come in. I read the message slip—*Anchors Aweigh. Will Try To Be At Sol Club 10:30*—and gave it to Sara.

She read it and looked at me. "Mac, this could be the last time we can be together. The car is locked. Let's go upstairs." She had the key card in her hand.

That was tempting. And it's sort of an Army tradition that you try to get laid before you try not to get killed. But I wanted to get out of the hotel. "Have you ever done it in the back seat of a station wagon in a mangrove swamp?"

She smiled. "I'll try anything once."

We left the Melia Hotel. I took the car keys from Sara, unlocked her door, and got behind the wheel. I fired up the Perkins boat engine, drove down the driveway, and headed west on the beach road.

She said, "This has been the best week of my life."

Were we in the same place? "Me too."

"You've got balls. And heart."

"And you've got guts and brains." And I meant it.

"We're a good team."

"We are."

"What time will we be in Key West?" she asked.

"In time for lunch."

"I'll buy at the Green Parrot."

Table for two? Or three? Maybe four with Jack.

"I'll tell Felipe after lunch that I'm not going back to Miami with him. And I'll tell him why."

Then maybe I should buy lunch.

"All right?"

I thought about all this—past, present, and future—and I came to the conclusion that Sara Ortega was my fate. This was where my journey had taken me. And this was good. I took her hand. "All right."

CHAPTER 53

We continued along the dark beach road. The sky was looking more ominous, with black smoky clouds racing across the face of the moon.

Sara said, "There's the sign."

I slowed down, and my headlights picked out a faded wooden sign: SWAMP TOURS. I turned left onto a dirt road that was hemmed in by thick tropical growth. The road was rough and the steamer trunks started to bounce, so I slowed down and shifted into first gear. My headlights showed a straight path through the ten-foot brush, and I switched to parking lights.

Felipe said it was half a mile to the floating dock, and within five minutes I could smell the swamp, and a minute later I could see the sheen on the water and huge mangrove trees rising from the dark wetlands.

I slowed to a crawl as I approached the water and stopped at the shoreline. Around me was a small clearing—a turn-around and parking area in front of the floating dock. There were no boats at the dock, no vehicles, and no people except us. I shut off the parking lights and we sat there, staring into the darkness.

Sara said, "Back the wagon up to the dock."

"Right."

I maneuvered the Buick wagon around in the tight space and backed it up close to the floating dock. I killed the engine and said, "Let's check it out."

We got out of the wagon and looked around.

The fleeting moonlight reflected off the black, shiny water, and as my eyes adjusted to the darkness I could see that a thick wall of vegetation crowded the small clearing. Exposed roots from the giant mangroves provided some traction and kept the Buick from sinking into the waterlogged mud.

I walked onto the floating dock, which was not much more than a log raft, held together with rope, about five feet wide and ten feet long, jutting into the swamp. The dock was tethered to stakes at the shoreline by two ropes. It would not support the Buick, but it seemed steady and sturdy enough to allow the transferral of the cargo between the wagon and our boat. I couldn't help but imagine that the station wagon was a big panel van, filled with a dozen steamer trunks. This would have worked. Assuming we'd made it to Camagüey. And here. Well, we'd never know.

"Okay. This is good."

Sara was staring out at the mangrove swamp. "Can the boat get through there?"

Hopefully, Felipe had already answered that question for himself.

I looked into the dark swamp. Mangroves grew up to the shore, but there was a channel through them, obviously man-made for boats to navigate the wetlands. It was hard to judge measurement in the dark, but it seemed that *The Maine*, with a 16-foot beam, could come sternway through the mangrove trees—very slowly and carefully—and reach the floating dock. The problem was not the channel through the mangroves—it was the depth of the bottom, which I guessed hadn't been dredged because swamp boats were usually flat-bottomed. *The Maine*, however, had a keel that was about five feet below the waterline. And even if we had seven feet of water at high tide, there were mangrove stumps out there, and roots that could foul the propeller. The good news was that we were light on fuel and cargo. Four thousand pounds of money might have put us too close to the bottom. Every cloud has a silver lining.

"Mac?"

"Well . . . it's doable." Which didn't sound like a sure thing. I added, "If The Maine can't get to us, we can swim to her."

"What about our cargo?"

"Well . . . I don't see why we can't use this dock for a raft and meet the boat in deeper water."

She nodded.

I was tempted to point out that Felipe was more of an optimist than a sailor, but this may have been his only option. And I didn't like to second-guess men under my command when they showed initiative—even if they had a stupid solution to a problem.

"We'll see how it goes at ten-thirty." I looked at my watch. It was now 8:45. We had a long wait. But I'd rather wait here for *The Maine* than wait in the Melia for the police.

I checked out the ropes that tethered the floating dock and saw they were one-inch hemp lines, easily cut with my Swiss Army knife.

Sara stood on the dock and asked, "If we have to make this dock into a raft, how do we move it into the swamp?"

Good question. The dock seemed too big and heavy for us to move it by hanging on and paddling with our feet against the incoming tide, but I suggested we could do that if we waited for the tide to start running out.

Sara replied, "I don't want to wait . . . Maybe we can do what the balseros do when they're launching their rafts from the wetlands."

"Which is?"

"They use poles—to push off into the deeper water."

Right. I think Huck Finn did that. "Okay. Good solution." I suspected she was smarter than her young boyfriend. Anyway, if we had seven feet of water here at high tide, as per Felipe, we needed at least a ten-foot pole.

I was about to go look for something in the bush, but I noticed that toward the end of the floating dock were two pilings—actually long poles, rising about six feet above the dock, and about the thickness of a baseball bat. The poles had been driven into the swamp mud to tie up boats and to keep the floating dock from swaying in the currents. I went over to one pole and Sara joined me. Together we pulled on it, trying to free it from the muck. We pushed it from side to side, and pulled again, and finally the pole started to rise out of the swamp floor.

We freed it and laid it on the dock. It was about twelve feet long, fairly straight, but waterlogged, so it had some flex in it, which was not good for raft poling. But if we had to use it, it would have to do.

We went to the other piling and after about ten minutes of sweating and swearing we got the pole out of the sucking mud and onto the floating dock. Teamwork makes the dream work.

We wiped our muddy hands on our pants, and I said, "Okay, we're all set to unload the trunks onto this dock, cut the lines, then pole into the swamp to meet The Maine. But we'll do that only if The Maine can't get to us."

"Should we unload the trunks now?"

"I want to hear my diesel engine before we do that."

She put her hand on my shoulder and we looked into the swamp, where an evening mist rose off the water. Tree frogs croaked, and night birds made weird sounds, insects chirped, and something leapt out of the water.

"It's spooky," she said.

But no spookier than the spidery caves I crawled through looking for UBL. Who knew the asshole was in Pukeistan? But at least in the caves, everyone had everyone's back. Here, I wasn't so sure.

She said, "Let's sit in the wagon."

I think I promised her a ride in the back seat, but now that I was here, I was reevaluating the situation, and I thought we should keep our pants on. "We need to keep alert. But you go ahead. I'll keep watch."

She walked to the station wagon, opened the rear window and tailgate, and pulled out the black tarp that covered the trunks. She spread the big tarp on the muddy ground between the wagon and the dock and invited me to lie down and relax awhile.

There might not be a next time for this, so we made love on the tarp—quickly, quietly, and with our boots on—listening to the sounds of the swamp and the mosquitoes buzzing around my butt. While we were going at it, Sara said, "Keep alert," and laughed.

Afterward, we sat on the tarp with our backs to the station wagon bumper and shared a bottle of water that she'd gotten from the Ranchón Playa. I thought about the remains of the men that were a few feet from the back of my head. If we all weren't soldiers once, I might think that I had somehow dishonored the dead; but it could've just as easily been me who didn't make it home. And those who did make it shouldn't feel guilty about anything. We all understood that.

Sara asked, "What do we do now?"

"We wait." I looked at my watch: 9:46. We had a long forty-five minutes before I heard the familiar sound of my Cat 800 diesel. Or longer if Felipe and Jack had decided to wait for high tide. Or never, if Felipe had left Jack at the marina and was now on his way to Miami. What I knew for sure was that Jack Colby would not leave Cuba without me.

Sara said, "Tell me that everything is going to be okay."

I assured her, "Within a few hours we'll be in open water, on a heading for Key West."

She took my hand. "That sounds nice."

Sara Ortega was not a clueless idiot, and she knew this was a very dicey plan. The mangrove swamp could damage the fiberglass hull of *The Maine*, but not as badly as a rapid-fire cannon. "Do you see that water?"

"Yes."

"That water is a road that will take you anywhere you want to go."

She nodded, and stayed quiet for a minute, then asked, "What if they don't . . . can't come?"

Well, that was the other problem. "Jack knows—you never leave a man behind." I wasn't so sure about Felipe, however. I mean, without the sixty million . . . But I was forgetting about Sara. I hoped Felipe still loved her enough to come for her.

She got quiet again, then said, "I'm thinking about the last week . . ."

"When we get back, we'll have some good laughs. Even Antonio was—"

"What's the matter?"

"Quiet."

We listened and I heard something out in the swamp. It got louder, and we could both hear voices carrying across the water.

Sara whispered, "There's somebody out there."

I pulled the Glock from my belt and got into a prone firing position facing the water, trying to peer through the darkness. Sara lay down beside me.

The voices got louder and it sounded like two males, speaking Spanish. I could hear oars splashing in the water.

I saw a movement, then suddenly a boat emerged from the mist, coming toward the shore.

As it got closer, I could see that it was a square-bowed swamp boat, and sitting in the flat-bottomed craft were two men. They saw the big Buick before they saw me and Sara lying on the black tarp, and they started jabbering.

Sara stood and called out, "Buenas noches."

There was a silence, then one of them called, "Buenas noches, señora."

I slipped the Glock under my shirt and stood, but I didn't call out buenas noches in my Maine accent.

The two men, who looked young, jumped out of the boat into the water, then took hold of a bow line and pulled the flat-bottomed boat onto the muddy shore. They made conversation with Sara as they dragged the small fiberglass boat farther inland.

Sara walked toward them, still chatting, and like fishermen everywhere, they showed her their catch, which looked like catfish. And they looked like poor fishermen. But this was Cuba, where everyone had a second job.

The men were barefoot, but they slipped sandals over their muddy feet and pulled the boat close to the Buick and glanced at the tarp.

They conversed with Sara, obviously about the station wagon, and gave me a few quick looks.

One of them went into the bush and came out pulling a small boat trailer. They put their fiberglass boat on the trailer, secured it with a line, and maneuvered the trailer around the Buick and onto the dirt road.

I can't remember how many times my night patrols had run into locals, and how many times I had to make the decision of what to do with those people. I started with the premise that no one could be trusted, and I worked out a solution from there.

The two young men waved to us as they pulled their boat and trailer—a little too fast—up the road we'd come in on. Buenas noches.

I looked at Sara. "Well?"

"I... don't know. They seemed... friendly." She added, "They're just fishermen."

"I don't doubt that."

"I told them we were waiting for friends to come in from fishing."

"All right ..." But if I had it to do over again, those guys would be looking down the barrel of my gun while Sara tied their hands and feet with their line, and they'd now be resting comfortably in the back seat of the Buick. But you don't get do-overs.

I looked at my watch: 10:04. Nothing to do now except wait for our ride. And keep alert.

———

It was 10:30, and though I didn't hear *The Maine*, Sara wanted to unload the station wagon. "They're coming," she assured me. We threw our backpacks on the dock, then Sara and I lifted the heavy steamer trunk filled with título de propiedades out of the rear compartment, walked it across the black tarp, and set the trunk down in the middle of the floating dock.

On our way back to get the second trunk, I heard the sound of an engine—but not in the swamp. It was on the dirt road.

Sara and I exchanged glances and I pulled my Glock.

There were headlight beams coming through the darkness, and the engine got louder, then the headlights illuminated the Buick and us, and the vehicle suddenly stopped about twenty feet away. Someone shouted something in Spanish. I don't speak the language, but I know what "Guarda Frontera" means.

Sara said, "Oh, God . . ."

I jumped on the rear bumper of the station wagon and aimed my Glock across the Buick's roof at the open Jeep vehicle.

A guy was standing in the passenger side, a rifle aimed at me above the windshield, and he shouted something.

I fired three rounds at him, and the blasts split the night air. I shifted my aim and fired three more rounds through the windshield opposite the driver, then fired my remaining three rounds, right to left, in case I missed anything.

The birds were silent now, and there was no sound from the Jeep except the idling engine. I quickly reloaded my second magazine into the Glock.

The rule is to wait fifteen seconds to see if your kill suddenly springs to life, so I waited, but there was no movement in the Jeep.

I jumped down from the bumper and made my way quickly but cautiously to the military vehicle. The guy slumped in the passenger seat was still alive, but the driver had caught one above his right eye. They were young guys. Maybe twenty.

I reached in and turned off the headlights, then shut off the engine and threw away the keys. I retrieved the rifle from the dying guy, which was an AK-47 with a thirty-round magazine. I found another loaded AK in the rear, along with an ammo pouch and four loaded magazines. I slung one of the rifles over my shoulder and started back toward the Buick, carrying the second rifle.

Well, I'd just committed murder in the People's Republic of Cuba. Surrender was no longer an option. It never was.

Sara was calling my name, and I said, "I'm okay—" There was

suddenly light around me, and I heard an engine behind me. I spun around and saw another set of headlights bouncing over the rough road.

I jumped onto the hood of the Jeep and knelt as I flipped the firing switch of the AK-47 to full automatic. The Jeep was less than thirty feet from me and slowing down as it approached the first Guarda Frontera Jeep. I could hear voices that sounded confused as to what was happening. Well, let me end the confusion. I squeezed the trigger and fired a long burst of green tracer rounds into the windshield left to right. The Jeep veered into the wall of brush and the engine stalled out.

I stood on the hood of the first Jeep and looked up the dark road, but there were no more headlights coming.

I jumped down and ran back to the Buick where Sara had already managed to get the steamer trunk full of skulls out of the wagon, and she was dragging it over the tarp toward the floating dock. "Mac! Are you okay?"

"I'm good." I grabbed a handle and we carried the trunk quickly onto the dock. I slapped a fresh thirty-round magazine into the AK-47 that I'd fired and laid both rifles on the steamer trunks.

I pulled my Swiss Army knife from my pocket and cut the two lines that tethered the dock to the shore. Meanwhile, Sara had one of the poles and pushed off.

The dock floated a few feet, then started back on the incoming tide. I grabbed the other pole and together we pushed off again, then stuck the poles into the muddy bottom and began poling away from the shore.

The floating dock was not floating very fast, and it took all our strength to push against the poles and move the dock a few feet against the tide. But we were making a little progress and the dock was now about twenty feet from the shoreline. A few feet later, the bottom dropped and we had barely two feet of pole to work with, so we knelt to give us more leverage.

I looked up to see how far we'd gotten and saw head beams reflecting off the mangrove trees on the shore. *Shit.*

Sara saw it too. "Mac . . . look . . ."

"See it. Keep pushing."

We got a few more feet out, but we were barely sixty feet from the shore and already we were getting fatigued. Meanwhile, where was *The Maine*?

The vehicle that had arrived was obviously blocked by my two kills, but he'd left his headlights on, which was not smart, because I could now see three men on the shore, silhouetted against the head beams. One guy was looking at the Buick and two were looking out at the swamp.

I grabbed one of the AK-47s and got down into a prone firing position. *Darkness distorts perception—aim lower than the target you see.* I held my fire, waiting to see if they spotted us. Then one of the guys shouted, and I saw a muzzle flash, followed by the buzzing sounds of green tracer rounds going high, and the almost simultaneous pop-pop-pop that the AK-47 makes. I hear that fucking sound in my nightmares.

I steadied my aim and returned the fire, raking the shore with six-round bursts, adjusting my aim as the streaks of my green tracers hit the shoreline. One man screamed and went down. I quickly changed magazines, and noticed that they'd shut off their headlights.

Tracers show where your rounds went, but they also show where they came from, and the return fire was more accurate. A few rounds hit the water in front of me, then one hit the steamer trunk next to me. Sara was still kneeling and pushing with the pole, and she was presenting too good of a target. "Get down!"

She got down a little, but kept pushing off.

There were a few more men on the shore now, and I saw at least six muzzle flashes. The sounds of automatic rifles filled the air and bullets were striking the water around us, and another one hit the trunk. They definitely had our range now, and we were basically sitting ducks, about to be dead ducks.

I was down to two magazines for the AK-47, and after that I couldn't put out enough suppressing fire with the Glock to keep their heads down.

I took aim at the shoreline, but before I squeezed the trigger, the sky lit up with a flash of heat lightning, followed by a roll of thunder. *I am the storm.* I shifted my aim to the Buick and squeezed the trigger. A stream of green tracer rounds impacted into the rear of the station wagon, and the incendiary material of the tracers ignited the fuel in the tank and the gasoline exploded in a huge red-orange fireball.

The shooting from the shore stopped, and when the echoes of the explosion died away I heard the sound of a boat engine—my boat, my engine.

Sara and I turned around and I saw the stern of *The Maine* coming toward us through the swamp mist. The boat was about fifty feet away, and as it got closer I saw Jack kneeling on the rear bench, aiming a rifle—the AR-15—at the shore, but he was holding his fire, obviously unsure of what was happening. I could make out the silhouette of Felipe in the darkened cabin, and I imagined he was glancing over his shoulder as he steered sternway toward us, maybe with a little guidance and encouragement from Jack.

Felipe was making less than five knots, which would be normal for these water hazards but too slow for getting our asses out of here under fire. In fact, it was probably the gunfire that made Felipe display an abundance of caution. But, to be fair, he was still coming.

Sara was kneeling, pushing off with the pole, and I was dividing my attention between the shore and *The Maine.* We were in thicker mist now, which was good regarding the guys with the AK-47s, who'd stopped firing, but I wasn't sure Jack had actually seen us. So I stood and waved silently. Jack spotted me and waved back, and as I dropped to one knee a loud burst of AK-47 fire streaked over my head. I spun around and dropped into a prone position and fired my last magazine at the shoreline, and when my AK clicked empty I could hear the sharp sound of Jack's AR-15 returning fire. Glad he remembered the extra ammo. Hope he remembered to put his vest on.

I had two magazines of 9mm left and I slapped one into the

Glock. We were about a hundred feet from the shore, well beyond the effective range of the Glock, but I emptied the magazine at the shoreline just to be involved. Jack meanwhile was pumping out rounds like he was surrounded by V.C.

I glanced at Sara and saw she was exhausted, barely hanging on to the pole, and I noticed that the incoming tide was carrying us back toward the shore. *Shit.*

The guys on the shore—maybe four or five of them—were apparently getting over the shock of the explosion and were starting to lay down effective fire. I saw tracer rounds streaking over *The Maine,* then it looked like a few rounds entered the cabin. I hoped that Felipe didn't lose his nerve and hightail it out. Would he do that to Sara?

The Maine was less than twenty feet from us, and if we could stop drifting toward the shore we'd meet up in a minute or two, but Felipe was not appreciating the situation and wasn't moving toward us as fast as the tide was moving us away from *The Maine.*

Sara suddenly called out, "Felipe! Faster! Faster!"

I don't know if he'd ever heard that word before in another context, but it worked, and I heard the engine growl and *The Maine* got closer.

I scrambled over the raft, grabbed Sara, and pulled her behind the two steamer trunks. The AK rounds couldn't penetrate the wads of paper, but they'd probably go through skulls—just as they had forty years ago in Villa Marista prison. I positioned myself between the trunks and Sara, then pushed her flat on the raft. I heard a round smack into one of the trunks but it didn't exit, so the trunks gave us some cover, and the dark and the mist gave us some concealment. Theoretically we were not in the line of fire—until we had to get ourselves and the trunks onboard.

The Maine was less than ten feet away now and I could see Jack's face as he took careful aim and kept up a steady volley of fire, and I could hear the crack of his rounds as they sailed over my head.

Then, for some reason, Jack suddenly stood, maybe to get a clearer shot of the shoreline, and I yelled, "Get down!"

But he kept standing, steadied his aim, and got off a few rounds before a green tracer knocked him off the bench and back onto the deck.

Sara saw what happened and let out a scream, then got herself under control and shouted, "Those *bastards!*"

Hey, they're just kids doing their job. Been there. Jack, too. *Come on, Jack. Get up.* "Jack!"

But he didn't answer.

The stern of *The Maine* was only a few feet from the raft now, and I heard Felipe shout, "Jump! Jump!"

I said to Sara, "Go ahead. Quick!"

"The trunks . . ."

"Go!"

"No!"

Shit.

Felipe shouted again, "Jump! I'm leaving! I'm going!"

Asshole. You'd think he'd never been shot at. *The Maine* was at idle, and the tide and current were starting to separate us again. I yelled out, "Reverse!" I grabbed Sara around the waist and started to lift her onto my shoulder. A few more rounds hit the trunks, and I saw a tracer hit the stern, putting a dot right above the "I" in <u>Fishy Business</u>. *Holy shit.*

Diesel doesn't explode like gasoline but . . . we didn't need any more incendiary rounds in the fuel tank.

Time to get aboard before we got shot or left behind. I said to Sara, calmly and slowly, "You have to get up and get on that boat."

She got into a crouching position, glanced at the two trunks that were between her and the gunfire, then looked at the boat, which was now about five feet from the raft.

I don't know what would have happened next—Sara jumping for the boat, or Felipe pushing forward on the throttle and leaving us there—but something hit me in the face, and it took a second for me to realize it was a line thrown from *The Maine*. I grabbed it and heard Jack's voice. "Secure the line!"

I dropped to the deck, looped the line through the hemp rope that bound the logs together, and shouted, "Forward!"

The Maine began to move forward, and the floating dock was towed away from the shore and the gunfire, and deeper into the mist.

Jack appeared at the stern, kneeling on the bench, and he was staring at me. I called out over the sound of the engine, "You okay?"

"What's it to you, asshole?"

He sounded fine. "You get hit?"

"Vest."

Good purchase.

We were clearing the mangroves, and Felipe put on some speed, and within a few minutes we were in the Bay of Dogs, on a westerly heading.

Sara sat up and put her arm around my shoulders. She was breathing hard, but getting it together.

"You okay?"

"I'm okay."

I glanced up at the cabin and saw that Felipe was checking us out.

It was time to come aboard and I called out, "Idle!"

Jack shouted to Felipe, "Idle!"

The engine got quieter and *The Maine* slowed.

Jack pulled the line, hand over hand, until the raft was against the boat's stern.

Sara and I stood, and Jack reached his hand out to her, as he'd done when she first came aboard *The Maine*—but this time I put my hands on her butt and she kicked her legs out to the stern while I pushed and Jack pulled. She tumbled onto the stern bench, and Jack said, "Welcome aboard!"

She gave him a hug, hesitated, then glanced at me and went into the cabin.

So Jack and I, with two secured lines, pulled the trunks on-board, and he set them on the deck. I pitched the two backpacks to him, scrambled aboard *The Maine*, then cut the line. Felipe opened the throttle and we picked up speed across the bay, leaving the floating dock behind us.

Sara was still in the cabin, talking to her boyfriend, and I was left with Jack, who complained, "I think I got a cracked rib."

"An AK-47 round will do that."

"You owe me combat pay."

"You owe me your life."

"No, you owe me *your* life, asshole."

"We'll work it out."

He asked, "What's in the trunks?"

"Well . . . the heavy trunk has a billion dollars' worth of property deeds, worth nothing."

"Yeah? And the other trunk?"

"I'll show you later."

"Worth risking our lives for?"

"It is."

"Better be."

"What are we drinking?" I asked.

"Whaddaya want?"

"Rum and Coke. Hold the Coke."

He turned and went below. I called after him, "Cigar, if you have one."

I plopped my butt into the starboard fighting chair and swiveled around, looking at the bay and the distant shorelines. When we got out of the bay, we were basically in the Atlantic Ocean, and we needed to take a northwesterly heading. If I recalled correctly, the Zhuk-class patrol boat was running west along the coast, and if he got the call he'd come around and run a course that would intercept us.

The Stenka-class patrol boat, the 120-footer that could make forty knots, would still be at anchor, but not for long, and she could come around from the marina and might overtake us before we got out of Cuban territorial waters.

I glanced at Felipe at the helm and saw he was looking at the console—the radar screen—and I was sure he'd figured this out for himself. I would have joined him in the cabin to discuss our options and strategy, but he seemed involved in an intense conversation with Sara. I'd give him ten more minutes at the helm before I kicked his ass out and took my ship back.

Jack came topside with two tumblers filled with dark rum and handed one to me. We touched glasses and drank.

Jack had taken off his Kevlar vest, and he had a T-shirt with a map of Vietnam on it that said: "When I Die, I'm Going To Heaven, Because I've Already Been To Hell And Back."

Indeed.

Jack asked, "You waste anybody?"

I nodded.

He thought about that and asked, "Are we protected as combatants under the Geneva Convention and the Rules of Land Warfare?"

"I'm afraid not."

"That sucks."

"You got a cigar?"

"Yeah." He pulled a cedar-wrapped cigar out of his jeans pocket and handed it to me.

I unwrapped it, bit off the tip, and lit up with Jack's Zippo. Jack had a cigarette in his mouth, and I lit him up and handed him his lighter.

He looked at it and said, "This is my good-luck charm. Kept me alive for a year."

"No it didn't."

"Everybody in my company had a good-luck charm. Mostly crosses, some rabbit's feet, or an AK bullet that was the bullet that would've killed you if you didn't have it on you. Stuff like that."

"Does that mean nobody in your company was KIA?"

"Yeah, guys got killed. But if you had a charm, you didn't *think* you were gonna get killed."

"Right. Well, thanks for lending it to me."

"It worked."

"Must have." I downed half the rum.

"What happened with the money?"

"It's a long story."

"I got time."

"We'll pick it up on the next trip."

He laughed.

I stood. "Look, if we make it back, this boat's mine, free and clear. We sell it and split the money."

"Okay. So you owe me half a million for the trip, half a million for combat pay, and four hundred grand for the Glock, and let's say another half mil for saving your ass. How much is the boat worth?"

"We'll figure it out." I asked, "Hey, did you get laid in Havana?"

"Ten minutes after I left you." He asked me, "Did *you* get laid in Havana? Or . . ." He cocked his head toward the cabin. ". . . Or did you get fucked?"

I wasn't sure. "Okay, stay here and look for unfriendly craft."

I put the rum in the cup holder and went into the cabin where Felipe sat at the helm, wearing a Kevlar vest. I noticed that the windshield had two neat holes in it, to the left of Felipe's head.

Sara and I exchanged glances, and I thought she was going to go below, but she remained standing.

I said to Felipe, "You did a good job," meaning you didn't do an excellent job. In fact, you got a little shaky back there, amigo.

Felipe kept looking out the windshield and nodded.

I sort of ignored Sara and looked at the radar screen. There were no craft in the bay, which was good for starters. I could see the surrounding shorelines on the screen, but not the open water outside the bay, and we wouldn't see that until we navigated through the archipelago of small islands that ran west from Cayo Guillermo. Then we could see if there were two craft on a course to intercept us.

Felipe seemed to understand the situation and said, "We can transit into the next bay, Buena Vista, and keep the archipelago between us and the ocean for about a hundred and fifty kilometers, then break out into the ocean around Punta Gorda."

"Do we have a chart?"

"I do. And we have the radar, depth finder, and GPS."

Life at the edge is all about life-and-death decisions. Pilots, sea captains, combat commanders, deep-sea divers, sky divers, mountain climbers, and other risk-taking crazies know this, and they see it as a challenge. You can get away with a bad decision, but not a bad mistake.

Felipe asked, "What do you think?"

"I think I don't want to be hemmed in by islands and shorelines. I want to be in open water."

"But—"

"You're relieved. Please leave the cabin."

He looked at me, then stood and went below. He probably needed to pee.

I sat in the skipper's chair and scanned the dials and gauges, including the fuel, then looked at the radar screen and took a heading that would put us into the Atlantic Ocean in about fifteen minutes.

The bay was choppy, meaning the ocean was going to be rough. I took a drag on the cigar.

Sara said, "I was scared to death."

"You really did fine."

"Jack is a brave man."

And Felipe is . . . ? Well, to be generous, not too many people do well during their baptism of fire. It gets easier each time, and one day you don't give a shit. I suggested, "Why don't you go below and get some rest?"

She glanced down the steps to where Felipe was, then asked, "Did you tell Jack what's in the trunk?"

"No."

"I'll show him."

"Okay."

She went out to the deck and took a key out of her pocket.

I thought I should be there, so I checked the radar, put the boat on autopilot, and went out to the deck.

I said to Jack, "You remember what Carlos said on this boat about the POWs in Villa Marista prison in Havana?"

"Yeah . . ."

Sara knelt, opened one of the trunks, and lifted the lid.

Jack stared at the skulls. "What the . . . ?"

"These are those seventeen men. They're going home, Jack."

He looked at me, then at Sara, then back at the skulls. He moved closer to the trunk, made the sign of the cross, and said, "Welcome home, boys." He took a step back and saluted.

I left Jack with Sara and went back to the cabin and took the helm. As we got closer to the ocean, the sea became rougher. The wind was from the southeast and we had a following sea as we headed northwest at twenty-five knots. This was going to be a hell of a ride.

I saw the western tip of Cayo Guillermo on the radar, and a smaller island west of that, and I steered for the passage between the islands, keeping an eye on the depth finder.

It started to rain, and Jack and Sara came into the cabin. Sara, maybe sensing that Jack and I needed a minute, went below.

Jack said, "She told me you met up with Eduardo."

"Right."

"He's a foxy old bastard."

"So are you."

"He told me when he left The Maine in Havana Harbor that he had something important he was going to give to you and Sara, and that when I saw it, I'd understand."

That sounded familiar.

"I guess what I just saw is it."

"It is."

"So now we're gonna go on TV and talk about it."

"Let's get to Key West first."

"Yeah, I guess those . . . those guys are gonna be used to fuck up the peace talks."

Sometimes, as someone once said, the dead past should just bury its dead. "I think those men should be identified, and returned to their families for a proper burial."

"Yeah . . ."

"What did Eduardo offer you?"

"Don't matter."

"Okay."

"You need help at the helm?"

"No."

"Okay." He started down the stairs, then said, "Get us the fuck out of here."

"Can do."

The military teaches you about the loneliness of command, and the weight of command that sits on your shoulders and is the combined weight of everyone whose lives you are responsible for. It is the worst feeling in the world. But that's what you signed on for, and no one ever said it was going to be easy.

I took *The Maine* through the windswept passage between the islands and I was out into the Atlantic.

I looked at my radar screen and saw only two craft—one was to the west, about ten nautical miles from me, and the other was to the east, only six nautical miles, traveling west.

These could be any ships on the sea, but I was fairly certain I knew who they were, and I knew I was about to earn my pay.

As I watched, both craft, having spotted me on their radar, changed course and began converging on *The Maine*.

We were in trouble.

CHAPTER 54

The Maine was getting tossed around by the wind and waves, though I was able to keep her on a straight northerly heading toward international waters, which were about ten miles ahead. But no matter how I did the math, the two Guarda Frontera patrol boats were going to intercept us before I crossed that imaginary line—which was imaginary enough for them to ignore.

In fact, the two patrol boats had by now been told what happened to their colleagues in the mangrove swamp, and it didn't take too much genius for them to figure out that the radar blip they saw was the boat used by the murderers in the swamp. A little more thought would draw them to the conclusion that this was the American fishing boat *Fishy Business*, and those patrol boats would follow us to hell to get revenge.

The rain was getting heavier, and I wasn't able to see much through the windshield, even with the wipers going full speed. There wasn't much to see anyway; if you've seen one storm, you've seen them all. The radar, however, showed a clearer picture of the danger, and it wasn't the weather.

Jack came into the cabin and looked at the radar screen. "Do I see what I think I'm seein'?"

"You do."

"Shit." He asked, "What're we gonna do?"

Well, we were going to get captured or killed. Unless the other guys made a mistake. Or unless I could make them make a mistake. "It's like a chess game. Except everybody gets only one move."

"Okay . . . what's our move?"

I looked at the radar screen. The Zhuk-class patrol boat was heading for us from the west, probably at his full speed, which was twenty-five knots. If I maintained a direct north heading, he'd veer north, and at some point his machine guns would be within firing range of us, but he couldn't actually overtake us. The real problem was the Stenka-class boat, which at forty-five knots was close enough at six nautical miles to be alongside us within maybe ten or fifteen minutes—or within firing range with his radar-controlled guns sooner than that.

I wasn't sure of the effective firing range of the Stenka's 30mm rapid-fire cannons, but that's a relatively small caliber, and the cannon shell was about the size and shape of a big Cohiba in an aluminum tube—but this was an *exploding* cigar. Guns like that were used mostly for anti-aircraft and ripping up a small ship—like *The Maine*—and I knew it was a close-range cannon. Maybe accurate at two miles.

The question was, did these guys want to kill us, or capture us? I would have said capture, except I'd left a lot of Guarda Frontera corpses back on the shore. So the guys in the patrol boats would fire first, no questions asked.

"Talk to me, Mac."

"I'm thinking."

"I think you gotta make your move."

I turned on the radio and switched to Channel 16, the international distress and hailing channel, where the Cuban gunboats might try to contact me. I could hear voices in Spanish, and they weren't singing "Guantanamera." I would have called below for a translator, but I understood "Guarda Frontera," and I was also able to translate "Feeshy Beesness," and that's all I needed to know. I shut off the radio.

Jack said, "Holy shit."

"What do you do, Jack, when any move you make is the wrong move?"

"You hope the other guy makes a bad move."

"Right. And what do you do when you're in contact with a superior force and you can't break contact?"

"You do the unexpected."

"Right." I looked at the radar screen. If I kept a northerly heading, I'd be intercepted from the east and the west. If I turned south, I could get back into the inter-coastal waters between the archipelago and the coast of Cuba, and maybe play cat-and-mouse with these guys for awhile, but that would just delay the inevitable.

I asked Jack, "So if the bad guys are pressing you from two sides and you can't break contact, what do they not expect you to do?"

"Attack."

"Right." I turned the wheel to port and took a direct heading toward the Zhuk-class boat that was coming at us from the west.

Jack said, "I guess you want to get this over with sooner than later."

"Correct."

Felipe came up to the cabin, wondering, I'm sure, about our new heading. "What are you doing?"

I tapped the screen. "We're meeting the beast. The Zhuk."

"Are you crazy?"

Why do people always ask me that? But I took a moment to explain, "We need to stay as far from the Stenka as possible, so we're heading directly away from him."

Felipe looked at the radar screen. "But you're heading right for the Zhuk—"

"I *know* where I'm heading."

He asked again, "Are you crazy?"

"Go below."

But he had a suggestion. "Turn around and get back into the archipelago."

"Go below."

Felipe was staring at the screen, transfixed. "Listen . . . if we get back into the archipelago, they'll lose us on their radar—"

"Until they follow us."

"Their radar is going to pick up shore clutter, islands . . . We can get into a mangrove swamp—"

"I've had enough mangrove swamps for awhile, amigo. Go below. That's an order."

But Felipe was not taking orders from me and he said, "You're going to get us killed."

We were as good as dead anyway, and Felipe knew that. He just didn't want to deal with it.

Jack said to him, "The captain ordered you below."

Felipe looked at him as though crazy was contagious. Felipe took a deep breath, stepped back from Jack, and pulled my .38 Smith & Wesson from under his shirt. "Turn this boat south."

I reminded him, "You promised to take orders."

"Now! Or I'll—"

Unfortunately, Sara came into the cabin, looked at Felipe, and saw the gun. "Felipe! What is going on—?"

"Looks like a mutiny." I suggested, "Take him below before I get pissed off."

Felipe explained to Sara, "He's going to get us killed."

Sara looked at me, then back at Felipe. She didn't know *how* I was going to get everyone killed, or what the debate was about, but she stepped past Felipe and stood between me and her boyfriend with the gun.

Well, I'm not comfortable hiding behind a woman, especially when I had a Glock in my belt and the woman was now in my line of fire. I said to Jack, "Take his gun and escort him below."

Felipe stepped back from Jack and descended a few steps into the lower cabin. "Stay where you are."

Jack made like he didn't hear him and put his hand out. "Give it."

Felipe realized he was outnumbered by crazies, but before he retreated, he had some advice for my crew. "Make him tell you what he's doing. And make him stop. Or we're all dead."

Dead anyway. Once you understood that, you were left with the one move—attack—that would either keep you alive or let you go out in a blaze of glory. Sara had said she would die before she was captured, and I was taking her at her word.

Felipe retreated below, still armed, but not dangerous. For now.

Jack offered to go and disarm him, but I said, "Just keep an eye on him. We'll need him if we get into a shoot-out."

Sara had no comment on that, but she was very interested in what I was doing that would get everyone killed.

I pointed to the radar screen and explained, "The faster boat, the Stenka that has the cannons, would intercept us quickly if we headed north at an angle away from him. But if we head directly away from him, he has a lot of catching up to do."

She looked at the screen and nodded, but then noticed the other blip heading directly toward us. "What's that?"

"That's the Zhuk—the smaller boat that goes the same speed as us." I was going to add, "The Zhuk has only machine guns," but that didn't sound reassuring, so I also explained, "The closer we are to the Zhuk, the less likely it is for the Stenka to fire its cannons."

Again she nodded, but pointed out, correctly, "The Zhuk is going to shoot at us."

"And we're going to shoot back."

She had no comment, and I had nothing to add, but Jack said, "We'll both be moving and shooting from unstable platforms."

Sara comprehended that and nodded.

I added, "It's sort of like a drive-by shooting on a bad patch of road, and both drive-bys are moving toward each other, so it won't last long, and when we pass in the night, he has to turn around to pursue, but he loses a lot of speed in the turn, and we're still making twenty-five knots." That, of course, assumed his twin machine guns didn't kill us all.

Again she nodded, but didn't comment.

I looked at the radar screen and saw that we were about five nautical miles from the Stenka, who was in pursuit, but who hadn't gained any ground on us, so maybe he wasn't able to get full speed out of his engines—or he was lying back, waiting to see if I made another crazy move.

The Zhuk was coming at me full barrel, though he was heading into the wind and waves, and maybe not making twenty-five knots. In any case, our closing speed was maybe forty knots and we would meet in about five minutes.

I asked Jack, "What's the ammo situation for the AR?"

"I got ten empty mags that need reloading."

"See if you can do that in three minutes. And get yourself into a firing position through the forward hatch."

He disappeared below and I said to Sara, "I need you to go below, get a Kevlar vest, and bring one for me." I handed her my Glock. "And get fresh magazines for this."

She nodded and disappeared below.

The Maine didn't have an anemometer, so I couldn't measure the wind speed or direction, but I was guessing the winds were about twenty knots, still blowing westerly, and I could see that the waves were cresting at about six feet and not breaking over the bow. But the bow was rising on each wave, and Jack would only have a clear shot ahead when the bow pitched down. The good news was that the Zhuk had the same problem with his twin machine guns mounted on his forward deck.

I looked at the radar screen and saw that the Zhuk was now three nautical miles ahead and still coming straight at us. He was playing chicken with me, which was my game—or more likely he thought that I understood I was finished and I was going to surrender. But if he thought that, he was being too rational.

I saw the vent hatch rise up on the bow, and I expected to see Jack squeezing himself up with his AR-15, but it was Felipe whose head and shoulders appeared, and I could see he had the five-round automatic shotgun that was loaded with deer slugs. This may be the worst and most inaccurate weapon you can have in this situation, but it was better than a .38 revolver, and maybe even better than a Hail Mary.

Felipe looked back at me and gave me a thumbs-up. Apparently he'd come to the only conclusion he could come to. Or he'd had a chat with Sara, who'd straightened him out. I knew Felipe was standing on something in the lower cabin, and I hoped it wasn't Jack's shoulders. But where was Jack?

I looked at the radar. We were about two nautical miles from meeting the Zhuk. I couldn't see him in the dark and stormy sea, and he couldn't see me, but we both knew, thanks to technology, that we were on a collision course. In a minute or two, we'd both revert to something less sophisticated—bullets and balls.

I glanced again at the radar and saw that the Stenka was still about five nautical miles behind us. He couldn't turn his 120-foot boat as fast as I could turn, so I guessed that the Stenka captain, knowing he had more speed than his prey, was just waiting to see if I broke to port or starboard—then, when he got in range, he could open up with his radar-controlled cannons without taking a chance of hitting the Zhuk. Or, like the Zhuk captain, the Stenka captain was thinking I was going to raise the white flag. I mean, why else would I be heading toward the Zhuk?

Jack appeared from below carrying a canvas bag of loaded magazines and the AR-15. He shouted over the wind and breaking waves, "I'm going up the tower!"

Meaning the tuna tower, which was eight feet above the cabin roof and about twenty feet above the water.

I didn't think that was a good idea, with the tower swaying about 20 degrees from side to side, but he'd have the advantage of not having the bow rising and falling in his line of fire. I would never order a man to do that, but before I could think of a reason why he shouldn't become the best target on the boat, he disappeared onto the deck and climbed up the side rungs to the tower. "Good luck."

Sara came up the staircase wearing a Kevlar vest and carrying another one that she handed to me.

I put on the vest and motioned to the windshield, which had three separate framed windows that could swing out on hinges and lock-arms. "Unlatch the window on the left, and when I give you the word, push it out, and it'll lock into place. You stand in the stairwell and take aim out the window."

She nodded and unlatched the window over the stairwell, then drew the Glock from her waistband.

"Don't fire when the bow starts to rise." I was going to add, "You might hit Felipe," but I figured she was smart enough to know that, so why mention it?

I glanced at the radar. The blip that was the Zhuk was about five hundred yards from us, dead ahead. Felipe was still standing in the hatch, his elbows on the bow deck, and the shotgun aimed straight ahead. Jack would be at the top of the tower by now, and Sara was standing beside me with the Glock in her hand and extra mags in her pockets, waiting for the word to fire. I was at the helm.

The Zhuk captain must have realized that I was not running to him to surrender my ship and crew, and I saw the double flash of his twin machine guns, then the streak of green tracer rounds that went very high because his bow was rising, but his gunner adjusted—or overadjusted as his bow fell—and the next streak of tracers went into the water about a hundred yards in front of *The Maine.*

The tracers showed where the Zhuk was, and I could hear Jack popping off a rapid succession of single shots from his firing perch.

Felipe couldn't see much from the pitching bow, but he did see the tracers, and he got off five rounds as the bow settled down, then reloaded as the bow rose, and waited to fire again.

Jack was popping off rounds as though he could see the target, and maybe he could from up there, but I couldn't see the Zhuk and I glanced at my radar. The blip was so close that I should be able to see him. I looked out the rain-splattered windshield and there he was—a black silhouette on the black horizon, and coming fast.

I called to Sara, "Fire!"

She moved quickly to the window, pushed it out, and raised the Glock with both hands as I'd taught her. The wind and rain were streaming through the open window, and as the bow dropped she emptied the nine rounds in a few seconds, but instead of dropping below the windshield to reload, she stared straight ahead at the on-coming ship.

"Bastards!"

"Get down!"

I saw that Felipe hadn't been hit by enemy fire—or friendly fire—and he was firing at the Zhuk, which I noticed was not firing back. And the only reason for that would be because the gunner had been hit. In fact, I heard Jack shouting at the top of his lungs, "Got him! Got that asshole!"

The twin guns would have an armored shield, but Jack had the high ground and apparently he'd scored a hit. The Zhuk, however, had no shortage of gunners, and as we got within a hundred yards of him, the twin guns opened up again, and the tracers went high as his bow rose. But this gunner didn't overcorrect, and he kept a steady stream of rounds coming, and as his bow settled down, so did the tracers, and suddenly the cabin was filled with the sound of breaking glass and impacting bullets.

Sara screamed, then dropped into the stairwell, but she didn't appear to be hit. I caught a brief glimpse of Felipe and he was still firing. Sara was sitting on the steps now, slamming a fresh magazine into the Glock. She stood and emptied her second magazine at the looming ship.

The next burst of machine-gun tracers went high, not because the Zhuk's bow rose, but because that's where the gunner was aiming, so he must have caught sight of Jack in the tuna tower.

We were on a collision course, and the collision was going to happen within the next ten seconds, and I knew I wasn't going to change course because *The Maine* and everyone on her were as good as dead anyway. So he was going to change course, and all I had to do was wait to see if he was going to break to port or starboard.

We were within fifty yards of each other now and I could actually see the windows on the high bridge where the captain was either at the helm or giving orders to the helmsman. Easy shot if I had a rifle. But I didn't, and I didn't hear Jack's AR-15. I did, however, hear the twin machine guns open up, but *The Maine* was so close to the Zhuk and his forward deck was so high that the gunner had to depress his barrels to the max to get a burst off, and the tracers streaked over the cabin and impacted on the rear deck. And that was his last shot at me because the Zhuk suddenly veered hard to port to avoid a collision, and I caught a glimpse of his twin machine guns as the gunner swung them to starboard to try to get a burst off, but I was moving fast along the starboard side of the 80-foot Zhuk, so close that I could see men on deck.

Just as I reached the stern of the ship, I cut hard to starboard, directly into his wake, which sent *The Maine* airborne, and when we came down it felt like we'd hit a brick wall and *The Maine* bounced wildly. The rear gunner was either not at his station, or if he was he didn't know what was happening or it was happening too fast for him to react, and his stern swung to starboard, away from me, as the Zhuk continued its swing to port.

The Maine was more maneuverable than the bigger ship, and I cut hard to port so that my stern was lined up amidship to the Zhuk, and moving away from him. His forward- and aft-mounted guns could swing only one hundred and eighty degrees, so there was a blind spot about forty feet wide at his midship point, and I kept glancing over my shoulder, trying to stay perpendicular to him as he continued into his port turn. The Zhuk's crew, however, armed with AK-47s, had no blind spot and I could see muzzle flashes from the forward and aft decks, but the tracers were going wild as the oncoming waves started to slam against the starboard side of the Zhuk. The captain changed course to get his stern lined up so that his rear gunner had a shot at me, but I changed course to keep that from happening, and it was a little like a dog chasing its tail except that the tail—me—was getting some distance from the dog's teeth.

He finally gave up on trying to outmaneuver me, and came around hard so that he was now following me as I took a direct northerly heading toward international waters, which were about eight miles ahead—maybe twenty minutes if I could maintain twenty-five knots.

I couldn't visually see the Zhuk in the darkness now, but he'd lost some time and distance with his maneuvers and my radar showed he was about five hundred yards behind me. And that's where he'd stay if we both maintained our max speed. But with this weather, the Zhuk, which was big, could more easily cut through the waves and might be able to maintain a speed that *The Maine* couldn't match. If I saw him gaining on me, I could run a zigzag course—like trying to outrun a big, fast alligator—and because the Zhuk wasn't as responsive as my smaller boat, that might slow her up more than it slowed me up if he tried to mirror my moves. Works with an alligator.

Meanwhile, he was apparently pissed off and he'd decided to open up, but from five hundred yards in the dark rolling sea, his tracer rounds were all over the place, and mostly falling into the sea behind me.

I looked at the fuel gauge and saw we'd burned some diesel, but we could still make it to Key West—or if I had to, I'd head for one of the closer Florida Keys, maybe Key Largo, or even Andros Island in the Bahamas. I didn't have to make that decision yet, and maybe not at all. Key West was where I started, and that's where I wanted to finish. We weren't out of the woods yet, but I could see daylight ahead.

But then I saw something else. I'd adjusted my radar to get a tight picture of the Zhuk coming at me, but now I readjusted the picture to twelve miles out to see where the Stenka was, and I saw a blip to the east—the only blip on the stormy sea—and it was on a course to intercept *The Maine*, so it had to be the Stenka, and it was about eight nautical miles away. *Shit.*

If I maintained a due north heading, I'd be out of Cuban territorial waters in less than twenty minutes, but the Stenka might get within cannon range before I crossed that boundary. If I changed course to head northwest toward the Keys, I'd be in Cuban waters longer than I wanted to be, but I'd also be running away from the Stenka and also ahead of the storm. I kept looking at the radar blip, trying to do the math and the geometry, like thousands of sea captains before me. *You only get one shot at this, Mac.*

Sara was sitting in the chair beside me, and she may have been there awhile, but typical male, I was so wrapped up in my own problems, I didn't notice.

I said to her, "How you doing?"

She nodded.

"Can you do me a favor? Go see if Jack . . . Go see how he is . . ."

"He's alive," said Jack as he came into the cabin, drenched from the rain. Then he turned around, went out to the deck, and threw up over the side. That happened to me once when I came down from the tuna tower in rough seas. Not the worst thing.

I noticed that Felipe had disappeared from the hatch, and he appeared from below with a bottle of Ron Santiago, which I'm sure he had already sampled. He passed the bottle to Sara, who handed it to me. I said, "I'm driving."

Sara took a gulp.

Jack came into the cabin, and Sara offered him the bottle, but Jack looked a little green and went below. I heard the head door open, then close.

Felipe was starting to notice that the cabin windows had holes in them and that some of the wood and plastic was chewed up. He said something in Spanish that I guessed was "Holy shit."

Felipe moved behind the chairs, between Sara and me, looked at the radar, and pointed. "Is that the Stenka?"

"It is."

"Shit!"

"And behind us is the Zhuk." I let him know, "You did an excellent job, amigo."

He didn't reply immediately, but then said, "I think I got the gunner."

Jack was halfway up the stairs now and said, "I nailed that bastard right between his fucking eyes."

Which was more likely, but for all anyone knew, Sara had one of those impossibly lucky shots that no one would believe, including the guy who caught the bullet.

Felipe asked, "What are we going to do?"

I reminded him, "We are going to let the captain make that decision."

He didn't reply, but kept looking at the radar screen. He said, "The Zhuk . . . he seems to be too far behind . . ."

"He's gaining on us, but not fast enough to get into firing range unless he keeps following us into international waters." Which he'd do, because the Zhuk captain was very pissed off and he had a score to settle, and he had superiors to answer to who I was sure were reaming his ass in Spanish over the radio. I've been on both ends of radio transmissions like that.

Felipe concluded, "If we maintain this course, the Stenka's cannons will get within effective firing range of us in . . . maybe ten minutes."

"Who told you about thirty-millimeter cannons?"

"Amigos."

I need a few amigos like that. "What's his effective firing range?"

"Four thousand meters." He did the math and said, "About two and a half miles." Felipe also pointed out, "He could begin firing even sooner."

Right. The Stenka's rapid-fire cannons could put out a lot of shit from the twin barrels, and even if it wasn't accurate fire from a long distance, something could hit you. Or you could be having an exceptionally good day and you could sail through the shit storm. It could go either way.

Felipe gave me his unsolicited opinion. "We need to turn away from him."

That seemed obvious, but I pointed out, "If we keep a straight course north, we'll be in international waters in maybe ten minutes."

Felipe informed me, "He doesn't give a shit. That bastard would follow us to Miami if he thought he could get away with it."

"I know that," I assured him.

Jack also gave me his unsolicited opinion. "We gotta head west."

"Sara?"

She agreed with Jack and Felipe, but also said, "Do what you think is best."

Well, there was no best. I reminded everyone, "If we head west, we'll be running along the coast of Cuba, and if we do that there will be other Guarda Frontera boats sailing out of their ports that can intercept us along the coast."

No one had any opinion on that, so I continued, "But if we continue north, away from the coast, the only patrol boats we need to worry about are the two that are already on our ass."

My crew understood the dilemma. And that's all any captain can ask for. I turned on the radio, which was still on Channel 16, and listened, but the Cuban patrol boats had gone silent. Basically, they had nothing to say to me, or to anyone else who might be listening to Channel 16.

I handed the mic to Felipe and said, "Broadcast a distress message, give our location, heading, and speed, then repeat it in Spanish for our Cuban amigos behind us." I added, "Say we are being pursued by Cuban gunboats."

He took the mic and asked, "Our current heading?"

"No. We're taking a heading of . . . three hundred degrees." I turned the wheel to port and picked up a heading that would take us northwest, toward the Straits of Florida. This heading would keep us a little closer to the Cuban coast than I wanted and keep us in Cuban territorial waters longer than I liked. But it was the most direct route home.

Felipe began broadcasting, first in English, then in Spanish. English is the international language of the sea, but I wanted to make sure that the Guarda Frontera understood, in Spanish, that we were ratting them out. So even if we didn't make it, they couldn't claim, "No comprende." But to put myself in their position, they were justified in pursuing and firing on a boat full of murderers.

Meanwhile, the Zhuk had changed course in response to my change of course, and so had the Stenka. The Zhuk was gaining on us a bit. Now that I'd changed course and was moving almost directly away from the Stenka, he wouldn't be in firing range for about fifteen or twenty minutes if my calculations were correct. All we could do now was maintain this heading and hope that the Guarda Frontera boats received orders to give up the pursuit. I mean, hopefully the regime wouldn't want to cause an international incident on the high seas. True, we were no longer innocent tourists—we were wanted killers—but the bastards in Havana had to decide how to deal with that problem at one in the morning— militarily or diplomatically. I hope they were having as bad a night as I was.

I turned on my chart plotter for the first time and pulled up a view that took in Key West, which was about three hundred and fifty kilometers away—about two hundred miles. I corrected my heading and hit the autopilot, which would continue to correct for drift caused by the weather and currents.

I had the wind at my back, riding ahead of the storm, which I assumed was still tracking on a northwesterly course, and I was getting a full twenty-five knots out of *The Maine*.

The chart clock said it was 1:57 A.M. I should be in Key West by 10, maybe 11 A.M., and in the Green Parrot for lunch. If anyone had an appetite.

The only problem with this plan was the two Cuban patrol boats, which I assumed still wanted to blow us out of the water.

I glanced at my radar screen. The Zhuk was still gaining on me, but he'd have to follow me halfway to the Keys before I was in range of his machine guns. And he might do that. I didn't think I wanted to take him on again. God gives you only one miracle to save your ass. The next one is on you.

The real problem was still the Stenka. He was doing about forty-five knots, and I remembered him anchored outside the marina—a big bastard, bristling with mounted machine guns, and two gun turrets, fore and aft, that housed the twin rapid-fire cannons. I also pictured him now, cutting through the waves, and the captain staring at his radar, watching the distance between him and me beginning to close.

I looked again at the chart plotter. I was already too far west to shoot for Andros Island. I would have had to do that soon after I'd exchanged fire with the Zhuk. Now I was in the middle of nowhere, committed to my heading for the Keys, which was the closest land—if you didn't count Cuba.

We'd crossed into international waters about fifteen minutes before, and as I suspected, the Guarda Frontera boats also crossed that line without a pause. They were in hot pursuit, and international waters didn't mean much except that anyone could go there without permission. U.S. territorial waters began twelve nautical miles off the coast of the Keys, and no matter how I did the math, it didn't look like we were going to get that far before the Stenka caught up to us.

Jack came into the cabin. "How we doing?"

"What's the radio frequency for Dial-a-Prayer?"

He looked at the radar. "I think you need a higher frequency."

"Right."

"You got any more tricks up your sleeve?"

"I'm thinking." I asked him, "What's happening below?"

"Sara's in the port stateroom, maybe catching some Zs. Felipe's in the galley lightening our load of rum."

"He earned a drink."

"You want one?"

"No. But you go ahead."

Jack remembered one of his T-shirts and said, "I only drink a little, but when I do, I become a different person, and that person drinks a lot."

I smiled. "I'll take a smoke."

He fished his cigarettes out of his shirt pocket, and I could see he was in some pain from where the AK round smacked his vest.

I took a cigarette and he lit me up with his Zippo, then lit himself up and said, "These things are gonna kill me."

"You should live so long."

He looked at the fuel gauge, checked out the radar again, then the GPS and chart plotter, but didn't say anything.

The seas were getting calmer as we traveled west, and outside the windshield I could see stars peeking through the racing clouds. We had the wind at our backs, and *The Maine* was making good time. But not good enough.

My radar was set for six miles, to keep a close eye on our pursuers, whom I'd code-named Asshole A and Asshole B. Asshole A—the Zhuk—actually seemed to have lost ground, and it occurred to me that he may have a fuel situation. If he wasn't topped off when he left Cayo Guillermo for his nightly patrol, he'd need to calculate how far he could follow me before he ran out of gas in the middle of the ocean.

I glanced at Asshole B—the Stenka—and saw he was chugging along, making maybe forty-five knots, and closing the gap. This asshole wanted to kill me.

I adjusted my radar to take in the whole fifty-mile radius of its range, and Jack and I looked for other ships out there, but I saw only two—one to the west heading west along the shipping lane through the Straits of Florida. The other ship was on a heading that would put it into Havana Harbor. The storm had pretty much cleared out the sea to the east and no one was in our vicinity. Even the drug runners were taking the night off.

I said to Jack, "Broadcast a distress call."

He took the mic and began broadcasting, giving our position and heading, and who we were, and the nature of our problem, which he described as two fucking Cuban gunboats trying to kill us.

I advised him, "Say we also have a fuel situation and an injured crew member."

"Who's injured?"

"You, asshole."

"Right." He glanced at the fuel gauge, then continued his transmission.

The rules of the sea—the customs and traditions—say that you need to come to the aid of a ship in distress. But if the distress is a shoot-out on the high seas, there might be a lot of sea captains who'd rather avoid that, on the theory that your distress was not the elements, or an act of God, and not the kind of distress that obligated them to risk their own asses or the asses of their crew or passengers. The fuel situation, however, and the injured crew member might awaken a captain's sense of brotherly obligation. I suggested, "Tell them we're running out of booze."

Jack, whose dark humor is darker than mine, asked me, "Should I say we came in second in a Cuban fishing tournament?"

"Worth a try."

Jack transmitted again, sticking to the facts, but no one replied. I mean, we could have not mentioned the Cuban gunboats, but that's not fair. If you ask someone for help, you need to lay out the dangers. If I'd heard this transmission . . . it would depend on whom I had aboard. Or I might wonder what the ship in trouble did to get chased by Cuban gunboats. Or I might think it was a hoax, or a trap to pirate my boat. Lots of stuff happens on the high seas that wouldn't or couldn't happen on land. It was a different planet out here; a watery grave, waiting to receive the dead and the soon-to-be-dead.

I said to Jack, "Okay, we'll try again later." Meanwhile, I'd listen for a response. I said to Jack, "I need a damage report."

He replied, "It is what you see."

"What do I *not* see?"

"You don't see that a few rounds passed through the head, and I think the fresh-water tank sprung a leak."

"How's the beer?"

"Good. But I think we have a small leak in the fuel tank."

I glanced at the fuel gauge and nodded. If we had daylight, I could see if we were leaving a diesel slick behind us. I wasn't sure if we were leaking diesel or burning it in the rough sea. In either case, Key West was looking less possible. But Key Largo was still within reach if the fuel gauge stopped going south. Fuel, however, was the least of my problems. The Stenka was still the main problem, and he was gaining on us. I tightened the radar image. He was three nautical miles behind us.

Sara came into the cabin, and Jack, who looked like he was

about to pass out, said he was going below to make some coffee. "You want some?"

"Sure." I asked Sara, "How're you doing?"

"All right."

"How's Felipe?"

"He's in a stateroom."

I let her know, "He did good back there."

She nodded, and sat in the chair next to me, noticing that I'd turned on the GPS and chart plotter, which reminded both of us of our sunset cruise when we'd looked at Havana Harbor. If we knew then what we knew now, we'd probably both have said buenas noches and have a good life.

She said, "Talk to me. What's happening?"

"Well, we've come about eighty miles since our encounter with the Zhuk, and we have maybe a hundred twenty to go before we get into U.S. territorial waters."

She nodded. "Will they follow us?"

"They will break off five or ten miles before they reach that line." I explained, "Closer than that is a provocation, which will likely lead to a radio warning, and may cause the Coast Guard to send a cutter out."

"Okay . . . so we're halfway home?"

"We are," which was true in terms of navigation.

She looked at the radar screen. "They seem closer."

"They are."

She didn't comment.

We sat at the control console, side by side, looking through the bullet-pocked glass at the clearing sky. The sea was calming down and it was turning out to be a nice night.

It was 2:46 A.M. now, and if I could maintain twenty or twenty-five knots, and if the fuel held out, and if the Stenka didn't get in firing range, we'd be okay for a mid-morning arrival at Charter Boat Row.

I heard something coming out of the speakers, then Bobby Darin started crooning, "Somewhere beyond the sea, somewhere waiting for me, my lover stands on golden sands . . ."

I would have preferred my Jay Z CD for morale boosting, but Jack wanted to use my CDs for skeet shooting.

So we cruised along, like this was a sunrise cruise, or a ship of fools singing in the dark.

I looked at my radar. The Stenka was closer, but I noticed that the Zhuk seemed a bit farther. Then, as I watched, the Zhuk changed course and took a southwesterly heading, toward the Cuban coast. I looked at the chart plotter. It seemed that if the Zhuk maintained his new heading, he'd sail into Matanzas Harbor. I assumed he had a fuel situation. Why else would anyone go to Matanzas? I mean, I've been there. The place sucks. But don't miss the pharmacy museum.

Sara asked, "What's happening?"

I explained, "The Zhuk has broken off the pursuit." I added, "Must be low on fuel."

"Good." She added, in case I forgot, "God is looking out for us."

"Ask him about the Stenka."

Jack came into the cabin with my coffee and I advised him of the Zhuk's change of course, and also asked him to play a CD that was recorded in this century.

He ignored that and said, "Maybe the Stenka is going to break off."

I looked at the radar screen, but the Stenka held his course, and as I tightened the image, I estimated that he was about two miles behind us—and we were within range of his radar-controlled 30mm cannons.

I said to Jack, "Take the helm."

I got up and retrieved the binoculars from a well on top of the console, then exited the cabin.

Sara called out, "Where are you going?"

"Be right back."

I climbed the side rungs up the tuna tower and stood holding on to the padded bolster, which I felt had a hole through it. Jack was a lucky guy.

I focused the binocs on the horizon to the east. I couldn't see the Stenka, but I saw his running lights, so he wasn't running dark as we were, and there was no reason he should run dark; he was the meanest motherfucker on the water.

I kept looking at the lights on the horizon, then I saw the unmistakable flashes of rapidly firing guns. *Holy shit!* I called out, "Evasive action!"

I expected Jack to hesitate as he comprehended that order, but *The Maine* immediately cut hard to port, just as I heard the sound of large-caliber rounds streaking past the boat, then I saw them impacting into the sea and exploding where we would have been.

The Stenka captain wasn't using tracer rounds, which he'd only use if he could see his target, and with the radar controlling his guns the only thing he wanted to see now was an explosion on the horizon. Meanwhile, I heard Bobby Darin belting out "Mack the Knife."

The Maine cut to starboard, held course for a few seconds, then cut to port again. Jack was running a tight zigzag, which hopefully was too erratic for the radar-controlled guns to keep up with. But that didn't stop the Stenka from trying, and I could see the guns on his forward deck lighting up, and now and then I saw the point of impact on the water where the multiple rounds hit and exploded, then I heard the faint sound of his guns, like rolling thunder on the horizon.

There was nothing more to see here, and I started to climb down the tower as *The Maine* kept changing course quickly at twenty-five knots, making the boat roll hard from side to side. I nearly lost my grip a few times, but I got down to the side rail and jumped onto the deck and shoulder-rolled to starboard with the deck, then rolled to port when *The Maine* quickly changed course.

I couldn't stand, so I scrambled into the cabin on my hands and knees and pulled myself into the chair where Sara had been. I assumed Jack had ordered her below.

Jack was standing at the helm, so I let him keep the wheel because he seemed to know what he was doing, and what he was

doing was cutting the throttle as he changed course, then opening the throttle, so he was varying our speed and our course at the
same time. He was also singing a duet with Bobby Darin: "Oh, the
shark, babe, has such teeth, dear, and he—"

"Jack, shut the fuck up!"

"Okay."

I had no idea if the fire-control radar system was sophisticated
enough to keep up with the changing target, but if those twin cannons were also employed as anti-aircraft weapons, they could react
quickly. And yet we hadn't been hit yet.

Jack glanced at me. "You got any suggestions?"

"Yeah. Don't get hit."

"Thanks."

"I'll take the helm."

"I got the rhythm and I don't want to lose it."

"Okay . . . Tell me when you get tired."

"We don't have that long."

All of a sudden, a deafening explosion cut through the noise of
the sea and the engine, followed by another explosion that shook
the boat and knocked me to the deck.

Jack shouted, "We've been hit!"

I could see down the steps, and saw smoke and fire in the lower
cabin. I got to my feet, grabbed a flashlight and the fire extinguisher
from the bulkhead, and charged down the steps into the smoke.
The only good news was that the entertainment system was silent.

I didn't see Sara or Felipe, but I did see that the galley was ablaze
and I emptied the fire extinguisher at the flames, then grabbed the
galley extinguisher and emptied that, which killed the fire. The
smoke was thick, but I could see a gaping hole in the starboard
hull of the lower cabin, and smoke coming through the door of
the starboard stateroom where the second round must have hit.
The wind was streaming in through the hole above the galley, dis-
sipating the smoke, and I ran into the starboard stateroom, which
was dark.

There was a six-inch hole in the hull above the berth, which was empty, but then my flashlight fell on Felipe, who was on the floor. I didn't see blood and I saw his chest heaving, so I left the room and kicked open the door of the portside stateroom. Sara was curled up on the floor and I knelt beside her. "You okay?"

She looked up at me, eyes wide, but didn't reply.

"Get a life vest on and come to the bottom of the stairs, but stay below until you hear from me. Understood?"

She nodded.

I was about to leave, but I asked her, "Where's your Glock?"

She didn't reply so I shined my light around the stateroom and saw the Glock on the berth. I didn't want her using it on herself, so I took it and said, "Felipe is in the other stateroom. See if he needs help." I added, "There's a first aid kit on the bulkhead in the head— the bathroom. Okay?"

She nodded and started to get to her feet.

I left the stateroom, stood under the hatch, and emptied the Glock into the Plexiglas to vent the smoke.

I went up to the cabin where Jack was still standing at the helm, and I saw he was lighting a cigarette with his magical Zippo, while turning the wheel left and right. He asked, "How's it look below?"

"Under control."

"Everybody okay?"

"Felipe might not be." I told him, "Go below and check him out. Get the first aid kit, and get life jackets on everybody."

"We abandoning ship?"

"Maybe."

"It's still floating, Mac."

"It's a fucking target, Jack."

"So you wanna get eaten by a shark, or you wanna die in an explosion? Which?"

"I want to get into the water before the Stenka blows up The Maine."

"Okay. You think we'll be picked up by a luxury liner or by the Stenka?"

"Go below!"

"Don't forget the sharks."

He moved aside, I took the wheel, and he retreated below.

I continued the evasive action, cutting the wheel from port to starboard, and I also varied the time between turns. I left the throttle alone, so we were making maximum speed in the hard turns, but the maneuver caused the boat to heel sharply. I didn't know how best to confuse the radar that was directing the guns, but I had to assume there was some mechanical lag time between the radar locking on and the gun turret moving left or right as the twin guns elevated or lowered to follow the radar-acquired target. Also, there'd be some lag time as the projectiles traveled four thousand meters. I also didn't know if the guns were fired automatically with the lock-on, or if they were command-fired by the captain or a gunner. All I knew for sure was that the twin 30mm cannons could be outmaneuvered. That's why we were still alive. But we'd gotten hit, and the odds were that was going to happen again.

Meanwhile, I couldn't see any rounds impacting on the water, and just as I thought the asshole may have run out of ammunition, I heard what sounded like a flock of wild geese with rockets up their asses streaking overhead. *Shit!*

Jack stuck his head up the stairwell and said, "Felipe's okay. But he has a suggestion."

"What?"

"Transmit a surrender to the Stenka, come around, and head toward him." He added, "He says he'll do it in Spanish."

"Tell him to go fuck himself in English."

"Sara sort of told him that already."

"Good."

Jack also informed me, "It's a fucking mess down here."

"Everybody have life jackets?"

"Yeah."

"Everybody topside."

"You want a drink?"

"Later. Move it."

Jack, Sara, and Felipe came into the cabin and I said, "Go out to the deck, and if we get hit again and if there's a fire, or if we start taking water, we all go over the side."

Sara said to me, "I told you, I will not let them capture me."

I assured her, "They won't see you in the water."

She seemed to recall my spiel on our sunset cruise and said, "I will not be eaten by sharks."

Felipe looked like he was in a daze, but he said to me, "You have to surrender. I'll transmit—"

"Forget it!" We seemed to be running out of bad options— surrender, abandon ship, get eaten by sharks, or get blown up. And when you run out of bad options, it's okay to do nothing and let fate do something. I said, "Move out to the deck—"

I heard the explosion at the same time that I saw it, and the top of the bow erupted into a ball of fire. Debris flew into the windshield and I instinctively ducked as I held on to the wheel and held the boat in a sharp port turn.

I stood and looked at the damage. A hole the size of a pie plate had appeared in the white fiberglass bow deck a few feet in front of the hatch. If anyone had been in the cabin below, they'd be dead or badly injured.

Jack ran below to check for fire, then came up and said, "We're okay."

Relative to what?

I realized I'd been in my port turn too long, and I could almost see the barrels of the twin cannons tracking me. I cut hard to starboard, knocking Sara and Felipe off their feet, and sending Jack tumbling back into the cabin below. Again, I heard the flock of wild geese, but this time they were off my port side and I knew they'd have caught me broadside if I'd continued into my left turn. I resumed my evasive zigzagging, thinking of that alligator on my ass. Alligators never give up, because they're hungry, so you can never give up, because you want to live. Eventually somebody makes a mistake and loses. It can't go on forever.

Sara and Felipe were on the rear deck now, lying face down with their arms and legs spread to keep from rolling as I took *The Maine* through its wild maneuvers. Jack was in the chair next to me, lighting up. It occurred to me that I'd missed an option, which was to just cut the throttle and drift until a full salvo of 30mm rounds obliterated *The Maine* and us. I looked at the throttle and Jack saw what I was thinking.

He asked, "You want a cigarette?"

"No."

"They're gluten-free."

"I gotta tell you, Jack, your sense of humor is annoying."

"You shoulda said something."

"It just occurred to me."

"Yeah? And you know what just occurred to me? It occurred to me that I told you this Cuba shit was fucked up."

"Seemed like a good idea at the time."

"Yeah. Lotsa shit seems like a good idea at the time."

"Why don't you go out on the deck and keep our passengers company?"

"I like it here." He added, "Pay attention to what you're doing, Captain."

"You're distracting me."

"And don't even think about touching that throttle."

I didn't reply.

I kept at my escape-and-evasion game, trying to vary my maneuvers, but I realized that by trying to veer away from a salvo of cannon shells, I could just as easily run into them. This was not as skilled a game as I was trying to convince myself that it was; a lot of this was just luck. This was really my lucky day.

Felipe had apparently come to a different conclusion, because he was in the cabin now with the Smith & Wesson in one hand, hanging on to the door frame with the other. "Give me the mic."

Jack said to me, "Ignore him and he'll go away."

I ignored him, but Felipe said, "I'm counting to three. If you don't give me the mic—"

"Felipe," I said calmly, "I am not giving you the mic. We are not surrending the ship. We are—"

"One."

Jack said, "Put the gun down."

"Two."

Jack added, "You get one shot, asshole, then the guy you didn't shoot is going to take you down and shove that gun so far up your ass that the first round'll blow your tonsils out."

Felipe processed that and I glanced back to see his gun hand shaking. "It's okay, amigo. We're all scared. But we're doing okay."

Well, not that good. The Stenka captain had changed to tracer ammo, probably to add a little mind-fucking to the game, and we all saw the streaks of green tracers flying along our starboard side, not twenty feet away. I saw them drop into the dark sea in front of us, and I counted eight explosions. *Holy shit*...

I turned hard to starboard and the next flight of green streaks sailed about five feet above the cabin. I liked this game better when I couldn't see how close they were coming.

Another flight of eight green tracers streaked toward us and hit the water about ten feet from the stern.

Jack said to me, "Just keep doin' what you're doin' and pay no attention to the incoming." He reminded me, "You can't stop it and you can't change its trajectory. You just gotta keep runnin' and swivelin' your hips."

"Thanks for the tip."

I didn't look back at Felipe, but Jack was keeping an eye on him and I assumed Felipe was having a catatonic moment. I did glance back at the deck and saw Sara still sprawled out, blissfully unaware that the Stenka was now showing us what we couldn't see before. As I was about to turn my attention back to the wheel, I saw streaks of green coming right at our tail and two cannon shells impacted in the stern and I heard a muffled explosion, followed by the sound of the sea, but not the sound of the engine. We were dead in the water.

Sara seemed almost unaware that we'd been hit, but then she realized something was different and she got slowly to her feet and started coming toward the cabin. Behind her, I saw smoke from the engine—but no fire.

Everything seemed to go silent, and I heard the waves and the wind, and the firing from the Stenka seemed to have stopped. I looked out at the horizon and saw in the far distance the Stenka's running lights coming toward us. He should reach us in about ten minutes. Which was enough time to go to Plan B. Whatever that was.

I looked at Jack, but he had nothing to say except, "Shit."

Sara looked at me and I said, "Sorry." I thought a moment, then said, "The captain will stay with the ship. You will all abandon ship now." I also said, "Good luck."

But no one was moving from the cabin.

Jack said, "We all go together, or we all stay onboard together."

Felipe spoke first and said, "I'm staying onboard."

Sara said, "I will not be captured. I'm going into the sea." She looked at me. "And you're coming with me."

Jack said, "I'm not sure what I'm doing, but I want a hand to bury those . . . those remains at sea."

So we all went out on the deck and Jack and I lifted the steamer trunk by its handles and rested it on the gunnel.

Sara said a prayer for the dead that began with, "Heavenly Father," and ended with, "we commend the souls of these brave men into your hands."

Jack and I were about to tip the trunk over the side when we both heard a familiar sound and looked out at the horizon. Coming toward us from the north, a few hundred feet away, and not fifty feet above the water, were two huge helicopters. I recognized their profiles as Black Hawks.

They tipped their rotor blades, then turned east toward the Stenka.

One of them fired a long stream of red tracers across the sky, his way of saying to the Stenka's captain, "Game over. Go home."

The other Black Hawk turned and came toward us and I saw a big rescue basket hanging from a line below the open door.

We pulled the trunk back onboard, but no one had anything to say until Sara said, "We're all going home. Together."

Apparently this was true.

PART IV

PART IV

CHAPTER 55

So this guy walks into a bar and says, "Corona. Hold the lime."

And the bartender replies, "Lime's on me."

The cocktail hour in the Green Parrot begins when the doors open and ends when the lights go out. It was 2 A.M. on Monday morning and the lights were about to go out.

The place was nearly empty, so Amber had time to chat. "How was Cuba?"

"It was okay."

"How were the people?"

"Most of them were okay." A few tried to kill me, but why mention it?

"You have pictures?"

"No." Well, yes, on my cell phone, but my cell phone was in my backpack and my backpack was at the bottom of the ocean.

Amber pushed a bowl of corn chips toward me. "I haven't seen Jack around."

"He's off the island."

"How'd he do in the tournament?"

"Came in second."

"Good." She asked, "Did you see him there?"

"No."

She said, "You heard that they cancelled the last few days of the Pescando tournament."

"I heard."

"And they kicked out a tour group."

I'll bet I know which group.

"Weren't you with a group?"

"I was. But then I did independent travel."

"Did it feel dangerous?"

"Well . . . I guess it could be. But not for the average tourist."

"I thought the Cubans wanted better relations."

"We all have a ways to go."

She changed the subject. "What are you going to do now, Mac?"

"I was thinking about retiring."

She laughed. "Yeah. Me too." She said, "Couple of captains asked me if you were available."

"I think I've had enough of the sea."

"Lots of guys say that."

They must also have been shot at by Cuban gunboats.

A guy at the end of the bar wanted another drink and Amber moved off.

I sipped my Corona. It had been five days since my Black Hawk ride to Coast Guard Station Islamorada on Plantation Key. It's a bit of a blur, but I do remember the second Black Hawk firing a rocket into *The Maine* and she exploded, burned, and went down. I don't think I was supposed to see that, and when I asked about it at Islamorada, a Coast Guard officer told me the boat was a hazard to navigation and had to be sent to the bottom. Actually, as I came to understand, *The Maine*—*Fishy Business*—was evidence that needed to be buried at sea. She deserved a better fate.

Amber came back and said, "Kitchen's dumping some fries and wings. You want some?"

"I'm okay."

Amber looked at me. "You lost some weight. *Are* you okay?"

"I'm good. How've you been?"

"Good." She found her cigarettes behind the bar. "Mind if I smoke?"

"It's your bar."

"I wish." She lit up and blew a nice smoke ring. She asked, "Did you make it to Fantasy Fest?"

"Missed it."

"How come?"

"I wasn't back yet."

Actually, I was a guest of the Coast Guard on Plantation Key. Along with Jack, Felipe, and Sara. They said we needed medical attention. Actually, only Jack did. The X-ray showed a cracked rib. No big deal. So we wanted out of there, but a Coast Guard doctor said we were quarantined for seventy-two hours, though we were actually being held incommunicado.

On day two, a guy named Keith, who had been with us on the Black Hawk, told us that the Cuban government had implicated me, Sara, Jack, and Felipe in a criminal act that might include murder. This was not good news, but also not unexpected.

The Black Hawks, by the way, were unmarked, as was Keith, and they had nothing to do with the Coast Guard. Keith was in fact a CIA officer, though he never actually said that.

Regarding the murder charges, Keith assured us that we had no extradition treaty with Cuba and this matter could drag on for years. Or be settled diplomatically. In the meantime, Keith was interested in what happened and he needed statements from us, which we said we were happy to give with our lawyers present.

I thought back to what happened in the mangrove swamp. Murder? I could make a case for justifiable homicide. Or even lawful combat. The Guarda Frontera guys were not civilians, and they were armed. On the other hand, I wasn't a soldier anymore, and we were not at war with Cuba. But . . . it *was* Cuba. If the same thing had happened in Sweden, I'd have surrendered. Instead I'd used deadly force. Which was why I was here having a beer at the Green Parrot, and those guys in the mangrove swamp were dead. I did feel some remorse, as well I should. *One Human Family.* But I would eventually come to terms with what happened in Cuba as I did with what happened in Afghanistan. And as Jack did with Vietnam. Survival is a strong instinct, surrender is not an option, and all combat is justifiable homicide. But you pay a price.

Amber broke into my thoughts. "That guy Carlos who you met here last month came around a few days ago looking for you. Said he went to your house, but you weren't there."

"What'd he want?"

"Didn't say."

Well, one of these days I needed to talk to Carlos about financial and legal matters, and other things. Did I still have his card?

"He said you weren't answering your cell phone." She added, "I tried to call you."

"Lost my cell in Cuba." I thought back to our air-sea rescue. Age and infirmity get rescued first, and that was Jack, but he said, "Beauty first," and Sara went up in the basket, then Jack. Captain goes last and I reminded Felipe that he'd mutinied and wanted to be captain, but he also wanted off *The Maine* quickly in case the engine blew, so he took the third basket into the chopper, and I went last.

We argued with the crew chief about bringing the two trunks up, but Keith, who seemed to be in charge, said they'd be retrieved by the second Black Hawk. But when we got to Plantation Key and asked for the return of the trunks—our trunks—the story changed, and a Coast Guard officer said they'd gone down with the ship. Which of course was bullshit. And there was more bullshit to come.

Amber glanced at her watch. "Last call."

"I'm okay."

As for Carlos, I hope he had insurance on his boat. More importantly, I think he owed me at least fifty grand, and I think I owed him a kick in the nuts. What I knew for sure was that there wasn't going to be any press conference in Miami. In fact, our new friend Keith strongly suggested to me, Jack, Sara, and Felipe that because of the legal and diplomatic issues we shouldn't discuss our Cuba trip with anyone—except him. Felipe agreed, and urged me, Jack, and Sara to heed Keith's advice. Felipe, of course, had worked with Keith's colleagues—or maybe with Keith himself—on our escape plan from Cuba, and it appeared to me that Felipe was still working for the Company. I mean, you don't have to read Richard Neville novels to figure that out.

On the more important issue of my money, Eduardo had

promised me a consolation prize in lieu of my three million dollars, in exchange for my cooperation and my appearances on radio and TV. But that press conference wasn't going to happen, and also Eduardo was either dead by now or in a Cuban jail. Or he was wandering around a cemetery. I asked Amber, "What day is this?"

"November second."

"Day of the Dead."

"The what?"

"All Souls' Day. The Spanish call it Day of the Dead."

"Weird." She glanced at her watch again. "I gotta run the register and do some stuff. You want to wait? We can go for a beer."

"I'll take a rain check."

"Sure." She let me know, "I'm off tomorrow."

"Me too." I spontaneously suggested, "Let's go swimming."

"Sounds good."

I stood. "I'll call you."

"You lost your phone."

"I have a house phone." I gave Amber the number. "Call me if you get a better offer."

"See you tomorrow."

I went out to Whitehead and began walking toward my house. It was a nice night, the kind of breezy, balmy night you get in the Keys by November, like the nights you get in Portland in summer.

A block from the Parrot was the Zero Mile Marker of U.S. Highway One and I stopped there and looked at the marker, which was actually a standard highway pole with traffic signs attached. The sign on the top said BEGIN, the next one said 1, then NORTH, and finally a small green sign at the bottom said MILE 0.

During the day there're dozens of tourists here having their pictures taken—thousands every year. And you can get a T-shirt of the sign on Duval. Some people come here believing that the marker has telepathic powers or something, so I stood at the Zero Mile Marker, waiting for some profound thought or a divine message directing me toward the road I needed to take. I thought I heard a voice say, "Go get Amber, get drunk, then take her home and bang her. That will make you feel good." I don't think a divine voice would say that. But that's what I would have heard and done before Sara Ortega.

On that subject, the Coast Guard had offered us rides home, and Sara and Felipe went to Miami together. Jack wanted a ride to Miami Airport, destination Newark Airport, to see his sister in Hoboken, which was good. Me going to Miami with the three of them would be awkward, so I asked for a ride to Key West. That was two days ago. Sara and I hadn't exchanged landline numbers, so we both had good excuses for not calling. She had said, however, "Let me work this out and I'll come see you in Key West."

I guess she was still working it out. If it took two more days, we'd be passing each other on the Overseas Highway as I was heading north to Maine. I'd always thought about making that trip by car, starting right here at Zero Mile, and following old U.S. One to Portland. So now I decided to do this. Should be interesting. And give me time to clear my head. My parents will be pleasantly surprised at the return of their prodigal son.

I started walking home, but my feet took me toward Charter Boat Row.

On my way through the quiet, palm-lined streets, I gave some additional thought to Cuba—not to what I'd seen, heard, and experienced, but what I hadn't.

As best I could figure—drawing on my limited knowledge of clandestine operations—Eduardo and his amigos had gone to their amigos in the CIA with a plan. The CIA obviously liked the plan and offered to back it. They were suckers for any plan that included screwing Cuba, even if it wasn't their own plan. But the CIA likes to control other people's plans, and take credit if the plan goes well, or take a hike if it goes south.

Bottom line, I was certain that the CIA was more interested in the remains of the American servicemen murdered in Villa Marista prison than they were in Sara's grandpa's money hidden in a cave. I was sure the money once existed, and that was Sara's deep belief. But there was no way of knowing if the money was still there, and if it was, the CIA didn't care. It wasn't their money. As for the property deeds, I think the CIA thought these documents might be useful to have in their possession—and not the possession of the Cuban exile community who had their own agenda and did crazy things.

I could imagine the Company seeming to be enthusiastic about Eduardo's press conference in Miami, and about the storm of outrage it would cause in Congress, the media, the public, and within the MIA and veterans' organizations. Bye-bye Cuban Thaw.

The CIA, however, had no intention of leaving something as important as American foreign policy to the Cuban exile community. In fact, the Company, while approving and backing the plan of Eduardo and his friends, pictured a different outcome: The Company would take charge of the evidence and control how, when, and if it would be revealed.

I mean, this was a no-brainer, and I was surprised that Eduardo and his amigos didn't see how the last act was going to be re-written by their CIA partners. And the reason they didn't see this, I think, is that the Cuban exile community, like the CIA, had such a big hard-on for screwing the Castro brothers that they couldn't see or think straight. Blinded by hate, the way guys get blinded by lust.

I had no idea what the CIA intended to do with the contents of those two trunks, and for all I knew, the Company—maybe on orders from the top—had come onboard for the Cuban Thaw, and they were going to bury the evidence that would screw it up, like they buried *The Maine*. Or maybe they'd reveal to certain people in Washington the existence and contents of the trunks, to be used as a bargaining chip in the negotiations. Not my problem, except that I'd like to see those remains returned to their families. And maybe they would be. Quietly. Someday. But in the meantime, the CIA's story was that the trunks had gone to the bottom of Davy Jones' locker. Keith said he was sorry about that.

Bottom line, Eduardo, Carlos, Sara, Jack, and I had been used and screwed. As for Felipe, he was obviously the Company's man in Cuba. He had worked with the CIA on our escape plan, but when the escape by boat became a naval battle, he wanted to broadcast a surrender to the Cuban patrol boats—or more likely he was actually broadcasting a pre-arranged message to his CIA friends that we were in trouble. In either case, it seemed to me that he'd lost his nerve, and maybe lost his trust in his CIA amigos. It happens. But all's well that ends well; the Black Hawks came to the rescue.

The CIA's motto, "The truth shall set you free," was kind of an understood joke, while Key West's motto, "One Human Family," is a sad joke. Somewhere in between the cynical lies and a naïve trust in the human race was the true human condition: complex and capable of anything from heroism and self-sacrifice to betrayal and murder. That's what I saw in Afghanistan, and what I saw in Cuba.

And my final thought on all this was that if we and *The Maine* had made it to Key West, Keith and his colleagues would have been there to relieve us of the trunks. In the end, there was no way those trunks were going to wind up at a press conference.

The Black Hawk's timing was a little off, however, and I didn't know if that had to do with the storm, or if it had to do with Keith not fully understanding our situation, or if it had to do with typical chain-of-command inability to act quickly and decisively. Or maybe, to be cynical, the Company was trying to decide if this whole mission needed to be buried at sea. As I said, I'd worked with CIA Special Ops in Afghanistan, and they were good at what they did. And when they made mistakes—like directing a drone to launch a Hellfire missile into a house full of civilians—it was not a mistake; it had a purpose, and you'd never know what that was, because dead men tell no tales.

So, that was my post-action report and my estimation of the completed but unsuccessful mission. More importantly, my DEROS—Date of Estimated Return from Overseas—had come, and I was home.

My post-action report regarding Sara Ortega, however, was more complicated, and that awaited further Intel.

In life, love, and war, there are usually identifiable winners and losers. But with this Cuban mission, it was hard to tell if anyone won. I think Sara understood that Felipe hadn't been completely honest with her, and I was sure that the CIA hadn't been honest with Felipe—or Eduardo. And those two certainly hadn't been honest with me. Nor had Sara, for that matter, but I'm sure she thought she was lying to me for my own good. That's the way we justify lies to people we love. As for Felipe, he lied for his own good, but I fucked his girlfriend, so we'd call it even. Did I miss anyone? Well, Jack, who never trusted anyone from the beginning. Old guys have seen too much, and they trust no one. That would be me someday if I lived long enough. As for Carlos . . . well, Fishy Business indeed.

And all of this reminded me of Antonio quoting Hemingway about how the Cubans always double-crossed each other. I guess Hemingway lived in Cuba long enough to come to this conclusion—and he hadn't even met Antonio, Carlos, Felipe, or Eduardo. Or Sara Ortega, who hadn't actually double-crossed me, but who'd lied to me. It occurred to me that the Cuban exile groups and the CIA deserved each other.

I mean, this was all one big circle jerk, and if anyone was a winner, maybe it was the CIA. They needed a win in Cuba. They were long overdue.

I arrived at Charter Boat Row and walked out to the end of the long dock where *The Maine* had once been berthed, as I'd done so many times in the early-morning hours before sunrise.

The last slip was empty, so no one had yet taken it over.

I looked out at Garrison Bight, at the harbor lights reflecting off the water, and at the clear, starry sky and the moon setting in the west.

I recalled the last time I'd seen *The Maine* here, the night before Jack drove me to Miami International Airport. I think I'd had a premonition then that I'd never see her again, but that had more to do with me not making it home than *The Maine* not making it home.

I thought, too, of the time that Carlos, Eduardo, and Sara had come walking down this dock, and Jack saying, "Hey! She's a looker." He should have added, "I see trouble coming." Not that it would have made a difference.

I didn't feel like going home, so I sat on the dock with my back to a piling and stared out at the water and the sky and smelled the salt air, which always reminds me of being a kid in Maine.

It seemed to me that there was a purpose to all that happened, and the purpose was to free me of all my worldly possessions, my debts and obligations, and also to free myself from what had become the equivalent of my job on Wall Street.

Also, I'd more than fulfilled my wish to have a new adventure. I could have done without the shoot-out in the mangrove swamp or the drive-by shooting with the Zhuk, and for sure I could have done without the 30mm cannon fire. But everything was within my skill set, and a return to combat duty was just what an Army shrink would have ordered to make me healthy and happy. The best cure for post-traumatic stress is new stress.

And now I needed to decide what to do next, which I would do tomorrow. Or the next day. My road trip to Maine sounded good.

I think I drifted a bit, and in those unguarded minutes of half-sleep, Sara's face and voice crept into my thoughts.

I'd obviously fallen hard, but the reality was that we had not a single thing going for us outside of Cuba. Holiday romances can be intense, but as the old song said, too many moonlight kisses seem to cool in the warmth of the sun.

Aside from the good sex, there was the question of trust. I don't know as much about women as I think I do, but I was fairly sure that Sara's lies were situational, a requirement of the mission, and not who she was. That's why she gave me a copy of the treasure map: to show she trusted me, but also to atone for her lies. I could forgive the lies she'd been instructed to tell me, and the lies of omission—except the lies about Felipe, which were more personal than professional—and she'd lied to him, too. And that could be a peek into the future. And what the hell was she doing in Miami?

So I should consider myself lucky that I'd dodged that bullet along with the others. Mac was free at last.

———

The sky was getting lighter and the gulls were squawking.

I stood, yawned, and stretched. I'd spent a lot of nights sleeping on my boat, but not many sleeping on the dock.

Charter Boat Row was coming alive and I saw crews and captains getting their boats ready for customers who'd be along in an hour or so. Now that I was not part of this, I could admit it wasn't so bad, and I would miss it.

I took a last look at *The Maine*'s empty slip, and I pictured her there, then I turned to walk back along the dock to go home for a cup of coffee and start packing for Maine. Did I own a sweater?

At first I thought I was still half asleep, or my brain was still conjuring up ghost images, or maybe like a lot of guys who've loved and lost, I was seeing her face on every woman walking by. But the woman walking toward me on the dock was wearing white jeans, a blue Polo shirt, and a baseball cap. She had a nice stride.

She waved to me and called out, "I had a feeling I'd find you here."

We didn't exactly run into each other's arms, but we did move pretty fast, and within a few seconds we were embracing, and she said, "Permission to come aboard."

"Welcome aboard."

Corny, I know. But . . . what the hell.

THE END

ACKNOWLEDGEMENTS

All good fiction is based on fact, and I am fortunate to know people who know more things than I can find on the Internet.

First, I'd like to thank a man who I met in Cuba, and who gave it to me straight about contemporary Cuban politics, culture, and life. He wishes to remain anonymous for obvious reasons, but he's given himself the code name "Lola." Thank you, Lola, wherever you are, and take care.

There are many nautical scenes in this book, and growing up on Long Island I know many weekend sailors. I asked four of them to read and vet the scenes set on the high seas. Any mistakes in those scenes are mine alone.

First, thanks to my longtime friend Tom Eschmann, who, like my main character, "Mac," has fished and sailed the waters of Key West, and there's little that Tom doesn't know about boats. Tom is not only an avid fisherman and a great sailor, he's also an avid reader of fiction, and this happy combination has helped me lend realism to these scenes.

Similarly, my childhood friend Dan Barbiero has spent what amounts to years on the water. Dan (Yale '66) and his wife, Helen, accompanied me and my wife to Cuba on our Yale educational travel trip, and we learned a lot about Cuban rum and other things. To help me research this book, Dan took lots of notes and many pictures of daiquiris and mojitos, and a few photos of Havana. Thanks, Dan and Helen, for making the trip lively.

I've often thanked and acknowledged my great friend John Kennedy, labor arbitrator, and former Deputy Police Commissioner of Nassau County (NY) and Member of the New York State

Bar, for sharing with me his expertise in criminal justice and the law. And now I'd like to thank John for sharing his knowledge of the sea. John is a true Renaissance man.

My fourth sailor, Dave Westermann, is also a great friend, a great lawyer, and a great sailor. Weekend cruises with Dave on Long Island Sound and around Manhattan Island on his luxury cabin cruiser that I helped pay for have been a mixture of business and pleasure, and tax deductible to the extent allowed by law.

After thirty-five years with the same publisher, you may have noticed that I am now published by Simon & Schuster, a venerable institution in New York publishing, where I was welcomed with open arms, as though my reputation had not preceded me. Most welcoming were Carolyn Reidy, President and CEO, Jonathan Karp, President and Publisher, and my new and terrific editor, Marysue Rucci, whose own reputation as an excellent editor and author wrangler is well deserved. Thanks to everyone at S&S for making the transition easy and fun.

I would not have been at Simon & Schuster if it weren't for the efforts and good advice of my savvy and hardworking literary agents, Jenn Joel and Sloan Harris of ICM Partners. Jenn and Sloan love the written word and it shows in the passion they bring to their profession. Sometimes we even talk about money.

This book is peppered with Spanish, and my Spanish is limited to "Corona, por favor," but I was fortunate to have Spanish speaker Yadira Gallop-Marquez working down the hall from my writing office. Gracias, Yadira, for your patience and your time.

My good friend Michael Smerconish, novelist, journalist, TV and radio host, and political gadfly, was kind enough to share with me his experiences in Cuba, which inspired some of the scenes in this book. Thanks, Michael, for your years of support and enthusiasm for my writing.

As I've done in my last dozen or so books, I want to take this opportunity to thank my two fabulous assistants, Dianne Francis and Patricia Chichester. If it's true that no one wants to see how sausages or laws are made, then it's doubly true that no reader wants to see how books are written. It's not pretty. But someone has to see this, and Dianne and Patricia see me, hear me, and put up with me during my many months of sausage-making. Truly, this book would not have happened without them. Thanks again, and know I am appreciative.

Social media has become a mixed blessing for authors. I love that I can reach out to my readers, and vice versa, but the nuances of social media sometimes present a challenge. The solution is to hire someone who's less than half your age, and I did that when I engaged the services of Katy Greene, CEO and founder of Greene Digital Marketing. Thanks, Katy, for all your help, advice, professionalism, patience, and creativity. I have seen the future, and it is you.

And many thanks to my daughter, Lauren, and my son Alex, who are the perennial early readers of my manuscripts and who are repaying me for all the homework I helped them with. And thanks to my son James (age eleven), who is coauthoring his next funny novel with me.

The last shall be first, and that's my wife, Sandy Dillingham. It's not easy living with a writer (Cosmos help) but Sandy, a former book publicist, understands how to deal with authors—be patient but firm, compliment their writing, but be honest, and ignore their moods. Love you.

———

The following people or their families have made generous contributions in charity auctions in return for having their name used as a character in this novel:

Alexandra Mancusi—Cancer Center for Kids at Winthrop-University Hospital; **Scott Mero**—FACES (Finding a Cure for Epilepsy & Seizures), NYU Langone Medical Center; **Dave Katz**—Robert F. Kennedy Center for Justice & Human Rights; **Ragnar Knutsen**—Cold Spring Harbor Laboratory; **Ashleigh Arote**—Crohn's & Colitis Foundation; **Professor Barry Nalebuff**—Robert F. Kennedy Center for Justice & Human Rights.

I hope they all enjoy their fictitious alter egos and that they continue their good work for worthy causes.